U.C. Berkeley, where she majored in theatre and minored in everything that Berkeley has a reputation for. After college she moved to Los Angeles, where she has made an interesting living doing novel adaptations and selling original suspense and horror scripts to various Hollywood studios, with one film made so far: an adaptation of novelist Sabine Deitmer's thriller, *Cold Kisses*.

Alex is a former Director of the Writers Guild of America, West; she's also the founder of WriterAction.com, a large and unruly cyber-community of professional screenwriters. Next to writing she loves dance more than breathing: jazz, ballet, salsa, Lindy, swing – she does it all, every chance she gets.

Alex's debut novel, *The Harrowing* was nominated for Bram Stoker and Anthony awards for Best First Novel.

Visit her website at www.alexandrasokoloff.com

THE PRICE

'It scared, exhilarated, uplifted, frenzied, and made me green with envy'
Ken Bruen

'Sokoloff is simply amazing'
Bookreporter.com

'[A] sublime second novel...Her gooseflesh-inducing imagery jumps right off the pages, and her rich, graceful prose calls to mind names like King, Saul and Levin'
Dark Scribe Magazine

'A heartbreakingly eerie page-turner'
Library Journal

'Sokoloff's straightforward writing style perfectly enhances her chilling and mysterious novel, in which she blurs the lines between what is real and what is merely a hallucination'
Romantic Times Book Reviews

'*The Price* is another notch in this author's golden belt – a psychological roller-coaster that keeps the reader on edge throughout. I couldn't put it down. Miss Sokoloff is an author not to be missed'
Heather Graham, bestselling author of
The Seance

Praise for
THE HARROWING

'*Poltergeist* meets *The Breakfast Club*'
Kirkus Reviews

'A pyrotechnic climax … a cinematic finale'
Publishers Weekly

'An eerie ghost story that captivates readers from page one.
The author creates an element of suspense that builds until
the chillingly believable conclusion'
Romantic Times Book Reviews

'Good, engrossing fun'
Booklist

'*The Harrowing* is a real page-turner. Alexandra Sokoloff raises
a fine crop of goosebumps and shivers. A first novel of
unusual promise'
Ira Levin, author of *Rosemary's Baby*

'*The Harrowing* is more than an impressive debut novel; it is
an impressive work, period … highly
recommended'
Bookreporter.com

THE UNSEEN

ALEXANDRA SOKOLOFF

piatkus

PIATKUS

First published in the US in 2009 by St. Martin's Press, New York
First published in Great Britain as a paperback original in 2010 by Piatkus

A CIP catalogue record for this book
is available from the British Library.

ISBN 978-0-7499-4168-0

Typeset in Baskerville by
Action Publishing Technology Ltd, Gloucester
Printed and bound in Great Britain by
CPI Mackays, Chatham, ME5 8TD

Papers used by Piatkus are natural, renewable and recyclable
products sourced from well-managed forests and certified
in accordance with the rules of the Forest Stewardship Council.

Piatkus
An imprint of
Little, Brown Book Group
100 Victoria Embankment
London EC4Y 0DY

An Hachette UK Company
www.hachette.co.uk

www.piatkus.co.uk

For my partner, Michael Bradshaw, and my father, Alexander Sokoloff: both perfect blends of the scientific and supernatural

Chapter One

The hall ahead is dark, a tunnel of black.

She is in bare feet, wearing just a T-shirt, her steps slow and reluctant on the polished hardwood floor.

The warm Southern California breeze breathes through gauzy curtains at the windows, wafting the fragrance of night-blooming jasmine ... but the smell is cloying, gagging, and dread rolls like black waves around her as she approaches the door, their door.

The sounds are louder, now ... the grunts and moans are like physical blows. She wants to scream, wants to run ... and she can't breathe, can't breathe, something is wrapped around her chest like a vise.

In the night outside, a dog breaks into hysterical yapping; somewhere far away a siren wails. Beside her, the Art Deco clock on the wall clicks to 3:33. She steps past the ghost of her own reflection in the large gold-framed mirror ... takes a jerking step forward into the doorway.

And stops, sways at the sight—

They are in the bed, their bed, Matt and—

I don't even know her name, what's her name?

Tracey.

She can hear their breathing, Tracey's soft moans, Matt groaning, "Baby ... oh baby ..." She can smell them, feel their frantic writhing—Matt's quickening thrusts, Tracey's legs

1

flexing and tightening around his thighs ...

Every move, every thrust, every sigh, is like being stabbed, all over her body. She can feel the jabs, feel the blood pouring from her flesh, the coppery stink of blood ... she is wrapped in barbed wire and it is tightening, tightening ... Matt and Tracey cry out together on the bed ...

Inside her mind, she is screaming, her cries echoing against the walls ...

Please ... please no ...

And behind her, the mirror shatters ...

Laurel awoke with a shuddering gasp, felt her heart pounding crazily against the mattress, shaking the bed. The room around her was blindingly sunny, white and high-ceilinged, with crown molding and a ceiling fan.

Ceiling fan???

Where am I???

She lay against the pillows in total disorientation, waiting for the dream to subside, to regain some kind of reality.

Then she sat up slowly, in the bedroom of her house in—her mind scrambled briefly for it—Durham, North Carolina.

She had been there for three weeks and four days, after living all thirty-one years of her life in California.

And she had moved in a blind rush of escape, after finding her fiancé in bed with his graduate assistant, in exactly the scenario she had dreamed, down to the very last detail.

She swung her feet out of bed and stood, reached for a robe, avoiding looking at the mirror on the wall.

She belted the robe around her as she walked out into the hall, past the door of the spare bedroom with its unopened moving boxes stacked against the walls, and down the stairs of her house— *her house!*—her feet bare on the cool of the polished wood stairs, her left hand gliding down the satiny curve of railing. So different from the right-angled, modern condo in West Hollywood, with its recessed lighting and skylights, and stainless steel, granite-countered kitchen.

2

And that's the point, isn't it? I'm as far away as I could get.

The dream had followed, and it never felt like dreaming; it was always the same, like walking into the living past, into a parallel world that existed intact and constant, with her trauma captured, her silent screams echoing forever on the walls.

But it was less frequent, and she no longer awoke from it with barbed-wire welts in her flesh. *That's some kind of progress, right?*

It was the dream that had told Laurel that Matt was cheating on her. She'd jolted awake in her Santa Barbara hotel, where she was staying the weekend at an American Psychiatric Educators conference, with raised welts in her flesh and a shattered feeling in her chest. She didn't believe in psychic flashes, had never won so much as two dollars in the California lottery, didn't know who was on the other end of the phone when she picked up; she never even read her horoscope in the newspaper or online. She had a doctorate in psychology, for heaven's sake; she lectured on personality and theories of the self at Cal State L.A.; she had multiple job offers at universities in various parts of the country (all of which she'd turned down to stay in Los Angeles with Matt ...).

But the dream had been more than a dream. She'd *known*.

At 1:23 a.m. she left the hotel, got in her car, and drove two hours back to their condo in L.A. ... and it was just as in the dream, every detail: the smell of jasmine, the blowing curtains, the yapping dog, the clock clicking over to 3:33 as she walked down the dark hall through waves of black dread, toward the sound of moaning coming from their doorway, their bedroom, their bed ...

And the mirror ...

In her mind she heard the shattering and halted on the stairs, gripping the banister, squeezing her eyes closed to shut it out ...

Matt had moved out immediately, they had never even talked about it. It was almost as if he'd staged the scene for Laurel to find, to spare himself the awkwardness of an actual

3

conversation. He was out of her life, shacked up with Tracey. Just like that—unengaged.

Stop it, Laurel ordered herself, clenching her nails into her palms. *What's the point? You were living in a dream world.*

She had no illusions about what the real problem was. Los Angeles was a 24/7 candy store. Beautiful young people came in droves from all over the country, hoping to make their faces their fortune. Laurel knew she was pleasant enough to look at in a sexy librarian kind of way: glasses and braces long gone, and her unruly mane of red-gold hair less of a disaster than it had been in her coltish adolescence. And of course there were the legs that had stopped Matt in his tracks the night they met at a faculty Christmas party—or so he'd said at the time. But Laurel knew she didn't even register on the Hollywood scale.

She'd never really understood what Matt had seen in her, other than the fact that she simply listened well; she'd been sympathetic and available when he was shattered and mooning over being dumped (*By a model, no less—and shouldn't* that *have been your first clue?*).

No, she'd been an utter fool, blindly trusting, delusional, stupid in every way.

Better to know now, Laurel's friends, colleagues said. Of course she would heal, of course she would move on, laugh again, find someone new, someone worthy of her. *We love you, you'll be fine*. All the things that well-meaning people say.

Laurel had nodded and thanked them and gone home and given notice on her condo, then called the Duke University psychology department to accept a tenure track professorship that she hadn't even been considering, in the middle of North Carolina, a whole continent away.

She said all the right things to her dismayed friends: she couldn't stay an associate professor at a state college forever, tenure track jobs were almost nonexistent in California, she was doing the best thing for her career.

All true, and all lies. The truth was she ran—ran away from Matt, away from L.A., away from everything she'd known. She wanted to be someplace that no one knew her, where there was no place that she could run into people she knew, where they could ask, brightly oblivious, about the wedding—or worse, look at her with pity, even edge away from her as if she had a communicable disease. The cheated fiancée, the abandoned bride ...

She became aware that she had reached the bottom of the staircase and was just standing, unfocused, at the foot of the stairs.

She looked around her, breathing in, letting her present surroundings chase away the memories of L.A.

The house was bright, airy, and empty, two stories of old Southern charm, with a wide wraparound porch, ten-foot ceilings, heart-of-pine floors (the realtor had said "heart pine"), a screened back porch, a walk-in pantry (with a window!), and curious small square doors in the walls of the master bedroom and hall and kitchen, which to Laurel's utter amazement turned out to be functioning laundry chutes. The windows were hung on counterweights and had thick glass that rippled like water; the front and back yards overflowed with wisteria and honeysuckle. The quiet of it all still astonished her—not just of the house, but of the surrounding blocks and the whole town.

Laurel had been looking for a rental but she'd gotten lost on the way to an apartment appointment and found herself driving through a quaint and timeless neighborhood with gently curving streets and wide porches with white Southern rockers, a haphazard collection of bungalows and Victorians and barnlike Cape Cods. When she saw the OPEN HOUSE sign in front of a gingerbread house with eight-paned windows, she stopped on a whim. The house was captivating and the price so surreally low (compared to the still-stratospheric prices of Southern California) she'd found herself writing a down-payment check on the spot (stunning the chatty realtor into silence), and moving into the place two inspections and a scant two and a half weeks later. It was a huge and outrageous decision that she'd made in a matter of minutes, unlike her in every way.

5

But she was not herself; she had no sense of what "self" meant anymore. And buying meant it would be harder to ever go back.

She walked now like a white-robed ghost through the empty rooms—literally, empty: she'd spent her entire savings on the purchase, therefore furniture was not really an option. She maxed out a credit card on a bed, a kitchen table with chairs, and a very large desk for her upstairs study. The kitchen boasted a refrigerator, a stove, and an eating alcove. The rest of the house was entirely bare—but then, so was Laurel, so the emptiness suited her.

She moved across the empty hallway and turned the latch of the door.

She opened it and looked out, like Dorothy in *The Wizard of Oz*—and felt the familiar wave of unreality to see, instead of flat, sunny West Hollywood, the curved, tree-lined street, regal houses with their own wraparound porches with rockers and ceiling fans and hanging baskets of ferns, and yards with huge and lushly flowering trees. A car might pass once every ten minutes or so, and then the thick silence would descend again, laced with the subdued twittering of birds, the low hum of cicadas, wind chimes, an occasional faraway train whistle, even the tolling of church bells.

A white-and-orange kitty with luminous gold eyes sat on the porch, centered exactly halfway between the doormat and beginning of the stairs, and looked up at Laurel expectantly.

"Still here, hmm?" Laurel said to it wryly. "You're a trouper."

The cat waited beside the door while Laurel fetched the newspaper and then walked, flowingly, in front of her into the house, through the center hall, straight to the kitchen, where it sat beside the pantry door, waiting to be fed. The morning after Laurel had moved in she'd opened the front door and the cat had walked in as if it owned the place. The cat was light years ahead of Laurel in confidence, and she figured she could learn something from it, so they had been cohabitating ever since, the cat on one pillow of the new bed, and Laurel on the

6

other. Laurel had yet to name it, but felt certain that the cat would let her know in its own time how it wished to be addressed.

She tried not to think what it meant to be so vulnerable that a strange cat could dictate her life.

She reached for the coffeepot that she'd programmed the night before, and her eyes fell on the window.

She looked out on her lovely, alien neighborhood and thought for the millionth time, *What am I doing here? What have I done?*

But it turned out to be the day that she found out.

Chapter Two

Late, late, late.

Laurel gunned her Volvo out of the driveway and hit the road with a squeal of tires. *The entire day? I slept the entire day?*

But it happened alarmingly often these days. Avoidance. She'd been dreading the Psych department's welcoming faculty cocktail party all week. For the whole first week of school she'd successfully avoided colleagues and gatherings; she couldn't bear the thought of having to fend off personal questions. Now, of course, she realized the huge flaw in her plan. She would have to meet them all at once.

At least I made it through the first week, she thought wryly, as she drove across the railroad tracks out onto the highway.

She had a light teaching load for the first semester, just two lecture classes. The class sizes were amazingly small, and she could teach the Intro to Psychology and Intro to Personality courses in her sleep. Teaching was something she was good at, something safe and known, that kept her mind off Matt and *the dream.*

Yes, she'd survived the first week of classes well enough. After all, she had no reason to talk about her personal life with her students.

Tonight would be a different story. She'd have to say something. So after her coffee she'd simply crawled back into bed.

And slept the whole day.

Luckily the first clothes box she'd sliced open in a panic had had her favorite outfit practically on top. Luckily she lived only fifteen minutes from campus and traffic as she knew it was nonexistent.

"I'm not late, I'm *fashionably* late," she mumbled, with a touch of hysteria, and pressed down her foot on the gas pedal to exit onto Main Street, toward downtown.

Duke University was the center of the city of Durham, a former tobacco town. Through no conscious plan of her own, Laurel had landed in one of the fastest-growing areas in the country. The area boasted three major universities and a burgeoning software park within a half-hour's drive of each other, and development had exploded in the Triangle cities of Raleigh, Durham, and Chapel Hill, all of which consistently made "Top Ten Places to Live" lists.

Durham—the whole Triangle area—was much smaller than Los Angeles, of course. Anywhere would be. The up side was that getting around town was as easy as teleporting. Locals complained about the traffic, but Laurel had no idea what they were talking about; she often drove on the streets feeling as if she'd woken up in some postapocalyptic movie in which all the people on Earth had been vaporized.

She drove too fast now on the surreally empty streets, as always marveling at the sheer number of trees. There were many things about North Carolina that Laurel knew she would never get used to, but above all were the trees.

The trees were *everywhere*. So dense they formed walls—walls lining the highways, walls obscuring the houses and the businesses, vast green walls preventing her from seeing any direction except in a straight line. She sometimes felt as if she had been dropped into an enormous hedge labyrinth. The trees made the nights darker than she'd ever experienced (although that meant you could actually see stars, which was thrilling), and made navigation around town practically impossible. In L.A. Laurel was used to triangulating off buildings. A tree looks like a tree, especially when surrounded

9

by hundreds and thousands of other trees.

She'd spent her first few weeks in a perpetual state of lost, metaphorically and literally, until she'd broken down and bought a GPS for her car. The implacable digital voice was unnervingly like her mother's. She hadn't figured out how she felt about that, but on the other hand, also like her mother, the device was rarely wrong, and so far it had kept Laurel from driving off the map entirely.

Prompted by the GPS, Laurel made the turn onto Campus Drive and another sharp right to skid to a stop in the faculty lot. She zapped the car locked and hurried up a stone staircase that opened onto the long, rectangular main yard of West Campus, lined with its magnificent old oaks.

The campus was a Gothic castle of a school, with graystone walls and turrets and gargoyles (actual gargoyles!), arched walkways, a gorgeous medieval chapel, and fifty-five acres of world-famous gardens.

At the top of the stone stairs, Laurel veered onto one of the meandering paths, breathing faster as she hurried, wobbling on too-high heels, following her vague recollection of where the Faculty Club was.

There was apparently some formal event scheduled for students as well; Laurel found herself navigating around packs of young men dressed in what she'd come to learn was the Southern uniform of the privileged: tan khaki pants and navy-blue sport coats and light blue Oxford shirts—and brightly chattering bevies of blond, blue-eyed young women in flowered dresses, today even adorned with pearls and gloves. (*Gloves!* Had she ever even owned a pair?)

The students were ... well, interesting. Bright and motivated young people, both wealthier and more driven than the ones Laurel had taught at Cal State. And more homogenous than that melting pot, for sure. Duke accepted students from all over the world, but the vast majority were white, and a good third of them pledged frats and sororities; the Greeks dominated the campus social life.

It all added to Laurel's constant time-warp, *Twilight Zone* feeling.

10

A group of the slicked-out boys looked her over as they passed, and Laurel was suddenly uncomfortably aware of how alien she must look to them, in her short black knit dress and matching long black sweater and twisty silver belt.

Yes, I'm from Los Angeles, and we have this color we like called "black." She lifted her head defensively. The boys stared back. She turned her head and kept walking, struggling to keep her balance on her heels.

They look and look and never crack a smile. At least in California men smile at you when they check you out.

And they were amazingly predatory for their age.

On the first day of classes Laurel had been trying to acquaint herself with the campus (not an easy task, as almost none of the buildings had names above the doors—evidently people were just supposed to know). She'd stopped in front of a graystone building with medieval-looking leaded-glass panes in the windows, and stared down at the blurry campus map, counting the buildings she'd passed since emerging from the walkway from Bryan Student Center, when a lazy drawl of a voice came from above her.

"Lost?"

She looked up, startled. A young man with longish black hair and a Cheshire cat smile was draped on the stone railing of the—balustrade? Balcony? She needed an architectural dictionary to describe it. The young man who so aesthetically adorned it was elegant and feline, and had obviously been watching her for some time.

"Um . . . I'm looking for Perkins Library?"

He reached behind to the graystone wall behind him and patted it, a staggeringly sensual gesture.

Laurel felt herself blushing. "Oh."

"Anything else I can help you with?" the young man said, so suggestively she felt her face burn even more crimson.

You're the one who's supposed to be in charge of these kids, she reminded herself. *No matter how you feel, you can't show fear.*

"I'm fine, thanks," she said coolly, and all but scurried up the stone steps, like a mouse under his watching gaze. The whole

11

encounter had a prescient feeling of significance, and she was not surprised when on the first day of school the boy with the black hair and Cheshire cat smile strolled into her Intro to Personality class. He slouched into a chair with the same privileged grace with which he had lounged on the balustrade and smiled down at Laurel so smugly she knew instantly he was nothing like a Psych major, not even close, but had signed up for the class for the express purpose of playing with her.

Trouble, she thought grimly. *There's always one.*

But the young man—Tyler Mountford was his name—turned out to be well-enough behaved in class, although he looked at her as if he knew far too much; Laurel sometimes had the feeling he was just biding his time until he made some startling revelation.

Laurel slowed on the wooded path and looked around her at unfamiliar buildings and a wall of—yes, trees—in front of her.

Completely and totally lost. *Again.*

And just as she thought it, there was a lazy and irkingly familiar drawl. "Lost *again?*"

Laurel turned to see—of course—Tyler Mountford. He was stopped on the path behind her, dressed in the same uniform of khakis and sky blue Oxford shirt, but the shirt was unbuttoned at the neck and the navy blazer was thrown casually over a shoulder, and the long black hair and the slouch in his hips made him look more like a cheeky English rocker than a Duke frat boy.

He looked Laurel over, dress, belt, legs and all ... and smiled, a slow, lazy smile. "That's twice now I've had to rescue you. You ought to put me on retainer."

I ought to put you on a leash, she thought back, but she kept her voice even. "Mr. Mountford."

"Lookin' for the Faculty Club?" He turned and pointed down a side path. "Takes you right to the door."

He swiveled back to her and raised an eyebrow. "I don't want to go to my shindig any more than you do. We could get a drink instead."

Laurel felt her face heating in spite of herself. "Thank you, Tyler, no. I'll be just fine."

"Have fun now," he said mockingly, and slouched off down the path after the packs of frat boys.

What am I doing here? What have I done? Laurel thought for the two millionth time, and turned down the path through the trees, in the direction Tyler had pointed her.

Chapter Three

Laurel drained her champagne glass in one gulp, which she realized seconds too late was probably not the brightest idea, given that she'd had nothing but the one cup of coffee all day. But the bubbles ran through her in a warming rush and it was all she could do not to dash after the waiter to grab another.

Instead, she put the empty glass down on a table of hors d'oeuvres and forced herself to focus. Around her the elegant, high-raftered University Club teemed with the cocktail-fueled chatter of her thirty-five new colleagues on the faculty of the Department of Psychology and Neuroscience, mingling, jockeying, and cruising.

She took a breath and moved into the crowd, swallowing terror. As she'd started to suspect after that look Tyler had given her, the leggy aspect of her attire was turning out to be not her greatest idea, either. The minimalist black that would have been understated in L.A. made her stand out like, well, like a runway model amid the colorful (and baggy) Chico's casual of her older female colleagues. Even as she thought it, a short, wiry, bespectacled woman with bad skin turned and gave her a blistering look that made Laurel practically desperate for more champagne.

And she was attracting far more attention than she'd wanted from the male contingent, many of whom couldn't seem to raise their eyes above her hemline. She glanced back over her shoulder and realized she was still being stalked by a large and flat-footed associate professor with a ruddy face who'd cornered her with obvious lust, eyes crawling over every inch of her body even as he continually called her "Ma'am." Laurel wondered fleetingly if anyone in the history of hookups had ever actually gotten laid by "Ma'am-ing" the object of his affection, though she didn't expect the associate was a representative example.

As the associate started for her, she quickly stepped up to the nearest cluster of colleagues, nodding and smiling as if she were completely absorbed in the conversation.

But no one in the circle acknowledged her, and the topic of conversation was being ominously uniform.

"—just got the Peabody grant . . ."

"—proposals due on the nineteenth . . ."

"—book comes out from Macmillan in the fall . . ."

There seemed not a single faculty member in the group, or in the room, who was not talking about his or her most recent publication or pending grant proposals. Laurel shifted on her feet, her smile dying by the second. She knew her position at Duke was contingent on publication or the bringing in of grant money—preferably both. That stipulation had been clearly spelled out in both her qualifying interviews and her contract.

The "publish or perish" aspect of university careers was not new to her; she'd grown up seeing her professor mother slaving over articles after a full day of lecturing. The truth was, even though Laurel had faked her way through the Duke interview with what she knew sounded like an impressive overview of her research and publication plans, a series of interconnected articles on Myers-Briggs personality types and test scores as a factor in choosing professions, she'd had not the slightest hint of passion for the project since—

Since Matt. Since the dream.

How can I write anything about personality and the self when I have no self left?

Laurel murmured "Excuse me" to the circle, and edged herself out of the group. She paused by another table of appetizers with her stomach churning in anxiety, and again scanned the room full of her colleagues, looking for a remotely friendly face.

A ripple of feminine laughter drifted from across the room and Laurel turned to look. Beside the grand piano, a dynamic, dark-haired man in his early thirties, with broad shoulders and crackling blue-gray eyes and a dusting of Irish-looking freckles over his handsome and lively face, was surrounded by young female grad students, all hanging on his every word.

Laurel's face shadowed. *Shades of Matt. Definitely the last thing I need.* She looked quickly away from him.

She reached for an appetizer—some kind of chicken sate—just to look busy. *Relax,* she ordered herself. She glanced around the room and started a categorizing game to calm herself—classifying the people around her according to Myers-Briggs basic personality factors. The good-looking professor was definitely an ESFP (Extravert, Sensing, Feeling, Perceiving), a combination of qualities that inevitably resulted in more charm than was good for anyone. The hostile woman in the baggy suit: ENTJ, the self-proclaimed judge. And that bearded man holding court by the fireplace—

Laurel started as she recognized Dr. Unger, the department chair, whom, of course, she'd met during her interviews. Like most psychology department chairs he had a hint of Freud about him, even though Duke's academic reputation leaned toward neuroscience. Laurel swallowed the last bite of chicken, took a breath, and forced herself to go up and say hello.

"Laurel MacDonald," she prompted the chair, as he turned toward her with a quizzical look.

"Of course, Dr. MacDonald," he said smoothly, and she started slightly at the "Doctor." He grandly managed not to sneak a look at her legs.

Laurel smiled what she hoped was a competent and professorial smile. "I just wanted to say thanks for the welcome and the party. It's so nice to meet everyone all at once," she lied.

Dr. Unger gave her a complacent and toothy smile back.

"Yes, we want the faculty to know each other. The department encourages interdisciplinary collaboration, particularly on grant projects, so don't be shy about approaching anyone with ideas. We're on the books to discuss your proposal, aren't we?"

Laurel's heart skipped a beat. Had she missed something? It occurred to her that she hadn't checked her phone messages for probably a week now—but she couldn't exactly ask him the date of their appointment. Instead she stammered, "I'm looking forward to it."

"Excellent," Unger said heartily. "Your aunt has been a credit to the university. We expect great things from you as well."

Laurel blinked and had to scramble to remember what he was talking about. *My aunt?*

"Your Aunt Margaret?" Unger prompted her, frowning.

Aunt Margaret. Yes. Right.

Laurel had only met her Aunt Margaret twice, both times when she was little more than a toddler, had not seen her since she'd arrived in Durham. The truth was, when Laurel had called to accept the Duke position she had not remembered the North Carolina family connection at all, not until she'd called her mother at Stanford to announce her decision.

Meredith had gone completely silent—in fact, the silence had gone on and on—until Laurel realized that she had for the first time in her entire thirty-one years succeeded in astonishing her dry and unflappable mother.

"North Carolina?" Meredith finally said, with an unaccustomed hint of Southern accent. And it had not been until that second that Laurel recalled that North Carolina was her mother's home state—that even though she'd left right after high school, Meredith had grown up not half an hour from Duke, that her older brother and sister were Duke alumni, that Laurel's Aunt Margaret was a celebrated professor on the medical school faculty.

To be fair, it was not a case of total amnesia on Laurel's part. Meredith rarely mentioned her past. She'd left the South at seventeen, and headed for California, never to return for more than a few weekend visits.

17

And why was that, exactly? Laurel was just starting to wonder when a voice broke through her thoughts.

"Professor MacDonald?" The department chair was speaking to her, an edge in his voice. Laurel forced herself to focus and return to the party.

"Yes ... thank you. I'll certainly try to live up to that," she said lamely.

Thankfully, there were others waiting behind her to pay homage and she stepped aside so the next supplicants could have their turn.

Laurel turned and very nearly collided with a bespectacled, somewhat unkempt little man hovering beside her. He gave her a shrewd look. "Hope your proposal is a knockout. Because he's serious as a heart attack." Laurel recognized the little man from the departmental Web site: J. Walter Kornbluth, the department's acknowledged prodigy. At the age of thirty-two he'd already published two acclaimed popular psychology books on abnormal psychology, one of which, *Head Cases,* had been optioned for television.

It's not enough to teach anymore, Laurel thought glumly. *You need an agent and manager.*

Kornbluth didn't bother to introduce himself; he seemed to expect her to know him. "If you want a tip—forget about articles or grants, although bringing in some money doesn't hurt. But these days anything less than a book doesn't cut it."

A book? Laurel thought. *I can barely get dressed in the morning.*

He continued smugly. "They dumped two associate profs last semester when they didn't get the publishing deals they were angling for. No book deal, no grant money, no job."

Kornbluth had taken out his Treo and was scrolling through his e-mail as he talked, a habit Laurel had found appalling in Los Angeles and which seemed to her even more pretentious at a faculty party.

She felt her hackles rising. "I can't imagine that will be a problem. I'm excited about what I'm doing."

"And what would that be?" The pompous little man peered at her over his horn-rims.

18

"Oh, I never talk about writing projects. Stops the internal momentum," Laurel said lightly. *And I wouldn't talk to you about it if I did have an idea,* she thought to herself. *I know your kind. Sharks.*

And even as she thought it, a voice spoke behind her.

"Don't trust him."

She turned, startled. Hovering on her other side was the good-looking professor she'd seen with the groupies, now sans nubile hangers-on. He was even more attractive up close ... Laurel could feel his energy as a kind of heat radiating from him.

There was obviously a history between the two men—she could sense Kornbluth beginning to bristle.

"Excuse me, but I hardly see—" Kornbluth started.

"No, obviously you don't. Don't you have anything better to do than bully the new hires? This guy"—the tall, freckled young professor leaned in closer to Laurel and nodded at Kornbluth, whose face had turned three shades of red—"the legend in his own mind. Don't trust him. He'll stab you in the back just as soon as look at you, won't you, Kornbluth?"

"Now see here, Cody—" Kornbluth started.

The other professor—Cody?—cocked his head and looked at Kornbluth with a frown. "Is that your phone? Might be your agent calling." He gestured to Kornbluth's hand and Kornbluth automatically glanced at his Treo.

"Hah!" Cody pointed at him. "Made you look."

Kornbluth shot him a disgusted look and tromped off through the milling faculty, leaving Laurel and Cody behind.

"Consider yourself rescued," Professor Cody grinned at her.

Why does everyone think I need rescuing? Laurel wondered, but she had no time for a response before Cody barreled on. "Kornbluth is the Great White of the department. Shark, I mean—no race allusions intended. Don't let the diminutive stature and lack of any quantifiable social skills fool you. He's a killer. Any new hire is looked on as a threat to be annihilated."

"A threat—" Laurel started, but he was already answering her.

"—to his rise in the department. Isn't that what we all want, here in the Bermuda Triangle of academia?"

It certainly was beginning to occur to her.

"The man is just about strangling himself with his own ambition," Cody said. "Of course, when I use the term 'ambition' about this crowd I'm using it very, very loosely. He is right about one thing, though—it's all about the money."

The brash and annoyingly attractive man in front of her had not a trace of a Southern accent. In fact, there was a suspiciously Valley lilt to his voice. As if he'd read her mind, he pointed to his own chest.

"Brendan Cody, CBT." He meant Cognitive Behavioral Therapy. Everyone in the room so far—besides Kornbluth—had introduced themselves by their specialty. Brendan Cody continued, rattling off: "BA/MA Berkeley, doctorate USF, thirty-three, six-one, black and blue—that always sounds ominous, doesn't it?—love piña coladas and getting caught in the rain."

He was so jovial and was talking so fast that Laurel wondered if he might be manic as well as being a little drunk; certainly he radiated the kind of slightly out-of-control charisma you often found in cyclothymic bipolarity. Also, she knew USF, University of San Francisco, to be a Jesuit school. Which meant Irish probably. *More shades of Matt, which means you steer away.* Laurel opened her mouth to excuse herself, feign a bathroom run or something, when he said abruptly:

"What were you doing before, when you were looking over the room? Categorizing?" She was surprised that he'd noticed, and guessed what she was doing. He nodded sagely. "You Myers-Briggs people are all alike. I'm ESFP, by the way. Myers-Briggs passes the time, but what's way more interesting is identifying the out-and-out psychotics."

"The—what?" she said, startled.

"Because statistically, there are some. Thirty-six full professors, twenty associates, twenty-five teaching assistants—chances are we've got three full psychotics, two associate psychotics, and two and a half assistant psychos. Makes you think, doesn't it?"

It did, but Laurel wasn't entirely sure *what* it was making her think.

Cody reached out to a passing waiter and snagged two more glasses of champagne, handing Laurel one without missing a beat in his monologue. "The university environment is a hotbed anyway," he informed her, as he clinked his glass with hers and took a healthy swig of champagne. "Cheers. It's a virtual Petri dish for nurturing neuroses. Gifted and sensitive minds, ambition, stress, sex, debt. It's a wonder more people don't snap." Despite the weirdness of the conversation, Laurel was beginning to suspect he was hitting on her, which must have been an automatic gesture on his part rather than a sincere one, as clearly he had his pick of teaching assistants.

"Not only that, but I think the collective angst of previous generations imprints on the entire environment. And magnifies with each subsequent generation."

By this time Laurel was almost certain Brendan Cody was manic—or even on something. At the same time, she was acutely aware that, one-sided as it was, it was the longest adult conversation she'd had since her arrival in North Carolina.

"Your specialty has been occupational testing, right?" He faked a yawn. "Earth-shattering—"

"I love occupational testing," she said, bristling. "It's about helping people recognize their own talents—and potential— things they didn't even know they could do."

"Why, that's delightfully fresh and uncynical of you, Dr. MacDonald. But what about *your* hidden gifts? Is conducting occupational testing tapping your hidden potential? Is *this* what you wanted to do when you grew up?" He was being facetious, of course, but to Laurel's dismay she found herself suddenly on the verge of tears.

Brendan Cody seemed oblivious. "How did you end up in God's country, anyway? You look like you're practically dying of culture shock. Nice dress, by the way. No one in this room can look at anyone else," he said, and his voice was casual, but he bent closer to her when he said it, and her heart tightened in her chest.

Exactly like Matt exactly like Matt exactly like Matt

And suddenly she was back in the dream, in the dark hall ... with the curtains blowing, the smell of jasmine, the mirror ... the mirror ...

No. No. Not again.

She backed up from Brendan Cody who was looking at her with concern, and she saw he was speaking but she couldn't hear a word, a word ...

And once again, she fled—fled the room, fled the party, fled brash young Professor Brendan Cody, fled her colleagues and her department chair, without so much as a good-bye.

Chapter Four

Outside the University Club, Laurel walked blindly on the oak-lined paths into the deepening sunset, with the dark spiked silhouettes of Gothic buildings around her, and no idea where she was going.

Great ... that's just great. You can't even make it through a cocktail party. How do you think you're going to survive the year? she berated herself.

What am I doing here? What have I done? I've torpedoed my entire life, I've landed in the middle of nowhere, and I'm going to be fired if I don't come up with some knockout proposal by ... I don't even know *by when.*

She laughed, but it was a strangled sound; she was again dangerously close to tears. Brendan Cody's questions taunted her, like hives prickling under her skin: *"And what about your hidden gifts, Professor MacDonald? Is this what you wanted to do when you grew up?"*

A dry wind whispered through the towering trees above, swirled leaves at her feet. She forced herself to breathe, to look around. There was a medieval-looking archway in front of her and she realized she was coming up on the Page Auditorium, with its turrets and heraldic crests. Instead of heading back to her car, she'd started like a homing pigeon for the main yard of West Campus, in the direction of the Psych building.

Laurel turned on the path and looked up at Perkins Library,

a looming shadow against the reddening sky. Suddenly she longed for the comfort of books around her. No matter how bad she felt, a library could always make her feel better.

She walked up the granite steps, and pushed through the fortresslike doors.

The entry of Perkins was a soaring three stories of graystone, with a domed ceiling and arched windows that in the sunset streamed pink light into the column of space—a medieval chapel of a building. Even chattering students hushed when they walked through the heavy wooden doors. Laurel could feel all the molecules in her body rearranging into something peaceful and serene as she stepped through the gates and entered the sanctum.

She breathed in ... and moved into an inner hall which led to a set of double doors of dark walnut with a brass plaque: SPECIAL COLLECTIONS LIBRARY.

The library was a long, dark-paneled study with a fireplace at one end and heavy needlepoint drapes at the windows, with groupings of antique sofas and divans, and recessed shelves— a cocoon of intimacy and concentration. Four other smaller rooms branched out from the first, each entirely lined with glass-paned bookshelves housing gorgeous volumes with gilt lettering on hand-tooled leather.

The first day Laurel found Special Collections she couldn't believe that it wasn't packed with students, assistants, and professors clamoring for any available space. She now suspected the emptiness had more than a little to do with the Special Collections librarian, Dr. Ward, a stout, quietly terrifying force of a woman who presided from a rolltop desk near the front door. Ward wore thick round glasses that made her look vaguely like an enraged owl and her black hair was cut in a severe pageboy. Her gaze could cut a student down at twenty paces.

On her first day, Laurel had approached the desk with no small amount of trepidation. "I'm Laurel MacDonald. I'm a new professor in the Psych department."

Dr. Ward looked at her unblinkingly through Coke-bottle lenses, without speaking.

Laurel summoned her courage. "I wondered if study time in the reading room had to be reserved. I'd like to sign up for a regular time, if that's possible."

The librarian looked at her, unsmiling, and answered, "No reservation required. Help yourself to a table."

Laurel glanced around the magnificent, empty room. "But ..."

Dr. Ward looked up at her, waiting.

Laurel half-laughed. "I just can't believe there aren't more people here."

"That would require taking the initiative of asking," the librarian replied dryly.

"Oh. I see," Laurel said, unable to believe her luck.

After that, almost daily she brought her notes and journals and texts with her and found a table in one of the small, leather volume-lined alcoves off the main room, where she could immerse herself in preparation for a lecture or let her mind wander to possible research topics. Dr. Ward always nodded to her—the briefest of nods, it was true, but even that was somehow comforting, the beginning of familiarity and routine, when everything else around her was so uncertain. And under that, perhaps, was even a hint of adventure.

Of course, Laurel immediately had a favorite room, which was probably why she missed the display case in her first few days of haunting the Rare Books room.

But tonight she nodded back to Ward—who was completely alone at her command post—and just wandered through the chambers, actually looking at them for the first time. Beyond the superb collections of hand-bound books, each room contained large glass exhibit cases displaying parts of the collection: fine sketchbooks open to drawings of native birds, yellowed maps documenting Blackbeard's journeys on the Carolina coast, architectural renderings of the campus buildings. Laurel moved into another, smaller alcove room. Like the other rooms it had a large glass exhibit case, this one on four legs, tablelike. She drifted over to the exhibit, expecting more sketchbooks.

What she saw instead froze her in her tracks.

She was looking down at a set of five cards of playing-card size, glossy and with a grayish tinge, as if they were of some age. There was something both archaic and strikingly familiar about the bold black symbols: a circle, a cross, three wavy lines, a square, and a star—

She *knew* those symbols.

Chapter Five

The Duke University parapsychology lab was founded in
1927 by Dr. William MacDougall and Dr. Joseph Banks Rhine,
with the mission of searching for scientifically quantifiable
evidence of paranormal, or psi phenomena, such as ESP and
psychokinesis.

Even as Laurel began to read the explanatory placards, a rush
of connections and memories was flooding into her
consciousness. The cards with their strange symbols were
Zener cards, designed for use in the groundbreaking ESP tests
of Dr. J. B. Rhine.

Laurel was experiencing a rush of emotions she was having
trouble identifying. And then a childhood memory swept over
her, shocking as ice water.

*Laurel at eleven, camping out in her school library, working for two
weeks on a science report on Rhine and his ESP experiments, illustrated
with diagrams and sketches: two students seated at a table with a black
screen between them, one looking down at a card, the other
concentrating intently, trying to guess which of the five symbols the other
student held.*

Laurel had slaved over the report, had even made up her
own set of Zener cards, and had proudly presented the project
to her mother. Meredith had gone white and swept the cards
off the table, a reaction which, coming from her normally

27

clinical and detached mother, had confused and frightened eleven-year-old Laurel. Meredith proclaimed Rhine a "kook" and parapsychology a sham, and by the end of her tirade Laurel was in tears; she ripped up her report, and hastily wrote another on right and left brain function. But her interest in psychology and the mysteries of the mind had taken root and grown, though effectively channeled into a more scientific groove.

But I didn't remember any of that, she realized with an uneasy feeling. *Not the Zener cards, not that the Rhine Lab was at Duke, not any of it. I came straight to the Rhine Lab—without even knowing what I was doing.*

The coincidence was unsettling ... and thrilling.

Laurel turned back to the glass case and quickly read through the rest of the historical placards of the display:

The Duke laboratory was the most famous parapsychology lab in the United States. Over the lab's thirty-eight-year history, Dr. Rhine and his researchers scientifically proved the existence of ESP, using "forced choice" testing with the Zener cards, in which a test subject would attempt to guess each card turned up from a deck of twenty-five cards, consisting of five sets of five simple symbols. Pure statistical chance would be a guess of five cards out of twenty-five, or 20% correct. Any score significantly greater than 20% correct was an indicator of psychic ability, and Rhine discovered test subjects who could predict the cards with accuracy far beyond statistical chance.

Rhine went on to perform laboratory tests of psychokinesis, the movement of objects by the mind, using motorized dice-throwing machines, and in the early sixties his researchers conducted field investigations of poltergeists.

Poltergeists? Laurel thought, startled. *They were investigating poltergeists?*

And then on the last placard she found the sentence that stopped her dead.

When the Duke lab closed in 1965, seven hundred boxes of research material from the parapsychology lab were sealed and stored in the basement of Perkins Library. Now for the first time in forty-five years, those boxes have been made available for public viewing.

Laurel had to read that last part three times before it fully sank in.

Seven hundred boxes of original parapsychology research material? Right here in this very building? And available to anyone who wanted to look?

She felt behind her for a chair and sat down hard, a little breathless.

It was sensational. It was unbelievable, really, that she hadn't read or heard about any of this.

Surely someone had already claimed this topic, was writing articles, papers ...

J. Walter Kornbluth's voice suddenly spoke clearly in her mind. *"These days nothing less than a book will do."*

Laurel looked over at the glass case, and thought with crystal clarity: *This is my book.* Her whole body was tingling, her face warm and flushed.

"Whoa, whoa, whoa. What are you thinking?" she muttered to herself. *You're a psychologist, a research professor. Parapsychology has nothing to do with your life's work.*

Oh, yeah? What life's work is that? some alien voice whispered back, mocking.

And she hadn't felt a rush like this, hadn't felt so enthused, since, well, since before *the dream* had shattered all her ideas of reality.

She stood from the chair, moved past the glass case in a daze, and went into the main reading room to find the librarian.

As always, Laurel approached Dr. Ward with some caution, and hovered some distance from the tall dark desk. Ward looked her over with a slightly raised eyebrow, and Laurel remembered that she was still in cocktail-party attire. She felt blood rising to her cheeks, and surreptitiously tugged the hem of her dress down.

"I was just reading the exhibit about the Rhine Lab," Laurel began. "I guess I somehow forgot all that happened here." Now that she was thinking about it, it hit her that the auditorium downstairs in the Psych Building was called Zener Auditorium. *I must have been asleep not to put it together.*

"Thirty-eight years," Ward agreed laconically. "Put the university on the map."

Encouraged by a whole two sentences from the librarian, Laurel pressed on. "I'd like to know more about it—all. Is it really true that there are seven hundred boxes of original research files right here in the library?"

"There are indeed," the librarian said, without smiling. Laurel had never seen her smile. "Seven hundred boxes."

"And anyone can just look at them—any time?"

"Any time."

Laurel hazarded another question. "Is there some study being done, then?"

"A study?" The librarian repeated.

"A research project, or a book being written, or ... I mean ... if seven hundred boxes of original research have just been opened to the public, isn't someone going through them?"

"There have been a few," the librarian said noncommittally.

"Of course,"_ Laurel said. There was no reason to think otherwise, after all. She stood for a moment, then suddenly asked. "Do you know why the department was shut down?"

The librarian raised her eyebrows.

"The parapsychology lab was so famous, and then ..." Laurel nodded back toward the display case. "The placards say it shut down entirely in 1965 ... and I wondered why."

"Dr. Rhine was approaching retirement age and wanted to move his research to a private institution where he could continue his work," Dr. Ward recited without inflection.

"That makes sense," Laurel admitted. "But why shut the whole lab down?"

Again the librarian looked up at her without speaking. This

time Laurel didn't notice; she was off on her own train of thought.

"And *why* were they sealed?"

The librarian regarded her impassively.

"The boxes," Laurel elaborated, for some reason feeling uneasy. "Why were they sealed, for all those years?"

"I couldn't tell you," Ward said.

"Thanks," Laurel said. Her mind was already a million miles away. "Thanks."

She walked out of Special Collections, out of the library, moving in a daze through Gothic stone arches, her face lit from within.

Seven hundred boxes.

What in the world might be in them?

Chapter Six

Precognition—*the ability to see or predict a future event or occurrence.*
Clairvoyance—*the ability to see an event as it happens without being physically present.*
Telepathy—*the ability to read or communicate thoughts directly between minds.*
Psychokinesis—*the ability to move objects with the mind.*

It was Sunday, and Laurel had lain awake all night in a state of overloaded excitement, and now pretty much felt as if she'd been hit by a truck, but she was at the front door of Perkins Library when it opened.

She marched through the ethereal front hall with its medieval tapestries and lambent light, straight to the intricately carved dark-wood doors of the Rare Books Room. She took the fortifying pause required to face Dr. Ward, and pushed through the doors.

Ward was unblinkingly in place behind the looming rolltop desk. Laurel walked forward, stopped before it, and said all in one breath:

"I'd like to put in a request to view the parapsychology lab files."

Ward took a good long time looking Laurel over before she reached for a library request form. "Which boxes did you want to see?"

Laurel lifted her chin. "All of them."

After summoning a library minion of indeterminate sex who scurried into place behind the rolltop desk, clearly as intimidated by Ward as Laurel was, Ward took up a massive set of keys and walked Laurel down to the basement of Perkins Library.

It was two long flights of stairs down to double doors ... which opened onto a dim and high-ceilinged basement space that was larger than anything Laurel would have dreamed lay beneath the corridors she moved through every day.

She followed Ward in a daze, down through rows of shelves that reminded her of nothing so much as the warehouse in the classic last scene of *Raiders of the Lost Ark*, in which a janitor wheels a trolley carrying the deadly Ark, enclosed in a wooden crate, through stacks of thousands of similar crates.

In this case the crates were cardboard office file boxes, but the sight was no less labyrinthine and ominous ... and the contents perhaps even more mysterious.

Ward abruptly turned down an aisle and stopped. Laurel followed her gaze to the massive wall of shelves, all lined with identical boxes.

"This is the first aisle," Ward informed her without expression. "Where did you want to start?"

Seven hundred boxes, covering thirty-eight years of laboratory research. It was monumental.

Laurel sat at a long basement table, staring at the first seven boxes of the seven hundred, neatly lined up in front of her. She had worked her way through the first third of the first box, and was beginning to get a glimmer of what she was up against.

The files were remarkably inclusive. Overwhelmingly so. The scientists, professors, researchers, and staff of the Rhine Laboratory seemed to have saved every scrap of correspondence, accounting, lab test results, employment applications, and field research reports that had ever passed through the lab. Laurel found scribbled notes on sessions with

33

trance mediums, pored over mind-bendingly tedious statistical analysis reports of ESP tests with the Zener cards, leafed through letters to the lab from clearly paranoiac, borderline personalities claiming alien abduction and governmental thought-control.

And the files were in no discernible order whatsoever.

In fact, it seemed as if whole drawers had been dumped randomly into file boxes—even more—as if the entire lab had been turned on its side and its contents poured into one box after another. Among the letters and memos and files were old cigarette packs, movie stubs from 1965, a petrified candy bar, Sen-Sen breath mints, a tarnished silver teaspoon. It was more like looking at the contents of a recluse's basement than the official department files of a major university.

After partially working through the chaos of the first box, Laurel checked several more boxes, hoping Box Number 1 was an anomaly. It wasn't. If anything, Boxes 2 through 7 were even more chaotic than the first.

Laurel had done a semester of fieldwork in a mental hospital for her PhD, cognitive therapy for schizophrenic patients. Reading through the boxes was like that—waves of delusion with occasional startling glimmers of insight. After the first hour, her head was swimming. After the second, she felt like a candidate for an institution herself. She would have to learn to skim if she was ever going to get out of that basement in her lifetime. Yet as soon as she started reading, she was hooked.

She read letters from parents who had experienced an overwhelming sensation or a vividly detailed dream of danger to their children, who had kept them from school, off flights, from getting into cars—and averted certain death by random accident.

She read story after story of ordinary people who had dreamed, or actually seen, a loved one appear to them—only to learn later that that relative or friend had died at the exact moment the apparition came to them.

She read accounts, backed up by testimony from witnesses,

from family members who had experienced phantom pain in a limb at the exact moment a relative had been injured.

And as she read, she felt a rightness about it—there was an unmistakable ring of sincerity and truth to the accounts. She believed them.

At the end of the day, Laurel returned the boxes to the front desk of the basement archives and used the call button to page Ward, then stood in a daze beside the desk, every muscle in her body and her mind sore.

The dour librarian appeared in less than a minute, as if she'd been poised and waiting for the call. She looked over Laurel and the boxes without a trace of expression.

Despite herself, Laurel blurted out, "So there's no order to any of this?"

"Not that anyone's seen so far," Ward said dryly. "Had enough?"

Somewhere deep inside Laurel, something flared. "I'll be back tomorrow at nine," she said defiantly.

"Huh," Ward said, and began stacking the boxes.

As Laurel drove home through the dark maze of trees, her mind kept straying to her own dream. Finally, she pulled the car over to the side of the road, stopped the engine, and sat back against the seat, letting herself experience the memory . . .

Step by step down the long, dark hall, bare feet on the cool hardwood floor . . . the sick-sweet scent of jasmine and the sound of moans . . .

And the shattering . . .

Laurel gasped and pulled herself out of the memory. She was breathing hard . . . and she could feel the beginning of welts rising on her chest.

She clenched her hands around the steering wheel, and closed her eyes, trying to calm herself.

As much as she had tried to dissect the dream in logical terms: she was subconsciously aware of Matt's infidelity; she'd gotten real life hints that Tracey was his lover, there had been clues, there had been signs all along . . .

None of those hints and clues explained the time on the

clock, the siren and the dog, and the smell of jasmine—all details she dreamed, exactly as they happened, before they happened.

And the mirror ... the mirror ...

Without realizing it, she spoke aloud into the dark. "It wasn't broken before. It shattered ... while I was standing there."

For the first time she allowed herself to consider the possibility that there may have been more to the dream.

Much, much more.

Chapter Seven

> **If indeed we have this ability, then why are we not devoting every waking hour to the exploration of that possibility?**
> **—Dr. Alaistair Leish**

In the early morning before class, Laurel sat in the darkness of a basement library carrel, the light from a black-and-white sixteen-millimeter film flickering on her face. The film was of an interview: On the small screen in front of her a man was speaking from a leather armchair in front of a wall lined with books, in what looked like a private study or library. The man was tall, lean, blond, and gorgeous, dressed in an elegantly tailored suit with a narrow tie. His voice was as rich and refined as the voices of the best actors and news broadcasters of the time.

He leaned forward in this chair with an intensity that sent chills through Laurel's entire body; he seemed to be speaking directly to her, in that velvety British accent.

"Perhaps that which we call 'reality' is no more than an agreement, a social contract that the less imaginative among us have decided upon, for the sake of convenience. But what if life is—in reality—more like the dreaming state? If time is a spiral, then is it possible to remember the future as well as the past? Might that begin to explain ESP?"

The black-and-white film had the grainy quality of a

newsreel and seemed like a jolt from history. The only marking on the film can was ALAISTAIR LEISH, 1965. Laurel had found the can of film in one of the file boxes and was now watching it on one of the library's machines, completely riveted to the screen.

An off-camera interviewer was asking: "Dr. Leish, what are the implications if ESP really exists?"

Leish looked into the camera, straight at Laurel, into her very soul. "It means everything we know about reality is in question. It means that we are on the threshold of a whole new world."

His voice was so quietly confident, so clearly in awe of the possibilities, that Laurel felt a thrill running up her spine, ending in a tingling behind her ears. She was barely aware of her body in the chair.

The film cut to overhead shots of the Duke campus in the sixties. Laurel was enchanted by the agelessness of it, the time-machine feeling of seeing the same buildings she walked by and worked in every day, in another era. The camera lingered on a distinctive Greco-Roman building with a copper dome and four tall white pillars on the portico. Laurel felt another shiver at a shot of a wooden door, with a window of frosted glass and the lettering: PARAPSYCHOLOGY LAB.

Then she leaned on her elbows and watched, mesmerized by the footage of Zener-card tests: the volunteers in their 1960s dresses and suits sitting at opposite sides of a small square table with a dark-wood screen partition in the center of the table that hid the cards on either side from view of the researcher and the test subject.

The next shot was of a machine consisting of a stand and a long lever that rotated a two-foot-long rectangular cage with rolling dice inside it.

Both shots were so familiar Laurel felt she must have seen some similar film before, if not the same reel. But she had no idea where that would have been.

The film moved back to a voice-over of Leish telling his own story, while Laurel was treated to a series of photos of the younger Leish, breathtakingly, arrogantly handsome, with thick blond hair and light piercing eyes.

"My first poltergeist investigation took place at a farm in Sussex in 1951. The family had reported knocking and scratching in the walls, bedclothes being pulled off the children as they were sleeping, the radio going on and off at odd hours." Leish's voice dropped into a storytelling hush and Laurel leaned forward, entranced. "I was convinced that the twelve-year-old son of the farmer had been faking all the 'poltergeist' effects: pulling out drawers when no one was watching, spilling sugar and salt on the kitchen counters and floor." Leish paused. "But one night, in the middle of the night, long after this boy had gone to bed, I was sleeping on the couch in the living room, and I suddenly awoke to intense cold. A fire was blazing in the hearth, but I could see my own breath in the air. Then with my own eyes I saw coins begin to fall from the ceiling. They appeared just below the ceiling and fell to the floor without a sound, like rain."

Dr. Leish paused again to let the story resonate. Laurel felt chills through her entire body now.

"Such an experience changes you on the most profound level. How can you not halt everything in your life, and devote the rest of your life to pursuing that question—of whether a thing like this *could* happen ... and how?"

Laurel pushed back her chair to stand ... and found her legs were too weak to hold her. She sat, shivering, wanting to shout, *Yes! It happened to me, too! It happened and nothing has been the same.*

The film continued, but Laurel had no idea what was playing on the screen. Her face was flushed, her own blood pounding in her ears. She knew what she was looking for, now: Leish had just spoken her inmost feelings aloud. How could she not stop everything to pursue how such things happen? How she could have had the dream, how could she have seen it all, known it all?

How?

*

39

Laurel drove home from campus with wind gusting through the streets, whipping at the trees around her, turning the green wall into a moving ocean of branches and leaves. A storm was coming; she could see it in the roiling dark clouds above. The frequent and sudden thunderstorms were another unnerving but strangely thrilling aspect of her new Southern life.

She reached home just as the sky opened, and she ran toward the house through pelting rain, soaked but exhilarated.

Up in the study, the cat sat watching in the doorway as Laurel patted her hair dry with a towel and logged on to the Net to learn more about Dr. Leish. She had never heard of him, and she had to admit it was not just the thrill of the unknown; it was the man himself who was mesmerizing. She Googled him (which was cheating, she knew, but she needed the instant gratification), and clicked through several links, skimming eagerly. And all she got was a mystery wrapped in a mystery.

Leish had begun his career as a psychologist with a specialty in hypnotism, but became converted to the study of parapsychology after his experience on the farm in Sussex. He made a name for himself in Europe by investigating haunted houses and lecturing to parapsychology societies, and was a member of the British Society for Psychical Research. He wrote a book specifically about poltergeists, on which he continued to do field investigations into the 1960s.

So was he here at Duke? Laurel wondered. The film had shown footage of the Duke campus, and the shots of Leish testing students with the Zener cards and dice machines in the film certainly looked like photos she'd seen of the Duke lab. She tried Googling "Leish + Duke University," but found no matches beyond a few articles that mentioned both in general reference to the subject of parapsychology—nothing to indicate he was ever part of the Duke parapsychology lab.

Next she Googled Leish's book, *The Lure of the Poltergeist*. It

40

was out of print and going for a staggering $1,800 on Abe Books, when it was even available.

"Well, that's out," she murmured wryly.

She returned to clicking through articles online and skimming. As a personality psychologist, she found the whole idea of poltergeists fascinating: that random, inexplicable movements could have a mischievous, teasing quality, even an intention—although surely those qualities were simply projected onto the phenomena by human observers. But that in itself was tantalizing: the psychological projection of human qualities onto inexplicable phenomena.

She was intrigued by Leish's take on the subject. He'd headed up poltergeist investigations in Europe and reported that poltergeist manifestations almost always increased over the course of an incident—and actually stepped up once outside investigators were on the scene. Leish advanced a theory that a poltergeist was fed by a spiraling group dynamic, that started with the family and then was fed by the expectations of investigators, researchers, even law enforcement officials and the media—in other words, that a poltergeist was actually created by human intention.

A kind of group hypnosis, Laurel thought, *or shared madness.* There was something that made sense about it, and admittedly, was fascinating.

She clicked onto another article—then her eyes stopped on a phrase:

After Leish's death in April 1965 ...

She sat back in her chair, thinking, *So he must have died not long after that film was made.*

She felt a curious sense of disappointment, even loss.

She made a notation in her notebook and circled it. After a moment she added a row of question marks as well.

Leish died April 1965
???

She stood from her table and stepped to the window, opening it to let in the cold, wet air. She stood leaning against the sill, watching the rain, and thinking about the maze of boxes.

The initially daunting lack of order to the files had become intriguing. Laurel had a growing suspicion that the chaos had an order of its own, that someone had *deliberately* scrambled the contents of the boxes so that only someone with a road map could decipher the patterns. The mystery made her even more determined to crack the code.

"There's something else, too," she said aloud into the cool dimness of the room.

At first, it was just a question that surfaced again as she worked her way steadily through the boxes, a question she filed away to consider later, but which kept popping up in her mind and then gradually took over her thoughts.

Why the hell did the lab shut down?

She went back to her desk table, and sat in her chair to open the notebook in which she'd been compiling her random notes.

In 1965, the Duke parapsychology lab had shut down completely. All right, Dr. Rhine had retired from the Duke faculty, and he moved his research off campus, continuing his work with the other foundations he'd set up. Laurel could understand that—to a degree. *But why shut the entire lab down?* All records stopped short in 1965, just when it seemed that the parapsychology lab was more famous than it had ever been, garnering national media attention on the Seaford poltergeist investigation—"The House of Flying Objects"—and the subsequent "Project Poltergeist" case in Newark. The entire world had known about the Duke parapsychology lab.

And even more puzzling: Why had all those years of research been sealed?

Why seal it all up for so long?

42

"Why?" she said aloud.

Across the room there was a sudden scraping slide and crash.

Laurel leaped out of her chair, which toppled to the ground behind her as she spun in the direction of the crash.

The window had slid shut on its own, falling violently against the sill.

Laurel stood staring at it with her heart racing in her chest. After a moment she approached cautiously.

The window was old, of course, an archaic counterweight device, the ropes of which were either cut, or sprung, or painted shut on half the windows in the house.

"It's an old house," she told herself, unaware until she heard the words that she'd spoken them aloud. "And the wind . . ." Her voice sounded shaky in the twilight silence of the room.

But right there: a perfect example of what she'd been reading.

I actually psyched myself into believing for half a second in some kind of paranormal visitation. Just exactly what happens in these poltergeist incidents.

She moved back to the long table and looked down at her notebook, at the notation she had made:

Leish died April 1965
???

It bothered her. It didn't merely bother her, it gnawed at her. Why?

It was a genuine mystery. Leish was only forty-one when he died. Did he die in the middle of some investigation? Without realizing it, she spoke aloud: "He died the same month that the lab shut down. Within weeks."

And then a thought struck her that sent chills through her.

Could his death possibly have anything to do with the lab shutting down?

She grabbed her notebook and a pen and wrote quickly.

43

Leish was at Duke in 1965?
Leish died in 1965
The lab shut down in 1965
What happened?

Then she almost jumped out of her skin—as the phone shrilled on her desk behind her.

Chapter Eight

Laurel shot to her feet with a rush of guilt, as if she'd been caught doing something illicit. The number displayed on the phone screen was her mother's and Laurel picked up to Meredith's no-nonsense voice.

"Are you in the middle of something?"

Although Meredith could not possibly see what she was doing, Laurel closed her notebook and slid it into her desk drawer as if to hide it from her mother's eyes.

"Just doing some work on my research proposal," she said, and instantly regretted saying it aloud. *Try explaining to Meredith that you're researching poltergeists—that will go well. Maybe I left my entire mind back in L.A. . . .*

"Is everything okay, Mom?" Laurel asked quickly, to divert any questions, but in truth she was wondering. Meredith never called, never did anything, without a good reason.

"It's your Aunt Margaret. She's been trying to get through to you, to ask you over for dinner."

Laurel felt another stab of guilt. Since the *dream* breakup, she was in the habit of going a week or more without checking her phone messages. It was another symptom of her disappearance into oblivion.

"I'll call her tomorrow, Mom," she promised. "I've just been . . . settling in. I've been busy with this project—"

"What project is that?"

"It's an educational testing series I'm developing," Laurel lied. There was a long silence on the phone. Laurel didn't try to fill it.

"Laurel, are you sure you know what you're doing?" her mother said bluntly.

Laurel felt her cheeks burn. *No, Mother, I have no idea whatsoever.*

Aloud she said, "I'm adjusting, Mom. Really. I—Duke is great, my house is lovely. I'm sure I'll be happy here."

Whatever happy is.

Meredith sighed. "Call your aunt."

"I will." Laurel promised, and characteristically, Meredith hung up without a good-bye or another word.

Laurel set down the phone and looked around at her study: the teetering stacks of books she'd already collected on psi, telepathy—*and poltergeists, don't forget poltergeists . . .*

She glanced uneasily up at her calendar on the wall. Her appointment with Dr. Unger was circled in red—only two weeks away and she was no closer to a research proposal than she had been on her first day. But there was something here, something she didn't understand, but something big.

"I know it," she said softly.

Outside the window, lightning cracked, branching white light through the sky.

Chapter Nine

The French psychologist Jacques Lacan said, "Trauma repeats almost inevitably." Freud called this the "repetition compulsion." Both psychologists were talking about the psychological traumas passed on within families, from generation to generation. But one theory of hauntings is that houses repeat trauma as well.

—Alaistair Leish, *The Lure of the Poltergeist*

Aunt Margaret lived in an elegant older Durham neighborhood of doctors, scientists, professors, and other professionals. The house was Federal-style, with slender white columns and dark shutters at the windows, austere against the two stories of white brick. Towering magnolias lined the brick walkway; Laurel could smell their faint and waxy perfume as she walked up the path toward the door, fighting anxiety. Her aunt and uncle might be blood relatives but they were virtual strangers to her.

Laurel's mother had fled the South at seventeen, as soon as she graduated high school, and headed for Berkeley on a full scholarship to the biology department. It was 1965, but Meredith hadn't been looking to join any hippie revolution—she'd just chosen a school as geographically far from the South as she could get without leaving the continent, and had never looked back. As far as Laurel had been able to glean, she herself was the unintended consequence of a graduate-school affair with a professor, and for some reason unfathomable to Laurel, Meredith had decided to keep her. Meredith had never married; had bounced around from university to university in the Bay Area with Laurel in tow until she landed a tenured position at Stanford, and Laurel had grown up in university day care and in magnet schools, with a brilliant and distant parent who was more like a roommate than a mother. In all of Laurel's life Meredith had barely mentioned her family, and Laurel had met them only twice, when she was barely out of diapers. Meredith had always seemed to her like her own continent, not part of a family at all— it was the reality Laurel had grown up with and had not thought to question.

Laurel had only the sketchiest memories of those two visits to North Carolina: lush green fields and brilliant flowers, butterflies as big as birds, a grandmother she had adored who was as maternal as her own mother was not, a stern aunt who was, if it was possible, even more aloof than Meredith, and a sweet, vague uncle with a disarming smile.

Laurel flashed back to the phone call with her mother, when she'd told Meredith she'd accepted the Duke job. In that drawn-out minute of Meredith's silence on the phone, Laurel had realized how very little she really knew about her mother's childhood.

"Mom? Is something—wrong?"

"Of course not," Meredith snapped. The silence continued.

"Well," Meredith finally said. "It's a fine school, no question. Congratulations on the job. Call Aunt Margaret when you get in—I'm sure she'll introduce you around." She paused, and then added dryly, "And stock up on insect repellant—you're going to need it."

Laurel had hung up with a sense of confusion, feeling distinctly odd about the phone call. There was something about the undercurrents there that went beyond her mother's constant need for control. The feeling Laurel had gotten instead was a deep sense of unease, as unlikely coming from Meredith as finding her in the kitchen baking cookies. But that

48

was quickly forgotten in the whirlwind of packing and selling, of arranging and departing. Now Laurel felt it again, that deep unease …

Why?

She looked up at her aunt's house, took a breath, then stepped onto the porch and rang the bell.

The door was opened by an older and sterner version of Laurel's mother, austere, trim to the point of boniness, but with the same auburn hair and blue eyes. Laurel tried to swallow her surprise, and saw that Aunt Margaret gave her an equally startled, appraising look before she reached to embrace her stiffly, with a brusque, "Welcome to North Carolina."

She ushered Laurel in to a darkish entry with a curving staircase up to the second floor with a baby grand piano beside the landing. A double doorway to the right opened into a formal dining room; the double doorway to the left led to an equally formal living room. The furniture was antique and somber. Laurel felt her back stiffening, her posture straightening just stepping into the hall.

"It's a beautiful house," she said aloud, dutifully, but in truth she found it weighty and depressing.

Life with her mother had had its awkwardness, but Meredith's sprawling clutter of books and professional papers, and predilection for old California bungalows and disregard for mealtimes (or anything to do with food in general) had given their life a sort of casual disorder. Laurel felt the gloomy rigidity of her aunt's house working on her senses and thought she finally had a glimmer of why Meredith had gone so far away and with such finality.

Margaret didn't offer a tour of the house, although as Laurel followed her aunt to the sitting room (or was it called a parlor?) she got glimpses of an updated cook's kitchen, a dark-paneled study with recessed bookshelves, a screened-in porch with crisply upholstered Cape Cod furniture, and a breakfast alcove with a round table and arched windows on three sides.

Laurel paused for a moment, frowning in at the breakfast

room … and felt some kind of memory stirring, just out of reach. Then she realized her aunt was stopped in the hall, waiting for her to follow, and she turned and moved after Margaret through the den.

Everything was spotless and more floral in pattern than Laurel would have expected her aunt's taste to be, but Laurel was finding that flowery bent typical for the South.

She felt movement from the doorway behind her and turned with a start—to see a ruddy, sweet-faced man of around sixty hovering shyly behind her, in the doorway of the study. His eyes were an amazing crystal blue: Carolina blue, they called it here.

"Well, come in, Morgan—say hello." Margaret spoke irritably, as to a child. The man blushed and dipped his head. "Morgan, you remember Laurel. Laurel, your Uncle Morgan."

Laurel smiled at her uncle and he sidled into the room, peering at her worriedly. Laurel was starting to wonder if he could speak at all. Then suddenly he beamed at her, his whole face lighting.

"Meredith."

For a moment Laurel thought he was in a fog of age, mistaking her for her mother. Margaret frowned and opened her mouth to speak, when Morgan shook his head.

"You look just like her," he said softly, and Laurel felt her eyes brimming with unexpected tears.

Dinner, thankfully, commenced almost immediately, with Margaret serving from a sideboard and delegating a few trivial tasks. They sat down to the formally laid table with no grace said or even alluded to; in that, family was family.

There was no sign of a cook or any other household help, though Laurel couldn't imagine that Aunt Margaret had made the gargantuan dinner on her own. Along with both fried chicken and steak, there were biscuits, three kinds of casseroles, and two kinds of pie, along with bottomless glasses of sweet tea. Laurel kept murmuring, "Yes, please," to refills, even though one of the first things she'd had to learn was to order her iced tea "unsweet"

50

to avoid the syrupy concoction that was the regional standard.

Even with the distraction of eating, Laurel was almost paralyzed with awkwardness. Every few minutes she found herself straightening her spine, anxious to sit properly. Questions about her mother were quickly floated and answered, Margaret's work in recombinant DNA discussed, and Morgan's reduced hours at the tobacco shop he had owned for years took mere minutes to relate, as Margaret did all the talking and clearly had no use for her brother's shopkeeping activities. Morgan himself barely said a word beyond "please" and "thank you" throughout the entire meal, and Margaret answered any questions directed toward him for him. Laurel began to think her uncle might be simple ("simple" was the word that went through her head, instead of "autistic" or "borderline" or "schizotypal" or "developmentally disabled"). She was vaguely aware that he had lived with Margaret for some time, but had no idea if that was because he was unable to take care of himself on his own or simply that, as a lifelong bachelor and spinster, the living arrangement was more convenient and economical for both of them. But she also knew he was educated, a Duke graduate himself.

Something doesn't fit, she thought. *I wonder.*

She became aware that an appalling silence had fallen around the table, and she leapt to fill it without entirely thinking.

"So I've been doing some research into the Rhine Laboratory."

Margaret instantly stiffened. The air around them seemed to thicken. Morgan was industriously bent over his plate, cutting his steak, his face not visible.

Margaret touched her napkin to her lips. "What"—her tone added "on earth"—"is your interest in the Rhine Lab?"

Laurel felt as if she were walking around mines. She realized instinctively she should not mention her book. If she'd been thinking at all she would have taken the clear warning in Margaret's tone and dropped the subject altogether, but the fact was, she didn't know what was driving her fascination with the lab, and she had no one else to talk to about it. And somewhere in her mind, without being aware of it, she'd done the math: both Margaret and Morgan would have been at Duke in the early sixties, so surely they had anecdotal knowledge of the parapsychology lab. It had been too famous by the 1960s—the entire world had known about Rhine; as Duke students, they must have been acutely aware of the lab. She tried to keep her tone light, to diffuse the strange tension.

"I'm not sure exactly. It hadn't even occurred to me that it was here, at Duke. I've heard so much about it ..." She laughed slightly. "Well, it's almost mythic, isn't it?"

"Mythic," Margaret repeated, tonelessly.

Laurel pressed on. "I was wondering why it was closed. So abruptly. I haven't been able to find much about that."

Margaret set down her glass with a thud.

"It was closed because people came to their senses. Balderdash. All of those years—all of those resources squandered on something purely unprovable. People wanting to believe and making up facts to support it. Gullible people buying into a fraud. I'm surprised you'd waste your time on something so silly."

Her aunt was near trembling with anger. Laurel was stunned into silence. Morgan had not once raised his gaze from his plate during the entire exchange.

"I was only ... curious," Laurel stammered.

"Curiosity killed the cat." Margaret stood, and lifted her plate. Suddenly the storm had passed and her face assembled itself into something more dignified. "If you'll excuse me, I'll get dessert."

As Margaret left the room, Laurel could have cut the silence with the silver butter knife she still held limply in her hand.

Morgan had raised his head and was looking at her from across the table. "I did it," he said quietly, conspiratorially.

Laurel looked at him, startled that he'd even spoken. She had no idea what he was confessing to.

He nodded solemnly. "I did the tests. Dr. Rhine tested me. I did it."

Margaret's steps clicked in the hall, approaching, and Morgan went back to mopping up gravy on his plate as if nothing had happened at all, leaving Laurel stunned speechless.

After dinner Morgan promptly disappeared for the rest of the evening, which didn't last much longer beyond dessert. Laurel helped Margaret clear the dishes and load the dishwasher; they talked of her house purchase and of reliable plumbers and yard services, and steered far clear of the Rhine Laboratory. Morgan had retreated to the dark-paneled study; when Laurel stopped in to say good-bye he rose vaguely from a large leather armchair, book in hand, and bowed graciously. His blue eyes were so hazy Laurel had no idea if he was even aware of who she was.

At home in bed, with the still-unnamed cat purring like a diesel combine on the pillow beside her, Laurel tossed restlessly and pondered the chances that she would be related to an original Rhine test subject.

Not so entirely surprising, is it? Rhine and his researchers had conducted their experiments for thirty-eight years and had used hundreds, maybe thousands of student volunteers. Morgan had been attending the university at the time. Why wouldn't he have participated?

She rolled over, resettled her pillow, stared up into the dark.

But why is Aunt Margaret so angry about it? Not even just angry . . .

Laurel lay still for a minute, trying to identify what she had felt from her aunt's reaction.

Frightened.

What Aunt Margaret was, was frightened.

53

Chapter Ten

She is at a table, a round breakfast table, in a sunny room, arched glass windows on three sides. She is tall but small, not just small, in a high chair, a child, a toddler giggling through wisps of red-gold hair. The sun is dazzling through the windows, warm on her cheeks.

At the side of the table, a beaming man with a round, ruddy face laughs with her, blue eyes sparkling ...

... as the forks and spoons dance by themselves on the table in front of them ...

Laurel's eyes flew open. Her cheeks were warm ... as warm as if she'd been sitting in sunlight.

But the electronic shrilling she was hearing did not belong in that sunny breakfast room. She moved under the blankets, shaking off sleep, and realized her cell phone was jangling on the stand beside the bed.

To her vast and groggy surprise the caller was her mother. Adrenaline shot through Laurel and she bolted up in bed. "Mom? Is everything okay?" Meredith never called two days in a row, and it was shockingly early in West Coast time.

"Of course," Meredith's voice was gravelly, irritable. "I was just calling to see how it went."

Laurel wrested her co-opted pillow away from the cat and leaned back against it. She wasn't entirely buying her mother's sudden attempt to be an involved parent, but saw an

54

opportunity to mine some information herself.

"It was nice," she said neutrally. For a moment she wondered if Margaret had already reported about the dinner, if there was some conspiracy between the all-but-estranged sisters. *And why would you be thinking that?*

"So everyone's well?" Meredith was asking, equally neutrally.

"They seem fine, Mom," Laurel answered. "It was nice of them to have me." Then before she could lose her nerve, she blurted out. "Did you know that Uncle Morgan was a test subject in the Rhine parapsychology experiments?"

There was an instantaneous, live silence on the other end of the phone. After an eternity, Meredith said slowly. "Yes, that's right. I'd all but forgotten about that." Then she said something that threw Laurel more than anything else that had happened. "He always was like Mama that way."

Meredith's voice was far away, and she'd reverted to a Southern accent that Laurel had only heard her use in times of extreme stress. Laurel held her breath, wondering if her mother would say more. When she didn't, Laurel hazarded:

"Like Grandma—in what way?"

"What?" Meredith snapped, and there was a hint of outrage in her tone. "I don't know what you're talking about. How in the world did that business come up, anyway?" Meredith's tone was back to her usual crisp irritability, and the Southern accent was gone.

"Oh, I saw an exhibit in the library and wondered if they remembered the lab," Laurel said vaguely. She hesitated, then took the plunge. "All of those experiments must have been a huge deal on campus when Aunt Margaret and Uncle Morgan were there, at Duke."

The silence on the other end was icy. "I hope you haven't been upsetting your uncle."

What? What was that?

Laurel swallowed. "I don't think I have, Mom. What do you mean?"

Her mother ignored that entirely. "I have to run. I'm

55

speaking at a conference this morning—"

"Wait—Mom," Laurel said quickly. "I wanted to know … when we visited Aunt Margaret and Uncle Morgan and Grandma—when I was three or four—were they living in the same house? The two-story with that glassed-in breakfast room?"

Her mother paused. "Yes, the house on Steeple Street. Why?"

Laurel closed her eyes and saw the sunny alcove from her dream, the silverware dancing on the table in front of her uncle.

"I thought I remembered it. I just wanted to know."

Again, silence, something unspoken. Then Meredith said, "Don't forget to write your aunt a thank-you note; they live and die on those things there."

As usual Meredith disconnected without saying good-bye, but Laurel had gotten what she needed: Uncle Morgan wasn't fantasizing; he really had been a test subject in the lab. And Meredith's unexpected admission kept playing in her head.

He always was like Mama that way.

The thought, coming from her supremely rational mother, gave Laurel an eerie thrill. It meant Meredith believed that Morgan, and their mother, had some kind of—and Laurel had to pause even mentally before she even thought the word—

Power.

She felt caught in something huge, something bigger than herself, and yet *about* herself—something almost inevitable.

I have to know what happened.

Chapter Eleven

Laurel was barely able to focus on her "Theories of Personality" lecture, a fact that was not lost on Tyler Mountford, who smirked down at her knowingly from his front and center seat every time she drifted off in thought and lost her place.

As soon as she uttered the last word she dismissed the class without discussion and raced through a morning drifting with gray fog across to the Administration Building.

"No Alaistair Leish on staff," said the blond clerk in the registrar's office, with red, white, and blue salon nails clicking on the computer keys.

"Could you check for other years besides 1965?" Laurel asked. "Or how about as a guest lecturer?"

"It would have come up in the search," the clerk said. "There's no record of an Alaistair Leish ever being on the university payroll."

Laurel turned away from the counter, murmuring thanks, and stood for a moment on the marble floor, frowning and frustrated. *But Leish must have been at the lab. All those shots of Duke in the film . . . so why no record of him?*

She left the Administration Building and crossed the quad under the massive oaks. She paused on the path and stared through the fog at the Psych Building.

Now what?

She knew there might well be professors in the department who would have been at Duke in the sixties, but she felt an instinctive reluctance to approach any of her department colleagues on the subject. It wasn't paranoia, really, but she didn't want someone co-opting her project, even though she didn't exactly have one, yet.

And there was no one yet that she *could* talk to, anyway. She'd seen Brendan Cody around campus, of course, in the halls of the Psych department, holding seminars outside on the lawn under the trees. It was impossible to miss his constant whirl of energy and exuberance.

He was always surrounded by coeds, psych students who obviously had more interest in the young professor than in the study of the mind. And the sight of Brendan surrounded by sighing females made Laurel even more determined to avoid him, for her own self-preservation.

She turned on the path and glanced toward the circle of oaks where she often saw him with his study groups, but on this chilly day the lawn was empty, dotted with little white daisies.

She was not aware that she herself sighed, as she turned away from the tree.

It's fine. I can do this by myself. She stood for a moment, looking at the buildings around her, then she started off through the drifting gray fog across to East Campus.

It was unmistakably the same building.

She stood on the rough marble of the portico, looking up at the building from the Leish film, an elegant copper-domed structure, Greco-Roman, with four tall white columns on the portico.

Laurel stepped forward and tried each one of the heavy double doors. Locked. She moved back to look up at the building again.

The sign above the doors read BALDWIN AUDITORIUM, and it was not the kind of building she would have expected to house an academic department. So, had a building of original classrooms that had contained the parapsychology lab been converted into an auditorium? Or had she made some sort of mistake? Perhaps the shot of the building from the old film she had seen had been an aesthetic choice rather than the actual building that had housed the Rhine Lab?

She was fighting an almost crushing sense of disappointment as she walked down the steps. *But what did you really expect to see? It was a lab, not a haunted house,* she told herself.

It was a cold day, overcast and misty from the night's rain, a hint of winter before fall, and the drifting fog made Laurel feel even more alone in the vast and strangely deserted quad. Most of the former academic buildings had been converted to freshman dorms, and compared to the constant activity and traffic of West it seemed like a ghost campus—only an occasional student going in or out of the residence halls.

At the foot of the grass circle below the auditorium was a towering bronze statue of Duke University founder Washington Duke, seated in a bronze easy chair. Only "seated" was not exactly the correct word. The founder was more precisely "slouched" or "sprawled" in the chair, cigar in mouth, bronze hands loosely gripping the rounded armrests of the chair, legs flung carelessly wide apart, with the ease and arrogance that only comes with vast wealth, and looking pretty much as if he still owned the place. Laurel circled the statue in a sort of awed admiration; she'd never seen a statue with quite such . . . attitude.

A voice spoke behind, her, a low, lazy drawl. "Thinkin' of climbing up?"

She turned, startled—and was even more startled to see Tyler Mountford standing on the grass, watching her.

"Everyone does it." Tyler's eyes flicked up to the statue of Washington Duke, then back to Laurel, with insolent amusement. "That ol' dog has had more sorority girls in his lap than three generations of lacrosse teams."

Laurel almost laughed. "I'm sure," she said, willing her face not to redden under the boy's sly smile. She suddenly wondered if he had followed her from class. "I think I'll pass, though."

He glanced around the deserted quad. "What are you doing all the way over here on East? Nothing but freshman and theater geeks over here."

I might ask the same thing of you, she thought. While she was annoyed at his intimate and knowing tone, she realized she might be able to get information out of him, so she smiled as she answered.

"I'd seen photos of that building"—she turned and indicated the domed auditorium—"and I wanted to come take a look ... but it's locked. Do you know—was it always an auditorium? Or did there used to be classrooms there?"

"Looking for the Rhine Lab?"

She started, and he smiled slowly at her, enjoying her discomfort. *How did he know?*

He shrugged. "You're from California, aren't you? Y'all are into all that spooky shit." He looked at her challengingly.

"I don't know," she found herself responding without thinking. "From all I've been reading, you have a whole lot more ghosts here in the South."

"Yes, we do." His drawl extended all vowels for at least three syllables, and she was uncomfortably aware of feeling the words like an illicit caress. She was immensely irritated at this automatic sexual response she was having to a kid who was at least ten years younger than she was. *That's the last thing you need,* she thought. *Leave. Now.*

Instead she found herself saying aloud, "So the Rhine Lab *was* in that building?"

"Oh yeah," he said, his eyes gleaming.

"How do you know?" she demanded.

That lazy shrug. "I've worked crew on some shows."

This seemed to her unlikely in the extreme and she was about to say so, when he smiled crookedly. "Gut class. Easy five units."

She studied him, still skeptical. "I can't see it."

"I had a band for a while," he said, and his face was suddenly closed.

60

Now that makes some sense ... that musician indolence. And probably didn't have the guts to risk the family inheritance by telling Daddy he was going into music.

"What's your major, anyway?" she asked casually.

His smile twisted again. "Business, what else?"

"Ah. Oldest son?"

"Oh, yes, ma'am."

His voice was light and mocking, but she could hear the simmering anger underneath. She supposed his family went to Duke, too, the father at the very least, but probably a whole line of them. She decided not to push the questions, for the moment.

She turned and looked at him straight on. "Who told you where the lab used to be?"

He leaned back against the base of the statue, hands gripping the marble edge, a pose strikingly similar to the captured arrogance of the statue. "The old guys from the scene shop talk about it. Say it's haunted, because of all the Rhine experiments."

"Haunted?" She stared at him.

"Oh, they're just mainly trying to haze us, I know. But things go missing down in the shop, and sometimes the lights go weird, and they say it's because of all those kids that Rhine brought in and tested. The kids from the haunted houses. The shop guys say they brought the ghosts in with them."

Laurel was strangely electrified, even though she knew the prevalent theory was that poltergeist phenomena had nothing to do with ghosts.

She realized she was holding her breath, and was suddenly annoyed with herself. *What are you looking for? What do you expect, here? What the hell is this about, anyway?*

Tyler was watching her like a cat. He smiled slowly. "You're really into it, aren't you?"

"Curious," she said, briefly. "It's all curious. So what else have they told you, the 'old guys'?"

He shrugged, pushed off the granite slab on which he was

61

leaning. "What were you looking to know?"

Good question, she thought to herself. "Has anyone ever said why the lab closed down?"

He smiled, a strangely humorless smile. "Well, it's kind of a shock they ever let it happen at all, isn't it? Studying ghosts and such on a college campus?"

"Have you ever seen anything happen, in there?" she said suddenly.

He looked at her, and after a long moment he smiled. "Can't say I believe in that stuff, Dr. MacDonald." His smile broadened. "It was just you were interested, and all. Has anything spooky ever happened to you?"

She found her skin heating. "I—no. You mean ghosts? Nothing."

He sat back, studying her. "Ghosts—or anything. You're into this for a reason, aren't you? Doesn't just come out of nowhere . . ."

She looked into the drifting fog, and her dream came back to her. The clock that read 3:33 A.M. The dog barking in the distance. The fire siren. The curtain blowing at the window.

I saw it all.

She snapped back to the present. Tyler was still watching her, leaning on the base of the statue again, ankles crossed, smiling faintly.

"Well, thanks, Tyler," Laurel said stiffly. "You've been very helpful."

"Anytime," he drawled, and dipped his head, a mocking little bow. She could feel his eyes on her back as she started off across the lawn.

She suddenly turned back to him and called out. "Have you ever heard of a Dr. Alaistair Leish?"

He looked at her for a long moment. "Can't say I have." He tilted his head. "Why?"

Laurel had a strange impulse to answer, when she noticed two coeds with Duke sweatshirts approaching the statue behind Tyler. One scrambled up into Washington Duke's lap,

62

while the other giggled and aimed a camera phone. At the flash of the camera, Laurel halted in her tracks.

"Of course," she said aloud. "Of course." Before Tyler could speak, she had turned and was running, across the grassy yard again toward Perkins Library.

Chapter Twelve

Laurel pushed through the doors of the Special Collections room and approached the rolltop desk. Ward gave an exaggerated sigh and reached for the keys to the basement.

Laurel gasped out, still breathless from her mad dash across campus. "Actually ... I was wondering if the library kept a collection of school yearbooks ... and where I might find those."

On the third floor, Laurel sat at a table with stacks of yearbooks in front of her and a panoramic view out the window in front of her. After two weeks in the basement it was strange to sit at a library table with a view of trees and Duke Gardens and the spires of the Chapel, rather than the windowless gloom of the underground.

As she began to browse the yearbooks, one thing was immediately clear: the parapsychology lab had been a vital, vibrant part of university life. In nearly every yearbook since the lab's opening there were candid and posed photos of Dr. Rhine, his wife and colleague Dr. Louisa Rhine, other professors and assistants, and students. Laurel turned the pages and saw history go by in the progression of photos on the lab, the evolving postures and attitudes of the students, along with the changing hairstyles and tie widths and skirt lengths.

She skipped through to the sixties, reached for the 1965 yearbook, and opened it to the inevitable section on the Rhine Lab. Her eyes were immediately caught by a candid black-and-white photo of a mesmerizingly handsome, light-haired man. Laurel felt an electric thrill: the man was unidentified in the photo caption but she recognized Dr. Alaistair Leish from the film.

"Yes!" she said aloud, so forcefully that several students looked out from their study carrels. Laurel blushed to the roots of her hair, but she felt a rush of triumph at this proof of her intuition.

So it's true: Leish was at the Duke lab. I knew he couldn't stay away from the poltergeist research.

He was here, and he died.

She sat very still ... then started turning pages impatiently. When she found the photo, she recognized it instantly: a handsome, ruddy, round-faced young man with bright, clear eyes that she knew were blue, Carolina blue.

Uncle Morgan ...

There were no captions identifying the students, either. In the photo he was standing beside a lab counter, watching a dice machine with its rotating oblong cage.

To be sure, Laurel flipped to the senior portraits, and found his photo in the Ms—Morgan MacDonald. It was the same boy. He was laughing and glowing with youth and health, his eyes and face animated. There was a string of initials and notations under his name: Varsity Football, Varsity Baseball, Kappa Alpha ...

Laurel felt an ache in her heart.

What happened, then? He was at university, he was in a frat, he played sports—he was alive and sound. He had a life.

She stared down at the yearbook.

I have to know what happened.

She was still brooding on the question as she halted in the upstairs hall of the psych department and reached for the door of her office, carefully balancing the armload of yearbooks

(1960–1965) she'd persuaded the reference librarian to loan her, as she fished for her keys. A gratingly familiar voice called from behind her.

"I'll get that for you."

She half-turned, almost losing her stack completely, and saw J. Walter Kornbluth bustling up behind her. He deftly plucked the books from her arms. Unable to protest, Laurel forced a smile, unlocked her door, and pushed it open. Kornbluth marched into the tiny office and unloaded the books on the desk.

"Thanks, I appreciate it," Laurel said dutifully from the doorway.

"Happy to help," Kornbluth said expansively. He looked over the volumes he had deposited with a frown. "Yearbooks?" Laurel thought his eyes lingered on the dates.

"Yes, my ... my aunt is an alum ..." she hedged.

Kornbluth turned, took in the office with a sweeping glance, and sat on the edge of the desk. "How are you settling in?"

Laurel paused, disoriented by the sudden and seemingly unwarranted attention. "Well ... it's a big change from L.A., that's for sure. At least I'm not getting lost every time I get on the freeway. I'm enjoying the teaching—the kids are top-notch. And the campus is gorgeous ..." She stopped, painfully aware she was rambling, but Kornbluth smiled at her tolerantly.

"You've been putting in a lot of library time," he said, and she froze. *So there* is *an agenda here*.

"Yes, it's like working in a castle, really—" she started, flustered.

"And then there's the lure of the Rhine files," he said cheerfully, but the look he gave her was shrewd. He was firmly planted on her desk, and short of leaving him unattended in her office, she wasn't going to be able to avoid this conversation. Also, she was suddenly acutely aware that she had parapsychology notes all over her desk: all he had to do was glance down at a page and he'd know exactly what she was up to.

"It is fascinating, that all of that actually happened here," she agreed, inching toward the desk.

"Finding anything of particular interest?" he pressed on.

"It's *all* interesting, isn't it?" she countered. "But it would take about twenty years to go through everything properly. They saved everything from soup to nuts." (She had in fact found a can of petrified peanuts in one of the boxes.) "At a certain point . . ." She gave what she hoped would come off as a nonchalant shrug.

"It's overwhelming, I know." Kornbluth smiled with easy and completely false camaraderie. "Seven hundred boxes." He widened his eyes.

Laurel smiled back, tightly.

"And it's not really your thing, after all. Vocational testing, Myers-Briggs, a little Allport, a little Maslow . . ."

She fought not to let her surprise show. He'd obviously been checking up on her. *So he's interested in the files. He thinks there's something there, and he wants to make sure I'm not going to beat him to it,* she thought, and was immediately annoyed by her own paranoia.

"Yes, I did a lot of vocational testing analysis in Los Angeles," she agreed.

"And I thought everyone there just wanted to be stars," he quipped.

True enough, but Hollywood's not the only place you find aspiring stars, she thought, while on the surface she laughed at his wit.

"So are you doing work with the files?" she asked, when they'd finished their mutually artificial chuckle.

"Oh no," he said, heartily. "No no. You've seen them—it's just a mess. Total waste of time. It seems the entire lab was operating under a mass delusion."

"My thought exactly," she said, and immediately wondered if she'd said too much, as the idea of mass delusion was increasingly interesting to her. "A total waste of time," she repeated, to clarify.

"Well," he pushed off from the desk and stood, energetically. "Feel free to run your research by me any time. I know a thing or two about proposals."

"How nice of you to offer. I will do that," she said sweetly, half a second from batting her eyes.

She was still smiling a strained smile as she closed the door on him. Then immediately was flooded with a surge of possessiveness the likes of which she had never felt before.

Oh, no you don't. This is my book. Mine. *And you can't have it.*

It was more than a book. It was looking very much like her life.

Chapter Thirteen

Dr. J. B. Rhine and Dr. William Roll, of the Duke parapsychology lab, developed the theory of RSPK: "Recurrent Spontaneous Psychokinesis," to explain poltergeist phenomena. Dr. Roll coined the term in a research paper cowritten with Duke researcher J. Gaither Pratt, detailing their investigation of the "Popper Poltergeist" at a house in Seaford, Long Island, in 1958. According to Rhine and Roll, the poltergeist energy originates in the mind of a single human agent, or focus, who deliberately or unconsciously projects that energy outward, causing the movement or breakage of objects, inexplicable noises, and apportation characteristic of poltergeist occurrences.

—Dr. Alaistair Leish, *The Lure of the Poltergeist*

It was two more days before Laurel could contrive to catch Morgan alone. It had to be alone; her uncle was clearly not willing to talk in front of Aunt Margaret. She headed over to her aunt's house on Steeple Street on a crisp fall day, the temperature suddenly cooler, and the air laced with a light wind that rustled the still-green leaves.

Laurel stood between the white columns of the porch and rang and knocked. She waited for a good ten minutes, knocking several more times, and was just turning to give up when the door opened behind her with a soft creak. She looked back to see Morgan peering out from a crack in the door. Seeing her, he pulled the door open a few inches more, his face both bright and uneasy.

"Hello, Uncle Morgan." He shuffled shyly behind the door, without speaking. She stepped forward. "Can I come in?"

"Margaret isn't here," he offered. Laurel knew that, of course—she'd been careful to check her aunt's schedule at the hospital and had chosen a day when she was sure Margaret would be tied up in consultations.

"I came to see you."

He looked pleased, and then alarmed. "Oh, no no no. Probably not. Most probably not." His eyes were hazy and she thought possibly he had been drinking. He started to close the door, but she reached out and held it, gently but firmly.

"But I did. Won't you let me in?"

He stood in the door for a long moment, then backed up into the hall. Laurel stepped inside cautiously, careful not to make any sudden moves. She eased the door shut behind her.

"Can we sit down?" she asked.

Morgan looked around him vaguely, shifting from foot to foot. "How about in the study?" Laurel suggested, as the stiff-backed chairs and low divans in the parlor hadn't seemed in any way conducive to conversation.

Morgan turned on his heel abruptly and scurried down the hall. Laurel followed him down the windowless corridor to the walnut-paneled room. The light was clear through a triple window, but the built-in bookshelves and dark wood of the ceiling and walls kept the room dim. As Laurel had suspected, Morgan relaxed considerably in the encompassing quiet of the room; she'd noticed long ago that bookstores and libraries were both alluring and calming for people with troubled minds.

Morgan remained standing until she remembered to sit down herself (she was still getting used to these ingrained Southern manners), then he settled happily into what was obviously a favorite soft leather armchair.

Laurel noticed a leather-bound book with an embroidered marker on the marble-topped end table beside the chair, and a pair of half-spectacles beside it. There was a faint, sweet smell of Scotch.

"What are you reading?" she asked.

He shyly held up the volume: Edgar Rice Burroughs's classic science-fiction fantasy *A Princess of Mars*. Laurel felt a pang. It couldn't have been easy for this gentle, dreamy man to grow up in a house with two Amazonian sisters. No wonder he'd retreated into a fantasy life ... maybe retreated so far he hadn't come out.

She forced herself back to the matter at hand. She smiled at him and spoke in her gentlest voice.

"Uncle Morgan, I need your help with a paper I'm doing. When we were talking about the Rhine Laboratory, you said that you were tested. What do you mean?"

Already the words, "Rhine Laboratory," had made him flinch and blink rapidly, nervously. He started to shake his head and Laurel said quickly, "Aunt Margaret isn't here. And I won't tell. I just want to hear about it."

Morgan glanced behind him toward the kitchen as if to verify they were alone in the house. After a moment he leaned toward Laurel stealthily. "I was good at cards."

She felt a thrill. "The Zener cards, you mean?" She reached into her purse for the pack of the cards she'd printed out that morning. She'd found templates easily available on many Web sites on line, formatted for printing.

But before she could draw out the pack, Morgan was shaking his head. "Cards. I was good at cards. Always won. Fellows said I should go get tested."

"What fellows, Uncle Morgan?"

He extended a shaky hand, displaying the heavy gold ring on it like a proud new bride-to-be. Laurel saw the Greek letters—KA—and realized it was a fraternity ring.

"Your fraternity brothers?"

He smiled with a touch of smugness. "I beat them. I beat them all."

"So they said you should go to the Rhine Lab ... when was that?"

71

Her uncle looked vague, and then worried. He twisted the ring on his finger, without responding.

"What did you do in the lab?"

Her uncle brightened. "I won. A-plus."

Now Laurel did take out the pack of Zener cards and showed them to him. "You won at these cards, you mean?"

He beamed, nodding. "A-plus. One hundred percent."

Laurel felt a thrill of unreality. "You got every card right?" Except for very short trials with one exceptional subject, only two of the cases she'd read about so far had come even close to perfect results, even when the scores were far above chance.

"A-plus," he repeated. "And the dice."

She knew he must be referring to the dice-throwing machines, which could test either ESP through prediction of the toss, or PK, psychokinesis, in a test in which students attempted to influence the fall of the dice with their minds.

"Did you guess the dice?" she asked.

He shook his head adamantly. "You think hard and you make them fall."

Not just ESP but PK? Laurel glanced toward the kitchen and flashed again on the dancing forks and spoons from her dream.

"Can you show me?"

The look of alarm on his face was immediate and overwhelming. "Oh, no no no. No no." He stood from the chair, shifting back and forth on his feet as if about to break into a run. "No more. Margaret says no."

He shot a frantic glance toward the hallway door, then the study window, then the door out onto the screened porch. He was making soft worried sounds like the crooning of a pigeon.

"It's okay, Uncle Morgan—it's okay. I'm sorry." Laurel hastily gathered the cards and put them back in her purse. "I didn't mean to upset you. Maybe we can just play, then?"

He lit up and scurried to an end table that she just then realized had an elegant poker caddy on it, with stacked chips and packs of cards.

It had been a long time since Laurel had played two-handed

bridge, but her mother was an avid solitaire player and had taught her Hearts and bridge and gin rummy (Laurel always suspected it was so they wouldn't actually have to talk). Laurel was able to keep up with Morgan's hands, although it was clear he was a professional-level player and was beating the tar out of her. But winning was of no importance to Laurel: her uncle had completely relaxed into the game, his concentration completely on the cards, the worried wariness gone.

"I've been reading more about the lab, Uncle Morgan," she said casually.

Morgan didn't lift his eyes from the cards. "Your trick," he said, and for a moment, she had the distinct feeling he was being literal, instead of referring to the game.

"I'm very curious," she continued after a minute, more carefully. "And I wondered if you knew. I just don't understand why the lab was closed so suddenly."

"Your draw," he said, looking down at the cards. He would not look at her, and she suppressed a sigh. It was clear he didn't want to talk about it, and she didn't have the heart to press him.

Dutifully she reached for a card—and Morgan abruptly stopped her hand with his. "No," he said, and she looked at him, startled. "You're not paying attention."

His gaze locked hers ... in the moment his rheumy eyes were startlingly clear. He looked down at the cards, passing his hand gently over them—and then reached for a different card than the one she had been about to draw.

He turned it over and she saw the Jack of Diamonds—the precise card she needed to complete the hand. She drew in a breath, and looked up at him.

"You need to pay attention." He reached his index finger and touched the center of her forehead.

Her heart was beating faster and she felt tingling behind her ears.

Morgan didn't look at her as he collected the cards and shuffled them, shuffled them again. Then he started dealing cards face down in two piles. The majority of cards he dealt into one stack, but every few cards he put one card aside in a smaller stack. Laurel watched, mesmerized by the soft slapping of the cards. When he had gone through the entire deck, he took the smaller pile and laid them out in a row, face down, in an order known only to him. He looked down at the row of cards, changed the place of one, then started at the head of the row and turned over one card after another, to reveal a complete set of hearts, in a perfect Ace-to-King order.

Laurel stared at the cards in complete awe.

"Uncle Morgan," she said, and her voice was barely a whisper. "Why did the lab shut down?"

"It was the house," he said softly.

"What house?" she asked, not daring to breathe. "The Seaford House?"

He shook his head slowly. "The Folger House." He met her eyes with a clear gaze, but before she could speak, his eyes clouded again with confusion, and yes, a hint of fear.

He collected the cards silently and began to lay them out, and would not speak again, no matter what she did to engage him.

Chapter Fourteen

There was no record of a Folger House, or a Folger investigation. Not on the Internet, not in the catalog list Laurel had been carefully compiling of the Rhine files, not in any of the texts she'd been using as supplemental material to her research into the boxes.

It was almost dawn when Laurel finally looked up from her computer. Rain was pouring outside the window. Lightning branched across the sky, illumining the street in blue-white light.

Laurel stood from her desk and paced her study (which had somehow acquired a red couch and bookshelves, already filled almost to overflowing with what had now become several hundred books, library books, new purchases, almost entirely to do with psi and the paranormal). She stopped and stood facing the array of books, flooded with doubt.

Is any of this real at all?

Her uncle's grasp on the present, the past, on reality in general could not by any stretch of the imagination be called solid.

But the card trick!

No, even the perfect layout of cards, as dazzling as it had been at the time, could have been nothing more than a common magician's sleight of hand.

But she had a feeling—no, more than that, a nagging,

tickling certainty—that there was such a thing as a Folger House, and it was exactly what she'd been looking for all along, the mystery that had shut down the parapsychology lab for good. In her mind she kept seeing Uncle Morgan holding up that Jack of Diamonds, and she believed.

She reached for the 1965 yearbook and opened it to the page she'd marked, the one with Uncle Morgan's senior portrait. She studied the photo, his smile, his clear and sparkling eyes.

What happened?

Thunder rumbled through the dark again, and the wind hurled rain against the windows.

Laurel went downstairs to the kitchen to make coffee, sleepy but wired. She stepped out on the front porch to watch the rain, brooding as she sipped the hot, bitter liquid, staring out into the dark.

We're going to have to be careful, now.

The encounter with Kornbluth made it clear that she was not alone in her interest, and Kornbluth was as competitive a competitor as she could have drawn. But she felt on the verge of a breakthrough, and she had a plan. She stepped up to the porch railing and tipped her face up to the rain.

Chapter Fifteen

The Duke Parapsychology Lab became the model for parapsychology labs throughout the U.S. and Europe. Rhine's scientific methods were employed at both university laboratories and privately funded research centers such as, among others, the Paranormal Research Center in Raleigh.
—Dr. Alaistair Leish, *The Lure of the Poltergeist*

The Paranormal Research Center was a disappointingly plain and provincial building: a cheaply made and functional two-story beige-and-tan block with a tacked-on triangle-roofed facade and shuttered windows.

Laurel parked outside in the lot, filled with about two dozen cars, and contemplated the building.

After Dr. Rhine retired in 1965, he and his wife founded the private Rhine Research Center; he was already making provisions to continue his work. Another Duke poltergeist investigator, Dr. William Roll, moved on to a position at the University of West Georgia, and another group of researchers had broken off from the Duke lab earlier to found the Paranormal Research Center, located in Raleigh, just a forty-minute drive from Duke. Leish had made several mentions of the PRC in the articles Laurel had been able to find of his; it was clear he had ties to the organization, and Laurel hoped someone at the Center would be able to give her more answers about Leish's work at Duke.

Laurel had phoned the Center and spoken with a receptionist, explaining she was a new Duke professor interested in the history of the Duke parapsychology department and the Research Center. "I wondered if I could arrange to get a tour, at the Center's convenience, of course."

"I'm very sorry. The PRC is a private facility. We don't conduct tours."

Laurel pressed, but both the receptionist and the administrator that Laurel insisted on being transferred to held their ground. "I'm sorry—the Center is not open to the public. You are perfectly welcome to attend one of our open lectures, though. We have one tomorrow night at seven."

Laurel decided to go to the lecture and take it from there.

She was as jumpy as a cat as she got out of the car and moved up toward the building. It was unaccountable, the feeling of going into enemy territory, but her instinct was to proceed cautiously, not to let too much slip.

Her uncle's voice whispered in her head. *You need to pay attention.*

The double doors of the lecture hall led into a hundred-seat auditorium connected to the main building. There were about three dozen people scattered in the seats, most older than fifty. A volunteer, a small elderly woman in a St. Pete's sweatshirt and jeans and red Keds sat at a back table, surrounded by stacks of literature on the Center, program schedules, flyers calling for study volunteers. There was also a schedule of the bimonthly lecture programs: nothing Laurel hadn't seen advertised at bookstores and yoga studios and community college seminars all over Los Angeles: "What Do We Know About Auras?"; "Healing Through Meditation"; "Coping with Spiritual Emergencies"; "The Implications of Parapsychology for Religion and Spirituality."

Laurel collected one of each, and took a seat in the back row, where the dimness of the auditorium gave her some anonymity. The pamphlets were disappointingly lightweight— there was nothing of the groundbreaking potential she had been finding in the Rhine Lab files. Browsing through them, she realized that the bottom line of all of the brochures was to solicit contributions for the Center's research. Just as she was wondering if donors might get tours of the Center, another elderly volunteer walked out on stage to introduce the speaker: the director of the Center, Dr. Richard Anton.

Anton took the stage to a murmur and scattering of applause from the audience. He was an arresting man in his forties, with thick dark hair and eyebrows and piercing black eyes. His black trousers and sweater and rich maroon scarf were all of fine quality and even from a distance Laurel could see the glitter of real gold in his watch. *They must be getting money from somewhere, then,* Laurel thought. When Anton started to speak, his voice was deep and compelling, and Laurel was instantly reminded of Dr. Leish, though the swarthy Anton did not physically resemble the cool, elegantly blond Leish in any way.

Maybe all parapsychologists are charismatics, Laurel thought. *That's how they convince people that the impossible is real.*

The topic of the evening was remote viewing.

As a native of California, where New Age trends were as much a part of the culture as sunshine, Laurel was somewhat aware of the concept of remote viewing. As she understood it, it was the most recent catch phrase for ESP experiences, in which a subject could see something happening from a distance, sometimes a great distance. According to Dr. Anton, remote viewing had been tested in top-secret experiments by the military with apparent success.

But really it's just another fad, isn't it? We're trying to put scientific explanations on something that exists, but can't be explained.

On the stage, Anton was speaking about the PRC's remote viewing experiments in their custom-built Ganzfeld rooms. "It was parapsychologist Charles Honorton who developed the concept of the Ganzfeld, the 'empty field.' We know from statistics that the vast majority of ESP or psi experiences occur while the subject is in an altered state: while dreaming, in a state of relaxation or meditation. Honorton theorized that ESP experiences were subtle communications that are easily drowned out by the cacophony of internal and external stimuli flooding our brains during normal, waking consciousness."

Laurel sat up straighter in her seat. She knew from her reading that Leish had used the Ganzfeld technique in his experiments. She eased a notepad out of her purse and began to take notes.

"Taking as a model the practices of mystics and psychics throughout the centuries, Honorton adapted the Ganzfeld technique to reduce all distracting sounds and visuals. The ESP subject is seated in a soft, reclining chair in a soundproof room. Split halves of Ping-Pong balls are taped over the receiver's eyes to eliminate visual distractions, and headphones play a relaxation tape, all to produce a mild state of sensory deprivation.

"A sender is in a similar room, and goes through similar relaxation exercises. Then the sender is shown a photo or a film clip, and for the next thirty minutes, the sender tries to mentally communicate the image or images to the receiver."

Laurel already felt a nagging dissatisfaction with the structure of the tests. The whole concept of laboratory testing ignored the fact that telepathic and precognitive experiences seemed to manifest under conditions of extreme stress and trauma, which would be difficult if not downright unethical to create in a lab.

On the stage, Anton launched into a recitation of eye-glazing statistics from the Center's latest remote-viewing study. Laurel saw movement at the corner of her eye and turned to see the elderly volunteer at the back table rise unobtrusively and head for a side door. In the dark of the back row, Laurel quietly rose from her own seat and followed her.

The side door opened into a hall with a men's and women's restroom. Another door on the other side of the door was just swinging shut. Laurel took three quick steps across the hall and caught the edge of the door just before it closed, then stood close to it, straining to hear anything beyond the door—steps, movement . . .

There was nothing.

Laurel pushed the door open cautiously ...

It opened into a hushed, deserted hallway. There was a dark, glassed-in office to the left and a walled-in office to the right, and a long dim corridor with other doors leading to other rooms off it.

She could hear the murmuring of voices somewhere from the back—a meeting, maybe, with doors open.

But instead of calling out, or ringing the bell on the front table, she hovered quietly in the entry hall, looking around.

A narrow table beside the door held more informational flyers and brochures. On the other side of the hall a standing rack displayed several dozen display copies of books for sale, all with addictively intriguing titles: *The Gift* ... *This House Is Haunted!* ... *Entangled Minds* ... *Life Among the Dead* ... *Seven Experiments that Could Change the World*.

The murmuring of voices from the back room continued, but still no one emerged to check on the hall. Stepping quietly, Laurel moved further into the building, past offices and common rooms with exotically patterned rugs and lush indoor trees and arresting art from different cultures: shamanic masks and primitive fetishes. There was a quiet resonance about the place Laurel found unnerving—a quality of waiting, of listening.

Ahead of her a door opened into a room with comfortable and expensive high-backed couches and chairs. Laurel caught her breath at the sight of a familiar object on a dark mahogany end table: an original dice-throwing machine—a stand holding a long rectangular Lucite tube with seven dice in the bottom and a series of shutters through which the dice could fall. Even though the device was anachronistic and somehow naively simple Laurel felt the same strange thrill, seeing the real machine in front of her.

She backed out of the room and continued her illicit tour.

The intersecting hall was hung with black-and-white photos from the early days of the Duke parapsychology lab. Laurel passed by scene after scene of austerely dressed, serious scientists, in offices that were as uncluttered as the time, as formal and familiar as stage settings. But in none of them did she find Dr. Leish.

She turned and looked further down the dark hall, wondering. *So where are the poltergeist shots?* she thought wildly. *If I keep going, will I find a photo of the Folger House?* She had a sudden urge to laugh.

The last door of the hall was open into a long room lined with bookcases filled with many older and leather-bound volumes, the spines all affixed with what looked like new white library catalog stickers. Just inside the doorway stood an old-style walnut card catalog ... Laurel couldn't remember the last time she'd seen one. She glanced back down the dim hall with its gleaming floors—but there was still no sign of anyone. She quietly stepped into the library to the cabinet and scanned the file titles.

Well, why not?

She pulled open the F–J SUBJECT drawer and quickly flipped through the cards, looking for FOLGER, passing through a variety of wild subjects: FAE, FAIRY, FAKIR, FETISH, FIELD INVESTIGATION, FIR DIRECTOR. But the cards skipped from FIVE-FOLD KISS to FORCED CHOICE TESTING, with no entry for FOLGER.

Laurel pushed the drawer back in, and tried FOLGER in the TITLES drawers and also the AUTHOR drawers—but no luck, either place.

Laurel slid the file drawer back in and turned—and jumped.

A man stood in the inner doorway of the library, watching her. Dark hair, thick dark brows, black trousers and sweater, expensive watch. Dr. Anton.

Have I been here that long? The lecture's over? Laurel's thoughts were fast, disjointed. Her heart had started beating frantically.

"Something you're looking for?" Anton asked, his face expressionless as his dark eyes took her in with photographic intensity.

Laurel felt her face reddening, though she tried to keep cool. "I'm Laurel MacDonald. I got lost on the way back from

82

the bathroom, and … well, then I'm afraid I was snooping."

The dark-haired man studied her without speaking and Laurel had the uneasy feeling that he was reading her mind, or at least reading her. She tried not to fidget. "I just joined the faculty at Duke. The psychology department. The legacy of the parapsychology lab is so much a part of the department's history that I—"

He interrupted her. "What's your field?" he demanded—yes, it was a demand, even though his voice never rose.

"Personality psychology," she replied, looking him straight in the face. "I'm particularly interested in how various personality types bring their own agenda to social situations."

His eyes narrowed, and she thought she had gone too far. Needling this man was no way to get the information she was here for.

"And you have an interest in parapsychology?" Anton's voice was barbed with sarcasm.

Laurel surprised herself with her smooth reply. "I'm always interested in every aspect of human potential. I believe human beings are infinite. Don't you? We're not even half aware of everything we're capable of."

Those black, black eyes were fixed on her … she could almost feel the air between them vibrating with the intensity of the connection. Finally, he spoke softly. "Indeed, Dr. MacDonald. Indeed."

Winning that admission from him made her reckless. "Actually, there *is* something you could help me with. I was looking for information on the Folger House."

It was his sudden stillness that made her think she'd hit home. His eyes contracted to black pinpoints and he simply stared at her.

Sensing her advantage, she pushed it even further. "Folger," she repeated helpfully. "Like the coffee. I understand it was an important part of the Duke lab's research."

"You're mistaken," Anton said flatly.

"I don't think I am," Laurel said. "Folger. I'm sure that was it. I'm very interested in what happened in that house."

They locked eyes, and his face was like stone. "I'm sorry. It's not something I'm familiar with."

Laurel could sense a deep animosity coming from him, and she was suddenly acutely aware that she was alone with the man in a deserted building, and no one knew where she was. And yet with a boldness that shocked her, she persisted. "Then I wonder if you could tell me a bit about Dr. Alaistair Leish."

Anton raised an eyebrow. "Dr. Leish. What about him?"

Laurel took a wild stab in the dark. "I understand he was on staff at the Paranormal Research Center before he died."

Anton smiled thinly. "Again, your information is faulty. Dr. Leish was never on staff at the Center."

"But you do know of him."

"It would be unusual to work in my field and not have heard of Dr. Leish. But the Paranormal Research Center is dedicated to scientifically quantifiable results. Leish was exclusively interested in field work, and was notorious for not gaining permissions for his unconventional studies. Since the founding of the Center, our board and researchers have been dedicated to carrying out its research under the most rigorous conditions."

Laurel had the clear impression that Anton was reciting a policy he might not completely believe in himself. She felt her way carefully.

"I don't know much about it, but as a researcher I have to wonder ... how can you study a phenomenon like a poltergeist in a laboratory setting?"

Anton smiled at her strangely. "You can't." As she stared at him, trying to interpret this, he half-turned. "And now, Dr. MacDonald, I'll see you out."

There was no option of refusal; the interview was over.

She followed Anton back out into the spotless corridor and he opened the front door for her.

Just before she stepped out, she suddenly turned to him. "How did Dr. Leish die, do you know?"

Another beat of stillness. Then Anton said, "It was a heart attack, I believe."

They looked at each other, and Laurel was sure he was lying. "At forty-one," she said. "What a shame."

"I agree. Good night, Dr. MacDonald." He shut the door on her.

As she drove home on the nearly deserted highway through the dark tunnel of trees, her unease grew.

He's lying.

Partially or even totally, but he was lying. Laurel struggled to regain her bearings. Had she completely given away her game by asking Anton about the house? On the other hand, she'd gotten exactly the information she'd come for: the Folger House was not only a real thing, but something significant, if not top secret— that was clear from the mysterious and arrogant man's reaction.

And the confluence of dates—Leish at the Duke lab just before it closed—if Uncle Morgan was right and Folger closed the lab, then whatever the Folger House was, she was sure Leish had something to do with it.

She turned onto her block and parked her Volvo by the curb outside her house on the quiet, deserted street. All up and down the block, lights were on above the wide porches, but there was not a soul in sight beyond the shadow of a prowling cat. Wind whispered through the oaks and crape myrtles.

Laurel shut the car door and moved to the trunk, opened it to get out her wheeled book bag.

And suddenly the sense of being watched was overwhelming.

She turned under the diffuse light of the streetlamp. A breeze picked up and dry leaves rolled past her feet in a small flurry.

She could see no one, not on the porches, or inside a car.

She grabbed her bag, heaved closed the trunk lid, and hurried up her walkway for the door.

On the porch she pressed the book bag into the door frame, holding it up with her body as she dug in her purse for her keys. Her heart was pounding, completely out of proportion to the situation, but she was overwhelmed with a sense of urgency.

She found the keys, fumbled the door open, and slammed it behind her, locking it.

All right, now? she chided herself, as she leaned against the wall—but she was shaking.

Nothing to be afraid of . . .

Then she thought of Anton's cold dark eyes, and was not so sure.

Chapter Sixteen

There is no question that each of us has inherent psi ability. This is the bedrock of all modern paranormal investigation. The more pertinent question is—do we have the courage to claim it?

—Dr. Alaistair Leish, *The Lure of the Poltergeist*

Her notebook was gone.

Laurel stood with hands on hips, surveying her Psych department office—now even more chaotic than usual, an explosion of papers and files and pulled-out drawers after her increasingly frustrated search. The gargoyle outside the window leered in at her as if it were in on the joke.

She'd returned to her office that morning after her troubling visit to the Paranormal Research Center, started to pack her roller case for another foray into the basement of Perkins, and realized the notebook was missing: the three-subject Blue Devils notebook from the student bookstore that she'd been taking notes in. It was the ninth notebook she'd filled with notes from the Rhine files. The others were at home, lined up on a shelf in one of her overflowing bookcases.

She'd looked through, under and around every single piece of paper and file on her desk, in the three desk drawers, through every bookshelf in the tiny office. Nothing.

Am I losing my mind?

She thought briefly of the feeling she'd had of being watched, last night.

Okay, now that's crazy. Isn't it? Who would want my random notes? Who could even read my handwriting?

But she had no time to ponder—it was Friday and she had a full day of classes, plus office hours. The carillon bells in the clock tower were chiming five before she was able to lock the door of her office and hurry down the stairs and across the quad through a blustery wind and rush of escaping students to Perkins Library. Down in the basement she checked her table, and the coat closet; she even went back to the shelf and looked through the last box she had been sorting through yesterday morning to see if she'd absentmindedly put it back into the box with the actual files.

It wasn't anywhere.

Which means nothing, she thought. She'd once turned her entire condo upside down for a book that she found a week later in the freezer beside a quart of Honey Vanilla Häagen-Dazs.

But the more she looked, the more certain she was that she had left the notebook on her desk in her locked office.

She sat on the edge of the long table, and thought back to Kornbluth's unsolicited visit to her office. He'd been sitting on top of her desk, obviously scanning the materials on the desktop.

Did I see the notebook after that? I don't think I did.

But would he really be brazen enough to steal a colleague's research material? Should she confront him?

There was a step behind her and she turned, startled.

Ward stood behind her, between the shelves. "It's Friday night," the librarian informed Laurel dryly. "I'm leaving for the evening. But you can lock up behind you, if you're staying. Just pull the doors shut as you leave. Closing bell's at quarter to ten."

Laurel was surprised and grateful for the vote of confidence. "I appreciate it," she said.

Ward looked behind her at the rows of boxes. "Well," she said, and turned to go.

"I have a question," Laurel said suddenly, and Ward turned back, waiting. "I wondered if you had ever seen anything, or heard anything, about a Folger House."

Laurel didn't know why she was asking the librarian, except that for whatever reason she trusted her. At least, she trusted that the librarian had no vested interest in the research Laurel was doing, the way that others in the department would have.

"I haven't been into these files," Ward said.

"But ... maybe someone else has asked? I just wondered if you had ever seen anything or heard anything about a Folger House ... if it was familiar at all." Laurel was painfully aware that she was grasping at straws.

Ward looked at her through the thick owl glasses. "Folger. No. Never heard of it."

"Well ... thanks," Laurel said. "Enjoy your weekend," she added with effort.

"Oh, I will." Ward walked off with a bit of a spring to her step, leaving Laurel with the sneaking feeling that the dour librarian had a more active social life than she did.

Laurel stood in the middle of the tables. Though she did not hear the door close, she knew Ward was gone by the sudden absence of energy—the dim, cool, faintly moving air surrounded her and she was alone.

Alone with seven hundred boxes of unfathomable mystery.

She felt like crying, something very near defeat. She knew she had already spoken the word "Folger" aloud far too many times, was being far too obvious about her intentions. And she now had only a week until she had to meet with Dr. Unger and she had nothing. Nothing.

She looked around her at the aisles and aisles of bookshelves, the hundreds of file boxes with their frustrating chaos.

Their carefully engineered chaos.

How many weeks had she been doing this, now? And what had it gotten her?

The book seemed more and more like an elusive dream. The truth was, she was looking for something she'd probably

89

never find. She was like the poltergeist investigators, wanting so much to find some proof that they chased the most intangible wisps.

Yet a defiant voice rose from somewhere inside her: *Somebody else thinks there's something real, there. Kornbluth, Anton— whoever stole my notebook . . .*

But where? Seven hundred boxes and she'd been through thirty-two, and she was no further to finding anything remotely like a pursuable topic. *What chance do I have, after all?*

"Might as well hire a medium," she muttered to herself.

And that thought stopped her still.

Well, who needs a medium? she thought recklessly. "It runs in the family, doesn't it?" she said aloud into the cool silence.

It runs in the family, her uncle agreed, inside her head.

Everyone has inherent psi ability, Dr. Leish added, also inside her head. *The more pertinent question is—do we have the courage to claim it?*

Laurel stood, and surveyed the shelves filled with file boxes. "All right, then," she said under her breath. "If everyone has it, let's see what we've got."

She walked slowly to the middle of an aisle and stood, closed her eyes and took a breath, uncertain how to proceed.

"You have to pay attention," her uncle whispered in her head.

Great. Attention to what?

"The Folger House," she said aloud, her eyes pressed shut. "Anything on the Folger House. I need to find it. Where is it?"

She could hear the distant whir of a fan, the cool rush of air on her face from above.

It's here somewhere. There are records for everything else. It's as easy as opening one of these boxes.

She pictured herself lifting a lid, seeing the word FOLGER on top of a page.

Leish's voice was in her mind again. *"Perhaps what we call reality is simply an agreement that the less imaginative among us have decided upon."*

She took a step in the aisle without opening her eyes, and

paused ... her whole body relaxed, but poised ... listening with something other than her ears.

She took another step, and then another, hands hovering by her side, working her way down the aisle, moving with a slow, trancelike step. At the end of the aisle, without opening her eyes, she moved deftly around the end of the shelving, surprised at how clearly she felt the presence of the shelves. In her mind's eye she could see the boxes around her as if they were in a white room, with indistinct contours, as if the walls were actually a fog of white. Time had stopped: she was suspended in a sense of being that was beyond physical; her body seemed to have lost its boundaries, and she registered the information in the boxes like touch on her skin.

She moved slowly, down one aisle, up another ... all the time in the world. And then she felt it. In the middle of the third aisle, something like a magnetic pull.

It was so clear and yet so subtle that she was afraid to breathe.

I'm making this up, I must be.

The backs of her ears were tingling ...

She eased another step forward ... and the feeling was gone. She froze ... then slowly, slowly stepped back ...

... and again felt the subtle pull ... the fine hairs on her forearms were standing straight up.

Okay ... okay ...

She reached out a hand—and felt the magnetism like a gentle vacuum, pulling at the center of her palm. She let the pull take her palm, forward, forward ...

... and suddenly felt her hand flat against the side of a cardboard box.

Her eyes flew open.

Her hand was pressed up against a box, number 642, at about eye level on a shelf. She was no longer in a dreamy trance; her heart was beating a mile a minute.

She breathed in, and reached up to pull the box from the shelf. It was heavy, like the others, obviously full to capacity.

Too impatient to haul the box back to her table, she put it on

91

a lower shelf and lifted the lid, staring down into the box at the row of files and documents and pages. Her palms were sweating. She wiped them absently on her skirt.

Unlike in her mind's eye, there was no document with FOLGER clearly spelled on the top.

Well, go on, she told herself, crossly, to dispel the almost unbearable nervousness.

She took out a stack of papers from the front. By now she was used to skimming, and she zipped through the pages, searching only for the words: *Morgan MacDonald, Folger House, Alaistair Leish*, and *1965*.

The documents were discouragingly familiar: bills, memos, pages and pages of personal letters.

Just breathe, Laurel told herself. *It's there. Just look.*

She reached into the box for another stack of papers . . .

And then there it was. She knew it the second she saw it: a thin paper-clipped sheaf of pages, all test-result charts—the same Zener-card test charts she'd already seen hundreds of in the files. The names of the subjects had been redacted (she held them up to the light but was not able to read any names through the slashes of black marker), and relabeled SUBJECT A, SUBJECT B, SUBJECT C. But all three of the test scores were through the roof, the highest she'd come across: 51 percent correct, 55 percent correct, and an astonishing 75 percent correct.

And on each test, someone had scribbled at the top in bold spiked handwriting, the same authoritative slash of penmanship:

FOLGER EXPERIMENT—start date 4/03/65

Chapter Seventeen

Laurel realized she'd been holding her breath for some time, and forced herself to exhale. She shuffled through the test forms again, just to make sure she really was seeing what she was seeing.

It was what she'd been looking for. There *was* a Folger Experiment. Whatever it was, it took place just before the parapsychology lab was shut down. And it had involved test subjects with ESP scores higher than any other recorded test subjects she'd ever come across in the literature.

(She wasn't even going to think about how she'd actually *found* the test packet, yet.)

The room suddenly felt colder, as if the air-conditioning had kicked into high gear, although she hadn't heard any kind of mechanical change. She felt the fine hair on her forearms rising, and then the tingling began in back of her ears ... the same chilling feeling of being watched she'd experienced at her house the night before.

She clutched the sheaf of test papers, inched toward the end of the aisle and peered out.

The central area of tables was deserted, just as she'd left it. She exhaled silently and shook her head. *All right, stop freaking yourself out.*

She walked back to the middle of the aisle and grabbed the box, hoisting it off the shelf, and walked out of the aisle, back to her work table. She set the box down—and froze, staring down at the table top.

Five Zener cards were laid out on the table in a row.

There was someone in the basement with her.

It was long after dark, too—she hadn't noticed how late it had gotten.

Instinctively she darted into an aisle of shelves, and hovered, listening with every cell of her body.

She realized she was still clutching the packet of tests she'd found. Without really understanding why she was doing it, she slipped them into the waistband of her skirt, hiding them underneath her pullover sweater.

She breathed shallowly and silently, fighting a rising panic, the irresistible urge to scream or make any kind of noise that would alert the person in the basement to where she was.

Stupid stupid stupid. After all her years in L.A., all her precautions of never being caught alone in a parking lot or a deserted building—and here she'd been for weeks, alone in the basement, a total target . . .

She silenced the panicked voice in her head with sheer will and concentrated on listening, while simultaneously calculating the fastest route to the door.

The basement shelving was set up in a large rectangle: two long rows of about two dozen shelves on either side of the long vertical, and two shorter rows of shelving completing the rectangle at the head and foot. In the center of the rectangle was an open space with several long tables.

Laurel was at present hovering between two rows of shelves on the long right side of the rectangle. She slipped off her shoes and walked, stepping silently, to the far end of the aisle. She stopped, took a breath, and eased her head around the edge of the shelf.

The corridor against the wall was dark and empty.

She pulled her head back, and glanced behind her. No one.

Her heart was pumping out of control; she could hear the

blood rushing in her ears, but she seemed to be able to see with hyperclarity.

If I run down that aisle and go right, in an L-shape, I have a straight shot to the door ...

But even as she was plotting her escape, and wondering if she had the guts to actually do it, it was dawning on her that her stalker was no ordinary creep. Whoever was in the basement with her knew enough about what she was doing to lay out the Zener cards—he knew they were significant.

So what's that supposed to mean?

She immediately answered herself. *What does it matter what it means?* She was alone in a dark basement with someone who was playing games with her. None of it was good.

She pressed her back against a cold metal shelf and resolved to make a run for it along the aisle. She took a breath, then took a look behind her—

And nearly jumped out of her skin.

There was a tall shadow there, hovering at the head of the aisle.

But right before she screamed, a pleading voice spoke quickly. "Sorry sorry sorry—I didn't mean to scare you. It's me. It's me."

Who the hell is "me"? she thought in a blind rush of panic, at the same time that her mind was registering the man who stood before her. It took a moment for her adrenaline-jolted brain to come up with a name: Brendan Cody, from the faculty welcome party: blue-gray eyes, curly dark hair, freckles, and all.

"What the *hell*?" Laurel blazed at him.

"I know, I'm sorry ... ," he started.

"What do you think you're *doing*?"

Her heart was racing, even now that she knew she wasn't in danger. Although come to think of it, there was no real reason to think she *wasn't* in danger; all she knew of this guy was that he was on the faculty with her. It didn't prove he wasn't a serial killer. She lifted the shoes in her hand, threateningly.

He was backing away from her now, holding up his hands,

95

an open, conciliatory gesture. "Please please please. Just let me explain."

She was backing away from him, too, down the aisle, and he stopped in his tracks and just stood still, as if to show he was no threat.

"Look, I didn't know it was you," he said appealingly. "I just saw the Rhine Lab boxes out and I was so shocked that someone else was looking into them that, well, I was just going to take a look and see who it was—"

"You laid out the cards—" she said accusingly.

"I know, I know, it was stupid. But I had no idea it was *you*. I was—never mind."

"You were *what?*" she demanded, now advancing on him. She was aware her voice was shrill, fishwife-like, really, but she was still on the edge of panic.

"I was mad," he said sheepishly, and for a moment he looked all of ten years old. "I was pretty well furious, actually. I've been busting my ass going through the files and I came down here tonight and there were all the boxes laid out, meaning someone else was doing it too, and I guess ..." He trailed off. "I wasn't feeling all that mature about it in the moment. That happens, sometimes," he admitted.

She was starting to feel less fight-or-flight about it, her terror replaced with a limp adrenaline-crash sense of relief, although she still had no idea what she was in the middle of.

"I'm really sorry I scared you," he said. "You scared the shit out of me, too, if it's any help."

"It's not," she snapped.

"Totally understood." He glanced behind him at the rows of long tables. "Look, can we sit down? I'm feeling a little shaky."

"*You* are?"

"I know. Just let's—sit down." He backed up slowly, toward the center table section, hands lifted.

After a long moment, she followed him, warily.

When she stepped into the center space, he was standing beside her table with its row of boxes. She glanced pointedly at the five laid-out Zener cards and he grimaced. "Not my

96

brightest idea," he said again, and hastily scooped them up, shoving them into a front pocket of his khakis. Then he eased himself into a seat, keeping his hands well above the table.

Laurel sat slowly across from him, as if they were gunslingers in the Wild West, sitting down for a summit.

Brendan looked at her across the table and suddenly smiled, a huge great heartfelt warming smile.

"Well. I guess we've got a little more in common than California," he beamed.

Laurel felt herself closing off immediately. She stared across at him stonily.

His smile dropped a few watts. "Um. So—what's your interest in the Rhine files?"

"Uh-uh," she said coldly. "You first."

"Okay, okay, fair enough." He looked at the boxes on the table, and broke into that grin again. "Well, it's just freaking awesome, isn't it? Forty-four years these things have been sealed and suddenly we get access? Criminy."

Criminy? She thought, bemused.

"And obviously there's something someone was trying to hide. I mean, the chaos in those boxes. Nothing is that random." He looked around them at the shelves and shelves of boxes. "There's a treasure trove of knowledge in there. But it's like—like someone took the whole history of research in the lab and shattered it into a million little pieces and dumped it willy-nilly into all those boxes. And then sealed it up, to boot. What are they hiding?"

She had to force her face to keep still, not to give away that he'd just voiced the precise thought that had been plaguing her for weeks.

He leaned his elbows on the table, looking across at her with those earnest blue-gray eyes. "But you know what really bugs me? The department was just shut down cold. Sure, Rhine was retiring, but obviously he had no intention of really retiring, because he worked another good fifteen years, right up until his death. But the school shut the whole department down, right? Not only shut the department down, they sealed the files. Why?"

97

Laurel was listening with a sense of unreality, hearing her own thought process spilling out of his mouth.

"Right," she heard herself saying, against her will. "Why?"

"So here's what I'm thinking. You gotta admit, things were getting pretty wild there, by '64, '65. The whole poltergeist stuff. The sixties were just starting to explode, and people were testing the boundaries of consciousness. The lab was sending researchers out into the field to study the weirdest stuff in the actual environment it was happening in."

His eyes sparkled at her with contagious excitement. "I think they did something revolutionary. I think that there was some experiment that was so trippy, that so freaked out the powers that be, it made Duke shut the whole thing down cold, and bury it. Not just whatever happened in that experiment, but *everything*. They just wanted the whole thing buried."

An experiment. The Folger Experiment, Laurel was thinking, but said nothing. She could feel the test charts with their amazing scores against the bare flesh of her midriff, scratchy and insistent and real.

Brendan Cody looked at her, and she found herself nodding warily. His face was intense in the dim light. "I don't know what it was, but it's in there." He looked at the boxes on the table, then off into the aisles. "And I'm going to find it." He turned that blue-gray gaze on her again. "Or we, if you like," he added hastily. " *We're* going to find it."

"We are?" she said, startled.

"Sure." He suddenly looked grim. "In case you haven't noticed—this department gives 'publish or perish' a new meaning. It's true, Duke might just not have been happy having the parapsychology lab here—but if there was some trippy experiment that shut down the lab? It doesn't matter what anyone thought or thinks. That's instant publication, no matter what the story is. And not just in some obscure journal, either. That's worldwide attention."

But it's my *book,* Laurel was thinking. At the same time, she was feeling a thrill that they had been thinking exactly the same things. All of a sudden it was all feeling real.

Brendan Cody looked like he was deciding something, perhaps struggling with himself, and then he leaned slightly forward.

"Okay, look. There was a new guy they brought in, as far as I can see, no more than four or five months before the department got shut down. Alaistair Leish. Ever heard of him?"

Inwardly Laurel froze. But she kept her face neutral, furrowed her brow. She was still light years away from trusting this man. *He may even have stolen your notebook, you don't know.* "Not that I remember," she said aloud.

He nodded. "I'm not surprised. I hadn't either, by the way, but for a while there, he was a big thing in British parapsychology circles. I've been going through the files—it's a bitch, isn't it?" he interrupted himself to say directly. She found herself smiling back at him in spite of herself.

"A bit of one, yes," she admitted. "Just a bit."

He beamed at her as if they were long-lost siblings. "I had to start somewhere ... so I've been concentrating on documents just from 1965, to see what they were up to right before the department shut down."

Laurel felt again that eerie excitement—to realize he'd been following exactly the same path that she had.

Brendan frowned at her from across the table. "What?"

She shook her head, fighting the completely irrational urge to tell him everything, to show him the tests, the scores of the anonymous students. *You know nothing about this man. Nothing.* She bit down on her lip and kept silent.

"Anyway, I found Leish's name several times in documents, although he was never on staff here—not officially, that is: I checked with the registrar. But I saw the name enough times that I looked him up. He was a parapsychologist from London—the Society of Psychical Research. Made a reputation investigating haunted houses, lecturing to parapsychology societies—and he wrote a book specifically on poltergeists. But I couldn't find anything for him after 1965. He disappeared."

Actually, he died, Laurel thought. *He died the same month the lab closed down*. But she kept the thought to herself.

"Except he was *here*. In 1965." Across the table, in the dim light, Brendan's eyes gleamed. "Like I said, he's not on record with the school as ever being part of the Duke parapsychology lab. But his name is on the roster in several memos, and he's listed as being present at some meetings."

More proof, Laurel thought, exhilarated. Her pulse spiked, but she kept her face neutral.

Brendan slammed his palm down on the table top, startling her. "He was definitely here. And there's no official record of him, no acknowledgement of having someone that big around, when they kept records of everything else under the sun?" He leaned back in his chair. "I think not. I'm pretty sure that anything really relevant has been lifted. They took his name off documents, and something happened that year that shut down the lab and sealed these files."

Laurel was reeling, although she was careful to keep her face expressionless. Her hands were pressed into the table so that she wouldn't move or betray her excitement. Between what Brendan had and what she had, there was a good chance they could piece together the Folger Experiment.

Brendan was already off again, talking a mile a minute. Laurel was sure by now that he was manic, maybe even clinically, and it wouldn't be much effort at all to keep him talking. In fact, he did exactly that.

"Now, as far as I can see Leish was involved in some way with the poltergeist investigations. He wasn't in on the ones that Roll and Pratt did, the obvious ones like Seaford and Newark ..." He glanced at her to see if she were following the references, and she nodded. "There was so much press coverage on those, it would have been easy to find out if Leish had been involved, and yeah, I checked. But he was reviewing *all* of the poltergeist cases. I know that because I found a requisition form for back files, signed by him." He stared past her shoulder toward the aisles of the Rhine boxes. "Sometimes I swear they burned everything relevant and just saved the memos. Anyway, his handwriting is all over some of the documents I found." Laurel started slightly at this, remembering the bold, spiked handwriting on the test documents, which were still tucked in the waistband of her skirt.

"My guess is that he was on another case, or maybe brought in specifically for one—but something went wrong and they've buried everything about it."

Laurel was fighting a whole spectrum of conflicting feelings. "Why are you telling me all this?" Her voice sounded hollow in the cavernous basement space.

"It hasn't been much fun working on it alone," he admitted, and his candor tugged at her. "And sometimes what I'm thinking sounds so trippy I've just wanted a reality check. I mean, you can tell me—I won't be offended. Does all of this sound completely nuts?"

"Well, it *was* nuts," she responded spontaneously. "They were seriously studying poltergeists."

He looked caught. "Okay, there's a point." Then his face lit up again and he leaned forward on the table so suddenly she flinched.

"I've been pulling documents. Some tests. Mostly stuff that I could figure out was in Leish's handwriting. I compared it to photographs of his writing in several of his books."

Brendan reached down into the backpack that he'd dropped beside the table and pulled out some manila file folders. He handed them across the table to her. There were pages paper-clipped together, with notes scribbled on top sheets that she assumed were Brendan's. She lifted a top sheet to look at the first original document, the handwritten notes there. It was without a doubt the black, spiked handwriting from the tests she'd found.

She looked down on the writing without reacting, and flipped through the paper-clipped pages. The documentation in itself was innocuous: standard personality tests, invoices for work-study students.

"I know, I know—nothing earth-shattering," Brendan said from across the table. "The point is, the notes are in Leish's

101

handwriting. And I know he wasn't here to be an office boy."

What quickened Laurel's pulse was that the dates on the tests and forms were within weeks of the dates on the extraordinary test scores she'd discovered herself. Brendan was right, Leish was up to something. What Brendan didn't know was that it was all leading up to something Leish had decided to call the Folger Experiment, that involved three of the highest-testing students the lab had ever seen.

She felt the cool rush of the air conditioner, and shivered.

Brendan was looking across the table at her and this time there was no hint of a smile on his face. "I think they brought him here for a poltergeist investigation. And whatever happened, it shut down the department permanently. They pulled the documentation concerning it—all of it they could find—and covered everything up. Which makes me think: maybe he actually found one."

Looking into his eyes, she realized it was not the air-conditioning that was giving her a chill.

At that moment a bell jangled through the basement, so loud that both she and Brendan jumped out of their chairs to their feet ...

... and then collapsed in laughter, recognizing the library closing bell.

Chapter Eighteen

They sat over Chinese food in a restaurant on Franklin Street, nearby Chapel Hill's main drag.

"Not so many Dukies, and if you half-close your eyes, sometimes you can imagine yourself back in Berkeley," Brendan beamed at her over a chopsticks-load of lo mein.

"How long have you been doing this?" she asked.

"Ages," he said glumly. "I moved here three years ago. I miss the Left Coast every day."

Laurel actually had meant his research in the Rhine files, but as his words spilled out she didn't feel like correcting him.

"At least the beach is close. The Outer Banks are out of this world." He brightened slightly. "And then there're the leaves."

Laurel had never seen the leaves change in the fall. There were the few scattered deciduous trees that you'd see around Southern California, but she'd never experienced a full-color East Coast autumn.

"Never seen them, huh?" he said, reading her mind. "It's a trip. You'll see. You can't even begin to describe it." He looked a little dreamy and she felt an unwelcome surge of longing, which she quickly pushed down, closing off.

"Actually, I was asking about the Rhine files," she said, her voice cool. "How long have you been sorting through them?"

"Mid . . . summer," he said vaguely. "I had no idea they were there, at first. The unsealing of the files has not been all that widely publicized, bizarrely. It's almost as if ..." He stopped.

"As if what?"

He shook his head. "I've been trying to find out. The official story is that the files were sealed for a generation to protect the privacy of study participants. But anyone who would have known the real dirt is dead, and no one associated with the university wants to talk about it."

"And why are you so interested?"

He broke into a huge, irresistible smile. "Oh, please. How much cooler does it get? You start reading this stuff, the field reports of clairvoyance, crisis apparitions, telepathy ... and it's like, whoa. It happens *all the time*. The dying relatives appearing to their family members. The brides-to-be who dreamed their fiancés' mistresses."

Laurel froze.

But Brendan Cody rolled right on, oblivious. "You read these same stories, over and over, and you *know* they're true. They're all the same. From all over the world. It happens. To perfectly ordinary people."

Laurel felt the cool tingling behind her ears, the excited fluttering in her stomach. It was exactly the way she had felt. Exactly.

"And then you get to the poltergeist stuff. I mean, *man*."

In front of them, the water glass suddenly slid across the table by itself.

Laurel gasped. Brendan's eyes were almost comically bugged out, glued to the glass. Laurel realized what had happened just as he laughed and reached for the glass, shaking his head.

"No, look. I couldn't resist." As she watched, he slid the glass over a puddle of condensation on the smooth surface of the table, then took his hand away. A few seconds later, the glass slid several inches on its own.

He shrugged apologetically. "Old bartender trick. Put myself through grad school behind the bar at O'Houlihan's on Geary."

Yeah, and I can just imagine the tips you were getting—from women

104

and *men*. Laurel pushed back her chair, overcome with the instinct to flee, when he reached across the table, practically lunging, and grabbed her arm.

"Come on come on come on. I was just trying to prove a point. You should have seen your face—you lit up like a Fourth of July sky when that glass moved." Before she could protest, he tightened his grip on her arm. "You know it's true. This stuff is exciting, home girl. It's out-of-this-world exciting."

Laurel felt a rush of blood through her body, to her head, as if the very fact of him saying "exciting" could elicit a physical reaction.

Just stop it, she warned herself.

But Brendan was not only oblivious, he was on a roll. He nodded to the long bar along the side wall. "I was reading the other night about a pub in Denver that had a ghost that walked down the bar and blew on the backs of all the women's necks." Laurel laughed, startled, and he grinned at her. "Yup. The bartenders said you could watch it happening. A woman sitting at the bar would suddenly turn around as if someone had touched her neck—and there was no one behind her. And then you could see it happening all the way down the bar, one woman after another turning to look. Only the women, ever." He laughed aloud, his eyes shining. "You want personality, Dr. Myers-Briggs? There's *personality* there, no doubt about it. Pure personality."

Well, he has your number, she thought in a daze. *Watch it,* she warned herself again.

He leaned forward on his elbows. "What I'm really interested in is the evolution of the character of the poltergeist. The word started appearing in general usage in the late nineteenth-century, with Catherine Crowe's *The Night Side of Nature*, and people were starting to use 'poltergeist' to differentiate a certain set of phenomena from more sedate hauntings. Poltergeists were the ones that threw things around, that made noises, that pulled pranks. Some psychic researchers wrote that boisterous ghosts tended to show up in houses where children were living."

105

"Children—or hysterical young female servants," Laurel pointed out.

"Hah. Exactly. I'm getting to that, just hold your horses." He slurped down another tangle of noodles, and took a large swallow of beer. It was his second pint, and it was already almost gone, and Laurel wondered about that, too.

"But no one disputed that poltergeists were ghosts—they were just a more violent or mischievous kind of ghost. It wasn't until Freud—psychoanalytic theory and unconscious motivation and covert sexual drives—that this person-centered theory evolved to explain what a poltergeist was. The afterlife was out; neurosis was in. So suddenly you have Nandor Fodor writing about how poltergeists are the projected sexual repressions of traumatized adolescent girls."

Laurel must have grimaced because Brendan nodded sagely. "Yeah, how Freudian, right? Blame it on the girls. Downfall of man, and all that."

That made her smile in spite of herself, and he winked at her.

"Then Rhine comes along just at the same time as the science of statistics was invented, and the scientific method is *in*. The space program kicks into high gear ... everything has to be scientifically quantified. So Roll and Rhine start in with the scientific terminology: focal person, attenuation—"

"Recurrent spontaneous psychokinesis," Laurel finished.

"*Yes*." Brendan pointed at her with his chopsticks. "Sounds great, right? RSPK—how scientific is that? The focus of the Rhine Lab was to bring parapsychology into line with the 'real' sciences. So here we go with all the scientific terminology and the flow charts and the quantifiable results. And because it's really tough to scientifically quantify the afterlife, researchers focused on the theory that poltergeists aren't ghosts at all, but projections of human energy. But *I* think ..."

He dipped into his noodles again, and scarfed them down in a prolonged slurp, before he continued. "I think that was all window dressing. Well, and the zeitgeist.

"Now, our man Leish was coming at it from a completely

106

different perspective. He'd headed up these poltergeist investigations in Europe and reported back that poltergeist manifestations usually increased over the course of an incident—and actually stepped up once an investigator was on the scene. Leish didn't think it was *one* agent at all. He thought it was a group dynamic that fueled poltergeist energy, that poltergeists were actually *created* by a spiraling group dynamic—which included the investigators." He quoted: "'The expectation and desire to experience a poltergeist factored into the manifestations.'

"Now look," Brendan waved a chopstick for emphasis. "The post-RSPK theory is that poltergeists and hauntings are facets of the same phenomenon. Haunted houses can host RSPK outbreaks, and hauntings may to an extent be person-oriented. Most contemporary researchers admit in retrospect that the combination of haunting and poltergeist features is the rule, rather than the exception."

His face grew serious and at the same time suffused with light. "But you know what I say? This isn't a science. Not nohow, not no way. It is, I submit, asinine even to try to find the science in it." He picked up the mysteriously moving glass and shook it at Laurel. "It's the unknown, for Christ's sake. But ... *but*." He paused, and waited until he had her absolute attention, then continued. "The psychology of it all is a different story. You can learn a lot about human psychology by studying test subjects' reactions to completely unscientific phenomena. And that's our book."

"*Our* book?" she stammered. At the same time she felt a thrill start from the base of her spine and sizzle through her body to the top of her head.

"Of course, our book," he said expansively. "It's obviously big enough for a book." He suddenly leaned across the table and snapped his fingers in front of her face. "Have you not been paying attention?" His eyes glowed with the candlelight. "This is *huge*. This is the meaning of life. Who are we? What are we capable of? What the hell other forces are we sharing this planet with? Do we have the freaking power or do we not?"

He was, she had to admit, completely mesmerizing. And he knew it, too, because he suddenly leaned back in his chair with his hands on his thighs, smirking, as if he'd won something.

"So what's the current psychoanalytical construct for poltergeists, hmm? What *is* a poltergeist, for us, today? What does it look like? What does it *want*?"

Laurel just stared at him, speechless.

"That, my dear, is an award-winning book. I guaran-fucking-tee it."

He leaned abruptly forward over the table, startling her.

"So we're going to do this, right?"

She looked at him, caught up in a miasma of feelings—helpless confusion, amusement, distrust, excitement. "Do *what*? How?"

"I—don't know," he admitted. "But whatever it is, we're close." His eyes were alight. "Don't you feel that? We're so close."

And he was right. She had the sense of standing outside a door that was slowly opening, beyond which there were worlds she'd only begun to imagine. Her entire body was cold, trembling, alive.

"We're on Leish's trail, now. What have we got to lose? At the very least we can write an article on how the prevalent psychoanalytic theories of the time influenced the actual experience of poltergeists. On the other end of the spectrum— we could prove they exist."

Chapter Nineteen

She didn't sleep that night, of course, but lay awake against her pillows in the jasmine-scented dark, in a dazed state of overload. The basement scene had been weird beyond belief, and in moments she wasn't exactly sure any of it happened.

Brendan had walked her to her car and there had been an awkwardness as if they had been on a first date—the weirdest first date in the recorded history of first dates: sitting in a basement with seven hundred file boxes around them, talking about poltergeists. The thought sent her into a fit of giggles that woke the cat, who stared at her from its pillow in unblinking reproof.

Get hold of yourself, Laurel ordered sternly. *This is madness. You're a tenure track professor at a major university and you're seriously thinking of doing some sort of study on poltergeists?*

And there was somehow another professor who was equally crazy enough to be contemplating it?

But you can end that right now—easiest thing in the world. It's clear he has no idea about the Folger Experiment. You don't ever have to mention it.

And really, she didn't have any idea what "the Folger Experiment" meant; all she had was the vaguest idea where to start.

A house, her mind whispered back to her seductively. *Uncle Morgan said, "The Folger House." It's a real place.*

Brendan had confirmed what she had been thinking herself: Leish had been at the Rhine lab conducting an investigation into the Folger House. Before he died.

In fact, in all likelihood he was conducting the experiment when *he died,* she reminded herself, and the thought shot through her body in an icy chill.

And what do you really think you're going to do if you do find the house? If she ever decided to tell Brendan that there was a house?

But she knew what they would do. It had been crackling in the air between them at the restaurant. Brendan wanted to follow in Leish's footsteps. He wanted to *find* a poltergeist.

The thought made her shiver again . . . but she had to admit there was an excitement running through the chill.

She could pretend all she wanted that it was a psychological experiment. Really, what it was, was magic.

Her cell phone rang beside her, and she bolted up. The phone rang again, vibrating on the bed table. She had no idea who would be calling her. But she did.

She reached for the phone, felt its ring vibrate through her hand. She punched it on. "Hello?" she said warily.

"This is going to be so big."

She wanted to laugh. She had no idea what was happening to her. She had no idea how he'd gotten her cell number.

"What is?" she asked, finally.

"You know." Brendan's voice thrilled through her, heating her to her core.

Now she did laugh. "I don't know."

"Yeah, you do."

There was a live, warm silence.

"Noon. In front of Bryan. I have something I need to show you."

The silence again.

"Okay," she heard herself saying into the dark.

By the time they met, of course, the doubts were back, gnawing around the edges of her consciousness. No matter how much she wanted to do this book, and no matter what a relief it was to think that she might not have to do it all alone, there was no reason to trust this man—none at all. But the day was gorgeous, trembling with the excitement of fall ... tantalizingly warm sun and teasing wind that brushed at her cheeks and her legs and played with her clothes and hair, and she felt her heart lift as she hurried on the flagstone paths toward the sprawling stone and glass student union.

Inside the lobby, Brendan turned from a theater poster, and heat shot through her at the way his face lit up at the sight of her. He was slow crossing the room to her and she felt again the awkwardness of a date. He touched her arm and by silent agreement they moved immediately out of the bustling thoroughfare that was the Bryan Center, through the glass side doors onto the outdoor walkway, where iron tables were scattered between umbrellaed kitchen kiosks selling salads, desserts, and various ethnic foods. The whole upper walkway looked out over the tops of trees, the pond of Duke Gardens glimmering below between the maples. A strong wind gusted leaves across the pavement and swirled the trees, a promise of mystery and adventure.

They chose a table surrounded by nothing but empty tables, but once seated kept their voices low and kept glancing around as if they were on the lam from some government agency. Brendan's voice was barely above a whisper.

"Look, there's no reason not to say it straight out. We both know what we're talking about, here."

She felt a wild urge to burst into not entirely sane laughter, but managed to keep control. "You want to track down a poltergeist."

He looked across the table at her. "Don't you?"

Now she did start to laugh.

"I don't even know what that *is*."

"It's the farthest reaches of human consciousness." He said it with radiant conviction. "It might be pure discarnate personality, who knows? However you want to say it, I'm fine with that."

111

Laurel's smile died and she watched the students passing by, in groups, in couples. All animated with the same quality of— of life, longing, promise. And she realized she was jealous ... she was tired of feeling worn out, discarded, used up before her time.

She thought of the test papers with Leish's notation about the Folger Experiment in her roller bag and was two seconds away from reaching down to pull them out and hand them to Brendan—when he reached into his own backpack and pulled out a file folder and removed a single sheet of paper. He looked at her and his blue-gray eyes were serious, now.

"All right, here it is. I think Leish was brought in to investigate this case." He handed her over a document, a police report form. She immediately noticed three things: it was old, typed on a real manual typewriter; it was dated March 13, 1965; and parts of the text had been blacked out. She glanced up at Brendan. He made a motion for her to read.

She bent over the page, and as she read, she felt a growing incredulity ... and then a powerful surge of excitement.

POLICE REPORT

NOTIFICATION: Complainant, **XXXXX** *reports to* **XXXXXXX** *Desk Officer, that strange occurrences had been taking place in and around the* **XXXXXXXXXXX** *in which she worked. Electrical appliances had malfunctioned, household items had disappeared or been moved, and on the day in question, a large number of rocks had been thrown on the roof and back veranda.*

DETAIL INTERVIEW: On Tuesday, 11 March 1965, the complainant, **XXXXX** *was interviewed by this officer,* **XXXXXXXX** *and Officer* **XXXXX**. **XXXXXXXXX** *is a housekeeper in the employ of* **XXXXXXXXXXXXXXXXXXXXXXXXXXXXXXXXXXXXXXXXXXXXX XXXXXXXXXXXXXXXXXXX** *groundskeeper on the estate,* **XXXXXX** **XXXXXXXXXXXXXXXX** *family occupy the servants' house, attached to the main house.*

Complainant stated that on Monday, 10 March, 1965, at about 1530 to 1615 hours, she was at home with her daughter **XXXX***, age 14*

112

years, and her son **XXXX**, *age 12 years. The complainant and the children heard pounding and rattling on the roof, for a period of approximately three minutes, on and off. When the noises ceased, the complainant went outside the house and found hundreds of rocks of various sizes lying on the back veranda. When she picked up a few of the rocks they were hot to the touch.*

The complainant then called the **XXXXXXXXXXX** *police department and I and* **XXXXX** *responded. Complainant proceeded to show myself and Officer* **XXXXX** *the scattered rocks outside the main house.*

Complainant stated that there had been other disturbances at the house in the previous weeks which the family had attributed to an electrical problem: lights and household appliances had turned on and off at odd times of the day and night and/or had refused to work at all. An electrician had been called and could find no fault in the house's electrical wiring.

Complainant further reported household items, including a sugar bowl, a serving platter, and a skillet had disappeared and subsequently reappeared in inappropriate places, such as the upstairs bathtub and in the complainant's bed.

While I and Officer **XXXXX** *were in the complainant's quarters, all the family was present with us in the living room when the complainant's son ran in from the kitchen, reporting that rocks had fallen in the kitchen as well. When Officer* **XXXXX** *and myself went into the kitchen with the complainant's family, we found the kitchen table and floor covered with rocks of various sizes, and the sugar bowl, a ceramic fruit bowl, and a glass plate smashed, though no rocks were nearby.*

I initially suspected the boy of placing the rocks in the kitchen and smashing the glass, but as I and Officer **XXXXX** *and the family stood in the kitchen, we heard pounding sounds all around us in the kitchen and the sound of glass smashing, although nothing was visibly occurring.*

At the time of these occurrences the entire family was standing in full view of myself and Officer **XXXXX** *in the kitchen. There were no tremors in the house, no movement of any kind that could be noticed. None of the appliances was going at these times and the complainant has no high frequency equipment at all in the*

*

113

Laurel reached the bottom of the page. As she turned the report over impatiently, a loud scraping sound made her jump nearly out of her skin.

Across the table, Brendan was on his feet, instantly apologizing, "Sorry. Sorry." She realized the horrible screech had been his metal chair scraping the concrete as he pushed it out. "I was just going to tell you that that's all there is. I could only find the one page."

Laurel felt a wave of frustration bordering on fury. She stared at him.

"I know—it's maddening, right?"

Her mind was racing so fast she didn't even respond. *It was a real poltergeist house. The Folger House?*

"Where was this?" she asked aloud.

Brendan shook his head glumly. "I have no idea what town, or even if it was in this state. But the time frame is too much to be a coincidence, right? The report was dated March 13, 1965, and mid-March is exactly when Leish's name started showing up on Rhine lab documents."

She looked down at the police report, the tantalizing details, the blocked-out portions. "I've been reading reports of poltergeist occurrences for weeks now," she said slowly. "The details are classic. But I haven't come across this particular occurrence. Not in 1965."

"Neither have I," Brendan agreed. "Believe me, I've been scouring the Net and the available literature. And it's much bigger than Seaford. The rock showers, the sound displacement—and those were *early* manifestations. So why wasn't this getting national attention?"

"What about the names?" She suddenly leaned back in her chair and held the page of the report up to the sunlight, trying to read the names that had been blocked out.

"Yeah, I tried that, too. You can't read anything underneath. The weird thing is, I'm not sure there *is* anything underneath." Brendan's face was serious, focused.

She glanced past the paper at him, then looked more closely at the sun shining dimly through the blacked-out sections of

114

the report. It was true—she couldn't see a single character underneath the black, and no impressions of typewriter keys under the blacked-out parts, either. "So what does that mean? It's a copy?" But she already knew that made no sense—she could see the impressions of typewriter keys under all the rest of the document.

"Well, it could have been retyped without typing in the names, yes, I guess, if they really wanted to preserve anonymity."

She lowered the page and stared at him. He tapped the page with his pen.

"But the date is too close to be coincidental. Leish shows up working at the Rhine Lab right after the date this sheriff's report is filed. I'm sure they brought him here to investigate a poltergeist."

"Or ... ," she said slowly, "they brought him here to create one."

Brendan looked at her, mystified.

The wind gusted, blowing leaves past them on the walkway, and Laurel felt a chill run through her, a palpable sensation of danger. She looked around them ... at students chattering in line at the food kiosks, professors striding by on the walkway. No one was looking at them, she couldn't see anyone she recognized, but the sense of not-rightness was paralyzing. She had a sudden, almost overpowering feeling of menace. She started to shiver.

"What?" Brendan said, automatically lowering his voice.

"I don't know ... something wrong ... something bad ..." She could barely speak through the overwhelming need to flee. "I think we need to go somewhere else."

He did not ask her why, just zipped his backpack and stood.

They found a private conference room in the library.

"Who did you see out there?" Brendan asked her, when the door was safely shut. The room was small, just a table and four chairs. Laurel took a deep breath. She felt shaky, but the amorphous feeling of danger was fading.

"I'm probably just being paranoid," she hedged, and glanced out the small glass window in the door.

"Doubtful. We've got some competitive people in this department. Ruthless, really. Next time we should meet off campus."

Next time? she thought. *Already there's a next time?*

Brendan's face had darkened, and he was silent for a moment. "So all right, what are we trying to get at, here?"

Laurel felt a conspiratorial thrill as she walked the small room, gathering her thoughts. "Leish's overall hypothesis was that it was the expectation of the group—the affected family and the investigators—that created a poltergeist?"

"Yes . . . ," Brendan said, raising his eyebrows.

"Then maybe—maybe that report *was* a fake." He looked at her, mystified. She sat on the edge of the table beside him, unconsciously lowering her voice, even though they were completely alone. "Maybe that's just the story he gave out to his team."

"What team?"

Without realizing she was doing it, she stood again. "What if you put a group of researchers together to study the effects of expectation on a paranormal investigation? Only you use research assistants who test off the charts for ESP and PK abilities?"

She turned and looked at him, watching comprehension dawn on his face. "So you tell these high scorers they're going in to investigate a poltergeist, provide some corroborating documentation . . . and see if one shows up? I think that would be freakin' awesome," he finished, delighted. "But how do you know—"

She reached to the floor, lifted and set her roller bag on the table, and removed the paper-clipped sheaf of high-scoring tests. Brendan was pacing behind the table, as if he no longer could sit still, either.

She handed the test charts across the table.

He read the first one while standing—and his eyes widened. "Holy shit." He pulled out a chair and sat at the table, flipping

116

quickly through the tests, then going back and looking a second time, his eyes moving rapidly back and forth between scores, comparing. "This is—"

"I know," Laurel said, her voice sounding giddy to herself. "Look at the dates."

"I know," Brendan said, with the same dazed exuberance. "Late March to early April. So Leish put together a team of super-scorers . . ." He looked up at her. "These are higher test scores than even Pierce and Linzmeyer."

"I know. I don't know how he found them—"

"It's like putting together a PK pressure cooker—"

"If you believed in that kind of thing," she said, with a straight face.

He stared at her, then burst out laughing. "Busted," he admitted. He looked over the tests again, and she saw him frown and point to the notes, in Leish's spiky handwriting. "What's this? 'Folger Experiment'? It's noted on all three of the tests. Who's Folger?"

In a split second she decided to keep that part to herself. *You've said way too much already. You don't know him. Not at all.*

She shrugged, hopefully casually. "I don't know. But there's a linear progression with the dates. The police report, dated right before Leish's name starts to show up on Rhine Lab documents, then Leish's notes on all the ESP and PK tests, then the high scorers being culled from that series of tests and pulled for 'The Folger Experiment.' And the notations on the test papers are definitely in Leish's handwriting."

"And then the lab shuts down just six weeks after the start date of the experiment," Brendan finished. "Something happened, all right. Something big. Let's review." He paced behind the table as if he were in front of a classroom. "One: The Rhine Lab is on a roll. They've reinvented themselves and taken paranormal investigations to a new level by starting field investigations of poltergeist activity. These investigations are getting them national attention. Two: A police report surfaces of electrical disturbances and rock showers and sound displacement at an undisclosed location." He paused. "The

117

report may or may not be real, but for the moment, let's take it at face value.

"Three: Paranormal investigator Alaistair Leish suddenly shows up at the Rhine lab, attending meetings, conducting tests. It's Leish's theory that poltergeists are created by the expectation of the involved parties, including investigators. Four: Leish does a series of ESP and PK tests and culls a group of high-scoring testers for an experiment he calls 'Folger.'"

He glanced at her and Laurel tried to keep from squirming uncomfortably. *I can tell him anytime,* she told herself. *Just wait.*

After a second, Brendan continued, pacing back and forth, gathering momentum as he thought aloud. "So, either A: Leish has made up a poltergeist house with classic manifestations to take his high-scoring team into to test his hypothesis that researcher expectation can create a poltergeist; or B: he's taking his high-scoring team into an actual poltergeist house to see how the presence of the team and its abilities will affect the manifestations." He stopped pacing dropped into a chair, and looked at Laurel, his face alight. "Either way it's revolutionary."

She found herself, against her will, warming all over her body.

Brendan held up an index finger. "And then—six. Within six weeks of the start date of the experiment, the Duke parapsychology lab is closed, and all the laboratory files sealed."

They sat in silence, overwhelmed by the implication.

Something big . . .

Brendan's face had taken on a faraway look. He suddenly slammed his hand on the police report on the table between them. "We need to find this house."

"What?" she said, feeling caught up in something far beyond her control.

He looked at her. "'How can we not devote our lives to pursuing that question?'"

She felt a shiver, as if she were hearing Dr. Leish speak directly through him, and she was two seconds away from

118

telling Brendan everything—about Uncle Morgan, about the Folger House, about her dream, all of it.

Then she felt herself pull back.

What is this "we" stuff? "We" this and "we" that. It was a technique commonly used by criminals, con artists, serial killers, called "forced pairing." Get the victim to drop her guard by pretending you and she were a team.

"You're leaving out the obvious, aren't you?" she said aloud, and there was an edge to her voice.

Brendan frowned, lifted his hands in puzzlement.

"That there might have been a good reason that the experiment was covered up?" she said pointedly. "That maybe something *bad* happened?"

"Like what?" he asked, perplexed.

"Do you know that Leish died in April 1965, the same month as the experiment?"

Brendan stopped for just a fraction of a second. "He died of a heart attack—" he started.

"At forty-one?" she demanded.

"It happens," he countered, defensive.

"How do we know it was really a heart attack, anyway?" The only evidence she had for that was Anton's word—another man she didn't trust.

"What are you saying, that he was murdered?" Brendan asked skeptically. "He was scared to death?" That stopped her. "I don't get what you think happened."

She hesitated. *What do I think?*

"I don't know," she said finally, "and you don't either. But whatever it was, it was bad enough to shut down a world-renowned department that had been functioning for thirty-eight years. It wasn't just shut down—someone locked up all the research files and tried to erase all physical trace of the department's existence. I mean, they turned it into an auditorium—"

He was staring at her, perplexed. "An auditorium—what are you talking about?"

"Baldwin Auditorium . . ." But she was having a bad feeling, suddenly.

Brendan shook his head. "The old Rhine Lab was in the East Duke Building. The building was torn down in 1978."

Laurel's face and chest flushed with the heat of humiliation. So Tyler had been completely having her on—it was all a big joke. *All lies. All of it.*

Her head was ringing; it felt as if the room were closing in on her. She pushed back her chair and stood—she just had to get out.

"I have a meeting with a student," she lied, and grabbed her book bag. "I have to go." In a flash she was out of the room.

Students looked up from their study carrels as she barreled past them toward the elevators.

"Wait a minute—Mickey!" Brendan had pulled open the door of the conference room to call after her.

Mickey? She registered in some part of her brain. But she just kept going, nearly running, through the library.

Chapter Twenty

She sat alone in her office with the door securely locked, lacerating herself.

How could you possibly have confided in him? You don't even know him. Are you that starved for company?

And Tyler, that whole ruse, the "haunted" auditorium … Her face burned again, thinking about it. *Are you so gullible that a twenty-year-old can fleece you now?*

Would she ever be able to tell the truth from a lie again?

She swiveled her chair from her desk and stared out her window on the quad. The gargoyle stared back in at her.

And suddenly she felt a surge of resolve.

They can all go to hell. I'm going to figure this out.

She shot to her feet and paced her office—as well as anyone could pace a five-feet-by-six-feet rectangle, and tried to arrange her thoughts.

What do I know about the experiment?

Leish was dead, and quite possibly had died in the middle of the experiment. No one wanted to talk about that, and she wouldn't trust anyone who did, anyway.

But there were three other witnesses: Subject A, Subject B, Subject C. A sudden thrill shot through her at the realization. Leish had collected three students with off-the-charts psi scores. Well, all right, she didn't exactly *know* they were students, but it was a good bet; she'd noticed from all her research that the Duke lab had favored student participants. They would have been enrolled in the school. There must be a way to find them.

She went to a bookcase for the 1965 yearbook that she had coaxed out of the reference librarian. She'd found one photo in it that she was certain was Leish, and one of Uncle Morgan, and she knew there were photos of other student participants. She stood by the window and paged through the volume impatiently, to the section of photos of the lab and the student participants.

She stopped on the photo of Uncle Morgan watching the dice machine ... and felt the same pang as before at the *life* in him.

Still holding the yearbook, she crossed the few steps to her office door, opened the door, and looked out carefully. The hall was empty. She stepped out of her office and walked quickly to the departmental office. She stopped just before the door and peered in—then breathed a sigh of relief when she saw the secretary's desk was deserted. Laurel moved past the wall of anachronistic mail slots, with their glass doors and old-fashioned keyholes, and stepped through the door of the copy room.

The room was also empty, and for five nervous minutes Laurel stood in the heat of the copy machine, making copies of all the photos of the lab in the yearbook. The lights of the machine flicked in a regular, steady beat as she paged through the yearbook and her copies snicked into the receiving tray.

She pulled the finished stack from the slot, looked around the small room, and grabbed an empty cardboard box, then returned to her office and locked the door again.

She swept everything off the top of her desk into the box, and lined up the photocopied lab photos on the desk. Then she sat in her desk chair and opened the yearbook to the beginning of the student portraits and started going through the photos one by one, page by page, to see if she could identify the students in the lab shots by name. She didn't know what she was looking for, exactly, and maybe she was just crazy, but she would start with that and see if that led to any interesting information.

As it turned out, it did.

The students in the yearbook photos of the lab were unidentified, but with the copies of the lab shots in front of her, she was able to match school portraits to all the students in the lab shots, and compile a list of twelve names . . .

. . . after which she had to do a mad sprint downstairs to her Personality 101 lecture (where Tyler Mountford was sitting front and center, grinning lewdly at her flushed face and tousled hair).

Lecture accomplished, she hurried back to her office, locked the door behind her, and called the Alumni House. She explained to a secretary that she was trying to track down a number of alumni to interview for a departmental project. The secretary was blessedly cooperative. Out of Laurel's list of twelve, there were four deceased. Of the remaining eight, the secretary provided contact phone numbers and addresses for six of them, one of which, of course, Laurel knew already.

The other two had never graduated.

Laurel hung up, thinking about this. It was a small piece of information, and it didn't necessarily mean anything. But the backs of her ears were tingling again. She reached across her desk to pick up a photo and put it in the center of her desk. She was looking down at two students seated on opposite sides of a square table with a black screen dividing it—one of the Zener card boards. On one side of the screen sat a young woman she'd identified as Victoria Enright, a creamy-skinned, dark-haired girl with a Jackie Kennedy bouffant, holding a card in the palm of her hand. On the other side another student made markings on a pad: Rafe Winchester, an unsmiling young man with unnervingly intense eyes, and black hair shiny with Brylcreem, which failed to tame a defiant cowlick.

Laurel picked up the phone again, and this time dialed the extension for the registrar.

The registrar confirmed that Rafe Winchester and Victoria Enright had both dropped out of the university in April of 1965 and had not been in touch with the school ever since. And for both of them, their last class, never completed, had been a work-study program with the psychology department.

Laurel hung up the phone with her face tingling ... she felt cold all over, and exhilarated.

Work-study. Leish's name was on some of those work-study requisition forms. And Rafe and Victoria never graduated. And Leish ... Leish died.

She looked up—and nearly jumped out of her skin at the sight of baleful eyes staring back in at her in the dark.

The gargoyle, of course, and it was already twilight.

Chapter Twenty-one

Back at home Laurel fed the cat and fixed a bowl of Raisin Bran for herself, and then went upstairs to her study with the list of all the students for which the Alumni House had given her numbers.

She spent the entire evening on the phone. She felt increasingly guilty that she was able to reach all but two of the former students in her very first round of calls; it was a heartbreaking characteristic of people of a certain age that they were so accessible by phone, making them vulnerable to canny predators. Laurel chatted generally with the alumni of the Rhine experiments, about the psychology department and the research experiments they'd taken part in. They'd all been tested with Zener cards and dice machines.

But not one of the senior citizens she spoke with admitted to being a high scorer—although Laurel got the wistful sense from several of them that they wished they had been—and when Laurel asked each of the alumni if they had been part of the Folger Experiment, not one of the people she talked to had heard of it.

She also asked about the two missing students: Rafe Winchester and Victoria Enright. Victoria was a dead end— although one elderly woman hesitated when she heard Victoria's name. When Laurel delicately probed, she finally said wryly, "Dear, in my day, sometimes young women just had to . . . disappear."

So was Victoria pregnant? Laurel wondered. But that didn't explain why Rafe Winchester had also dropped out.

She got lucky on Rafe, though. Another elderly alumnus recalled that Rafe's sister was also a Duke graduate, and Laurel was able to get a phone number for Becky Hapwell, née Winchester, from the Alumni House.

Thank heaven for the old school tie, because Becky Hapwell would never have talked to Laurel if not for the Duke connection. But once she got started, Mrs. Hapwell had a lot to say, and none of it pleasant. Laurel had to hold the phone away from her ear as the older woman's voice rose stridently on the other end.

"That department was the end of Rafe. He turned away from his family, and he turned away from the Lord. Magicians masquerading as professors . . . they infected his mind."

Laurel was both creeped out and energized . . . feeling the possibility of a lead.

"Mrs. Hapwell, did your brother participate in parapsychology experiments while he was at Duke?"

"Call it your fancy names. 'If any turn to mediums and wizards, prostituting themselves to them, I will set My face against them, and will cut them off from the people—' "

Laurel realized from the suddenly stilted cadence of her voice that Rafe's sister was quoting from the Bible. She hastened to interrupt the woman's trumpeting rant. "I know Rafe dropped out of school without finishing his senior year. Where did he go?"

"I warned him," the older woman said with a steely satisfaction. "We all warned him to turn away from the left-hand path. He wouldn't listen. It was the experimenting—"

Laurel's pulse quickened. "Experimenting? Do you mean at the university? The Folger Experiment?"

"I mean drugs. I mean those heathen, hippie practices. They ruined his mind. He ended up on the street, in dissolution and degradation—"

"Was that here in North Carolina?" Laurel broke in, trying to keep the conversation on track.

126

"Atlanta," Mrs. Hapwell said, as grimly as if she were saying *Sodom and Gomorrah*. "With the hippies and drunkards and prostitutes. Dissolute, depraved, and degraded—"

"Do you know where he is now, Mrs. Hapwell?" Laurel interrupted.

"He is dead to the family."

Laurel tried one more time. "Mrs. Hapwell, was your brother involved in the Folger Experiment? Did he ever mention the Folger Experiment?"

There was a pause, and then the rasping voice intoned, "Open the door to the devil and the devil will walk through—"

Laurel quickly thanked her and disconnected before the woman got caught up in another rant. She set her phone on the windowsill and stood, too restless to sit. She felt distinctly unnerved, not just by the fanatic religiosity.

She had no concrete proof, but her nerves were jumping, her mind racing:

Victoria Enright and Rafe Winchester dropped out of school—and apparently disappeared from public record—after doing a work-study project in the Duke Psychology department coinciding with the dates of the Folger Experiment.

She stood and pawed through her roller bag for the 1965 yearbook. She flipped the pages of the yearbook and looked down at the photo of the dark-haired girl and the sharp-eyed young man, seated across from each other at the table with the Zener-card board between them. Victoria and Rafe. She was sure of it.

Two students dropped out and were never heard from again. One famous guest lecturer dead. And another student who, while he might have graduated, is not like the other boys and girls . . .

Laurel stopped her restless pacing and looked at her desk. She approached it with reluctance and looked down at the last name on her list of alumni.

Then she picked up the phone again and called her mother.

She spoke as soon as she heard Meredith's voice. "I want to know about Uncle Morgan."

There was an icy silence on her mother's side. "Know what?" Meredith said finally.

"You know what I'm asking, Mom. What's wrong with him?"

There was a long silence, then Meredith sighed. "You're the psychologist, darling, what do you think?"

"But I don't *know*," Laurel said in frustration. "Was he always this way? Or did something happen to him?"

"He was always sensitive—"

"I'm not talking about sensitive—"

"Please, Laurel," Meredith said sharply. "Let me speak. He was always sensitive," she said again. "But he changed."

"When was that?" Laurel held her breath. She could feel her mother thinking on the other end of the phone, the other side of the country.

"The year I graduated. The year I left," Meredith said slowly, and there was the heaviness of guilt in her voice.

"Nineteen sixty-five," Laurel said. She felt hollow to the core. She sat down on the small sofa next to the window. "Mom, did Uncle Morgan ever mention taking part in a study called the Folger Experiment?"

Another silence on the phone as her mother considered. "Not that I recall. Remember, Laurel, I was only in high school. Your aunt and uncle were already at college and I only really saw them on holidays—"

"But when did you notice that Uncle Morgan had changed?"

Meredith took so long to answer that Laurel thought she wouldn't. "He came home from school in the spring, just before I graduated. I wasn't able to see him; Mama and Daddy said he was sick, they said he was in the hospital." She laughed shortly, not a pleasant sound. "I suppose that could have meant just about anything, couldn't it? A sanitarium, some equivalent of a drug treatment center. You have to remember the times—the whole world had gone crazy. And I was having my own rebellion; I wasn't the easiest child in the world . . . not like you."

That last admission startled Laurel so much she lost her train of thought for a moment. She willed herself back to focus.

128

"But you never heard anyone mention the Folger House, or the Folger Experiment, or a Dr. Leish?"

"No." Laurel could hear the frown in Meredith's voice. "Why? Do you think the school involved Morgan in some kind of testing? Mind-altering drugs?"

For a moment Laurel thought of Rafe Winchester's sister, raving about drugs and degradation.

Drugs, no, Laurel thought. *But mind-altering? Maybe.*

"I don't know, Mom. Do you know the name Rafe Winchester? Or Victoria Enright?"

Laurel could picture the abstract concentration in her mother's face as she paused to consider. "I think Morgan dated a girl named Victoria. Before he dropped out of school."

Dated? Now that could lead somewhere. But . . .

"But Uncle Morgan didn't drop out," Laurel said aloud. "He's listed by the registrar as having graduated."

"Well, maybe I'm wrong," her mother said wearily. "He left school before *my* graduation, anyway, because he was too sick to go. That's what they said . . ." She was silent again, and then her voice changed. "What good is it to dredge all these things up, Laurel? Your uncle's made his way. He's comfortable. And I don't want you bothering him with any of this, opening old wounds. I mean that. Promise me."

Laurel swallowed. "I won't, Mom."

"Life isn't always kind. Just leave it be."

Laurel put the phone down and stood, lost in a chaos of thoughts. *Two students traumatized. One disappeared. A famous researcher dead. And a lab closed down permanently, with all records sealed.*

What in God's name happened in that house?

A bell suddenly rang, loud and sharp. Laurel jumped, her pulse skyrocketing—before she realized it was her doorbell. She had never heard it before.

She moved out of her study. As she descended the stairs, the bell rang again. She crossed the hall and looked warily out the side window—and felt her heart drop. Brendan Cody stood outside on her porch hefting two large brown bags.

Chapter Twenty-two

Laurel pressed her back against the wall, but he'd already seen her—he grinned through the window and lifted the bags, nodded to the doorknob. She took a deep breath and opened the door. The night air was warm and laced with the sweet scent of honeysuckle.

Brendan cut off all objection with instant self-effacement. "I know, I should have called. But you are going to be so glad I came. When was your last decent Mexican meal?"

Annoyed as she was, Laurel was already starting to salivate ... she could smell pico de gallo, and cilantro, and real chile verde wafting from the bags. She had not, in fact, been able to find a halfway decent Mexican restaurant, or even a burrito, since she'd come to North Carolina, and there were some days she thought she would kill for a tamale.

"There aren't any," he said, as if he'd read her mind. "Only this one. And I'm not going to tell you where it is, because that would reduce my leverage. We need to talk, Mickey."

Mickey? she thought, confused.

Before she could respond, Brendan had moved past her into the hall, heading unerringly for the kitchen, where he deposited the bags on a counter and pulled a six-pack of Coronas from one of them.

"Church key?" he queried, and when he tapped the bottle top she realized he meant an opener.

130

"I don't think I—"

He was already pulling at drawer handles, finding, of course, one empty drawer after another.

He suddenly abandoned the search and fished keys from his pocket—There was a Swiss Army knife on the chain and he used it to open two glistening bottles. He removed a lime from one of the other bags—"Can you believe what a lime costs, here? And don't even get me started on avocados ..."—and snicked open a blade to cut two juicy green wedges. He garnished the bottles, then handed one to her with a flourish and clinked his bottle against hers.

"*Salud,*" he toasted, and took a deep drink. Then he was walking out of the kitchen, into the hall.

In the time it took him to cross the hall to the living room it dawned on Laurel how strange her house would look to a stranger. It was still, for most intents and purposes, empty. Not a single stick of furniture in the living room, for example.

She hurried out into the hall and nearly collided with Brendan, who had stopped still in the archway of the living room, she assumed in shock.

He stepped around her and walked the empty room with a poker face. "Love what you've done with it."

"I haven't been home much," Laurel started, defensively. Something brushed her ankle and she jumped ... looked down to see the cat had appeared to investigate the stranger.

Brendan stooped and held a hand out to the cat, who, annoyingly, came to him in a shot and rubbed her head luxuriously against his hand.

"What's your name, pretty girl?" Brendan cooed at her.

Laurel shifted, uncomfortable and somehow guilty. "I ... haven't named her yet."

Brendan stood with the traitorous animal, who was purring so loudly that Laurel could hear the sound echoing in the room.

"A little problem with commitment here?" Brendan suggested.

"I didn't—she's not exactly *mine.*"

"Cats never are," he agreed. "No stereo, either?"

Laurel bristled. "No." She had not been able to listen to music of any kind since the night she'd found Matt and Tracey together. It was too painful.

Brendan sighed dramatically and handed her the cat. "Right back," he said, and was out of the living room, out through the front door.

Laurel stood with the cat, feeling awkward, invaded, and on the verge of tears. Before she had time to formulate a plan, Brendan was back, with an iPod and speakers, beckoning her outside. "I think on the *veranda*, don't you?" he said, exaggerating the drawl.

She followed him through the entry hall in somewhat of a daze, and stood in the front doorway and watched as he deftly set up the speakers on the porch rail and powered on the music. A familiar piano trill sounded, and Laurel sensed the music before she actually recognized it. Van Morrison, of course ... what else from a man named Brendan Cody? The familiar music was clear and heartachingly sweet, and as if drawn by the music, fireflies sparked in the soft darkness beyond the porch.

Laurel steeled herself. *I will not cry,* she vowed, and immediately felt tears hot behind her eyes. She moved quickly back into the house so he would not see, swiping at her cheeks before she stepped into the light of the kitchen, where she swallowed hard and busied herself lifting take-out boxes out of the bags.

"No plates, either?" Brendan said behind her, and she jumped.

"I have plates," she said, defensively, and found all four of them, the sole occupants of one cabinet. Brendan leaned in the doorway, swigging from his beer and watching her as she scooped rice and beans and heavenly smelling enchiladas onto plates. She could feel his eyes on her.

"All right, enough of this mysterious act. What are you doing here, Mickey? What made you bury yourself in Durham, North Carolina?"

She put down the fork and turned, bewildered. "Why do you keep calling me Mickey?"

He looked at her with surprise. "MacDonald? Mickey D?"

She stared at him. "You're . . ."

"A nut, I know, thanks, you're not the first to say so. You didn't answer my question."

"What are *you* doing here?" she countered.

"Ah, well. There was a little problem with a loan shark."

She was wondering how to take that when he laughed. "Same as you, Mickey. The wait times for tenure track professorships in California are longer than the lines at Disneyland. You gotta follow the money. It hasn't been a total loss, though," he added, and eyed her in a way that made her warm and angry at the same time.

He held her gaze until she was breathless, then said "Dinner," authoritatively. He tucked the six-pack under one arm, picked up the plates, and carried them out into the hallway, toward the front door. She had no choice but to take the rest of the food and follow.

The enchiladas were more than decent, more like divine, and the Coronas and the balmy darkness and the gentle motion of the rockers lulled Laurel into a dangerously comfortable haze.

They ate in almost silence at first, then Brendan leaned back in his chair to study her.

"So, Mickey D. Why are you resisting this so hard?"

"Resisting what?" she said, flustered. "What is *this*?"

"Only possibly the greatest adventure of your life."

"Oh, only that," she said, secretly charmed. *And that's the problem,* she reminded herself.

He shook his head at her. "Please, it's so totally obvious you're just as into all this as I am. So what's the holdup?"

She hesitated, not sure how to voice her thoughts about how badly the experiment might have turned out. She'd had no time to process her own thoughts yet.

Brendan pressed on. "First of all, what spooked you the last time we talked?"

133

Laurel felt her cheeks burn in the dark, remembering with humiliation how she'd run out on their last meeting after she'd realized Tyler had conned her with his phony stories of the haunted auditorium. But she wasn't going to mention to Brendan that she'd been bamboozled by a student.

"I think a little too much of all this is just wanting to believe," she said. "Researchers and subjects ... they get excited and lose all objectivity. They miss the real life explanations that are right in front of their eyes." *The dream* hovered ... but she pushed it away hard.

"Absolutely agreed," Brendan said instantly. "Absolutely no doubt. But doesn't that make just as—well, *almost* as good a study? How desire and expectation influence perception?"

"It could," she conceded. She'd had the thought herself. *But that was before ...*

"And you've gotta admit that it's all a hell of a lot more interesting than vocational testing." And before she could protest, he barreled over her. "And don't start in on your human potential speech." He leaped up out of the chair, startling her. "This is exactly what we're talking about: human potential! The farthest reaches of human potential." He was suddenly on his knees in front of her, gripping the armrests of her rocker. "Psi doesn't happen all the time. It might not ever be scientifically quantifiable. But *it happens.*"

She could feel the excitement vibrating off him, like magnetism, like heat. He slowly released the rocker and stood, then sat back against the porch railing in front of her.

"So what's the problem, Mickey? What's bothering you so much that you'd turn away from an opportunity like this?"

And so she said it. "I told you. I think something bad happened in that experiment. I think that study might have gone terribly wrong."

Brendan was quiet, so she continued. "Leish died the same month. And I've been looking for the student researchers: Subject A, Subject B, Subject C ..."

Brendan frowned. "The high scorers? How did you do that? There was no information on them at all."

She thought of Uncle Morgan, and hedged. "I looked at photographs in the 1965 yearbook—candid photos taken in the parapsychology lab—and then I tracked down those students. I mean, I tried."

"How do you know the students in the photos were the ones from the Folger Experiment?"

"I don't," she admitted. "But I identified all the students in those photos, from yearbook photos, and I think I've found"— she hesitated—"two of them. There were two students who took work-study in the Psych department for the Spring semester of 1965." She paused. "Victoria Enright and Rafe Winchester. They both dropped out of school entirely in late April. I haven't found any information at all about them after that."

Brendan was frowning, very focused on her. "I'm still not following. Why would you think those particular students were involved in the Folger Experiment?"

"Work-study," she said again. "In the serious poltergeist studies I've read, the investigators went into the field. That was Leish's M.O. If you're right, and Leish came to the Rhine Lab to investigate the occurrences at that house in the police report, that would mean they couldn't take ordinary classes— he'd have to put them into a work-study program. And you said yourself Leish's name appeared on work-study requisition forms—"

"You're assuming a lot," Brendan pointed out. "But all right. I like how you're thinking about work-study; that makes a lot of sense. So these students took work-study and then dropped out of school in April . . ."

"They didn't just drop out of school. They dropped off the map entirely." Of course she was leaving something significant out, but she wasn't ready to talk to Brendan Cody about Uncle Morgan. She'd promised, and she agreed with her mother: she didn't want to involve her uncle at all if she could help it; he was too fragile. Aloud she continued, "I haven't been able to track down Victoria Enright at all, but I talked to Rafe Winchester's sister."

She relayed the conversation, watching Brendan grimace at her imitation of Mrs. Hapwell's religious rants.

"Rafe ended up on the street, and the family lost track of him entirely."

Brendan shook his head. "It was the sixties, Mickey. A lot of kids ended up on the street, or gone for good. And Atlanta was the South's equivalent of Haight-Ashbury. But let's say you're right. Something big happened in that experiment. Don't you want to *know?*"

He suddenly kicked the porch railing. "I am so sick of this burying crap. Isn't that what we went into all this—psychology—for? To *un*bury stuff? My family, God, they take the prize. Illness, addiction, alcoholism: don't talk about it, don't even look at it—"

Laurel sat very still in her rocker, taken aback by the outburst.

Brendan stopped and pulled himself together, with effort. "Sorry. Sorry. What am I talking about, anyway? We don't even know if the house exists."

"It does," she said suddenly.

He turned and looked at her. She hesitated. *Moment of truth.* Then she plunged ahead. "It does. I'm pretty sure it does. And I'm pretty sure how we can find it, if it's still standing." Going back to Uncle Morgan was a last resort, but she thought they might just be able to do it without involving him. She took a breath. "Tax records."

He stared at her, uncomprehending.

"We need county tax records for 1965. For Folger. The Folger House."

For the longest moment he was just staring at her, then he was on his feet with his arms thrown up in a "touchdown" gesture.

Chapter Twenty-three

He picked her up before nine the next morning and they drove in his Prius through the downtown of brick factories converted to condos and bistros and malls, toward Raleigh, the state capital. She couldn't help teasing him about the car. "How Bay Area is this, anyway?"

"The ozone is shot everywhere, doll face," he lasered back. "Not just in the People's Republic of Berkeley."

"I think it's sweet," she said innocently.

"Ahh, she thinks I'm sweet," he grinned. And just as suddenly he switched gears on her, metaphorically speaking. "So how did you know?"

She knew what he meant, but didn't respond until he added, "About Folger? That it's a house?"

She looked out the window beside her at the—well, at the trees, that ever-present wall of green, as she quickly calculated how to respond. After Uncle Morgan's distressed reaction to her last round of questions, she didn't want to bring him into this any more than she had to. She felt an overwhelming sense of protectiveness toward him. Finally, she said aloud, "I'd rather not say, yet. I have a source, but I'd like to find it this way, if we can."

Brendan looked at her sideways, one eye still on the road, and finally nodded. "Okay, *partner*," he said dryly, giving her exactly the stab of guilt she knew he'd been trying for, but she pretended not to register it.

137

I promised, she thought to herself. *We can spend one day looking without going to Uncle Morgan*.

They'd already looked up and printed out the tax records for all Folgers in every county in North Carolina. It was the magic of the Internet: Four hours on the computer last night had yielded 492 property owners named Folger in North Carolina. Brendan and Laurel had eliminated everything built after 1965 and still had 241 properties. They had the addresses for every one.

But Laurel had a feeling the house wasn't that far from where they were. It was just the way Uncle Morgan had said it, as if he were talking about a neighborhood place, a house he was familiar with. Laurel thought they might get lucky and find an obliging county employee who'd be able to help them narrow the search.

"Penny for your thoughts," Brendan said from the driver's side.

She regarded him obliquely. "I hope you're feeling charming, today," she said.

"You want charm, lady? I'll give you charm."

The courthouse in downtown Raleigh was a square block of marble. Laurel was shocked by the age and alienness of it—a classicist mausoleum of a building on the inevitable town square, canopied by the inevitable centuries-old oaks. And the inevitable Civil War Memorial to boot, some scarily realistic soldiers brandishing guns.

As they climbed the wide steps to the copper-framed doors, Brendan muttered beside her, "We aren't in California anymore, Toto," and she shot him an understanding look.

The lobby was all marble. The corridor was all marble. The Office of Records was all marble.

The woman behind the marble counter had on an electric blue dress stretched across a monumental bosom and wore half-glasses perched on a broad, freckled nose. Her hair was straightened and sprayed into an imposing helmet, and the nameplate on that bosom read EUNETTA, and Eunetta looked nohow interested in helping a couple of white professors stick their noses further into someone else's business than they belonged in the first place.

She listened with a faint air of disbelief and disapproval while Brendan explained that they were looking for any houses owned by anyone named Folger in the year 1965.

"In Wake County?" Eunetta asked warily.

"In any county. Just in North Carolina."

"Oh, *just* in North Carolina. Child, there are one hundred counties in North Carolina," she said with relish.

"That many? That's a lot." Brendan flashed that grin at her, undaunted. "Sounds like we're going to need some professional help here, then."

"Mmm-hmm," she remarked in that patented Southern prayer-meeting grumble that Laurel had come to find so charming—when it was not directed at her.

"I don't suppose there are back tax records that you can look up online," Brendan said, a tad wistfully.

Eunetta harrumphed. "You are right about that. There surely are not."

"And there's no central depository for tax records for the state of North Carolina." Brendan looked increasingly crestfallen.

"No, sir. None." Laurel suspected Eunetta was beginning to enjoy herself.

"So if we were looking for a house owned by a Folger somewhere in North Carolina in 1965, we would basically be shit out of luck, records-wise."

"That's *all* you know to be looking for?" Eunetta shook her head. "You best get ready to do some driving, son."

Brendan glanced at Laurel. "Well, it's a big house, we know that. There was an attached servants' quarters."

"And there was trouble in the house," Laurel said. "A police report was filed of a—strange—incident."

"Police got called out?" Eunetta looked at her appraisingly. "You don't need to go driving around for that. Police reports are public record. You got a date?"

139

Laurel was momentarily flustered until she realized Eunetta meant the date of the police report.

"Yes," Brendan practically leapt forward. "March 13, 1965."

Eunetta shrugged. "So, you call around to the county police departments."

"Except that we don't know the town or the county," Brendan said, frustrated.

Eunetta looked them over. "You have no clue where to start looking in the whole state?" Incredulity dripped from her voice.

Brendan was about to speak and Laurel said, "We think it's fairly close to Durham."

Brendan turned to her. Eunetta's eyes narrowed. "How close?"

"An hour's drive or less," Laurel heard herself saying, and had no idea what made her say it. Brendan shot a questioning look at her, which she ignored.

Eunetta considered. "The family was named Folger?"

"We think so, yes," Laurel said. She had a sudden, uncanny feeling Eunetta was about to be worth her weight in gold.

"And it was a rich family, a big house?"

Brendan and Laurel exchanged a glance. "We think so, yes. Tell me what's going through that mind of yours, Eunetta, my love."

Eunetta looked down her nose at them, shaking her head. "Y'all aren't from the South, are you?"

"What gave us away?" Brendan grinned.

Eunetta smiled and left that unanswered. She leaned back on her stool. "Shug, these small towns, they keep clip files on *every* prominent family. Richer the family is, the more files they'll have. You get yourself a map and work out from here. Call around to the libraries and ask for their clip files on the Folger family, see if you don't get you a fish."

Brendan leaned over the counter to kiss her and she held up a hand, stopping him. "None of that, now."

Chapter Twenty-four

They found it.

They sat in the marble hall with their cell phones, working their way down a county library list Eunetta had helpfully printed out for them. She had further narrowed their options by instructing them to start with the counties' main libraries first—and some counties had only one. After a mere half hour of calls, they struck gold. In the town of Five Oaks, the library was very familiar with "the old Folger House," and the librarian said that there were indeed clip files on the house and family.

Brendan was pacing the polished floor with the cell phone. "Yes. Yes. We'll be there in an hour."

He punched off with a whoop that echoed through the hall.

Five Oaks was under an hour away, in Moore County, a region known as the Sandhills.

They drove out of town on U.S. 1, and into the green maze. Within minutes there was not a building in sight, just the road and the walls of trees. It was not until the last buildings had disappeared that Brendan asked it.

"So how'd you know?"

Laurel looked over at him from the passenger seat.

"Under an hour. How'd you know it would be that close? Your *source* again?"

She half-shrugged, shook her head. "I just figured—work-study, student researchers ... they weren't going to take them that far."

"Hmmm." He narrowed his eyes and stared out at the road. "I think there's something you aren't telling me, Kemosabe."

Laurel looked out the window at the—trees—and didn't respond. It was not that she didn't trust him, it was that she didn't trust anyone. And yet here she was, driving into the vast green unknown with a total stranger, in search of—

A poltergeist.

The town was a fair distance off the freeway; they had to take several much smaller roads to get there.

"Freeways get built and these towns just die," Brendan said somberly. In fact the entrance to the town was a surprisingly extensive cemetery, and that after they'd passed several miles of farms and churches with their smaller, private plots. *A lot of dead*, Laurel thought, *and it's right there on the surface, all the time*.

According to the county Web site, the town of Five Oaks had a population of just under three thousand people, but driving through the almost-deserted streets, it was hard for Laurel to imagine where those three thousand people were keeping themselves. It was a quaintly pretty town, though, laid out roughly in a cross. There was a Main Street with old-timey shops, the requisite post office and barbershop and soda fountain, all with a certain *Twilight Zone*-meets-Mayberry feel.

Brendan had slowed the car and was staring out the windshield with a look of bemusement that matched what Laurel was feeling. "Can you say, 'time capsule'?"

The town square was in the center, with four startlingly large churches grouped around a nice little park with various Civil War memorial statues and benches, and of course, the ever-present oaks, though there were considerably more than five of them.

The county courthouse was another solid block of marble, and it appeared from the signage that the sheriff's department was contained in the building. The library was also on the square. Brendan parked (there was a spot right in front of the

142

library building, a circumstance Laurel had only ever seen in the movies), and they walked up the broad gray-white steps to another set of glass-and-bronze-gated doors.

The library was small, but had the feel almost of a college library: a main room with high molded ceilings and long, scarred old wood tables with built-in lamps running down the center. The aisles of books were off to both sides.

A gray-haired and elegant librarian obviously closing in on retirement, if not already past, looked up from the front counter as they walked in. "You must be the Duke people who called."

"That obvious, huh?" Brendan grinned at her.

"Just a bit," the librarian answered, wryly. "So you want the clip files on the Folger family."

"We'd love to look at the town newspapers, too, if you have them. We're interested in 1965 in particular," Laurel said.

"Of course. Right this way." The librarian escorted them to the glassed-in Reference and Periodicals room and pointed them to the shelves of bound volumes of old town newspapers. "In the mid-seventies we started putting the paper on microfilm. Before then—well, the *Courier* wasn't really big enough back then, and there's something about the feel of an old paper, isn't there?"

Laurel smiled at her. The librarian indicated a row of shelves. "1900 through 1975 are in those shelves. I'll go pull the clip files for you."

Brendan grabbed the *Courier* book for 1965 and he and Laurel sat at the long table to look at the newspapers. First, of course, they flipped to March 13, 1965. Side by side, they scanned the whole paper, and then the papers for the next several months, but there were neither reports of unusual goings-on at the Folger House, nor of any research investigation at the house in the few months after.

"So nothing about the rock showers or any Duke experiment taking place at the house," Brendan frowned.

Someone cleared her throat behind them and the two of them turned. The librarian stood in the doorway of the Periodicals room, looking distressed.

"I'm very sorry to tell you this, but the clip files on the Folger family are empty."

Brendan and Laurel exchanged a glance. "There's nothing *at all* on the family?" Brendan said, perplexed.

"No, what I mean is—the files have been emptied." The librarian crossed to the table to show them the manila folders she held in her hand. They were weathered and sprung—the creases of the folders sagging, as if the folders had once been stuffed with documents.

"When did this happen?" Brendan demanded, and Laurel elbowed him.

The librarian shook her head. "There's no way of telling. Obviously it was never discovered, so we would have no idea how long ago it happened." She hesitated, then added, "Unfortunately, it happens more often than you would think."

"Who takes them?" Laurel asked.

The librarian looked rueful. "More often than not, the families themselves. Disappear the dysfunction, so to speak. Obviously it's easy to do—you two could have walked out with anything you had a mind to, just now, while I was out of the room. I hope you can find what you're looking for in the newspapers."

"Do you know the house? I mean, where it is?" Laurel asked.

"I know it's out Wyndham Road ... about six miles out of town. Please let me know if there's something else I can help you find." She lifted her hands apologetically, then withdrew.

Brendan looked at Laurel. "So, our cleanup man—or crew—strikes again."

They both looked around them at the shelves of bound volumes. They hardly had time to go through a whole century of newspapers.

"Police station," Brendan said decisively. "Let's find out if that police report was for real."

The uniformed officer at the police station counter, whose nameplate read "P. Callaghan," was far too young to know

144

anything about an incident from 1965; in fact it was quite possible that even his father had not been born at the time of the year in question. He was freckled and towheaded, if a twenty-something male could be called towheaded, and instantly, obviously smitten with Laurel.

Brendan gave Laurel a nudging sideways glance, and Laurel realized he probably thought she'd get further with the young officer. She was just able to stop herself from shooting Brendan a baleful look. Instead she forced a pleasant and innocent tone into her voice and leaned on the counter with what she hoped was an appealing expression.

"Um. Hi. We're from Duke University. Dr. Cody and Dr. MacDonald. We're doing some research into an incident that took place in town, oh, quite a while ago ... 1965. We know that there was a police report filed and we'd like to see it."

"Nineteen-sixty-five," the young desk officer marveled, as if she were speaking of the Dark Ages.

"We know the date of the report, and we know this incident took place at the old Folger House." She passed Officer Callaghan a Post-it note with MARCH 13, 1965 and FOLGER HOUSE printed on it, and smiled at him with her best dazzling Hollywood smile. He blushed from the base of his neck all the way up to his scalp, and she knew they were in.

"I'll go on and check that for you, ma'am. Have to go downstairs for the files."

"Thank you so much," she fluttered, channeling some inner Southern belle.

The young officer shuffled toward the back stairs, so flustered he ran into his own desk on the way to the door.

"Cradle-robber," Brendan said softly beside Laurel, as Officer Callaghan disappeared.

"'Ma'am'?" she answered back, under her breath. She glanced around the office. There was a bulletin board with business cards for local establishments, a flyer with a forlorn photo of a lost dog, another flyer advertising a dance recital at the elementary school.

"I think we've fallen off the map, Mickey," Brendan said,

luckily under his breath, because at that moment Officer Callaghan appeared in the back doorway again. He was carrying a yellowed manila file.

"It was right there in the 1965 files," the young officer said, sounding surprised. He extended the file across the counter. Laurel and Brendan nearly knocked heads reaching for it. Brendan opened it to reveal what they both instantly recognized as the same report they had already read, but without the blacked-out sections and with numerous accompanying photos.

Officer Callaghan stood solidly in front of them, apparently intending to read the report along with them.

Laurel looked up at him. "Excuse me, officer, but weren't there others?"

"Others, ma'am?" he blinked at her sleepily.

"Other incidents. Other reports. That's all that's in the file?"

"That's all that's in the file."

She smiled at him appealingly. "Is there any way of checking—about other incidents at that same house, the Folger House?"

The young officer looked from her to Brendan. "Uh . . ."

"Just for that year," Laurel said, aware that she was simpering. "In fact, even within a month or so. It would help so much."

"Yes, ma'am. Let me check that for you." The young officer backed out again.

"You're scary good at this Mata Hari stuff," Brendan mumbled. She kicked him under the counter. He grinned.

They bent together and read the file. It was much easier to visualize what had happened with the names restored, and especially with the black-and-white photos of the house included in the file.

The Folger House was actually quite an extensive estate. The first photos were of a large circular gravel drive flanked by two tall stone gateposts, atop which statues of sleek, graceful dogs sat at permanent attention. Beyond the gateposts a dirt road wound into pine woods with no visible neighbors on either side.

The gravel circle led to a large turn-of-the-century house.

146

There was something off about it, though Laurel couldn't at first see what it was. It was two stories, with a large sleeping porch over the main porch, a brick exterior with white Southern columns and tall shuttered windows. There seemed to be other pieces of houses crowded close to it, but it was impossible to tell from the first photos.

The grounds were surrounded by walls of towering long-needled pines and included extensive gardens.

Laurel looked away from the first photos and read the unredacted report:

DETAIL INTERVIEW: On Tuesday, 11 March 1965, the complainant, Mrs. Peter Henderson, was interviewed by this officer, Sgt. Bryce Cutler, and Officer Robert Sorrenti. Mrs. Henderson is a housekeeper in the employ of Atherton, Humphrey, and Miles, current managers of the Folger estate. Mr. Henderson is a groundskeeper on the estate, and the Henderson family occupy the servants' house, attached to the main house.

Complainant stated that on Monday, 10 March, 1965, at about 1530 to 1615 hours, she was at home with her daughter Julie, age 14 years, and her son Ray, age 12 years. The complainant and the children heard pounding and rattling on the roof, for a period of approximately three minutes, on and off. When the noises ceased, the complainant went outside the house and found hundreds of rocks of various sizes lying on the back veranda. When she picked up a few of the rocks they were hot to the touch.

The complainant then called the Five Oaks police department and I and Officer Sorrenti responded. Complainant proceeded to show myself and Officer Sorrenti the scattered rocks outside the main house.

There were several photos attached. There were indeed hundreds of rocks scattered on the narrow back stairs of the servants' house.

Brendan flipped to the next photo. In that one they could see the servants' house was actually attached to the main house by an enclosed corridor, three or four rooms long. It was an odd, awkward design, and Laurel realized that even though she hadn't been able to see it from the initial photographs, the oddness of it still registered in front views of the house.

The report continued:

Complainant stated that there had been other disturbances at the house in the previous weeks which the family had attributed to an electrical problem: lights and household appliances had turned on and off at odd times of the day and night and/or had refused to work at all. An electrician had been called and could find no fault in the house's electrical wiring.

Complainant further reported household items, including a sugar bowl, a serving platter and a skillet had disappeared and subsequently reappeared in inappropriate places, such as the upstairs bathtub and in the complainant's bed.

While I and Officer Sorrenti were in the complainant's quarters, all the family was present with us in the living room when the complainant's son ran in from the kitchen, reporting that rocks had fallen in the kitchen as well. When Officer Sorrenti and myself went into the kitchen with the complainant's family, we found the kitchen table and floor covered with rocks of various sizes, and the sugar bowl, a ceramic fruit bowl, and a glass plate smashed, though no rocks were nearby.

There were photos of the kitchen, and the damage was minor, but still unnerving. Brendan and Laurel looked through close-ups of pieces of a smashed glass plate, and several close-ups of the broken sugar bowl, with small heaps of sugar around it.

I initially suspected the boy of placing the rocks in the kitchen and smashing the glass, but as I and Officer Sorrenti and the family stood in the kitchen, we heard pounding sounds all around us in the kitchen and the sound of glass smashing, though nothing was visibly occurring.

At the time of these occurrences the entire family was standing in full view of myself and Officer Sorrenti in the kitchen. There were no tremors in the house, no movement of any kind that could be noticed. None of the appliances was going at these times and the complainant has no high frequency equipment at all in the

That was as far as the page of the report that Brendan had found in the basement files had gone, and both Laurel and

148

Brendan eagerly reached for the second page.

But there was nothing more to the report, only a handwritten note on the next page that read:

Returned 3/22 to follow up on incident and found house closed—complainant and family moved out.

They stared down at the page for a moment, then Brendan said under his breath, "Holy shit, Mickey. It really happened. There really was a poltergeist manifestation. This is what Leish was looking into."

Laurel had a fluttery feeling in her stomach.

There was the sound of someone clearing his throat.

Laurel and Brendan looked up from the file. The freckled young officer was standing in the doorway of the stairs.

"Sorry, ma'am," he said, rather formally. "There are no other files in regards to the house. At least, nothing labeled 'Folger.'"

Brendan glanced down at the folder in front of them. "This is all there is?" he asked, wistfully.

"Yessir."

Brendan looked at the top sheet of the report again. "This Sergeant Cutler and Officer Sorrenti. I don't suppose they're still with the department."

"No sir. Both passed on, now."

"Do you know anything about the Folger House?" Laurel asked, on a hunch.

"Know where it is."

"Does anyone live there now?" Laurel asked, trying not to sound too eager.

"Aww, no. Not for years. Supposed to be haunted." The young officer chuckled, a hollow sound, like whistling in the dark.

Brendan and Laurel looked at each other. Laurel took a breath, then took her best shot at another charming smile. "So how might we find out more about the house?"

The officer blushed to his roots and said, "Real-estate agency? Four doors down from the train depot?"

Brendan looked at Laurel, raising his eyebrows.

149

"Yes, of course, you're completely right," she beamed at the kid, and he blushed crimson again. "Do you think we could get a copy of this report?"

"Heartbreaker. Jezebel," Brendan observed, sotto, as they walked out, photocopied report in hand.

"Shut up," she mumbled.

"Yes, ma'am," he said, straightfaced.

She held her smile all the way to the car. When he opened the car door for her, she kicked him.

"So sorry," she said, and slid into the seat.

Chapter Twenty-five

Young Officer Callaghan was right on the money. The real-estate office was exactly four doors down from the train depot. They hadn't really even had to drive.

As they walked across the sidewalk to the office, Brendan reached and took Laurel's hand. She looked at him, startled. "Darling," he said, pointedly.

"Oh," she said, realizing. *Okay, so now they were a young couple looking for a house.* She thought it was a premature bit of deception, but maybe they'd get more information if the agent thought there was something in it for—

Her. Definitely a her. The woman behind the desk by the corner window was on her feet in a flash, dazzling them with her smile. She was an archetypal real-estate agent, in her late forties, fake nails and lemon-yellow Talbots suit, over-whelmingly, positively cheerful. California agents had a little bit more subtlety going on, but that was really just a regional veneer. The overall driving quality was the same. It was about sales. Markets were depressed all over and it must be even more true in an out-of-the-way place like this.

Her name was Audra Lennox.

"Morning, ma'am," Brendan was saying cheerily, and Laurel felt the "ma'am" was a bit of overkill, directed at her. She resisted the urge to kick him again. "I'm Brendan Cody and this is Mickey. We're brand-new to North Carolina, and

Mickey here and I have been driving through the area, looking at properties. Finally occurred to us it would be a lot smarter to consult a professional."

"You couldn't be more right about that," Audra gushed. "I'd never in my life want to come into a new area without some reputable guidance."

Laurel was already thinking of a million ways this ruse was going to backfire on them, but Brendan breezed right on. "Thing is, we have a good idea of what we want. I believe people around here call it the Old Folger House."

The agent's face fell so fast Laurel thought she might have to scrape it off the floor.

"I can't imagine you'd find that property ... suitable. I have so many properties more ... more convenient to area amenities—" Audra started.

"Oh, we're not after convenience, are we, honey? We are looking to get as far away as we can, and that's a fact." He threw an arm around Laurel's shoulders and squeezed her. Laurel was starting to feel trapped in an episode of the *Andy Griffith Show*.

She smiled weakly and agreed, "Something out of the way."

"But my goodness—that old place is a handful. That's nothing a young couple like yourselves needs to be getting into." Audra's eyes grazed Laurel's left hand, ostentatiously bare of any rings, and Laurel saw her gaze narrow. *Busted already,* she thought. *Some cover story.*

"Oh, we're up for a challenge," Brendan beamed, oblivious.

"I wouldn't call the Folger place a challenge. It's more like a train wreck," Audra said, matching Brendan's wattage, but Laurel saw steel under her smile.

"Still, there's something about it that spoke to us, didn't it, hon?" He grasped Laurel's hand affectionately.

"Have you *seen* the house?" Audra demanded, more suspicious by the moment. Laurel tensed, but Brendan covered smoothly.

"We've seen photos," he said without missing a beat. "Even if it isn't the place for us, maybe if we could walk through it

152

with you; you would understand what it is we're looking for in a house, and we could go from there. A sort of shorthand, so to speak."

Laurel barely kept herself from cringing—it was so obviously a ploy.

And it worked.

They piled into Audra's vanilla-cream Lexus and she drove them out on a largely deserted road past gently rolling farmlands with sleek chestnut horses behind white rail fencing.

The huge advantage of having a real-estate agent in charge was that you could ask all the questions you wanted about the area—history, population, flora and fauna—and there was a good chance of getting a knowledgeable answer. Laurel had to admit—grudgingly—that Brendan had been right to persist. She also had to admit, also grudgingly, that he could charm a bird out of a tree. Which was not, in her opinion, a point in his favor. In the backseat Laurel narrowed her eyes at him and he returned her a butter-wouldn't-melt-in-my-mouth look. She turned her head to the window to look out at the landscape, a series of flat-topped sandy ridges and broad flat valleys, blanketed with extensive open forests of longleaf pine. She lowered her window and breathed in the cool air, laced with the spicy scent.

Despite her initial resistance to showing the house, Audra was warming up to playing tour guide. "We call this region the Sandhills. Early settlers called this particular area the Pine Barrens."

"Why was that?" Brendan asked, straight-faced, and this time Laurel did slide her foot past the seat to kick him. There were nothing but pine trees as far as the eye could see.

Audra laughed heartily. "Well, yes, the 'pine' part is obvious, but 'barren' is unfair. This place is anything but barren. We've got turkey and blackjack oak, American holly, sourwood, black titi, bay, gum, hickory, yellow poplar, persimmon and red maple ... and in the spring, the dogwoods are out of this world—"

153

"Beautiful," Brendan enthused. "Dogwoods, honey." Without missing a beat he barreled right back on point. "Has the house always been 'the Folger House'? I mean, did a Folger build it?"

"Had it built, yes. The first James Folger was a steel and railroad magnate. He came to Five Oaks from Pennsylvania in the last quarter of the century."

In the backseat, Laurel eased her notebook out of her purse and began to take notes.

"The North was riding a wave of prosperity, while Southern plantations—around here that would be rice plantations— were going bankrupt. Northern millionaires began putting spare cash into Southern plantation land. The locals called them 'Yankee Playtime Plantations.'"

Her tone of voice conveyed a hint of the illicit, and Laurel had a sudden flash of long drunken weekends, sexual escapades . . .

"James Folger purchased twelve hundred acres in the Sandhills and created an estate that—well, as you probably saw in the photos—included stables, tennis courts, and extensive gardens. The Folger family was very fond of fox hunting, and the house was used as a hunting lodge for the family and various friends."

Fox hunting. A hunting lodge. Horrible, Laurel thought with a shudder.

Audra continued blithely. "The lodge was quite popular among the rich and famous. James and Julia Folger held parties where the servants outnumbered the diners. According to news articles the hunt parties would shoot everything in sight."

"Charming," Laurel murmured, and she saw Brendan grimace.

"After James Folger's death in World War I, his grandsons divided the original house and the front half was moved to a neighboring town, by mule of all things—"

"What?" Laurel said, startled out of her fox-hunting thoughts. "They cut the house in half?"

154

"It was done with these old family houses," Audra said airily. "More often than you'd think."

What a strange history. No wonder that even in photos the house seems so—wrong, somehow, Laurel thought.

"Interesting," Brendan murmured, as if he were thinking along the same lines. He turned back to look at Laurel and their eyes met in a questioning look.

What are we thinking . . . that that weirdness could set the stage for a poltergeist? We're already looking for anomalies?

"Oh, the house is perfectly complete now, though," Audra said, apparently opening her mind to at least the possibility of a sale, however unlikely. "In the twenties one of the brothers, also named James, rebelled against the family business and moved away from Philadelphia to pursue a literary career. He had his half of the original home redesigned and enlarged for his new bride, Julia Neville Folger. The Folgers moved into the house as their permanent residence, and began their family. After the success of James Folger's first published novel, the Folger house became the center of a very lively social life in the 1920s and 1930s."

Then she seemed to realize that she had slipped into hard-selling a house she didn't actually want to sell, and hastily amended: "The whole area has a rich history. Whether it's a Civil War pedigree or a literary background you're looking for, I assure you, there's a house here for you.

Amazing, Laurel thought. *She's actually bought into the idea that we could afford something on the scale of the Folger House.*

But then she realized it wasn't just Brendan's charm that had convinced the agent. Audra had sized them up, and their California accents had trumped any estimation of their clothing. And for all Laurel knew, a decrepit manor house in the North Carolina Pine Barrens really was affordable, by California standards.

They had turned off the narrow road and onto a dirt one that led up to the stone gateposts from the photos. Laurel felt a little buzz of déjà vu at the sight of the sleek stone hunting dogs seated atop them, permanently frozen at attention.

A metal gate stretched between the posts, padlocked. Audra reached for the keys on the dash, and Brendan gallantly jumped out to unlock and open the gate for her.

As he did, Laurel caught Audra eyeing her in the rearview mirror and felt uneasily that they might not be pulling as much over on her as Brendan assumed they were.

But before either of the women could say anything, if either was going to, Brendan was back in the car, presenting the keys to Audra with a smile.

They drove forward, gravel crunching under the tires, past a perfect curve of pink-blossomed crape myrtles lining both sides of a split-rail fence along the road. Wind stirred the tall, spare pines around them. Laurel found herself craning forward to look. As the house appeared between the trees, she felt a jolt.

It was an English country house of white-painted brick with a steeply pitched roof of what looked like real gray slate, two chimneys, a round upper balcony with white-painted iron railing, and gray shutters. It seemed whole from the front, but the overwhelming feeling was that it was not. There was part that just seemed to be missing.

And angry, Laurel thought absurdly.

As Audra drove the circle to come up to the front, Laurel got a glimpse of the rest of the house, and realized what was so wrong. There was another whole house connected to the front one, this one much longer, made of brick with white columns and trim, set perpendicular to the white front part. Unbelievably, there seemed to be yet another white house behind that, at the other end of the brick part, but just as soon as Laurel had spied it that glimpse was gone. Audra stopped by the path leading to the front door and shut off the engine.

"Welcome to the Folger House."

Chapter Twenty-six

The solid oak door creaked open into a small entry with glazed brick floors, surprisingly dark compared to the lightness of the house outside. The room had a greenish tinge from the garden green-painted wainscoting running halfway up the wall. Laurel was reminded of the Spanish-style houses around Santa Barbara, and she had a sudden, painful memory of—*the dream*—and her midnight ride from the hotel. She pushed away the thought and forced herself back to the present as she followed Audra and Brendan into the house.

Across the green entry there were two steps up into a second, larger entry with a fireplace and a long wood bench like a church pew facing it. Laurel glanced over a family portrait above the fireplace mantel, a crude, colorful painting of two parents and two children that gave her a strange sense of unease, but she had no time to study it before Audra stepped forward to begin her narration. "This is actually the newer portion of the house," she explained. "The part that was added on when James and Julia moved in permanently." Laurel looked around her at the cool, quiet rooms.

Past the fireplace were stairs down to a small empty room of indeterminate function to the right, with the same glazed brick floors, and what looked like a bathroom beyond. On the left there was a short hall with a glimpse of a small dark-paneled library at the end. *Very odd rooms to have at the entry of a house,*

Laurel thought. There was dust like a fine sprinkling of baby powder everywhere, but otherwise the house was in surprisingly good condition.

"Hmmm," Laurel smiled vaguely at Audra.

On the fourth wall of the second entry there was a door into a much wider and taller hall with dark hardwood floors and white walls. Laurel and Brendan followed Audra into it. A beautiful staircase curved up to the right with a tall bay window that looked out over enormous, overgrown gardens. Past a window seat, the stairs took another upward turn and disappeared.

Brendan took Laurel's hand again as they walked forward. She frowned at him and he nodded ahead toward Audra, shrugging helplessly (with a *What-can-I-do?* look). Laurel pressed her lips together and went along. His hand was strong and warm around her fingers, and she was suddenly electrically aware of his presence beside her.

At the end of this hall there was an archway, with three short steps leading down, and then out of nowhere, a huge room, the size of a small ballroom, with two fireplaces, smoky mirrors in gilt frames lining the walls, and a wide, rectangular expanse of hardwood floor.

Laurel was about to follow Audra through the archway when she felt a chill run through her entire body.

"Here," she said aloud, and Brendan turned back to look at her. Laurel pulled her hand from his and touched the doorjamb and thought she felt the faintest shock, like static electricity. "They cut the house here."

"Yes, I believe you're right," Audra acknowledged, with an appraising glance at Laurel.

They all moved down the steps into the great room. Aside from a few end tables with marble tops, the only furniture in the room was a battered, dusty grand piano.

"This is the older house," Audra said, unnecessarily; the feeling of the room was completely different, much older and more complicated. The ceiling was high, with a raised ornamental design in the dome, and the crown molding had

158

plaster medallions at intervals all the way around the room. Two bay windows with dusty panes flanked a set of equally filmy French doors, which led out onto what must have been absolutely stunning gardens, several acres of them, now so overgrown with wisteria and yellow jasmine and honeysuckle Laurel thought instantly of Sleeping Beauty's castle.

The bare floors shone even through their layer of dust and Laurel noted they were heart of pine (*heart pine*) but far older than the floors in her own house: she could see the wide planks had been fastened by hand-carved wood dowels instead of nails.

Then she froze, staring at a spot halfway across the floor.

Brendan opened his mouth to speak to Audra, but Laurel dug her nails into his palm and pointed.

In the solid layer of dust on the floor, there were footprints. Smallish and soft-soled, like footsteps on the beach, headed away from them, toward the archway to the next room.

But they began in the middle of the floor, and left off well before the doorway, just five or six of them, and then nothing but undisturbed dust.

The three of them stared at the footprints.

Audra broke the silence, sounding exasperated. "No matter what you do, people get in."

Which was absurd, of course, unless someone had been airlifted into the room—the trail of footprints had no logical beginning or end.

"But—" Laurel said.

Now Brendan dug his fingers into *her* wrist, while he tsked sympathetically to Audra. "It's a shame, isn't it. No respect for property."

He took Audra's arm with his other hand and smoothly steered both women well away from the footprints, so as to leave the oddly isolated tracks undisturbed, all the while keeping up a bright and distracting dialogue. "But I have to say, we're loving it, aren't we, honey? I can tell this is going to cost me a fortune."

At the doorway on the other side of the ballroom, they stepped down yet again—*Was this house built on a hill?* Laurel wondered—into a dark-paneled room that had clearly been the dining room. There was a long walnut table and some terribly dusty chairs. A massive grandfather clock stood in one corner, its pendulum still and silent, and the inner wall boasted another large fireplace with an elaborately carved mantel and white marble hearth. Four sets of French doors with arched tops led out to a wraparound brick patio. *Veranda,* Laurel corrected herself silently. *Where the rocks fell.* The room was large, and there was nothing about it that should not have been graceful and lovely, but something about it made Laurel almost claustrophobically desperate to get out.

"For a while it was rented out for weddings," Audra said vaguely. "The gardens, you know." She gestured toward the arched doors. She seemed as uncomfortable in the room as Laurel was.

"How big is it?" Laurel asked. Her voice sounded tight in the echo of the room.

"Nine thousand square feet," Audra answered promptly. "Twenty-seven rooms in all." Brendan whistled, and Laurel felt an odd sense of awe.

Audra led them into the next room: a huge, modern kitchen—not a domestic kitchen, but an industrial one, of almost restaurant size. It was in startling contrast to the formal rooms they had just been in. Though the kitchen was merely functional, with none of the beauty or design of the previous rooms, Laurel found she was able to breathe again once they were out of the dining room.

"The kitchen was put in to accommodate the wedding parties and special events."

Brendan looked around, nodding. "Who owns it now?"

"The county Historical Society. There were plans to turn it into a writers' retreat and art institute ... but that hasn't materialized. No one wants to destroy it—but no one knows what to do with it, either. The Society keeps it up—barely."

Brendan nodded, his eyes far away, calculating. Then he turned to Audra cheerfully. "Can we see the upstairs, then?"

There were three staircases in the back of the house—a set

of stairs on the outside of the house, and an inside staircase on each side of the kitchen area.

To reach the back steps they went through a room that was set up as an office, with an antique desk and an elegant mailbox cubbyhole. "The house manager's office," Audra said, and Laurel marveled at the idea of a house so large that there would be a dedicated office simply for household affairs.

The stairs led up to a tiny servants' kitchen, the back door of which opened onto the back stairs leading down to the garden. Out the kitchen door the rest of the servants' quarters began, a rabbit warren of rooms, really so many that as they walked Laurel was having trouble keeping track of how many they'd seen. The rooms were strung out along a long corridor that bent and jogged at odd angles. Two bedrooms on either side of the kitchen, a half-sitting room across from a bathroom, then three steep and beautifully carved steps up into a small but cozy den, with nine-paned windows under slanting rafters. The grain of the floor was dark and rich, and Laurel could see through the windows that the roof was indeed, real slate. There were waist-high bookshelves with an assortment of volumes (not as elegant or expensive as the ones she'd glimpsed downstairs), and several framed front pages of old newspapers on the walls.

On the other side of the den, a door opened on to another hall with more steps up, then the hall continued with three bedrooms in a row on the left: the biggest bedroom so far, with two antique sleigh beds and a fireplace and faded animal wallpaper of lions and tigers and bears. The next room was a closet of a bedroom, clearly meant for a nanny or even a wet nurse. The narrow room had a single bed, a desk squeezed between two floor-to-ceiling cabinets, and a large and startling lithograph of a crow framed above the writing desk. Then the last bedroom: a nicely appointed one with a hearth and big windows overlooking the garden. All of these rooms opened onto a long, narrow balcony overlooking the garden.

"I've lost count of rooms," Laurel murmured. It seemed they had been walking down the same hall for ages. The hall

161

wasn't only crooked, it rose up and down in an unnerving way; the floor was not merely uneven, it seemed to roll under their feet like a sluggish snake. In fact, the odd bulges of the hall vaguely reminded Laurel of a cobra that had recently swallowed prey, with odd undigested lumps of rooms.

The realtor nodded. "Julia Folger was forever moving walls and changing doors; the house was in a constant state of flux."

"The Winchester Mystery House," Brendan murmured, referring to a California house whose heiress owner had added on rooms and halls in an obsessive belief that it would prolong her life. Laurel felt a warm rush of familiarity—to instantly know what he was talking about and know that he knew she knew. He looked at her without smiling.

"We're back in the main house, now," Audra informed them. Her cheerfulness seemed somehow subdued. "That large room of course was the nursery, built for James and Julia's children, Paul and Caroline. The children inherited their grandfather's love of the hunt; you'll see a number of hunting and riding trophies collected in the next hall."

On the opposite side of the hall there was another door, and it was closed. Brendan reached to try the knob.

Locked.

He looked back at the women. Audra took out the key ring, and compared a couple of the keys, tried them. Nothing fit, and she stepped back and shrugged. They walked behind her, continuing down the hall, through another sitting area with more bookcases and a pale green leather divan.

The wide framed entry opened up into a perpendicular hall, with polished wood floors and a corridor of much larger rooms. The whole feeling of the building changed as they stepped through that entry. The ceiling was higher, the floor more solid and level, the walls thicker. Laurel thought again that the white plaster and curved ceilings had a vaguely Spanish flavor.

"And here we're back in the newer part of the house," Audra said.

The hall was four very large rooms on one side and two

bathrooms on the other. Laurel couldn't imagine what the house must look like from an aerial view.

She stepped to the window and looked out over the gardens. Through the brambles and tangle of vines, she saw a white gazebo at the head of the garden, gleaming like bone, and to the far left a small garden house of river rock at the end of a long reflecting pool.

Laurel caught a rustle of movement, a flash of black—too big to be an animal but not recognizably human—there and then gone . . . or never there at all. She shivered and hurried to catch up with Brendan and Audra.

The room at the end of the hall was the master bedroom: a spacious rectangle with large sunny windows, a fireplace, and window seats on both ends of the room.

They continued down the hall, which was lined with built-in bookshelves, to the next room, which Laurel immediately thought of as the fox room. It had French doors that opened out onto the round balcony over the front porch. The built-in shelves were crowded with silver hunting and riding cups. The walls held paintings of the hunt and old photos, of riders and horses and dogs.

"So you've taken us up through the forties," Brendan said to Audra, and she looked at him blankly. "With the Folger family, I mean. James brought his bride Julia to the rebuilt house. The estate became a thriving literary community through the twenties and thirties. The children grew up as avid hunters and horsemen. Then what?"

"Well, then there was the war, of course," the agent replied. "James Folger was killed overseas. His son Paul returned from the war and he and his sister lived with their mother until she died, sometime in the fifties."

"And the brother and sister?"

"Remained in the house until they died."

Brendan raised an eyebrow. "Neither married?"

"I don't believe so," Audra said. Her voice was distant. "They both died in the sixties, and it was never used as a family residence again."

"Hmm," Brendan said thoughtfully, and glanced at Laurel. "Would that have been the early sixties?"

"I think so, yes," Audra answered.

Laurel felt a distinct uneasiness about the story. *Lots of dropped threads there.*

They moved on to the last door, facing them at the end of the hall.

As they stepped in, Laurel gasped.

It was large and dark—almost completely black, due to the solid wood shutters covering every window.

But her gasp was at the touch of the room. There was a sense of it like breath, a cool, live presence. Brendan stepped close to her and she could feel his warmth, although from far away.

They stood suspended in the breathing dark ... and slowly their eyes became accustomed to the room, illuminated only by the thinnest shafts of light from the shutters.

"Library," Audra's voice came from somewhere.

There was a sudden blinding intrusion of light. Laurel blinked against the assault, dazzled, and saw Brendan silhouetted by the window, opening the shutters.

As her eyes adjusted she saw the room was dark-paneled and lined against one long wall with built-in bookshelves of some fine hardwood. There were tables, cushioned window seats under every window, two fireplaces, a standing globe, and an elegant carved bar, above which was a large framed painting of a dashing man in his forties, wearing a crimson smoking jacket. The painting was powerful but crude, the same primitivism of the family portrait in the entry downstairs. On the walls without bookcases were hundreds of black-and-white photographic portraits of men and women, mostly studio shots.

It was a magnificent, resonant room.

Laurel moved slowly along the wall of bookshelves.

Audra spoke behind, her voice distant, abstracted. "You'll recognize many of the names under those photos: the authors who came here to work and play in the twenties and thirties—

even a few movie stars. This room has seen a lot."

Laurel had reached the end of the wall and turned to the next wall of bookshelves. A familiar navy blue volume caught her eye—a Duke yearbook, and she jolted at the date—1965.

Brendan spoke suddenly. "Audra, what is it you're not telling us?"

The agent turned vacuously inquiring eyes on him.

"You've skipped a good deal of the history of the house. In the interest of full disclosure, I think it's time you were straight with us. What exactly happened here, that no one has really lived in the house since the sixties?"

Audra's gaze burned with resentment, and Laurel could see her calculating, coming to some decision. When she spoke it was with no inflection. "James and Julia's son, Paul Folger, suffered from what they called dementia praecox."

Brendan and Laurel knew instantly what she meant. "Schizophrenia," Laurel said aloud.

"Paul Folger showed early signs of having a talent like his father's, in painting rather than writing, but the story was that he became ill in the military—delusional and violent. There were no antipsychotics at the time, of course, only frontal lobotomies, electroshock, or permanent institutionalization. He was discharged from the service and returned home.

"After James Folger's death in Iwo Jima, Julia and her daughter Caroline kept Paul at home. After Julia's death, Paul's sister oversaw his care for fifteen years. Caroline rarely left the house; Paul Folger never did."

Audra paused for a second, then continued tonelessly.

"Caroline killed herself in the house in 1960. At the same time that her body was discovered, her brother was found dead in his bed."

"She killed him and then herself?" Brendan asked.

Audra didn't answer. "No one has lived in the house since," she said.

They were all silent in the library: there was a pall in the air. Laurel just had time enough to wonder what could have taken place between a spinster sister and a mad brother in fifteen

165

years of living alone together, when Brendan spoke.

"Of course, people die in houses, all the time. As family histories go, that's not too gruesome of one. Are you certain there weren't more—occurrences?" Brendan suggested.

"I don't know of any *occurrences*," Audra said stiffly. "I've done some reading about the Folger family. The house has changed hands many times since then. That's the extent of my knowledge of the house."

"We'd like to rent it," Brendan said beside Laurel.

Both Laurel and Audra turned to him, startled.

Brendan looked at Audra guilelessly. "The house is just sitting here. Why not get some money for it?" He took Laurel's hand again, including her. "We can move in here and look for another place at our leisure. You can arrange that for us, can't you?"

Audra looked from one to the other. "Who are you?" she said softly.

The room was completely silent, waiting.

No. *Hovering*.

"We'd like to rent this house, Ms. Lennox," Brendan said again. "Who do we need to contact to do that? You'll be paid a commission, of course."

His certainty was chilling. Laurel felt she was standing beside a whole different person. Even his voice was different.

"I sincerely doubt that will be possible. But I will phone the Historical Society," Audra said flatly.

"You are an angel. We really appreciate it, don't we, hon?" Brendan said, back to his usual ebullient—*and false*, Laurel thought grimly—charm.

Chapter Twenty-seven

Audra's cell phone chimed as they stepped through the front doorway. She excused herself and moved off, pacing the gravel drive while speaking into the phone. Brendan drew Laurel toward a statue and bench under a magnolia tree, out of earshot. Laurel was momentarily arrested by the statue, the ambivalent look on the naked nymph's face. She forced her eyes away and turned to Brendan, speaking in low disbelief.

"You want to *rent* it?"

"We're going to replicate the experiment." As Laurel's eyes widened, he pushed on. "It's a perfect house. A weird history, a weird vibe, schizophrenia, suicide, reported paranormal events. There are established protocols for a previous experiment. We do the whole damned thing exactly the same way. Test for ESP and PK, bring the highest scorers into a house with a documented history of events, and see what expectation plus ability does in those circumstances."

Laurel could not at first speak through the surge of disbelief, and then Brendan was motioning her silent, as Audra made her way delicately across the overgrown lawn.

Audra dropped them back at Brendan's car on Main Street as evening shadows fell, and they drove the forty miles back to Durham on a dark road with the looming dark shapes of trees around them. Laurel kept feeling odd little flip-flops in her stomach. Brendan was positively manic, blasting the radio, singing along to Nirvana. Laurel tried to think over the music.

"I think we can safely say that the house has a history," Brendan interrupted his Kurt Cobain imitation to beam over at her.

Laurel suddenly realized something that had been nagging at her. "But how did Audra know all that? Where's she getting her information?"

Brendan considered. "The Historical Society, most likely. Also, we're thinking the clip files were stolen by the same person or people who erased Leish and the Folger Experiment from Duke's records ... but any one of the new owners could have disappeared the clip files as well—erase the sordid history of the house when he was trying to unload it. Audra could've read those before they disappeared."

He paused. "There's another explanation, of course," he said, and maddeningly, waited until she had to ask.

"Well?"

"Leish made up the entire story. Every bit of it. Except for the initial poltergeist report—the police report confirms that."

She stared at him. "But why would he?"

"Maybe he was testing expectation. For all we know he was just trying to prep his research subjects to anticipate something in the house. He stole the clip files himself to conceal the real and more boring history of the family and started rumors instead, and that invented story became 'fact,' and Audra was just parroting back to us what Leish had created as the history of the house."

Laurel tried to process the idea.

"We may never know," Brendan said cheerfully. "In any case it's a fantastic story to tell our own team. Schizophrenia, suicide, possibly murder ... poltergeists will be showing up no time."

Laurel stared out the passenger window into the rushing dark. Beyond the fact that—at least according to classical definition—the history he was rattling off so blithely was more conducive to ghosts than poltergeists, Brendan's exultant tone deeply disturbed her.

168

"We can't really duplicate the experiment, you know," she said, trying to bring it all back to some level of sanity. "Even if we did know all the details, which we don't, the original investigation took place soon after there was actual reported poltergeist activity. That was over forty years ago. According to all the literature, poltergeists don't generally stick around that long." Then something else occurred to her. "Actually, if we accept the theory that poltergeist activity is caused by human agents, the agent wasn't there, either. The housekeeper and her family moved out before the investigators moved in."

"I know. Interesting, isn't it?" Brendan said. "The family was long gone. And Leish didn't have his full team until April. What he did was bring his own agents. But clearly he thought *something* would happen. And it did, didn't it?"

"Yes, it did. It went totally wrong. Dangerously wrong," Laurel said, with a growing sense of disbelief.

He laughed. "Mickey, Mickey, you're classic. You're believing your own story. What single shred of evidence do you have for any of your disaster scenarios? Two students who dropped out of school in the sixties? One who ended up on the street? Do you know how many people end up homeless and in the streets? I have a couple in my own family, if you want to start counting."

And sometimes they don't have to be homeless to be lost, Laurel thought, but said nothing.

"But what if there *was* a good reason to bury it?" she said pointedly.

"Like what?"

She was silent. She had no idea what could go wrong during a poltergeist experiment that wasn't out of a bad horror movie. Despite her suspicions, she had not been able to come up with any kind of scenario that made sense. And part of her, the L.A. part, was well aware that if a book on poltergeists was commercial, a book about poltergeists and murder, or some other disaster, was moving into bestseller territory.

Brendan picked up her hand and squeezed it, which sent an electric current through her entire body, completely derailing her train of thought. "Don't go second-guessing this. We don't even have to know what really happened in the house—that might just taint our impressions. Let's strive for beginner's mind."

Laurel groped for an objection that would make sense. "You really think Dr. Unger will approve a study on how to create a poltergeist? How would we even propose it?"

"We don't," he said so grimly she felt a prickle of unease. He must have sensed her reaction because he smiled and took on a lighter tone. "What we propose is to run the original Rhine ESP tests with an emphasis on how personality factors affect results. We administer standard personality tests to study correlations between personality traits and psi scores. In the proposal we're just running the tests. But really we're scouting our team."

Laurel felt an unwanted thrill of enthusiasm. She forced it down. *We. Our. Forced pairing again.* She reminded herself that it was folly to trust him. But she kept all that to herself.

"There's no guarantee at all we're going to find high scorers like the ones in the Folger Experiment," she pointed out.

"True," he admitted. "But it'll be fun trying."

She had to fight not to smile. "Very scientific."

"It's a perfectly valid study and I'm shocked that no one else has jumped in to do it," he said primly. "We concentrate on how expectation influences results. Now, if while we're doing that, we happen to find our high scorers, well, the experiment ... evolves."

He grinned at her and this time she couldn't hold back her own smile. But just as quickly his grin faded, and his eyes took on an intensity that was almost mesmerizing.

"I want to see what it is that they did, back then. I want to see what they were doing that scared everyone so much that they completely buried it." He stared out the windshield into the dark.

Laurel felt there were so many things wrong with the idea she didn't even know where to start. But the conversation was entirely theoretical, anyway.

170

There's no chance anyone's going to rent us that house, the idea is completely absurd.

Of course, she'd be fired when she walked into Unger's office for her meeting and had nothing to propose to him, but she'd deal with that. Somehow. Tomorrow.

Chapter Twenty-eight

The next morning, when Laurel opened her eyes, something had changed. The light in her bedroom was a different color, a golden orange, pulsing with its own energy.

She walked downstairs in the same golden light. She opened the door onto her porch—and stopped dead in the doorway. It was, again, as if she had opened the door onto Oz—an Oz of autumn-toned Technicolor: hallucinatorily brilliant yellows, golds, reds, oranges.

The leaves had turned.

Laurel walked in a daze off the steps into the yard, gaping in awe at the jewel-toned trees: the blinding yellow of a poplar, the ruby glow of a Japanese maple, feeling as if the top of her head had come off and pure sensation was flowing directly into her brain.

It had happened everywhere. Overnight. She almost had an accident on the way to campus when she slammed on the brakes to stare at a tree that seemed on fire, glowing with an orange so pure and intense it was literally painful to look at. Her head was buzzing, she was tingling all over. By the time she got to the Psych building, she felt as if she were hallucinating, which was the only explanation she had for what happened next. She was walking down the second-floor hall toward her office in a weightless daze, when footsteps pounded behind her and Brendan caught up with her in the hall. "We're good to go."

She was still giddy from the trees and had no idea what he was talking about. "What?"

"Audra called. The Historical Society said yes. We can rent the house for a month as long as we take out our own hazard insurance and sign liability wavers. It's been empty for so long they jumped at the chance. I suspect they know they're never going to be able to sell it." His face was glowing like the leaves.

She was obviously still in shock from the trees because instead of saying, "No," she said, "How much?"

"I'll cover it," he said grandly. "It's going to pay off beyond our wildest dreams. We're already authorized for work-study money—I talked to Marcia this morning."

By now Laurel was listening to him with a fascination bordering on trance. *All this—overnight?* Maybe she was still asleep.

"Now, first, we put out a notice for test subjects." He motioned to the long cork bulletin board mounted on the wall ahead of them, heavily stapled with flyers and posters and work-study announcements. "Make up some flyers with tear-off phone numbers, put up a notice on the departmental Web site. Marcia authorized ten dollars an hour. That'll bring 'em in—beats working. Oh, and I already rescheduled your meeting with Unger so we can go in together—"

They rounded a corner and without warning he pulled her into a corridor and backed her against the wall, very close, only his book bag between them. She drew a startled breath, thinking he was going to kiss her. He leaned forward and shook his head slightly, mouthing, "Shhh."

He held her eyes as they stood there, frozen. Someone hurried by in the intersecting corridor behind him.

Laurel, flushed and completely unable to breathe, was fixed on Brendan's eyes. She had no idea who they were avoiding.

The footsteps continued down the hall and faded away.

Brendan took a slow step back from her. She let her breath out. Brendan glanced back toward the hall. "Kornbluth," he said, and looked around the corner in the direction the footsteps had disappeared, checking to see if he was really gone. "I don't trust him. He was very interested in the files when they first opened up. I think he never could get an angle ... but we don't want him guessing what we're doing."

Laurel nodded, trying not to let on that she was still completely reeling from their close encounter. *What is* wrong *with me?*

"He's definitely interested," she said, trying to keep her voice steady. "He came to my office and grilled me when I started looking through the files. I don't even know how he found out I was doing it."

"Academia. Nothing is secret."

"And someone stole one of my notebooks from my office," she said, without thinking.

Brendan stiffened. "You're kidding. When? What was in it?"

Now Laurel felt uncomfortable. She'd forgotten that she'd suspected Brendan of stealing it.

"It was last week—"

Brendan interrupted sharply. "Anything about the Folger Experiment? The high scorers?"

"No ... no, it was before I knew about all that," she said. "It was a notebook of notes I'd taken while I was down with the files. It was really just my own scribblings and I don't know if anyone else could even read most of it, but ... my office is always locked when I'm not in it."

Brendan's eyes were gray and moody. "Well, I know the guy. He won't give up. From now on we meet off-campus if at all possible. Your place or mine?"

And that was how they ended up back on her porch, in the blazing autumn sunset, planning a testing series.

The "Call for Subjects" flyers were easy enough to lay out on OfficePro and Brendan had brought colored paper. As the flyers printed out, Laurel and Brendan stepped out to the porch, where at least there were the rocking chairs to sit in.

"We really are going to have to get you some furniture, you know," Brendan smiled at her.

Laurel felt heat in her cheeks at the word "we." *Forced*

pairing, she reminded herself grimly, and busied herself by handing over copies of several personality tests. Apparently presciently, she had been collecting a file of the standard psychological tests that the Rhine lab had used. The NEO Personality Inventory, or NEO PI-R, was a psychological testing series of 240 questions that measured the Five Factor Model (FFM) or so-called "Big Five" personality traits: Extraversion, Agreeableness, Conscientiousness, Neuroticism, and Openness to Experience. The Myers-Briggs Type Indicator categorized subjects according to sixteen traits: Extraversion/Introversion, Sensing/Intuition, Thinking/Feeling, Judging/Perceiving.

Laurel was all business as she explained to Brendan, "We know Leish used the Zener card and dice tests to find his high scorers. But for our own study I'd first like to catalogue all our volunteers using Myers-Briggs, the Neo-PI-R, and the PBS."

"PBS?" Brendan asked, flipping through the test sheets.

"The Paranormal Belief Scale." She'd found it referenced in numerous articles in the literature on paranormal testing and had been intrigued enough to hunt down a copy. "It's a twenty-six item, self-report scale designed to evaluate the subject's preestablished paranormal beliefs in seven different categories: traditional religious belief, psi belief, witchcraft, superstition, spiritualism, extraordinary life-forms, and precognition. Test subjects are asked to rate their agreement with statements from: 'There is a heaven and hell' to 'A person's thoughts can influence the movement of a physical object,' on a scale of 1 to 7, a '1' meaning 'Strongly disagree' and '7' meaning 'Strongly agree.' It will help in assessing the level our subjects' expectations coming into the experiment."

Brendan looked up from the list and stated very seriously, *"The Loch Ness Monster of Scotland is real."* He waited, looking at her, and she realized he expected her to answer.

She hesitated. "Uh . . . one. Strongly disagree."

"Huh. I would have fought you for that, when I was ten." He moved on to the next question. *"There is a devil."*

"Oh, for . . ." she started and he raised his eyebrows.

175

"You want to ask our subjects to take a test you wouldn't take yourself?"

She rolled her eyes, but answered. "Strongly disagree."

A smile tugged at his mouth. "I'd watch who I said that to around here. Buckle of the Bible Belt, you know." He consulted the test, read the next question. "*Some individuals are able to levitate objects through mental forces.*"

Laurel opened her mouth to speak—and suddenly flashed on a sunny kitchen, the knives and forks dancing on the table in front of a sweet-faced, smiling man with Carolina blue eyes . . .

Brendan was watching her. He leaned forward suddenly. "All right, Mickey, what is it you're not telling me?"

Her face flushed. "I don't know what—"

"No evading." He stood from the rocker. It tipped violently back and forth, as if someone were still sitting in it, rocking angrily. He sat on the porch rail, directly in front of her, so there was no avoiding him. "You're holding back on me and it's time you came clean. What is it you're looking for, here? What *do* you believe of all of this? What do you know about Folger that you haven't been telling me? How did you know about it to begin with?"

She sat back her own rocker so hard she hit her head against the top slat with a jolt, but the tears in her eyes were not from the pain. "My uncle," she said. "He was one of the original Rhine test subjects, a high scorer. He's the one who mentioned the Folger House. That's how I knew it was a house that had shut down the lab."

Brendan stared at her with a look that was half disbelief, half growing excitement. "Was your uncle part of the Folger Experiment?"

"I don't know," she said again. "But I think . . ." She stopped.

"What, Mickey?" he said softly.

Now the tears ran down her face. She brushed at them, and looked out on the hazy lights of the streetlamps, composing herself.

"Tell me," Brendan said, leaning forward on the rail, until his forehead was almost touching hers.

"He's very lost," she whispered.

"Okay. Okay." He stood, and pulled Laurel gently up with him. "Let's go see your uncle, Mickey."

In an unexpected bit of luck, Aunt Margaret's Cadillac was just pulling out of the drive as they turned the corner of the block. "Wait, stop!" Laurel whispered, and Brendan did, and they watched as the Cadillac turned the corner at the end of the street and disappeared into the night.

They parked down the street, in case Margaret abruptly returned. Laurel felt like a spy as they hurried up the walkway under the shadows of magnolia trees. Glowing white flowers dotted the dark above them. On the stoop, Brendan rang the doorbell several times, with no answer. He looked at her.

Laurel stepped back on the porch and looked up at the house. She visualized the small, dark, cozy library at the back of the house; saw Morgan sitting in the chair with his half-glasses on, reading *A Princess of Mars*.

Uncle Morgan, she said, but it was inside her head.

They waited. Brendan started to ask, "You think we should—" but she shook her head slightly. "Shh."

And suddenly the door opened a crack in front of them and Morgan was peering out.

Seated in the study, Laurel and Brendan on the small leather couch across from Morgan's deep leather chair, Laurel introduced Brendan. "Uncle Morgan, this is my—friend, Brendan. He's a professor at Duke, too, in the psychology department."

Morgan looked them both over solemnly, without saying a word.

"We're—" Laurel gestured to Brendan, "we're going to be doing a research study together."

"We're covering ground broken by the Rhine parapsychology lab," Brendan jumped in helpfully. "I understand you might know something about that, sir."

Uncle Morgan looked off toward the door to the covered porch but Laurel had the feeling he was really looking a million miles away.

"Were you at the Folger House, sir?"

Laurel winced at Brendan's directness, but Morgan spoke instantly. "No," he said, and the word was startling in the quiet of the study. "No no no." Laurel felt a flood of relief, hearing it. Brendan glanced at Laurel.

"You weren't part of the Folger Experiment?" Brendan pressed.

"Experiment?" Morgan said, looking bewildered.

Laurel felt as if a weight had been lifted from her. *I was wrong*.

"But you did do some work in the parapsychology lab, didn't you, sir?" Brendan asked. Morgan just looked at him blankly. "I understand you're very gifted with cards," Brendan tried. Uncle Morgan looked at Laurel reproachfully and she felt her chest tighten with guilt.

"I'm sorry, Uncle Morgan," she said. "But Brendan's a friend. I wish you would talk to him. I think it would help—"

"They never came back," Morgan said.

Laurel stopped. There was a heaviness in the room; the air felt thick with meaning.

"Who didn't?"

"All of them. They never came back from that house."

Laurel's heart was beating practically out of her chest. "Uncle Morgan, we need to know more about that. Are you talking about Rafe Winchester?" Morgan blinked rapidly. "Victoria Enright?"

Morgan's eyes filled with tears. "Victoria ..." he whispered. His chest heaved with a sob.

Laurel reached out, covered her uncle's hand with hers. She felt the gentle pressure of his fingers. "What happened to her, Uncle Morgan?" Laurel asked.

He shook his head, mutely.

"What about Dr. Leish?"

178

Morgan shot to his feet, so fast Laurel fell back against the sofa. *"No. No. No."* His face was crimson, the cords in his neck stood out starkly as he screamed it.

Brendan leapt up and held his hands out in front of him, a gentle, appeasing gesture. "It's all right. No more."

Morgan sagged. "No more," he whispered.

Brendan took the older man's arms very gently and eased him back down into the chair. He looked over his shoulder and said to Laurel, "Go make some tea."

Laurel rushed to the kitchen, where she fumbled in the cabinet for a mug and found tea bags in a china jar. Her hands were shaking so badly she could barely tear open a bag.

They never came back.

By the time she returned to the study, carrying a steaming cup of Earl Grey, Uncle Morgan was slumped back in his chair with his eyes closed, his chest rising and falling in sleep. Brendan stood beside him, two fingers on Morgan's wrist, looking at his own watch. He set Morgan's hand gently in his lap.

"It's okay." He turned to Laurel, and took the tea mug, set it quietly down on the end table, and nodded to the door. "Better to leave him," he whispered.

Driving Laurel home, Brendan was silent, staring out at the dark tunnel of road, and that deepened her unease. She was about to speak when he said suddenly, "Well, I understand why . . ." He stopped. "Has he always been that way?"

He didn't have to explain what way he meant. Laurel swallowed. "I haven't seen him since I was a child. I really only met him again a month ago. My mother said he changed the year she graduated from high school, 1965," she said, her voice hollow. Brendan glanced at her from the driver's seat. "But he graduated, and the other two work-study students, Victoria and Rafe, didn't." She turned to look at him in the light from the dashboard. "What is it, do you think?"

Brendan shook his head, and his usual guileless grin was twisted. "I think he may have had some kind of trauma. But I'm

179

not a clinician, Mickey, and neither are you. Even if you were, it would be unethical and just plain not a good idea to diagnose a family member."

"Trauma," she repeated.

"But you heard him: he wasn't at the Folger House. So let's not go working this into your conspiracy theory."

"But what if he *was* there?" she asked, low.

Brendan turned and looked at her in the dark of the car. "Well, Mickey—I suspect there's only one way you're ever going to find out," he said to her, and she did not have to ask him what he meant.

The answer was in the house.

She tossed and turned in her bed (*alone* ...) for hours, until she finally gave up and went downstairs and out on the porch, where she stood on the steps, looking up at the black night sky.

She had no other proposal to offer to keep her job, no other plan. And despite her nagging unease, there was no record of anyone ever being harmed by a poltergeist, or by a ghost, for that matter.

But the bottom line was, she wanted to *know*. About the Folger House, about Leish, about Uncle Morgan, about her dream, about all of it.

She had to know.

Chapter Twenty-nine

Laurel announced the research project (which they were calling "Patterns and Personality Factors in Psi Testing" to draw the least attention to themselves as possible) to her Intro to Personality class on a windy fall day. Outside the windows the blazing trees were swaying and rustling, a kaleidoscope of bright acid colors in a warm, dry wind.

Laurel stood at the podium and looked out on her class. "Most of you have probably heard that Duke was the home to the first official parapsychology lab on an American university campus. For thirty-eight years, Dr. J. B. Rhine used scientific methods to test psi abilities like telepathy, precognition, clairvoyance, and psychokinesis in a laboratory setting." She saw a number of students nodding their heads.

"I'm teaming up with Dr. Cody to conduct a series of tests based on those original ESP experiments, and we're looking for student volunteers to be tested."

A ripple of excitement spread through the lecture room, as tangible as the wind outside. Laurel heard muttered exclamations of *"Awesome!" "That's killer . . ."*

"What exactly is the experiment?" someone called out.

"We'll be using Zener cards to test for psi, or ESP abilities." Laurel held up a cardboard strip with Zener cards mounted on it to illustrate. There were murmurs of recognition from some of the class.

181

"I know what Mayfield is thinking right now," a kid named Wooten called to his frat brother.

"What else is there to think about?" Mayfield shot back, and got a few laughs.

Tyler put his hand casually up in the air and slouched back against his chair, waiting for Laurel to call on him. She steeled herself mentally before asking, "Yes, Mr. Mountford?"

"Do you believe that parapsychology falls under the purview of psychology, Dr. MacDonald?" His voice dripped with respectful insolence. *"Believe"* was emphasized with a hint of incredulity.

Laurel did her best to hold her temper. *Trust Tyler to get right to the sticking point.*

"I absolutely think that what we *believe* falls under the heading of psychology, and that will be the emphasis of these tests," she answered evenly. "Anyone can volunteer, and we're looking for as many volunteers as we can get so we can collect the widest range of responses. You'll be taking several personality inventories as well. Pay is ten dollars per hour, and you can sign up on the sheet making the rounds, on the departmental bulletin board, or on the department Web site."

When the sign-up clipboard came back to her, as she'd expected, Tyler's name was the first on the list.

The response was overwhelming, to put it mildly. They had hundreds of student volunteers in the first two days. They couldn't put flyers up fast enough: the tear-off contact numbers were gone within minutes; between the flyers and the "Call for Participants" on the departmental Web site, both their e-mail boxes were filled to capacity.

Laurel couldn't believe how the idea captured the student imagination. Brendan was exultant. "What did I tell you? We're onto something. When you've got it, you've got it."

They'd had their meeting with Dr. Unger together and whatever doubts the Chair may have had about the legitimacy of the project were neutralized by his practicality: he knew a media-genic topic when he heard it. The project was approved instantly.

They were assigned two lab rooms in which to do the testing. First, they scheduled two large group sessions to administer the standard personality inventories to their volunteers, then they scheduled students for individual tests with the Zener cards.

Brendan had discovered a file box in the basement that was full of packs of original Zener cards, and they instantly agreed that they should use them. Just as exciting was their discovery of several of the original card displays and sorting boards in the equipment storage room of the basement, and several original dice-throwing machines, too.

Laurel and Brendan were in their lab preparing several sets of twenty-five cards—every set consisting of five each of the five symbols, each card encased in its own opaque white envelope— when J. Walter Kornbluth breezed into their testing room, bristling with casually collegial interest. He circled the room like an unhappy bee, his eyes drinking in the display board of Zener cards, the dice-throwing machines on another table.

"Well, this looks like déjà vu all over again," he said with forced heartiness. Laurel laughed politely from the lab table where she was sealing Zener cards in envelopes, and said nothing. Kornbluth tried again. "So you're replicating the Zener card tests for precognition?"

"With an emphasis on personality factors," Laurel answered, in her best professor voice. "Obviously, we're testing personality, not precognition," she lied. "We're administering NEO PI-R and Myers-Briggs to study correlations between personality traits and ESP scores."

"Nothing groundbreaking, but of perennial interest," Brendan said offhandedly, and passed another stack of sealed cards to Laurel.

Kornbluth stared at them suspiciously. "That's the extent of your study? Replicating the precognition tests?"

"Oh, no," Laurel said sweetly. "We're also replicating the dice tests for psychokinesis, using the original dice machines."

She had no idea if they were pulling it off; it seemed so patently obvious that they were completely hazing him. But Kornbluth wasn't so much paying attention to them as he was circling the testing board, staring at the cards.

"And Unger really approved department funds for this—study?"

The quotation marks in his inflection were unmistakable.

"Well, you know how it is," Brendan said humbly. "We can't all write *USA Today* bestsellers. Some of us are destined merely to footnote the giants."

Laurel kicked him under the table, thinking he'd really gone too far. But Kornbluth visibly perked up at the flattery. "I suppose." He circled the room once more and finally departed.

Brendan closed the door behind him, and the two of them broke into stifled but irrepressible laughter. Finally Brendan got hold of himself.

"I'm telling you, we must be doing something right. Inspector Kornbluth is on the trail."

The testing itself was amazing.

Each student volunteer was tested sitting at a table in front of a display stand of particle board, painted black, showing a row of the five cards with their different symbols: star, circle, square, two squiggly lines, and cross. Beneath each symbol was a built-in box big enough to hold a stack of envelopes. The test subject took one envelope-encased card at a time, held it, then placed the card in the box under the symbol he felt was inside it. A "run" was a set of twenty-five cards. Statistical chance would be five hits per run.

The students' excitement was palpable in the tests: they *wanted* to do well. And Laurel was giddy with the sense of adventure and discovery. She felt her own mind opening and her senses reactivating. There was no predicting who was going to score what. A wistful and bookish girl tested well below chance, while the clowning, sweetly boneheaded center of the basketball team scored 20 percent above chance—in fact at the moment he was their high scorer, though nowhere in the range that they were looking for.

Their findings were bearing out what past studies had shown: extraverts scored significantly above chance, and introverts scored significantly below chance. If Laurel believed in ESP—and that was still a big *if*—she would have started to wonder if extraverts did better in social situations because they had that little extra edge of being able to read what people were really thinking, what they secretly wanted, and what one might say or do to put an unsuspecting person at ease—or manipulate them.

It occurred to Laurel that even if they never found their high scorers, the extraversion factor was enough to do a decent article, and her spirits lifted. In fact, watching the Zener card tests, she found herself holding her breath during a good run of hits. She *wanted* the student subjects to score high. And once in a while, like the gangly center, one did, but not anywhere near the level they were looking for to replicate the Folger Experiment.

Until Tyler.

Laurel ended up testing him herself through no plan of her own. She had been careful to assign Tyler's card testing to Brendan. She was still furious with Tyler for having duped her with those phony stories of the haunted auditorium, although she had been careful never to let on to him that she knew he'd conned her.

But when she opened the door of the lab for her first test subject on Wednesday, he was standing there, smirking.

"Tyler," she said, caught off-guard. "I have Paul Mayfield signed up for this slot."

"We switched. Mayfield wasn't up for coming in this early in the morning. Big night last night. Hope that's okay," he said innocently and sauntered past her into the room.

When she didn't answer immediately, he turned to look at her. "Unless you don't *want* to test me?" His voice went up questioningly in that uniquely Southern inflection.

185

She bit her tongue and indicated the big leather easy chair at the back of the room. When he was seated, with his usual indolent slouch, she took a position as far away from him in the room as possible. "We do this testing in the Ganzfeld, which means 'empty field.' Previous studies have shown that test subjects perform better when their minds and bodies are relaxed."

Tyler smiled slyly. "It's all about the performance, isn't it?"

She ignored that, and showed him the sets of cards in their envelopes, explaining the sorting process. "After the relaxation preparation, you'll be sorting these cards into the appropriate boxes in this display." She indicated the board with the set of Zener cards posted above the boxes. "You hold each envelope for as long as you like and then put it in the box under the symbol you think it contains—that's all there is to it. The CD I'm about to play is to relax you, put you in a receptive mood."

Then she handed him the eye goggles. "Put these on, and you can either close your eyes or keep them open." He smiled at the Ping-Pong goggles, but put them on and sat forward, poker-faced, staring at her with Ping-Pong-ball eyes. She had to fight a surge of annoyance and amusement.

"Just sit back and make yourself comfortable in the chair, and the CD will lead you through some relaxation exercises. When that's done, we'll begin the card testing."

He leaned back in the chair. "Are you going to be watching me?" He made it sound like porn.

"I'll be here but not watching, no."

She was familiar with the relaxation CD by now: typical New Age meditation music with interspersed suggestions for letting go of tension in different parts of the body. Even though she'd heard it dozens of times, it was surprisingly effective, almost instantly relaxing, which at the moment was welcome, since Tyler always seemed to know exactly what to do to make her blood pressure skyrocket.

She started the CD, then sat at her desk to wait. As the music filled the room, she felt her own neck and back untensing, her muscles unclenching, her breathing slowing. The sterile lab

186

room seemed to soften, becoming a peaceful cocoon. Tyler had sunk into the chair like a big housecat (apparently relaxation was another one of his talents), and was thankfully silent.

At the end of the recording, she spoke softly. "When you're ready, you can take off the goggles, and we'll begin."

Tyler smiled lazily, without moving or taking off the goggles. "Well, I'm definitely ready for *something*."

He reached to remove the goggles, unfolded himself from the chair and resettled himself at the testing table, where he proceeded to sort five sets of twenty-five envelopes into the boxes beneath the symbols. He was the picture of nonchalance, almost lazily handling the envelopes, then tossing them into the boxes with the precision of an experienced cardplayer.

Laurel pretended to be scoring other tests, but she couldn't keep her eyes off him: Despite his practiced pose of boredom, there was a focused concentration in his every move that she found mesmerizing.

When he was finished, he pushed back the chair as languorously as he had slouched in it, and stood.

"Thank you, Mr. Mountford."

"The pleasure was all mine," he said, with a maddening half-smile. "So when do I get the results, Doctor?"

"We'll be contacting students throughout the week," Laurel said offhandedly. "Dr. Cody will be in touch."

Tyler raised his eyebrows, but said nothing more as he strolled out.

As the door shut behind him, she took her keys and locked it from inside, then sat down in the seat in front of the Zener-card board to tally his results. She'd already administered Tyler's personality tests in one of the large group testing sessions. Predictably, he'd scored very high in Extraversion (gregariousness, assertiveness, action, excitement-seeking) and Openness to Experience, and far lower in Conscientiousness and Agreeableness. She'd also noted with some surprise that his Neuroticism scores were also very high (anxiety, hostility, depression, impulsiveness, self-consciousness, vulnerability to stress).

187

But his Zener-card tests were off the charts.

She counted the cards out with growing incredulity, and checked them again to be sure. Tyler had correctly guessed a staggering average of twenty cards per twenty-five.

"He cheated," Laurel told Brendan, as she paced in their lab room.

"How could he cheat?" Brendan said, leaning back on a high stool, entirely puzzled. "You were right there watching him, weren't you?" Before she could protest again, Brendan barreled on, waving a sheaf of pages at her. "And take a look at his Paranormal Belief Scale scores. That kid doesn't believe in *anything*. He's a great control on the existing belief front."

"But he's *lying*," she said, agitated, aware that her voice was rising in a most unscientific way.

"Why would he do that?"

"Because that's what he *does*," Laurel said, with a definite feeling that things were spiraling out of control. "He's a total manipulator." She was also more than mildly unnerved that the one student who had grated on her from her very first days at Duke turned out to be their star test subject. *What are the chances?* The whole thing seemed orchestrated in some ominous way that she could not explain.

But she knew she was fighting a losing battle. There was no denying the scores, especially after Brendan tested Tyler again himself, and though Laurel was sure there was something they were not seeing about his test results, so far Tyler was the only one who came close to the kinds of scores they needed to replicate the Folger Experiment.

Like it or not, he was their best candidate.

Chapter Thirty

Poltergeist mediums tend to be between the ages of ten and twenty years, with their abilities coinciding with the onset of puberty, which has led researchers such as Carrington and Fodor to hypothesize that poltergeist phenomena are the externalization of developing sex energy.
                    —Alaistair Leish, *The Lure of the Poltergeist*

They had another.

A girl. Brendan had found her, and when he called Laurel in from the other lab room on his cell phone she could hear the subdued excitement in his voice, though he was trying to keep it neutral.

The girl was a sophomore, small, slim, and startlingly pretty, in both a catlike and doll-like way. Pale, pale skin, silky butter-colored hair, a small bow mouth, almond-shaped blue eyes, and a honeyed Southern accent. She was manicured and pedicured and waxed and plucked, and her embroidered camisole probably cost more than every piece of clothing Laurel had on. Laurel could see instantly that Brendan had worked his magic on her; the girl's eyes followed him around like a starved feline stalking a canary.

"Dr. MacDonald, this is Katrina DeVore."

"Hello, Katrina," Laurel said. The girl looked her over, and her eyes narrowed, but she didn't speak.

Brendan didn't seem to notice the deliberate snub. He motioned Laurel over and showed her his clipboard, where he'd recorded results for five consecutive card runs. The girl had scored from twelve to fifteen hits on each test, significantly above chance. What's more, her scores increased with each test, while generally a subject's test scores tended to decline over time.

Laurel had been reading about this phenomenon in an article titled, "The Role of the Experimenter in the Successful Elicitation of Psi Results." Dr. Rhine had believed that the kind of experimenter actually in contact with a subject was critical and that the experimenter's personality was a determinative factor in the psi-testing environment. Rhine assumed that subjects were made, not born, and that it was the experimenter's job to adequately prepare his subject for a psi test.

Laurel looked over Katrina's personality inventories. Her PBS indicated she had strong traditional religious beliefs, and no belief whatsoever in aliens or extraordinary life forms—but she did answer ambiguously about anything psi-related: reading minds, predicting the future, movement of objects with the mind.

Laurel put down the clipboard. Brendan looked toward the girl, who instantly lit up under his attention. "Katrina, I'd like you to do a second run of tests with Dr. MacDonald."

Katrina's face turned sullen; it was clear to Laurel that she didn't like that idea one bit. But she smiled sweetly and told Brendan, "Of course, Dr. Cody."

Brendan left the room. Katrina perched with a ballerina-straight back in front of the card display, ignoring Laurel entirely as she sorted the cards with maddening slowness. Her dislike wasn't merely obvious; it fairly rolled off her in waves. Laurel felt like a footservant.

When Katrina had finally made it through five sets of cards, Brendan came back in, and again, the blond girl lit up like a Christmas tree. "Can you wait outside for a moment, Katrina?"

Katrina shot daggers at Laurel with her eyes, and answered prettily, "Yes, Dr. Cody."

190

Brendan reached eagerly for the envelopes to tally the results.

They were abysmal. She'd only managed to get one or two cards correct in each of the five runs.

"I don't understand ..." Brendan fretted.

"I guess she was more motivated with you," Laurel said, keeping her voice even, while inwardly she rejoiced. *Dodged that bullet.*

Brendan looked devastated. He slumped back in his chair, staring at the cards as if he could will a different set of results. Then suddenly something seemed to hit him, and he shot forward in his seat.

"Wait a minute. Chance is five cards per run."

"Yes ... ," Laurel started, puzzled—and then it struck her what he meant.

"These results are *too* far below chance," Brendan said triumphantly. "She was deliberately failing. She's got control over this."

Yes, and a massive grudge against me, Laurel thought, unprofessionally, but she said nothing aloud. Not that Brendan would have noticed; he was already halfway to the door.

"Let's try the dice tests."

He practically bolted to the door and ushered Katrina back in, beaming. "How did I do, Professor Cody?" she asked guilelessly, managing not to look at Laurel.

"Very interesting, Katrina. Very interesting, indeed. I'd like to try another type of test, if you're up for it."

The dice machines tested ability to influence the fall of a set of dice. The dice were shaken mechanically, in a revolving Lucite tube, and the test subject was to concentrate on the dice and attempt to make the dice fall as sevens, or snake eyes.

With Brendan's encouraging presence, Katrina displayed a dramatic concentration on the machine, and the resulting falls of the dice were impressive, 31 percent above chance.

At one point Brendan stepped close to Laurel to murmur into her ear, "I think we're in business."

Laurel saw Katrina's face cloud, and at that moment, the slowly rotating dice machine suddenly went wild, flipping crazily around on its stand.

Laurel stared in shock. *Did that really just happen?*

"Whoa!" Brendan leaped to shut off the machine as Katrina cowered back, wide-eyed. "Sorry about that. What can I say— they're fifty years old ..."

Katrina slid an oblique look at Laurel and Laurel wondered if they weren't taking on more than they could handle.

They finally dismissed Katrina, who tendered Laurel another malevolent glare at as she left.

Brendan turned to Laurel and he didn't have to speak. They had tested over five hundred students in three weeks, and there was no one besides Tyler who was even close. And even Laurel felt a rush: *What are the chances that we'd find two so quickly?*

Brendan leaned on the lab table. His eyes were alight. "I say we do it with just the two of them, if we can get them to agree. We can't just keep running tests forever. And their scores really are exceptional."

"What about controls?" Laurel countered.

"We're the controls," Brendan answered immediately.

"No, I meant—"

"So did I. Non-psi-gifted subjects. That's us. I think we should keep this as small and controlled as we can. We add more people and we risk losing the quality of subjects."

Now that the prospect of actually moving into the house was looming, Laurel found herself dragging her feet, metaphorically speaking. "How much do we tell them about the history of the house?"

"We definitely let them know that we're going into a house that has a history of poltergeist activity. Absolutely." He paced the room, planning. "Maybe we show them the police report to set up expectation. Otherwise ..." he trailed off, turning to her, "otherwise, I think we say as little as possible, at least at first. Let them pick up on the history—or not."

192

Laurel opened her mouth to protest and he cut her off. "I know what you're going to say. I know you have doubts. But Mickey—one week. Just a few days even. Even just walking through the house with those two. At the slightest hint of anything dangerous we're out of there, I swear to you."

He picked up Katrina's and Tyler's test scores. "But with subjects like this—how can we not at least try?"

Chapter Thirty-one

There was always an odd feeling to Laurel about having just one or two students in a classroom, and it was even more odd to have two professors to two students; there was something almost illicitly intimate about it. Tyler slouched at his desk, openly checking Katrina out. Katrina sat straight in her chair, as if on another plane, pointedly ignoring him. No one was fooling anyone: There was an energy about these two that made the atmosphere fairly crackle. The sun slanted through the leaded windowpanes and flame trees were in full color just outside, blazing the red of a molten sunset and adding to the charge of the atmosphere.

Brendan clapped his hands together in a jolly, archaic gesture. "Well. First of all, thank you for the time you're already put into this project. Your contributions have been very helpful." He glanced at Laurel. "In fact, you were our high scorers."

Laurel watched as the two students absorbed this. Katrina blinked rapidly. Tyler looked at Katrina, then at Laurel, speculatively. She had the feeling that he was assessing something about her, and trying to position himself to use it.

"So we're psychic, that's what you're saying?" Tyler finally drawled.

Laurel answered evenly. "What we can say quantifiably is that you both scored significantly above chance in your forced-choice testing. That was the laboratory definition Rhine used for ESP abilities, and that's the definition we're using for the purposes of this study."

Again, Brendan looked to Laurel. "There's another project we have in mind that we're interested in using you for, if you agree. It would be full-time for three weeks, full work-study pay—or credit for a full five units."

That last clearly got Tyler's attention. "A whole class credit for three weeks? What's the catch?"

"The project involves moving into a house that has a history of psi activity."

"You mean, it's haunted?" Katrina asked, with her honeyed drawl.

She's not as detached as she looks, Laurel realized.

"There have been various reports to that effect," Brendan answered. "In 1965, a team of researchers conducted an investigation into a local house where there had been reported poltergeist activity. We've obtained a lease on the house and are planning our own investigation into it. We would be replicating the investigation that the parapsychology team conducted in 1965."

"Just us?" Tyler suddenly asked. He looked at Laurel as he said it. Katrina was looking at Brendan.

"Your test scores show that you are uniquely qualified—"

"Uniquely qualified, huh? The two of us." Tyler gave Katrina a sizzling look. The girl turned away, flipping her hair back in annoyance, but there were high spots of color in her cheeks. Tyler turned those eyes back to Laurel. "So we're going to go ghost hunting for a full class credit?" He laughed, a rich, lazy sound. "Oh, I am so in."

Brendan looked to the blond girl. "Katrina?" She looked up at him and her cornflower eyes were rather unfocused, as if she were in some kind of trance. "If you need some time to think about it, you don't have to decide tonight—"

"Yes, I'll do it, Professor Cody," she said abruptly, her eyes very blue in her pale face. The subtext was patently obvious: *"I'll do it for you."*

195

"Excellent!" Brendan enthused. "We'll be starting right away. We'll arrange academic extensions in your other classes, so you don't have to worry about missing out on classes ..."

As Brendan continued, Laurel looked at the two students, fairly brimming with hormones. *This is seven kinds of trouble,* she thought grimly.

But she had to admit, Brendan wasn't stupid. If there was any truth to the theory that poltergeists were a by-product of unharnessed adolescent sexuality, they were in business.

Laurel walked across campus to the tolling of the carillon bells in the clock tower of the chapel. The setting sun blazed through a yellow tree above her, momentarily changing the fading light to gold. Her emotions were in turmoil, running from exhilaration to deep anxiety. They had two students in their care now, and it was all feeling uneasily real. Could they be taking their young charges into danger?

That's silly, she told herself. *Outside of the movies, who ever heard of a ghost killing anyone? As far as that goes, we don't even know if anyone ever died in the house.* Her extensive searches of the Internet and library records, and a call to the Historical Society, had revealed no more information about the deaths of Caroline and Paul Folger than they already had: per a terse obituary in the Five Oaks *Courier,* Caroline Folger had died at home in 1965, and there was no record whatsoever of Paul Folger's death, or even any record at all of him after an announcement of his being deployed to Germany in the summer of 1944. As far as the record was concerned, he may have died overseas.

Laurel had reached the arched walkway beside the Chapel and was headed for the stairs down to the faculty parking lot when the sun suddenly dipped down behind the spires of the chapel, plunging the yard into shadows. Buildings loomed on all sides, Gothic and timeless; the silhouettes of gargoyles perched on the turrets, looking down. Laurel felt the chill of night, and suddenly her exhilaration dissolved to fear.

What had she been thinking? It was madness, all of it. *We have to cancel this now, before it goes any further.*

She turned on the brick path and walked briskly back toward the Psych building.

Laurel never liked being in campus buildings after hours; there were too many shadows, too many halls down which any sort of predator might lurk. The Psych Building seemed completely deserted; there was no sense of anyone left in the building, and in all corridors except for the central hall, the lights had already been dimmed to half-power. Her footsteps sounded hollow in the halls, and she could already see ahead of her that the lab they had been using was dark, the door shut and locked. So she'd missed him.

She knew she should have turned, then, and gone back out; she had a firm rule about not taking chances moving around empty campus buildings at night. But the thought that Brendan was in his office was strong. She reached into her purse for her cell phone to check ... but then dropped the phone back into her bag. She opened the stairwell door quietly and eased it shut behind her, then walked as noiselessly as she could up the stairs. Each step increased her unease.

At the top of the stairwell she heard voices coming from down the hall, murmuring, even though the lights in the corridor were down to half-power. Someone was in Brendan's office with him.

Katrina? she wondered instantly. Her face flushed hot, and she was just as instantly ashamed of the thought.

Nevertheless she was compelled. She walked down the corridor, slowing her footsteps, and placing her feet carefully so that she was making no noise.

She stopped just outside the doorway—and was startled to hear not Katrina's, but Tyler's voice.

She hovered, straining to hear.

The voices suddenly stopped, and Brendan's voice called out sharply. "Is someone there?"

Laurel stepped into the doorway.

Brendan looked startled, then said, too heartily, she thought . . .

"Dr. MacDonald, I'm so glad you came back. First of all, we're in luck. Apparently Mr. Mountford here is much more accomplished in audio and computer technology than I am, so we won't have to bring in an outside tech expert."

Laurel remembered Tyler mentioning that he'd run light and sound for the theater department. *If that wasn't just another lie,* she added to herself grimly. She looked at Tyler and he had the grace to look flustered.

"It's not rocket science," he muttered.

She turned away from him, back to Brendan. "And second?" she asked coolly.

"Second?" Brendan repeated, confused.

"You said, 'First of all.' I wondered what 'second of all' was."

"Oh, I see!" Brendan's laugh sounded forced. "Well, second, I should have offered to walk you to your car to begin with."

"It's all right," she said coolly.

"I insist," he said, and stood gallantly. "We'll meet to requisition the equipment tomorrow, Mr. Mountford." Tyler shifted in his seat and mumbled assent.

Moonlight spilled across the deserted lawn of the quad as Brendan and Laurel walked on the paths under the shadows of oaks. Laurel was silent and stiff beside him, too aware of the heat of his body.

There was a touch of chill in the air, a hint of coming winter. She shivered, and the next thing she knew Brendan was taking off his jacket.

"I don't—" she started, but he already had it off and was draping it over her shoulders. His hands lingered for just a moment on her shoulders, then dropped to his sides again.

They continued to walk in silence. The scent of his aftershave and his skin rose from the leather of his jacket, enveloping her.

Don't . . . , she warned herself, and walked more stiffly.

198

They were almost to her car when Brendan suddenly spoke beside her. "I can't tell you what all this means to me, Mickey." His voice was husky and low. "I feel like my life finally makes sense. All of it. I'm so glad—"

He paused, and she looked at him, in spite of herself. He shook his head slightly, but smiled at her.

They stopped beside her car and she fumbled for her keys.

She zapped open the lock and Brendan started to open the door for her. She tried to step by him but he looked down at her. She froze, her heart in her throat, her pulse pounding in her head . . .

Then he touched her hair, the lightest touch. "Sweet dreams," he murmured.

He closed the car door on her and she sat trembling in the front seat.

Chapter Thirty-two

Move-in day was blanketed with clouds. They had decided to drive down to Five Oaks separately; the house was isolated enough that multiple cars seemed prudent.

Laurel got on the road early. She stopped in to leave the cat with Aunt Margaret and Uncle Morgan, explaining that she was doing a three-week research project without actually saying where she was going. Uncle Morgan looked at her with sad reproach, which both tore at her heart and made her wonder just how much he knew, both about the past and about what she was about to do, but he refused to answer when she spoke to him.

Laurel closed her eyes briefly, thinking about it.

The cat, however, had gone to him immediately and jumped up in his lap as if she belonged there, and Uncle Morgan cradled the animal to his chest and disappeared with her into his library as if she were the only thing he'd been waiting for.

On her own behind the wheel, Laurel paid much more attention to the route. She passed through sleepy towns with no more than a thousand inhabitants, and some obviously with far fewer. "Town" was sometimes no more than a Food Lion, a Family Dollar Store, an Auto Zone, and two or three gas stations along the highway.

With each mile, Laurel had the sense that she was driving off the grid entirely.

She turned off the highway onto the six-mile road that took her out to the Folger House, passing horse pastures and patchwork fields bordered by split-rail fences, then leaving those behind, too, as she drove into the Pine Barrens.

At the foot of the estate the gate already stood open and she drove between the gateposts with their stone dogs, feeling a shiver of anticipation as the wheels crunched over the slate chips of the circular drive.

The house was bigger than she remembered, and more strange, crouched between pines, and white as a shell.

The enormous circular drive was empty—somehow she had beaten everyone here. She shut off the engine and sat for a moment, staring up at the house.

Fine. I'll wait. No way am I going in there alone.

The car door made a hollow *thunk* as she shut it—too loud in the stillness. The wind slipped through the tops of the pines, making the long and glistening needles shiver.

As she stood on the slate-chip path looking up at the house, she saw clearly for the first time that it was really three houses, joined by two two-story brick connecting walkways. The front of the structure was the original white house with its white-painted brick and patios and multiple archways and almost Spanish flavor. Then that smaller brick connector, two stories, attaching the Spanish house to the older main house, redbrick with white colonial pillars holding up its double porches. Then another small two-story walkway joining the brick main house to the separate white two-story shingled house that was comprised of the servants' quarters. The long snakelike corridor she remembered from their first visit must stretch across all three separate parts of the house.

The wall of pines that surrounded the house were taller trees than she could ever remember seeing before, except for maybe the sequoias of Northern California. The height of that green wall gave an otherworldliness to the place that was awesome and unnerving.

Gravel crunched behind her and she whirled, startled.

"It's okay, it's okay."

Brendan, of course, holding up his hands apologetically, flashing her that dangerously appealing grin. He was dressed in jeans and a cable-knit fisherman's sweater, and looked like he'd just stepped out of a J.Crew catalog. Laurel pulled herself together. "I didn't hear you. Where's your car?"

"I parked around back to bring in the equipment and food."

"How long have you been here?" she asked, surprised.

"An hour or two," he said vaguely. "I thought it would be good to have everything moved in before our subjects get here so their first impressions of the house are as undiluted as possible."

It made sense, she had to admit, but there was something about his arriving early that disturbed her, in a minor but nagging way.

"Let me help you with your stuff." He grabbed the box of clean linens and bedding from her trunk, and she lifted out her suitcase. "We'll go up the back way and save the main part of the house for a first walk-through," he said, fairly brimming with enthusiasm.

They crunched their way over a path spread with more slate chips, the same gray as the roof, and onto a concrete path that led them past the round span of grass with the marble nymph at the head of the circle, past the elegant enclosed porch with the Colonial columns in front of the old main house. Around and above them the wind made a silky sound through the pines. At the back stoop Brendan juggled the box of linens to open the back door for Laurel, and she stepped inside.

The spell of the house, as before, was instantaneous, settling on her like a provocative dream. The silence was a palpable weight. They moved through the back hall into the house manager's office and wound up around the creaky back stairs of the servants' quarters to the long narrowness of the upstairs, the endless rooms.

"How many bedrooms are there? Did you count?" Laurel asked, breathless.

"It depends on how you want to define 'bedroom,'"

Brendan said over his shoulder. "Six along this upstairs corridor, plus a kitchen, three bathrooms, a study, and four or five of those weird nonrooms."

As he spoke they passed through one of the nonrooms, where the corridor widened into a room the size of half a bedroom, with a divan and an end table under a window on the left, and a wall of linen closets on the right. Then the three extremely steep and beautifully carved steps leading up to the relatively large study on the right, with its slanted ceilings and nine-paned windows.

They moved into the study. Laurel noticed again the deep, rich dark grain of the wood floors. There were standing bookcases with sets of dusty leather-bound volumes and newspaper pages framed on the walls of the room; Laurel made a mental note to take time to read them. *Could be something interesting there*. The room was so much larger than the ones before it; she stepped to one of the windows to look out and realized that they had already left the tall, narrow white house in back; the study room was the start of a much larger corridor—built on top of the brick part of the house.

"I see—" she started.

"Yep. Now we're on top of the original house. That bizarre dining hall is right below us, I'm pretty sure." Laurel noted that he called the dining hall "bizarre." *So it wasn't just me,* she thought. *There's something wrong in that room.*

And then she wondered what she was thinking.

Out the study door the hall jogged to the right again and resumed, quickly opening into another wide space. To the right was a staircase leading downstairs (Laurel guessed to the kitchen, but was not entirely sure). There was a large bathroom to the right and a small bedroom to the left—then another four steep stairs to an archway, after which the hall continued into the three bedrooms in a row on the left: the large room with the twin sleigh beds and the fireplace, then the tiny, narrow room with an adjoining door (*the nanny's room,* she thought again), and then the nicely appointed one with the hearth and with big windows overlooking the garden. All of these opened onto the long, narrow balcony overlooking the gardens.

"Can you imagine living like this?" Laurel said suddenly. She didn't have to explain what she meant; Brendan gave her a look of complete understanding.

"No, I can't. Not in a million years," he said flatly. "Not for lack of trying, though."

"Where is everyone going to sleep?" Laurel wondered aloud, and just as suddenly felt flustered.

"We'll let them choose," Brendan said. "Might as well let them go with whatever vibe they feel. In for a penny, in for a pound."

It occurred to Laurel that she would be sleeping alone in a room in this ominous, resonant old house. *Brings real meaning to publish or perish,* she thought, with slightly hysterical humor.

She reached out and tried the knob of the single door to the right again. Still locked.

"Locked," Brendan said, simultaneously with her thought. "We'll have to do something about that"—he winked at her— "but we'll wait for the team." He waved a hand back the way they had come. "I just left my suitcase in the closet in the study—den—whatever that room is. Figured we'd wait to choose our bedrooms and unpack later, after we get the children settled."

She nodded assent and they headed back to get another load from the car.

At the car again, she scooped up her laptop case from the trunk and Brendan lifted out a box of books and files. As Laurel shut the trunk lid, they heard a roar of engine, and Tyler zoomed up the graveled drive in a Maserati.

Well, if I didn't know he came from money before, I guess I do now . . .

Music blasted from the windows, dark and British-sounding. Laurel recognized The Cure. *Very retro of you, Tyler.*

To her surprise, both Tyler and Katrina got out of the car, Katrina looking as removed and regally indifferent as if she'd just been dropped off by a chauffeur.

Interesting, Laurel thought. *Before she was acting as if she*

204

wouldn't give Tyler the time of day, and now they're riding together? But then, nothing would shock me from that one.

She was gratified to see the two students stop in their tracks, and stare up at the house in a sort of stupefied admiration.

"Holy shit," Tyler whistled. "Y'all weren't kidding around about haunted, were you? You sure there'll be any room for us, with all the ghosts?"

Brendan took charge, which Laurel was grateful for, as it allowed her to stand back and watch. "We'll take you up the back way to dump your stuff and—freshen up. Then we'd like you to take an official tour, so we get your first impressions recorded."

"You're the boss," Tyler said lazily. But he looked at Laurel as he said it, and she felt again that annoying flutter in her stomach.

They trooped up the outer back stairs and Brendan let them in to the tiny servants' kitchen. Laurel and Brendan hung back and let the two students go first. Laurel noticed Katrina looking around her with a faint moue of distaste. The house was fairly clean, considering how long it had been empty, but Laurel imagined Katrina was used to far more elegant circumstances. The girl's shiny pants and embroidered blouse were casual, but Laurel recognized couture when she saw it.

They moved through the kitchen, past the servants' bedrooms, the linen room, and the lounge. Both students stopped in the hall outside the lounge and Laurel could see they were suitably impressed by the weirdness of the long upstairs hall. Tyler had stopped joking and was looking around him shrewdly, like a camera recording everything he saw.

"There are about a million bedrooms," Laurel said. "Why don't you both just choose one that feels comfortable for now and we can always switch later?"

Brendan added. "There are larger rooms in the next wing, but let's stay close for the first night."

"No doubling up, huh?" Tyler murmured, but somewhat

lacking his usual swagger. "Where's the fun in that?"

He half-bowed mockingly to Katrina (*Too practiced, that gesture,* Laurel thought wryly) and said, "Ladies first."

Katrina unhesitatingly chose the best room in what Laurel had come to think of as the "upper hall"—the large one with the balcony and the hearth.

Then they followed Tyler as he walked deliberately down the hall, then back all the rest of the way, and then slung his Calvin Klein bag on the single bed in the room across from the kitchen and back stairs, without comment.

"Any particular reason?" Brendan asked.

Tyler shot him an oblique look, shrugged. "Bathroom, kitchen, quick exit. What more could anyone ask?"

Laurel noticed a definite charge between the two men, a masculine jockeying for power, but Brendan neutralized the moment by choosing not to respond. "First thing on the agenda is exploring the house. Why don't you two take about fifteen minutes to wash up and compose yourselves, and then come back downstairs to the office at the bottom of those first stairs and we'll explain your first assignment."

Twenty minutes later, with the group assembled in the house manager's office, Brendan handed out floor plans of the house, two clipboards with both blank paper and questionnaires, and two voice-activated microcassette recorders to the students.

"We're not going to tell you much to begin with," Brendan told them. "We'll get into that later. We simply want you to walk through the house at your own pace and record anything you think or feel. There's no right or wrong, here—we just want your impressions. If you come across a spot where you sense anything worth noting, then mark the spot on your floor plan and make notes about it, either with the recorders or by written notes. The questionnaire sheets give you a list of adjectives that may help you define your impressions; you can use those word sheets or not, that's completely up to you.

"But we'd like you to start by filling out a checklist relating to your current mood—it's the first sheet on your clipboard.

206

Just take a few minutes to answer the questions and then we'll begin the house tour."

A silence fell in the small office as Tyler and Katrina bent over their clipboards to do the questionnaires. They were simple checklists that Laurel and Brendan had culled from books and articles about haunting investigations, mostly lists of adjectives to get at the subjects' current emotional states, but Laurel knew the act of concentrating on the questions, of having to tune into your own mood, was a kind of meditation in itself, a preparatory relaxation and awareness exercise.

The two students finished their questionnaires and looked up at precisely the same moment, like unwitting twins.

"All done?" Brendan asked brightly. "Excellent. After you've been through the entire house, we'll give you a break, and we'll reconvene to talk about the walk-through and give you some more background information. Any questions?"

Katrina and Tyler looked at each other, then at their two professors. "Bring it on," Tyler drawled.

"Okay, then." Brendan propelled himself to his feet, in that familiar leap. "We'll split up and work from opposite ends of the house, so that you two can have your own independent perceptions. Dr. MacDonald, you and Katrina can start at the north end of the house, and Tyler and I will work our way forward from back here."

Laurel saw Katrina's face darken and sighed inwardly, realizing it was going to be a long tour.

Chapter Thirty-three

A prevalent theory of hauntings is the "imprint" or "recording" hypothesis: that in some way we have yet to understand, strong emotions or traumatic events can be imprinted or recorded in the place in which they occur, and from then on can be unconsciously or consciously felt or perceived by certain individuals, in the same way that they might respond to a film or audio recording.

—Dr. Alaistair Leish, *The Lure of the Poltergeist*

Despite Katrina's obvious displeasure, if not simmering wrath, at being assigned to Laurel for the house tour instead of Brendan, the girl threw herself into the assignment with an almost frightening zeal. They began at what Laurel was starting to think of as the Spanish part of the house, although that was surely a California quirk of her own; as far as she knew the Spaniards never came anywhere near North Carolina.

The two women stepped through the front door into the entry hall with its greenish tinge and glazed brick floors. Katrina turned to Laurel and said bluntly, "So do I have to actually tell you all of this? Or can I just write it?"

Laurel suppressed an urge to slap her and said neutrally, "Whatever works best for you."

The first floor of the Spanish house was an amazing little

warren of rooms, and there was no level floor anywhere. For each room they had to step up or down, sometimes several steps. There was no continuity to any of it: rooms blossomed off each other and then abruptly stopped, and nothing was in proportion.

Katrina headed straightaway into the little library off the second entry, and Laurel couldn't blame her—it drew Laurel, too, with its dark-paneled walls and luxurious glassed-in bookshelves and Art Deco mantelpiece with carved peacocks, and large windows looking out onto the back gardens; Laurel could see all the way out to the white gazebo. The room enveloped her with a hypnotic sense of calm and warmth. Katrina stood in the middle of the room with a dreamy expression on her face, then began to move through the room with a proprietary ease, gliding her hand over the white marble tops of the tables, opening the glass doors of the cabinets to look at the books. She was almost overly diligent, taking an excruciating amount of time drifting around the room. She paused to gaze into a display case with an intricate model of a sailing ship, then lifted the top of a table to reveal a backgammon board built into the piece. She opened up a carved standing globe to reveal various brandies and liqueurs, emerald and amber liquid gleaming dully through dusty bottles.

I can't believe all this stuff is just sitting here, Laurel thought. *Wouldn't it have been vandalized long ago?*

Apparently Katrina had decided she would not deign to share her thoughts with Laurel, so Laurel was forced to stand watching as the girl made her slow revolutions around the room, stopping to industriously and ostentatiously mark her floor plan. Laurel had the strong sense of being an audience; twice already she'd caught the girl stealing a sideways look at her.

Katrina finally moved out of the study into the inner entry hall with the churchlike bench across from the fireplace and the strange family portrait above the hearth. She stopped still in front of the portrait and didn't move for a long time. Laurel stood in the doorway of the library and looked up at it.

What an odd room: just the bench in front of the portrait, almost like—like a shrine, an altar to that painting, with the bench placed for contemplative viewing ...

But the more Laurel looked at the portrait, the more she thought that the painter must have had serious mental problems. The parents appeared fairly normal, if crudely done, but the two children looked like adults dressed in children's clothing, or children dressed in adult clothing: the girl in a demure blue dress with a Peter Pan collar and the boy in what was either a Boy Scout uniform or an army uniform. There was no possible way of telling how old they were from their facial features, which on top of the age disconnect were vaguely simian. *Is that Paul and Caroline, then?* Laurel wondered. The two sat too close to each other on the steps, though they did not look at each other. *It's a horrible painting,* Laurel thought suddenly. *I hate it.*

And then she remembered that Paul Folger was a painter.

Katrina was scribbling industriously on her clipboard, as if Laurel weren't there. Finally, she moved away from the portrait, over the glazed brick floor, through another archway into the third entry with the front door to the outside of the house and the archway into the main staircase, its huge bay window overlooking the overgrown gardens. At the end of the entry was the archway into the great room. And it was at the archway that Katrina had her first "hit."

She stopped in the archway and froze.

"What is it, Katrina?" Laurel asked, forgetting for a moment that Katrina didn't seem to be speaking to her.

"It was here," Katrina murmured, and Laurel started. She'd said exactly the same thing when she'd crossed through the archway.

"What was?" Laurel asked, neutrally.

Katrina turned to her slowly. "What?" she said, sounding annoyed.

"You said, 'It was here.' "

Katrina looked at her without expression and then bent to her clipboard and made a notation.

210

Fine, Laurel thought to herself. *Don't mind me.*

Katrina stepped down the several stairs into the great room and drifted across the floor as if she were hearing inner music. Laurel glanced immediately to the middle of the floor, where they had seen the footprints—but the fine coating of dust was gone; the floors gleamed dully as if they had been swept, if not polished.

But by whom?

Across the room Katrina stopped to play a few notes of the piano—it was wretchedly out of tune. "Have you and Dr. Cody stayed in the house already?" she asked abruptly.

Why, whatever do you mean? Laurel thought, but answered calmly. "No, we've only been through it once, ourselves."

Katrina narrowed her eyes and turned away.

At the other side of the room she paused, frowning at the spot where the footprints had been. Laurel watched her, holding her breath ... but Katrina continued on, into the dining room.

More steps down, into the dark-paneled dining room (that bizarre unevenness of the house ...). The sky had darkened considerably outside and the room was thick with the gloom of twilight. Katrina grimaced with distaste, and moved quickly past the long table and French doors and out. Laurel herself felt the same overpowering urge to get out of the room she had felt initially, and she noted that on her own clipboard. Then she flipped back to the first part of the floor plan and made a note about the family portrait as well.

Katrina barely glanced around the kitchen: it was obvious she "felt" nothing, or perhaps she was so unfamiliar with kitchens it seemed not worth the bother.

The women started upstairs via the servants' staircase beside the kitchen. There was something appealing about the idea of a servants' stairway; Laurel wasn't sure that she'd ever been in one before, and she lingered, moving slowly up the steps. Then as she stepped onto the curved landing halfway up the stairs, Laurel felt her face flush and a rush of warmth through her body, a palpable sexual feeling spreading from

211

between her legs, as if a hand had reached to stroke her there. She stopped with a gasp.

Katrina turned on the stairs above her and looked down, annoyed.

Laurel tried to summon control over her body. Her legs felt too weak to walk on. *Get a grip. You haven't gotten any in a while. Deal with it*, Laurel told herself, and forced herself to take a step up onto the next stair. The sexual feeling instantly disappeared, leaving Laurel with her heart still pounding in confusion.

Katrina turned and continued upward without a word. Laurel climbed shakily behind her. *What the hell was that?*

At the top of the stairs, Laurel was suddenly aware of a soft murmur of voices. The two women stopped still, and looked around them, listening.

"Tyler and Dr. Cody, I think," Laurel said. Katrina looked at her as if she were an imbecile and flounced on.

Katrina breezed through the first part of the upstairs with an indifference that fairly shouted, *"These are just the servants' quarters."* But she slowed again in the linens room with its surprisingly lush dark wood floors and intricately cut stairs leading up to the small study.

There was a rumble of thunder outside, and suddenly the sky opened, dumping rain on the gardens.

Laurel watched as Katrina sat on the divan in the linens room and looked out the window at the rain, even closed her eyes. When she opened them she marked something Laurel couldn't see on her floor plan.

In the study, the girl stared out the windows over the garden, frowning for a time at the gazebo, standing still and white in the drenching rain. And then came the upper hall and the long row of bedrooms.

They walked past the bathroom … and then Katrina stopped in the hall so abruptly that Laurel ran into her from behind. Katrina turned on her with her face twisted in fury. "Don't touch me!" she snarled.

Laurel was so startled that for a moment she couldn't speak. "I'm sorry. My fault."

Katrina's face slowly lost its look of animal rage, and she turned blankly to the door they'd stopped in front of—the locked door to the right.

"It's locked—" Laurel began. Katrina reached and tried it anyway. To Laurel's surprise, the knob turned for the girl, although when she pushed on it, the door refused to budge. Katrina stepped back, looking at Laurel expectantly. Laurel stepped forward and tried the door herself. The knob turned, but the door held firm. Laurel pushed her whole body weight on it, and then suddenly whatever was holding it released, and Laurel fell into the room, barely catching herself before she tumbled to the floor.

It was a little room with slanted rafters, a narrow antique bed, a closet door, and—inexplicably in such a small room—a fireplace across from the bed.

Katrina frowned into the room, stepped tentatively forward . . .

. . . then wrinkled her nose and shook her head, as if warding something away. She moved quickly out. Laurel lingered in the doorway after Katrina moved on. The one small bed in it seemed more like a prison cot than a bed, and it may have been her imagination, but the atmosphere was simply—thick. A hat stand stood in the corner beside the door. There was a dark **O** on the window, about three inches in diameter, painted, she thought, but when she stepped closer she saw it was not painted, but etched into the glass and then darkened in with ink. It gave Laurel a strong sense of unease. At the window, the filmy curtains stirred, trembling in some unfelt current of air, and Laurel felt the flesh on her forearms rise.

She remembered the clipboard she held stiffly at her side and lifted it, looking at her own copy of the floor plan. She hesitated about how to mark the room, and then put squiggly lines over it. *Electromagnetic,* she wrote; it was the only word she could think of.

She stepped out of the room, and experienced a palpable sense of relief. Katrina had drifted down the hall toward the next rooms. Laurel watched as she drifted slowly through them, without comment and without writing anything on her clipboard. She didn't stop again until the room with the faded animal wallpaper and the sleigh beds. Paul and Caroline's room, Laurel remembered. *But why would the room have been preserved as a nursery, obviously long after the children were grown?*

Katrina was frowning and writing.

At the end of the long hall they moved into the perpendicular Spanish section again, with its larger rooms: the master bedroom, the two smaller rooms in the middle with their corresponding bathrooms across the hall, and the large library.

Katrina seemed to enjoy the master bedroom with its sweeping views of the garden; Laurel sensed that given the chance she would be moving out of her smaller bedroom forthwith.

They both turned at the sound of voices behind them.

Brendan and Tyler appeared at the top of the main staircase as the women reached the end of the hall.

"Nice timing," Brendan remarked, and they all went into the big library together.

Brendan and Laurel stayed by the door as the two students wandered around the room under the watchful eyes of the rows of photographs. Rain blew against the windows outside in spatterings and lightning cracked across the sky, accompanied by the low rumble of thunder.

"Yeah, there's some major heaviness here, all right," Tyler drawled. "Almost feels like I'm being watched." Laurel glanced at Brendan and he shrugged.

As Tyler turned back to the bookshelves, Brendan muttered to Laurel, "Actually he's been pretty cooperative." The warmth of his breath on her neck made Laurel flush, her ears tingle. "What about her?" he queried softly.

"Loving the attention," Laurel murmured.

He smiled at her with sparkling eyes and she had to look away.

The two students were industriously making notes on their floor plans. Brendan waited until they were through and then spoke.

"Okay. Have we all gotten through the whole house?" Brendan looked to Laurel and Katrina, who nodded. The two students seemed more subdued than normal, almost as if they were drained by their experience.

"Great. Let's talk." Brendan indicated the center arrangement of small sofas and chairs, and they all took seats. To Laurel's discomfort, Tyler joined her on one sofa, and Katrina took the opposite couch, looking to Brendan with clear expectation on her face. Brendan remained standing, and Laurel could feel the girl's flare of anger.

"Just an overview first, and then we'll get more detailed," Brendan started cheerily. "Can we point to any hot spots? Specific rooms?"

Tyler looked to Katrina.

"The green entry hall downstairs," she said promptly. "The archway between the front hall and the great room."

Laurel noted she used the words "great room" as if she said them every day.

"That dining room," Katrina continued, wrinkling her nose in distaste. "Upstairs, the little room with the sticky door. The one with the sleigh beds." She looked around her at the library. "And this one."

Brendan looked to Tyler. "Mr. Bradford?"

"The stairs next to the kitchen," he said, and shot a glance toward Laurel. "This room, yeah, but that could just be all the damn pictures staring down." He smiled slyly and everyone laughed, which seemed to gratify him. He glanced at Katrina. "Gotta agree—that dining room doesn't feel right. Don't know why. And my own room is pretty hot—if anyone would like to come have a feel," he added.

"Thanks, I'm sure we'll all keep that in mind," Brendan said. "Let's talk about what you felt in the rooms, specifically."

"The archway—a lot of pain," Katrina said almost dreamily. "It feels heavy. The air."

Laurel felt a wave of irritation even though she had to admit she actually had a sense of what Katrina meant. The air just felt *denser*, there. But Katrina was performing like a professional psychic, as if she'd been doing house readings all her life, when her preliminary questionnaires had not revealed any previous psi experiences.

"What about the back staircase?" Brendan asked Tyler. "You said you felt something there."

Tyler smiled slightly. "Well, if you must know, it made me horny as hell. Don't ask why."

Laurel remembered the unexpected sexual feeling she'd experienced on the stairs and had to will herself not to blush.

"Thanks for sharing," Brendan said dryly.

"Don't mention it," Tyler shot back. "That *is* my job here, right?"

The air fairly crackled between the two males for a moment, so manifestly that Laurel was about to speak, when Brendan suddenly stood down, although she could not have said exactly how.

He wrote something on his clipboard and said, "What else?"

"The dining room . . ." Tyler said slowly. "I don't know. I just step inside there and I want to get out."

Laurel felt a chill . . . and then a rush of annoyance—and skepticism. *This is sounding a little too perfect. Everyone feeling the same things? Highly unlikely. And the chances of Tyler being serious? Even more unlikely.*

"It's bad," Katrina announced. "Something bad happened there."

Oh, great. They're already making up things, Laurel thought. *But that's the point, isn't it?* she answered herself immediately. *We want them to psych themselves out.*

Katrina addressed her next monologue directly to Brendan. "And that little room upstairs is bad, too, the one with the sticky door. And there's something very strange about the archway into the great room. I could *feel* it." She put her hand on her chest, in case Brendan had somehow not noticed her lushly rounded breasts. Laurel was appalled to find herself

216

tensing. To make matters worse, Tyler tipped his head back against the sofa and looked lazily from Katrina to Laurel to Brendan, as if he wasn't missing a thing.

"Good," Brendan said heartily, pointedly ignoring the unspoken dynamic that was like an electric charge in the room. "I think we're off to a great start. Now here's how it's going to go. No Internet, no television, no phones, no music, unless one of you plays the piano, in which case knock yourself out. We want you to carry these at all times, though." He passed out a phone-sized walkie-talkie to everyone. "If there's anything of note, or if anyone gets in trouble, you can hit 'Page All' and reach the whole group at the same time. I expect everyone to respond immediately to any page, is that clear?"

Everyone nodded, solemnly.

"We'll be having you run card tests every day, and dice tests. We'll also want you to record your dreams as soon as you wake up in the morning, anything you can remember, and do mood questionnaires twice a day. It's fine to walk around the house and the gardens, and read or write, but no going off the grounds. We want you to immerse yourselves in the house, and simply—see what happens. Understood?" He looked around at all of them. "Just observe the house."

"And let it observe us?" Tyler quipped.

Brendan smiled, and Laurel didn't like the smile. "Exactly, Mr. Mountford."

"Let the games begin," Tyler said.

Chapter Thirty-four

It was too wet to tour the gardens, and the sky was going black behind the rain, so they split up, then—Brendan and Tyler to set up the cameras and monitors and infrared equipment and magnetic readers, Laurel and Katrina to make dinner.

Look at us, already time-warping back into the sixties, patented sex-role division of labor, Laurel thought—but she didn't really mind. *Let's face it, I can barely program my own cell phone. Hooking up a poltergeist monitoring system? Forget it.*

As it turned out, Laurel made dinner by herself while Katrina disappeared into the house, clearly used to having her meals magically appear for her.

And I'm fine with that, too, thank you very much.

It was vastly more comfortable not having Katrina around and the food they'd brought was mostly heat and eat—thankfully Trader Joe's had recently opened several stores in the Research Triangle area. Laurel put a couple of spinach-and-feta pizzas into the huge stove and opened a carton of tomato basil soup.

They'd bought paper plates to keep the kitchen work to a minimum, but it just seemed wrong to use paper in such opulent surroundings, and the kitchen was well stocked with dishes, so Laurel decided to indulge. She found a large crystal bowl that was perfect for the salad, and turned on the water to wash it and some gilt-edged china plates for dinner.

It was odd how comfortable she felt, since she had never been in a kitchen this size. Big, yes, but the ceiling was surprisingly low, compared to the rest of the house. *I guess because no one but the servants were ever in it—why bother with high ceilings?* she thought wryly, as she swirled dishes in the sudsy water to wash the dust off. It was weird beyond words to be in a house that actually had full separate living quarters for the household staff, to walk through the small rooms in the back part of the house and realize just how many live-in servants there had been at Folger.

Not my world. None of this.

She turned to a cabinet to look for glasses—and froze—at the sound of loud thumping from the wall.

She knew there was a rational explanation, *knew* it, but inside her mind she panicked. A wave of primal fear washed over her and she literally could not move. The thumping continued, shuddering through the wall.

Then logic kicked in and she lunged to turn off the running water. The thumping stopped.

She took a moment to draw a breath, then reached slowly forward again and turned on the water.

Nothing but the sound of water rushing into the sink.

Then the thumping started again, slowly, then building to a frenzied pounding, coming from the same high spot in the wall above the sink.

Laurel turned off the water, laughed shakily at herself. *And remember, that's all a haunting probably is, ever: just the mind playing tricks on itself. Expectations creating an atmosphere in—*

A *THUMP* came from the wall behind her. She gasped, whirled toward the doorway.

Brendan was in the archway of the stairs, looking in through the kitchen door at her. "Sorry—missed a stair . . ."

She stared at him, pale and speechless.

"What? What?" He crossed to her with concern.

She leaned back against the prep table and laughed shakily. "Shit!"

"Mickey, what?" He took her arms, steadying her.

219

She stopped laughing. "Nothing. I'm just managing to freak myself out completely and it's barely past nightfall."

He smiled, relaxing. "Well, fasten your seat belt."

She became aware of the warmth of his hands on her arms, the touch of his fingers like a caress on her wrists. He must have realized it at the same time, that he was still holding her, because he released her slowly, with a reluctance that she found thrilling.

"Guess it's time to feed the children."

"But where?" she said suddenly, realizing that the logical place—the dining room—was the last place she wanted to spend time in.

He looked at her innocently. "The dining room, of course. That's what we're here for, isn't it?"

The dining room was a mass of shadows, the gardens an eerie unexplored country outside the French doors with the arched windows above them.

Brendan was unabashedly going for atmosphere; he'd brought out candles to light the long oak table rather than use the electric lights. The grandfather clock stood silently in the corner, frozen at 2:59.

Aside from an unspecific nervousness, Laurel was not experiencing the discomfort she had expected to feel in the room. *Maybe it's just ugly in the day.*

Katrina ate as daintily and sparingly as Laurel would have expected, barely touching the tips of her knife and fork to her food as she cut it. Tyler dug into the pizza, but used his silver on the salad in the European style. *There's one for the statistical analysis page,* Laurel thought. *Rich kids have higher psi levels than commoners.*

"So who died here?" Tyler asked bluntly.

Brendan looked at Laurel. They had decided for the time being not to reveal the—so far unsubstantiated—rumors of the mad brother and the murder/suicide.

"It's an old house," Brendan said noncommittally. "Chances are a lot of people died. But that's not necessarily what we're here to investigate. It might not be a haunting at all. What we do know is that people in this house reported poltergeist-like activity."

Tyler whistled the *X-Files* theme. Katrina turned up her nose—

A sudden loud knock reverberated from the middle of the table. Katrina gasped and drew back against her chair.

Laurel had one jolted moment—then looked sharply to Tyler. She could tell just by looking at him. "Very funny."

Tyler raised his hands in surrender. "Sorry, I must have been possessed or something." He stretched out a leg and tapped the toe of his boot against the underside of the table again, this time not concealing the movement. "But okay, seriously: ghost, poltergeist—what's the difference?"

"Good question," Brendan said, pointing his pizza slice at Tyler. "The classic theory about a traditional haunting is that it's an imprint of violence or emotion or trauma on a house or location, that gets replayed, like a tape. Then there's the family member or close friend who is visited by the spirit of a departed loved one at the moment of death or extreme trauma—known as a 'crisis apparition'—or by a spirit who has a specific message to impart. Those are generally one-time occurrences and specific to a certain person, they often come in dreams, and once that message is received, the visitations stop.

"The word 'poltergeist' was coined in the mid-nineteenth century—by Martin Luther, no less—to distinguish a certain kind of haunting: one with very kinetic elements: loud rappings and other sounds, furniture and objects moving or flying, showers of rocks, breaking of household objects. For a long time investigators made a sharp distinction between those manifestations and the more traditional haunting apparitions: mist, phantom footsteps, the recognizable shade of a loved one. The theory that these were two very different kinds of manifestations was hot for a while, and the Rhine lab is famous for theorizing that poltergeist 'hauntings' are not hauntings at all, but manifestations of psychokinesis—the ability to move objects with the mind.

"Later researchers started to admit that there were almost always elements of both kinds of hauntings involved in so-called poltergeist incidents." Brendan leaned back in his chair, spreading his hands. "So basically, we know nothing."

He looked across the table in the flickering candlelight. "There may be a ghost in this house, there may not. There may be a poltergeist, there may not. We're here to see what happens."

Tyler slid a glance toward Katrina. "And we're here because you think we might *make* something happen. Because of our 'exceptional abilities.' That's what all the testing was about."

Laurel saw Brendan jolt slightly in the candlelight, but she wasn't surprised at Tyler's guess. Neither of their young subjects were fools.

"It's possible that you will be able to sense more in the house than subjects with less psi promise. As far as precipitating it?" Brendan shrugged. "That's what we're here to find out."

Both students expertly vanished after dinner, leaving Brendan and Laurel with the clearing and dishes. *Slipping into the servants' roles, already, are we?* she thought to herself, but she was secretly, shamefully glad to have the intimate time with him by herself, doing the washing up together in the steamy kitchen, Brendan making *Father Knows Best*-style jokes about "the children."

They laughed about the violently knocking pipes, and when they were through, they walked up the spiraling servants' stairs to the second floor, and Laurel again felt her knees go weak with the rush of raw sexuality she felt at the curve of the stairs.

What is *that? Why there?*

Brendan walked behind her, completely oblivious, and she was grateful that he could not see the instant, telltale color rise to her face.

Out of the stairwell, they started the long walk down the crooked upstairs hall. Laurel was annoyed with herself to find that her heart was still beating hard, and she was far too aware of the heat of his body beside her. It didn't help that he brushed against her going up the odd, steep stairs to the linen room and lounge.

"Any sleep preferences?" he asked, with no hint of innuendo.

"I was thinking anywhere but here," she answered ruefully.

He stopped still in the hallway, to look at her. "Really?" The light was low, shadows in every corner; they had not brought enough light bulbs to supply every lamp.

She felt odd, defensive. "Yes, really. We're not exactly in Kansas, are we? If ever a house was haunted, I can believe this one is."

"Huh," he said, and she felt a wave of annoyance.

She suddenly asked, "What about you?"

He turned and looked at her. "What about me?"

"Did you feel anything during the tour?"

"Ah. I see," he said slowly. "Nope. Nada. I just must not be sensitive that way."

There was an edge in his voice that might have been regret.

Laurel ended up choosing the small room with the single bed and the desk built in between the cabinet closets, with the door out onto the iron balcony overlooking the gardens, and the odd lithograph of the crow above the bed. It was by far the smallest of the bedrooms, the one that she'd thought of as the nanny's room, and she couldn't have said why she chose it, except that it was about as far from Tyler's room as it could be, which under the circumstances seemed prudent. Katrina had already taken the best room, and Laurel didn't like the feel of the children's room, or the little bedroom; she had no intention of sleeping in either.

When she stepped into the doorway of the nanny's room, Brendan looked at her questioningly, and she shrugged. "My governess fetish." She was instantly mortified that she'd said it and felt herself blushing.

Brendan raised an eyebrow. "We'll have to discuss that at length, sometime," he said with such a suggestive tone that Laurel felt her legs go weak.

223

He turned in the hallway, and then just as she suddenly knew he would, he walked to the door of the strange little room, with the narrow bed and the hearth inexplicably set in a room so small, and that odd circle carved into the window. The door opened without trouble for him, but Laurel felt an instant wave of unease. "Are you sure?" she asked, without thinking, as he tossed his duffel onto the iron-frame bed.

"Why not?" he asked, genuinely puzzled.

She shrugged, lamely. "I don't know. I don't like it."

He broke into a grin. "Good. That's what I want to hear. Maybe I'll get some action tonight."

Their eyes met and she felt shaky again. "Good night, then," she said quickly.

"We'll see, won't we?" he said, and stepped through the door to the strange little room. She got a glimpse of the hearth, the monastic bed.

Then he turned back and added obliquely, "I'm right here if you need me."

When she shut her door behind her, she had to force herself to breathe.

In her sleep shirt, the door of her small room closed, she stood at her window, arms crossed over her chest, and looked out over the dark garden. The gazebo was as white as bone under the slight moonlight, luminous, as if lit from within. The drapes of the willowy plants were pale nets, barely distinguishable against the sky. Beautiful ... and alien. *Let the games begin,* whispered a voice in her mind that was not quite Tyler's.

Laurel shivered and turned to the narrow bed.

Chapter Thirty-five

When she woke, she at first had no idea where she was. Even more unnerving, she had no idea what *year* it was and no sense whatsoever of *who* she was; her mind was a complete blank and she lay with her heart beating, in a blind panic, as awareness slowly returned.

I'm Laurel MacDonald. I was from California, and now I'm not. I was engaged and now I'm not. I'm a psychology professor at Duke and now I'm ... looking for ghosts of mad heirs.

She felt a bubble of not entirely calm laughter rise in her chest. *Well, it's no wonder I'm disoriented—who wouldn't be?*

As she got out of bed, she noticed one of the blankets had slipped to the floor in the night and her robe had fallen off the hook on the door, as well. There was a chill in the air so she picked the robe up and shrugged it on. As she turned in the room she was caught again by the lithograph of the crow on the wall above the desk. *Or is that a raven?* she wondered. *Is there a difference?* In any case, it was a singularly odd bit of decorating.

And then suddenly it hit her, like someone speaking aloud in her head:

"Why is a raven like a writing desk?"

It's a joke, isn't it? From Alice in Wonderland. *The Mad Hatter poses the riddle to Alice when they meet.*

She looked at the desk, the raven.

But whose *joke was it, I wonder?*

She felt suddenly as if someone were playing with her, and she had a strong urge to leave the room. But she looked across the door to the balcony.

She crossed the room and opened the outside door to step out onto the iron balcony outside her room. The chill of the morning enveloped her. A fine trailing mist snaked through the gardens. Her eyes were immediately drawn to the strange white gazebo rising from the tangled growth, with its picture-window view of something she couldn't quite see. The view from where she stood was gothically picturesque but the iron railing of the balcony was unnervingly low—knee-height at best, certainly not designed to any modern safety code. And the fall would be a sheer drop to the brick porch below. Brain damage, paralysis, death. Laurel took a step back and pressed her back against the wall of the building, with a sudden feeling of nausea.

From this height she was startled to see that the part of the gardens she overlooked was actually a formal labyrinth, a square one of boxwood hedges and taller camellias and brick walls, with worn gray statuary hidden coyly in its corners and angles. All through the gardens there were pale sprays of white flowers, almost glowing in their whiteness. She felt again the sense of a life she would never experience: a richer, decadent, opulent life. But there was the ghost of it here, a shadow of the sensation . . . to wake up and look out over acres of land, to feel the weight of the mansion around her.

A flicker of movement out toward the white gazebo suddenly caught her eye. She turned to look—and was stunned to see a figure dressed entirely in black: black coat, black pants, black hat, standing beside a white pillar, staring straight up at her. She swayed in shock.

Then something loomed in her peripheral vision and she whirled, losing her balance . . .

Hands grabbed her by the waist and pulled her back from the railing, against the brick wall.

"Okay? You okay?" Tyler demanded. "Jesus." He held her

226

firmly. Laurel stood for a moment, steadying herself in his grasp, her heart pounding as she realized how close she had just come to falling. She looked out toward the gazebo—but the black figure was gone. *Was it ever there?*

Tyler pushed open the door behind them and pulled her through. Inside her room he sat her on the bed and crouched on his haunches before her.

"Jesus," he said again. "Are you okay?"

"I ... thank you," she said inadequately.

"Don't be stupid," he said sharply. He stood, stepped to the door and stared out the door at the balcony. "That's fucking lethal. Can you imagine being out there after a couple of cocktails? They must have had people falling off that thing left and right. No wonder the house is haunted."

She felt oddly like laughing—he was so right.

He looked back at her. "What happened out there? You looked like you'd seen—whatever it is we're supposed to be seeing here."

She glanced toward the open door. *Had there been someone?* But the clothing was so—not modern: the hat, the frocklike coat ...

Which was one of the reasons the sight was so shocking to begin with. It had felt ...

Impossible.

"I think coffee would help," she said, and stood from the bed.

"Are you mad at me?" Tyler asked bluntly as the coffee dripped its way down into the pot and they stood in the small servants' kitchen with the burnt-bean fragrance filling the air around them

"Of course not. Why?" she answered, though she knew very well.

"That story about the lab," he said, looking straight at her. "It was a lame thing to do."

"It points out the pitfalls of this kind of study, actually," she said lightly, and reached for the pot. "People tend to believe what they want to believe." *Like that figure in the garden,* she thought to herself. *There was nothing there—I'm just hyped to see things.*

He wouldn't let it go. "I just wanted you to know I'm not going to fuck around while we're here. Whatever happens, it's for real."

"I appreciate that, Tyler," she said, and didn't believe him for a minute.

She took her coffee and pretended she was going back to her room to write up some notes; actually, she didn't want to be alone with him any more than she had to be.

As she walked down the endless hall, no one else was stirring and Laurel was appalled to experience a brief, irrational stab of jealousy, a sudden paranoia that Katrina had already found Brendan's bedroom in the night.

Delusional, she chided herself.

She glanced toward a small window under the eaves, overlooking the garden.

And speaking of delusions, what about that—person—in the garden? What was that all about?

She stood at the window, looking down, then turned and headed for the stairs.

She stepped out the back door onto the back brick—*patio? Veranda?* Veranda. *Where the stones fell,* she thought, remembering the photos. But the brick surface was bare, now. Laurel crossed to the railing to look out over the jungle of gardens. At ground level it was impossible to pick out the labyrinth shape she'd seen from the balcony—it simply looked like a random maze of paths. The grounds seemed completely deserted, the only movement the rise and fall of the breeze.

Did I see anyone? Could there have been someone back here, someone real?

She swept her eyes over the gardens, looking for any hint of a black-clad figure. Not a sign of it, but her skin still prickled.

There was no one, she told herself firmly. But instead of stepping onto the stairs descending into the garden, she walked along the brick path beside the house. Circling the house to the front. With its long-deserted horse pastures and wide open spaces, it looked much more bleak than the back gardens, and the wind swept through the trees, unbarricaded by hedgerows. She shivered and pulled her sweater closer around her.

The unnervingly tall pines were all around her, with that slight and constant rush of wind, and the sense of isolation was almost overwhelming. *No wonder I couldn't remember where or who I was. I'm about as far out in the middle of nowhere as it gets.*

And how must it have been for Caroline Folger, then, living in this huge place with just a brother who was not in his right mind? A spinster sister saddled for life with a brother who was not quite there . . .

She stopped short as the thought hit her.

Like Aunt Margaret and Uncle Morgan.

All those years in that house together . . .

"Trauma repeats inevitably . . ."

She didn't know why the parallel felt so disturbing, but it did. She pulled her sweater up around her neck and walked faster.

By the time she rounded the servants' quarters to the back garden, Laurel was breathing hard, and had warmed up considerably. *No wonder there was no such thing as a gym in those days,* she thought. *You get enough exercise just moving around a house this size.*

There was movement above her and she looked up. Katrina stood on the brick veranda outside the great room and dining room, leaning on the rail and looking out over the gardens.

Laurel moved up a short flight of stairs and stopped a few paces away from the blond girl. "Good morning."

Katrina barely looked at her.

Laurel forced herself to take a calming breath. *Don't let this girl get to you.* She looked out over the gardens from this new angle, marveling at the massive wall of elegantly drooped trees lining a long and weed-choked reflecting pond. The trees weren't willow—no willow ever grew so tall. She was mystified.

229

"What *are* those trees?" Laurel murmured, mostly to herself.

"Weeping cherry," Katrina answered automatically. Laurel turned to her, surprised; the girl never spoke to her unless absolutely necessary.

"They're beautiful," Laurel said tentatively. "So big. They must be ancient."

"In the spring they're pink," the girl said dreamily. "So lovely . . ."

Encouraged, Laurel spoke again. "I've never seen garden trees grow anywhere near this tall in California. It doesn't even seem possible."

The girl's face abruptly closed, and she was looking at Laurel with her usual hostility. "That's one thing you don't have in California, then." She stalked off, back through the French doors of the dining room.

Laurel sighed. At this point she'd prefer the company of a poltergeist.

Chapter Thirty-six

When Laurel got back up to the tiny servants' kitchen, Brendan was awake, at least marginally, pouring coffee, still drowsy and slow-moving. He looked haggard, as if he hadn't slept.

Katrina, of course, was already firmly planted at the table, her gaze fixed on Brendan. She stiffened as Laurel stepped into the doorway.

Three weeks living with this girl's hatred, Laurel thought, bleakly. *I can't wait.*

"Where's Tyler?" Brendan asked. "I want to get started."

"He's been up for hours," Laurel answered, with more edge than she'd intended. "We've been waiting for you."

They convened downstairs in the great room. Brendan and Tyler had moved a couch, a low table, and several chairs in from the garden room, and now the central screen of the bank of monitors reflected them in the same room in which they now sat. Seeing their every move captured on screen, reality mirrored back at them, Laurel had a flash of feeling trapped in a performance art piece.

"How did everyone sleep?" Brendan asked.

"Not a single visitor," Tyler drawled. "How about you, Professor Cody?"

"I slept fine, Tyler," Brendan said coldly, ignoring the

231

double entendre. "Thanks for asking. Did anyone have any dreams?"

Tyler lifted his hands. "Probably nothing present company would care to hear." His eyes slid insinuatingly toward Laurel and she reflected again that if nothing else, they had the requisite free-floating sexual energy going for them.

"Katrina?" Brendan asked, and Laurel thought that there was a hint of unprofessional eagerness in his voice.

"Not that I remember," Katrina said reluctantly.

Brendan's face clouded with obvious disappointment. He forced an upbeat tone. "Both of you should fill out your dream journals, anyway. If you don't remember any dreams, write down how long it took you to fall asleep, any thoughts you were having before you fell asleep, what time you woke up, anything about the night you can remember—"

Katrina had been fixed on him. Now she interrupted. "Well, there was something . . . I just don't know if it was a dream."

Laurel could see Brendan tense. "What do you mean?"

"It was more like—someone pulling the bedcovers down. Tugging at them."

Brendan glanced at Laurel. Katrina was describing a common poltergeist occurrence, often described in the literature. Laurel felt a flash of anger. *How convenient—the very first night we're here Katrina gets a nice classic visitation.*

Brendan didn't seem to have the same suspicion—in fact, he was wide awake now. "Can you tell us more about it?" He kept his voice neutral, but his excitement was clear in his posture, in his eyes, and Katrina knew it, too; Laurel could see it.

The girl straightened her back, warming to her story. "It felt like someone was standing at the foot of the bed and tugging at the blankets. When I sat up there was no one there, but the top cover was off the bed, all crumpled up. It happened three times," she added helpfully.

"Why didn't you tell me this out on the veranda, Katrina?" Laurel asked sharply—not because she believed the girl, but to call attention to the distinct likelihood that Katrina was making the story up on the spot. *No more real than anything I saw.*

232

"I didn't know if I should say," Katrina said coldly.

"The protocol is that you report any 'occurrence' right away," Laurel said. She could hear her own voice rising, the skepticism underscoring the word "occurrence." The girl stared daggers at her.

Brendan quickly intervened. "That's all right, Dr. MacDonald, Katrina knows now, don't you?"

"Oh, yes," Katrina said breathily. "Do you think it was important?"

Behind Katrina, Tyler rolled his eyes, and Laurel felt a surge of affection for him.

"It's interesting," Brendan said. "The point is that nothing is too small. We're here to observe and record *everything*. You should fill out an incident report now, and write down everything that happened. If anything like that happens again, use your pager."

"Yes, Dr. Cody," Katrina said, practically preening.

Tyler smacked the heel of his hand against his head. "I just remembered. I was abducted by aliens last night. Little gray men carried me out to this big silver ship and . . . well, I passed out, but I think they implanted something in my head. And . . . maybe other places. Was I supposed to page someone about that, too?"

Laurel was struggling not to laugh out loud and Katrina turned a furious look on her.

"All right, Mr. Mountford," Brendan turned on him. "Both of you, fill out your morning reports and mood questionnaires."

"No problem," Tyler drawled. "Now that I know what—" He stopped himself.

"Yes, Mr. Mountford?"

Tyler lifted his hands insolently, but said nothing as he slouched out through the archway, toward the main staircase. Katrina drifted out after him, clearly reluctant to leave Brendan and Laurel alone.

Laurel barely waited until she heard their steps on the stairs before she turned on Brendan, keeping her voice low. "You don't for a second believe any of that?"

"Why not?" Brendan said defensively.

"You know why not. The first night we're here she has a bedcovers incident? No, I'm sorry: *three* bedcovers incidents? If you Google 'poltergeist' that's probably the first thing that comes up."

"Let's not dismiss things out of hand, all right?" Brendan began. "Maybe she exaggerated—"

"Exaggerated? She's looking for attention. We're not supposed to be jumping to conclusions—"

"That's right, we're not supposed to be jumping to conclusions—*any* conclusions. You're already judging her—"

"Because it's perfectly obvious what she's doing," Laurel said. Her voice sounded raw.

Brendan paced on the long bare floor, and Laurel was aware of the cloudy mirrors on the walls reflecting them, the monitors reflecting them, dimension upon dimension. She had a sudden, unnerving feeling of being watched. She shook her head, trying to focus on what Brendan was saying.

"We don't know that she knows anything about reports of bedcovers being pulled. We don't know anything. We observe, we listen, we record—without preconception." He paused, and then without looking straight at her added, "If you have issues with Katrina I hope you'll be able to rise above them for the purposes of the experiment. Remember that you're the adult and she's the student."

The barb hit home; Laurel flinched as if he'd struck her.

Brendan turned his back on her, sat in front of the monitors, and cued the recordings back to the beginning of the evening. He pressed a button to start the playback.

All right, then, Laurel thought, and moved for the archway leading to the front stairs. Brendan didn't look at her, didn't speak.

She hesitated just before the door. As she stepped through, she felt the slightest shock, like the buzz of static electricity. She stiffened . . . then moved forward.

She walked numbly past the stairs, into the entry with the bench and the family portrait with its crude, simian figures.

234

Her face burned with Brendan's accusation.

It's not true, I don't have "issues" with Katrina. Why would I? She's a spoiled little rich girl, but the only real "issue" I have with her is that she's plain lying. And you, Dr. Cody—you're just grabbing at straws.

"Talk about losing objectivity . . .," she muttered aloud.

She felt eyes on her neck and turned sharply. She saw only the portrait above the hearth . . . and needed to be away from it.

She hurtled out of the room, through the small library, through the garden room, and out the back door.

The "Spanish" part of the house had its own walkway, not brick but red clay tile. Laurel felt a pressure instantly lifting from her chest as she closed the garden room door behind her and stepped outside. She closed her eyes and lifted her head to feel the air on her face.

The wind was soft and cool, instantly both clearing and lulling . . . all around her was a silky rustling that she realized was the sound of the long pine needles. *I could live with that,* she thought suddenly, surprised.

She opened her eyes and looked out on the garden. The sky was crystal blue after the rain, with billowy fast-moving clouds. *I want a walk,* she decided. *If there's anyone out there, I guess I'm going to find out.*

She walked down the brick stairs, past a fountain with a fish statue with bulbous eyes.

The bed nearest the house was enclosed in river rock, and she recognized enough of the plants to realize it was a culinary garden, with rosemary still thriving amidst long dead tomatoes and squash vines. The first steps she came to were river rock as well, and they descended to several branches of paths paved with the same gray-stone chips as the front drive.

Even choked with what must have been years of overgrowth, the gravel paths were still accessible. Laurel chose a path and meandered, past a huge bed of roses, all the vines now entangled, going wild, but still with brilliant spots of red and white and orange among the brambles. Wary and keyed up as she had been, as she walked she found herself relaxing,

235

breathing, beginning to enjoy the design of the garden around her.

Every curve or corner presented some charming or bizarre piece of statuary: a bench with frog legs, a malicious-looking Cupid, a lily-petal birdbath, and a surprising number of dog statues, like the ones on the gateposts. *Well, it was a hunting lodge, wasn't it?*

She continued past a pergola of weathered wood, so overgrown that it had been completely invisible from the house. A leering satyr peered out from the bushes; a fat stone rabbit huddled under a holly bush.

She marveled at the size of everything, often slowing on the path and craning her neck to look up: the walls of camellias were as tall as a house and those odd drooping trees—weeping cherry—were a good five stories high, gigantic ghosts with their slim trailing branches. Some passages were so narrow she could hardly squeeze through; others almost looked as if they'd been pruned in the last few days. And the constantly changing fragrances were subtly intoxicating ... the spicy bite of pine, a sudden waft of roses, then lavender, then honeysuckle, then mint—

There was movement in the corner of her eye and she turned to look, staring for a long time over the garden. After a moment she saw it again, a flash of light. Her heart started to beat faster as she remembered the black-clad figure.

The imaginary *black-clad figure,* she reminded herself.

You can turn back ...

Instead she moved toward the light.

She passed a bench that rustled suddenly and she spun toward it—to see a large snake slithering off it. It dropped heavily to the ground and wound off sluggishly. Somewhere far away there was the rumble of thunder.

Laurel took a breath and rounded the curve of path. She faced a stone circle with a silver reflecting ball, mottled with age. The clouds moved above, exposing the sun, and the ball burst into brilliant light.

So that's all I saw?

236

Laurel stopped and breathed in ... enjoying the silent stillness. Then faintly, she heard water rushing. She turned toward the sound in surprise. *A fountain? But who would be keeping it up?*

Curiosity drove her to wind farther through the twisting paths, following the sound of water through white birches and towering pines, passing under an occasional trellis or archway, finding stranger plants as she progressed: bushes with a hollylike leaf and malevolent-looking fingers of berries, and other shrubs with lush berries that were too red not to be poisonous. The sound of water became louder, unmistakable.

She rounded another curve and stopped still.

In a clearing before her was a three-tiered white fountain, with three white benches placed in the curved circle around it.

The fountain was completely dry. Nothing but dust and leaves in any of its bowls.

Laurel swallowed. The air around her was still, silent.

The wind in the pines. That's what I was hearing, she told herself—and knew it was not so.

She felt watched from all sides, and suddenly she had broken into a sweat and chills. She whirled from the fountain, about to run ...

And found herself staring up at the gazebo she'd been seeing from her window.

It was looking up at the gazebo that did it, the whiteness of it, with the tangled rosebushes climbing up the lattice, the dry fountain behind her.

It's my wedding day, she realized with a shock. *This is the day we chose, the one on the invitations that never went out.* And instead of standing with Matt under a gazebo in the Palisades, overlooking the ocean, she was alone in the dead gardens of a haunted house.

The thought crashed in on her, buckled her knees, made her head swim.

She lurched to the side of the fountain and sat, feeling waves of nausea, and the telltale prickling of hives rising on her chest.

237

And she felt a black despair welling up, that she would dry up like the fountain, wither like this garden, that she would never live, never love, never leave.

Never leave.

Somehow she made it back to the house, and went straight to her room, where she slept for the rest of the day, not even stirring when someone knocked softly on the door calling her name.

Go away. I'm dead. . . .

At some point it started to rain, and at another point she was sure someone was in her room, standing over her with a clipboard in hand, but both times she turned over and fell back into a dark and dreamless sleep.

Chapter Thirty-seven

The sky outside was fading to dusk when she finally forced herself out of bed. She had been lying awake for a long time, with no desire to move, but someone was bound to come for her if she didn't show herself.

When she moved to the door, something brushed her ankle and she cringed away from the animal-like touch ... then realized her robe was on the floor again. She stooped to pick it up and tossed it on the bed before she opened the door.

The long upstairs hall was dark; they hadn't brought nearly enough lightbulbs to cover the entire house, and it was a long walk to either staircase. The house seemed empty ... no one stirring.

What if they've left me here? What if I'm alone? she thought, completely irrationally.

She quashed the thought and glanced down both sides of the hall. She decided that in her current state she didn't need to pass by the closed door of *that room*—Brendan's room—in the dim light. She walked instead toward the Spanish side of the house, and she hurried.

She passed into the perpendicular corridor and took the turn onto the main stairs. Through the huge arched window she could see the moon almost full above the gazebo, which glowed white in the dark shadows of the garden, like a deserted altar ...

All right, stop it.

She looked away from the window and hurried down the dark stairs. There seemed to be no light below at all, and panic started to rise, from her stomach to her throat. . . .

It was not until she reached the bottom that she heard the murmuring of voices in the great room, and the relief made her legs weak.

She stepped through the archway of the great room. The three of them were lounged in the chairs and sofa grouped at the center of the room, with a few candles lit in the candlesticks, reflected flickering in the mirrors. Katrina was curled like a cat on the sofa, Tyler propped on pillows on the floor, Brendan in a leather armchair. He looked up at Laurel.

"Dr. MacDonald. Are you all right?"

The concern in his voice made Katrina stiffen on the couch.

"I'm fine," Laurel said, and realizing she would have to say more than that, she added, lying, "I didn't sleep well last night—guess I needed to make up for it." She looked around at them, looking for anything that would divert attention from her. There were Zener cards spread out on the low table in front of the sofa, and another table had been set up for testing, with the Zener-card display board in the middle, sorting boxes beneath it. There were two straight-backed chairs on opposite sides of the board. "Did I miss anything?"

"It's been a slow day," Brendan said casually, but there was a note of anxiety in his voice. "Nothing to report at all. We ran some two-person tests, sender and receiver and vice-versa . . ." He trailed off and Laurel sensed some kind of concern in his voice. But he quickly continued on.

"We've been talking about past psi experiences." He stood, offering Laurel his seat, the leather armchair. Laurel was about to decline and take one of the straight-backed chairs, but she saw Katrina glaring at her, so with a touch of rebellion she crossed and sat in the leather armchair. It was warm from Brendan's body.

He moved to lean back into the curve of the grand piano. "Katrina was just telling us—"

240

"No," the girl said, looking stonily at Laurel.

On the floor, Tyler raised his eyebrows. There was a silence, then Brendan laughed awkwardly. "Mr. Mountford, then. Anything to contribute?"

"I'm lucky," Tyler said.

Everyone looked at him. He shrugged. "I don't know what that means scientifically. But cards, dice, raffles—I win things a lot. I kind of know when to get in and when to get out." He grinned, a twisted smile. "I don't always pay attention, mind you. But when I do, I pretty much know."

Laurel thought of Uncle Morgan: *"I'm good at cards."*

And where did that get him? A wave of unease swept through her. *What have we brought these kids into?*

Brendan was speaking. "That's how Dr. Rhine first developed the Zener-card tests, and the dice tests. He wanted to test assertions by gamblers that they could influence the fall of the dice, and the lay of the cards. His findings backed those gamblers up. Of course, Rhine asserted that we all have innate psi ability. So far I haven't had much luck with the lottery, though," he quipped, and Katrina laughed, a musical, lilting, inviting laugh.

"And Dr. MacDonald?" Brendan asked. He looked across the room at her in the moving candlelight. Katrina's eyes flicked to her with disdain, then the blond girl stretched on the sofa, crossing her legs, her eyes fixed on Brendan ...

and suddenly Laurel was back in the dark hallway, walking toward the open door, toward the moans, toward the end of her life ... stopping in the doorway ...

... and the mirror shattering behind her—

Shattering her, shattering her world ...

Laurel couldn't breathe, couldn't speak.

"Dr. MacDonald?" Brendan's voice broke through the agony of the memory. Laurel forced herself back into the present, forced herself to respond. "I'm ... I'm inclined to think that psychic flashes are just ordinary perception. We're picking up on verbal, physical, emotional cues all the time. Sometimes our dreams—our minds," she corrected quickly,

241

"assemble those into a visual picture of what's going on, and it feels psychic, but really it's just perception."

Brendan seemed annoyed by her analysis. Tyler just watched her with sloe eyes.

"What about you, Dr. Cody?" Katrina said, practically purring.

"Nothing myself," Brendan admitted. "I'm Irish, though, so . . ." He stopped for a moment. "My grandmother—anytime anyone in the family was sick, or in jail . . ." He winked and laughed to indicate he was joking, but Laurel had the sudden and distinct feeling he was not. "We'd get a call from her. It was like clockwork . . . She just knew." He shrugged. "But me—no. Not a thing."

"Then what's in it for you?" Tyler demanded, and Laurel could see both Brendan and Katrina stiffen at his tone. "Why are you so interested in all this?"

Brendan looked at him sharply, and then half-smiled. "Who wouldn't be?"

The candles flickered, reflected in the mirrors, and in miniature on the monitors, and they watched each other.

Chapter Thirty-eight

She was asleep and then she was not, and there was the sound of the piano downstairs, just one note played lightly, over and over. She lay frozen, listening ...

Then her blood turned to ice as she felt the bedclothes sliding down her body, a faint tickling.

Her eyes snapped open and she lay in the dark, barely breathing. There was no light at all.

She felt pressure on the bed, like someone sitting beside her, only so light that it couldn't be. ... *Could it?* And then she realized there was someone sitting beside her, and his hand was on her face, his thumb brushing her mouth, and then his mouth on hers. Her body was instantly on fire. His hands were under her sleep shirt, brushing and then squeezing her breasts, and her breasts were straining against his hands, the nipples painfully hard, and his tongue was thrusting deeper into her mouth, deeper. She was moaning into his mouth and he was on top of her now, shoving the rest of the sheets away and grinding on top of her; she could feel the hard bulge of him pressing rhythmically against her through their clothing, seeking ... She whispered, "Please ... please ... and she meant no, but the word wouldn't come. He reached between her legs and she almost fainted with pleasure at the brush of his fingers against her, then inside her, and he pulled her sleep shirt over her body, over her head, raking her skin, and his hand was over her mouth, now, silencing her moans, and his mouth was on her breasts, sucking and licking and biting and she was writhing under him, lifting her hips against his, wrapping her legs around his. He was somehow naked then and she gasped as the crown of his shaft shoved against her wet warmth ... throbbing against her ... he slid just the head of him into her, teasing, teasing, and she was whimpering, out of control, lifting her hips to find him and he reared back and thrust, all the way to the core of her. She dug her fingers into his ass and he took her hands and pinned her wrists above her and was thrusting, thrusting; his mouth covering hers again and sucking her tongue into his mouth ... she felt a wave of unbearable heat radiating and breaking through her whole body ... as he thrust and shuddered against her, spasm after spasm until she was gasping and soaked ... their bodies bucking and their hearts beating against each other in a mad tattoo ...

And then blackness.

Her eyes flew open and it was dark. For a long moment she was unable to move—she felt enveloped in a paralysis, almost drugged. She was naked under the covers and she was alone, and limply reeling with confusion.

I passed out? I must have ... what happened?

She felt weak, almost nauseous. Her womb ached and throbbed, tingling, swollen, on fire with the remnants of pleasure, she felt dazed with wantonness, incredibly, hungry again. And then the real horror dawned.

She had no idea what had just happened to her. She had no idea who had been on top of her, inside of her ... or if it had been real at all.

Chapter Thirty-nine

The morning sun streamed through the wavery windows, casting shadows like rippling water as she descended the main staircase, past the recessed window seat. She stopped in the entry, just inside the archway. The great room was empty but she could hear them. ... They were all downstairs already: Brendan had them at the table in the dining room, filling out their journals and mood questionnaires.

Laurel was afraid even to walk into the room, to feel her body flame with heat, her cheeks flush—it was obvious, so obvious; she felt everyone would be able to see her shame. But when Brendan looked up at her from the table there was nothing in his face. "Dr. MacDonald, you survived the night. So nice to have everyone still with us," he joked.

He was either the best actor she'd ever seen, or he actually didn't remember.

The alternative was something she didn't even want to contemplate.

She took a chair, and Tyler watched her with a secretive smile, until she felt quite insane with doubt.

But surely I would have been able to tell. Yes, they're both tall, with good muscles on slender frames. But I would have known. Surely. Surely.

The thought was creepily incestuous.

Katrina was looking at her and Laurel forced her face still. *Calm down. Calm down.*

"Miss Sugar had another interesting encounter last night," Tyler drawled, and for a horrified second Laurel thought he was talking about her, but Katrina stiffened and glared at him.

"Not an *encounter*. I said someone was in my room. A man with a clipboard. He was watching me sleep."

Tyler snorted. "If you were asleep, you knew he was watching—how?"

"He thought I was asleep but I wasn't," Katrina said loftily. "First I heard footsteps ..." She frowned, a pretty picture of concentration. "I thought they were coming from above me, but then they were in the hall. That's what woke me up. He was standing in the doorway. I wanted to scream but I couldn't move."

Laurel felt a paranoid surge of horror. *What if she's telling the truth? Was there someone wandering around last night?* She flashed on the black-clad apparition in the garden.

She tried to keep her voice level. "What did he look like?" Despite herself, she glanced across the table to Brendan and Tyler.

Tyler raised his hands in aggrieved innocence. "I swear, I never touched her."

"He was blond," Katrina said definitively. "Older ... maybe forty. Blond, with ..."—she raised her fingers high at the sides of her face—"cheekbones."

Laurel looked at her, startled. Blond, cheekbones. It was the thing she had noticed about Leish—the cheekbones. *But that's absurd. Leish is dead.*

"Don't stop now," Tyler prodded suggestively. "Then what?"

"Nothing," Katrina glared back at him. "He just stood there watching—and then ..." Her eyes widened. "I guess I fell asleep, because then it was morning and he was gone."

Laurel was torn. The girl was clearly fabricating and yet ...

Could there be someone else in the house? Who looked in on Katrina and then ...

She forced the thought away. *Not possible. It was Brendan or it was your imagination.*

"Hmm," Brendan said neutrally. "All right, Katrina. Since

246

that room seems to be active, I'd like to put a camera directly in your room."

Laurel jolted a little.

"Now this is getting interesting," Tyler said.

Brendan ignored him, focusing on Katrina. "You'd be able to turn it off when you want privacy—but when you're sleeping ... so that maybe we can catch some of this activity."

"Anything that will help," Katrina said breathlessly.

"Good," he smiled at her. "Mr. Mountford will set up another camera."

"Yaaas, boss," Tyler drawled.

"Good; let's get upstairs and do it." Brendan stood and gestured, letting the two students precede him through the door, but he lingered, looking back at Laurel.

Ask him. Say something, she ordered herself, but she could not.

"Are you feeling better this morning?" he asked suddenly, as she stood to leave.

"Just fine," she said, and felt herself going crimson.

She rose to leave and he stepped in front of her. "You would tell me if there was something wrong? You were really out, yesterday." He seemed completely guileless, merely concerned about a colleague.

"Of course," she said, and fled, leaving the room with no destination in mind and no idea what was happening to her, moving blindly through the great room, past the main stairs.

And again, she found herself in the green room with the painting. That hideous painting. She sat on the bench to catch her breath. Her mind was racing.

Last night was a dream, she told herself. *He obviously knows nothing. It was because of yesterday. It makes total sense. I was thinking of weddings. I was thinking of* my *wedding. My subconscious created a wedding night. Plus there's enough sexual jockeying going on in here to fuel a porn movie. It wasn't real.*

"It wasn't real," she said aloud.

I'm just going to focus on something else.

She looked up at the painting, at the two figures seated too close to each other on the steps of the house.

And that's where I'm going to start.

The Folgers, Paul and Caroline. What really happened here.

There's the library, and those newspapers framed in the lounge. Maybe the stolen clip files are somewhere in this house, even.

"I'm going to find you," she said to the painting.

The watched feeling was back as Laurel stepped into the library upstairs, but then of course there were hundreds of pairs of eyes staring out of the photos on the walls, not to mention the large portrait of James Folger above the bar. She looked across at it, the crude but powerful style.

She crossed to the bar to look more closely at the signature—but the painted line was an indecipherable scrawl.

Well, if it was Paul Folger, he had talent.

Laurel turned from the painting and looked over the rest of the room, then stepped to the long wall opposite the windows to look at the photographs. As Laurel walked slowly along the wall, she noticed that most of the photos were professional studio shots, and of only one person, or two. *No family shots*, she realized. *These are celebrity guests.*

Looking closer she also noticed that judging from the clothing there didn't seem to be any photos taken past the 1940s.

Which means they've probably been up since James and Julia Folger were entertaining, and for whatever reason Caroline left the room exactly as it was, as if life stopped, or time stopped, inside the house. There's no history past 1950.

She suddenly felt—not a chill, not anything so definable, and not static either. It was a *magnetic* feeling, in the most subtle of ways, and there was that faint tingling behind her ears. She turned to the wall and found herself directly in front of a photo of a slim and handsome young man in an army uniform, with dark curly hair and an aquiline nose. His elegant posture was more aristocratic than militarily rigid. And his eyes . . . deep set, almost sunken; there was a wariness about them and at the same time a profound sadness.

It's him, she thought. *Paul Folger.* She would have staked her

248

life on it at that moment, it was so clear to her. She felt a thrill that was almost sexual—that *was* sexual.

There was no identifying signature or caption. She lifted the photograph from the wall to check, but there was nothing written there, either. She studied the face, looking for any sign of the madness to come: the flatness of affect, the absence of life force, the disconnect that often showed itself in schizophrenics. But this young man was alive.

She replaced the frame on the wall and now circled the room looking at all the photos, looking particularly for more of the young soldier. On the wall behind the door, hidden from view unless the door was shut, she struck gold: a photo of the young man with a young woman who had the same hair, dark curls pulled back from a high forehead with a band. They were sitting on the brick steps of the house, this house; Laurel recognized the white columns of the Spanish section. The young man's knees were spread, his hands on his knees, and they did not touch each other, but the girl's hair fell against his shoulder and they both gave the impression of leaning in to each other, though they did not look at each other. The same pose so weirdly distorted in the painting downstairs.

Laurel felt gripped by an uncanny sense that she was looking at herself. She knew the young woman in the photo looked nothing like her but she had a feeling of overwhelming familiarity, or really, empathy.

There was a palpable eroticism about the photo, as well.

Don't read into it.

Alone in the house, for all those years . . .

You're making up a story.

Paul Folger would have been only twenty-two when he got back from the war . . .

Just stop it—

Someone stepped into the doorway from the hall and she turned to see who it was.

There was no one.

Her heart leapt in her chest and her mouth went dry as a bone.

249

There was still a sense of presence in the room—she felt absolutely as if someone were standing in the doorway.

Impossible. You see there's no one there.

But she was frozen, completely unable to move.

And then just as suddenly, the feeling was gone. She forced herself to take a breath in, and out, and then she could move again.

All right, look—you have got to get hold of yourself.

She turned away from the door and continued her walk-by of the photos, but found no others of Paul and Caroline. Then she remembered that there were photos in the other room as well, the fox room. She left the library with some relief and moved into the hall.

The fox room—*the trophy room is what it was probably called*—was painted a pale institutional green that evoked a hospital, even though Laurel could not herself remember ever seeing a hospital wall painted anything but some variation of white. French doors led out onto the round balcony over the front porch—again, with a distressingly low balcony rail. *Maybe people were just shorter, then,* she thought to herself. *A lot shorter.*

The built-in shelves were crowded with silver hunting and riding cups; in fact, the lamps in the room were themselves made of silver trophies. The walls held paintings of the hunt and riders in hunting "pinks" (though the pink was as red as blood), and strange long-billed caps. Laurel walked along this wall as well, looking over sketches and old photos, of riders and horses and dogs—dozens of dogs. She stopped still, fascinated, in front of one grisly photo of a grandfatherly man with two small children, a boy and a girl no more than six or seven years old, impeccably decked in hunting costume—both with dark smears of what looked suspiciously like blood painted on their faces. The boy held up the severed head of a fox and the girl held the bloody tail.

Paul and Caroline?

They were avid hunters, Audra said in her head.

What a way to raise children, Laurel thought, and shuddered . . .

250

"The mask and the brush," a voice said behind her and she spun around in shock.

Tyler was draped in a tall-backed armchair in the corner, one leg thrown casually over the armrest. He must have been there all along, but he seemed to have materialized out of thin air.

"God . . . ," she gasped.

He half-smiled and nodded to the picture behind her. "That's what they call the trophies, the head and the tail. 'The mask and the brush.' Nice photo, isn't it? Kinda *Friday the 13th*."

Her pulse was still pounding and she sat down hard at the table, the twin of one in the library, a round one of solid oak, with a lazy Susan built into the top.

Tyler watched her with those eyes, without moving a muscle, and she could hear her heart pounding, slow, steady thumps. *It couldn't have been him, last night. He wouldn't have dared* . . . And tried to make herself believe it.

He tipped his head back on the chair, without taking his eyes off her. "You're not very comfortable here, are you?"

She half-laughed in spite of herself. "You could say that."

He shrugged. "I could stay here a while, myself. I think it suits me. My plantation-owner roots and all."

She felt an uneasy jolt at the thought.

He laughed. "Oh, now, that's transparent of you. Yes, you're in the bad ol' South, now. Soaked in blood. You shouldn't trust him, you know."

The segue was nonexistent, but she knew exactly what he meant.

"Who?" she said stupidly.

Tyler didn't even bother responding, but went on as if she hadn't spoken. "I really don't think you should. I know guys like that." He shot a veiled look in the general direction of the door. "Always scrambling for money 'cause they never had it and don't know what to do with it when they do get it."

She felt a chill as he said it—there was the unmistakable ring of truth, there. She heard Brendan's voice in her head: *"A little problem with a loan shark . . ."*

251

Tyler was watching her with a knowing look on his face. "Uh-huh," he said, as if he'd heard her thoughts. "I'm telling you—you're dreaming if you think he's in this for science."

"There's not a lot of money in academic publication, Tyler," she said.

"Maybe he's thinking bigger than that," Tyler said cryptically.

But what money is there in this? she wanted to say. A movie? TV? Even if they did something more sensationalized with the book, she knew from her years in Los Angeles that the chances of getting anything going on that level were like winning the lottery, and Brendan certainly hadn't said anything about it.

Exactly. He never said *anything about it.*

Aloud she said only, "That's very interesting, Tyler; thanks for your input. If that's the way you feel about it, why are you here?"

He looked at her as if at a slow but cherished child. "Full course credit for three weeks of this? Please. Who wouldn't?" He thickened his drawl. "It don't matter to me none if we see ghosts or not." He dropped the country accent suddenly. "It's a cakewalk for credit. Not to mention Miss White Sugar is practically panting for it. Plan A is to get myself laid."

Tyler seemed unaware that Katrina wasn't exactly panting for *him,* and for a moment Laurel envied his brash adolescent confidence. She was also profoundly relieved to hear she herself was not the object of Tyler's intentions.

He eyed her speculatively. "No, the real question is, why are *you* here, *Chère?*"

She almost answered without thinking, *Because I have nothing else.* She barely stopped herself in time. "No matter what, it will be an interesting study in expectation and personality."

"Is that what you call Miss Priss making things up?"

She fought a smile, lost, and somehow felt better. "We're here to observe everything that happens."

He tilted his head back against the chair, looking at her. "But you don't really think this place is haunted. It's all just some big mind fuck for science."

She looked at him—the aristocratic features, the lazy indolence—and suddenly leaned forward on the table.

"Tyler, if you're just going to play around, you should leave. It might not mean anything to you, but this is my job, and Dr. Cody's job, and it's pretty fucked of you to be here just for a laugh."

He was still in his chair, gray eyes like ice, no expression at all, and then he half-smiled.

"But you're wrong, Professor. I want to prove something's out there, something real—just to see my father's face. He might just drop dead on the spot."

And for a moment his gaze was fevered; then in one of those instant, mercurial changes, he smiled at her. "That Freudian enough for you?"

So was all that a game, just now? she wondered. *Do you ever tell the truth at all?* Aloud she said, "Not bad. I'll make a note of it in your file."

"Always happy to be of service." His eyes gleamed at her and her stomach did an uneasy little flip.

No, she told herself. *There was no one in my room last night. It was a dream.*

She stood to leave, and could not resist a dig. "You're right. This place suits you."

She moved out of the library and through the hallway into the older part of the house. The conversation had left her queasy.

She walked the upstairs hall from the front side of the house this time, marveling again at the slow and sickening rise and fall of the floorboards.

Katrina's door on the right side of the hall was closed, but the door next to it was open into the nursery, with the sleigh beds. Laurel paused in the doorway, frowning in. *Why preserve it as a nursery?* she thought again. *If Caroline Folger was a recluse, it's not like they had children visiting that they would need the room for.*

She shook her head and continued down the hall. As she

253

approached the door of Brendan's room, she felt again a sense of foreboding. *How can a door be ominous? That makes no sense.* Still, she hurried by it, staying as close to the opposite wall as she could.

The hall ended with the small study ... *or whatever this room was used for—a sitting room, a communal room?*

As she looked around the room with its bookshelves and slanted ceilings, she noticed again the newspapers framed on the walls, and remembered her intention to read them. She moved to the wall. Someone in the house had collected front pages of significant events: there were front pages from December 9, 1941: WAR DECLARED!! August 7, 1945, the bombing of Hiroshima: IT'S ATOMIC BOMBS!! and then PEACE!!! in red ink and sixty-four-point type: August 15, 1945.

Laurel moved on to another framed page: November 10, 1947. Not a date that registered any significance for her, and she stood reading with increasing puzzlement. Unlike the others, it was not a front page: there were no eye-catching headlines, no sixty-four-point type; the articles on the page were completely mystifying in their ordinariness, compared to the apocalyptic events of the other framed pages. Laurel took down the framed page and sat on the small chintz-covered sofa to skim through columns on horse races, a garden show.

What on earth would inspire someone in the house to keep this page, much less frame it? Whoever it was who had framed the newspaper pages had been capturing world-changing events, life-changing events. Why this page?

And then she spotted it: an article on the Dorothea Dix mental hospital in nearby Raleigh. On a spring day in 1947, a main building had caught fire. All the patients were successfully removed from the building, with no injuries but minor scrapes and smoke inhalation, but the entire building burned and the institution lost a full quarter of its capacity.

Among the patients who were displaced were two dozen servicemen who were housed in a separate ward ...

Laurel raised her head and looked up at the faint square outline on the wall from where she'd removed the framed newspaper.

Had Paul Folger been at Dix, then? If Audra's story was to be believed, was the fire the reason he was brought home to this house?

Laurel read carefully through the rest of the article, but the patients' names were not listed.

She lowered the framed article and put her head back against the sofa, looking up at the slanted roof above her.

Would Dix Hospital tell me about a former patient? Can I call?

She stood, and replaced the framed newspaper article on the wall before she left the room.

When Laurel opened the door of her room, her robe was on the floor again. She frowned and stooped to pick it up, hung it back on the hook of the door. Then, thinking better of it, she lifted the robe off the hook and stepped to the clothes cabinet to hang it up there. She opened the cabinet door—and gasped.

Every single piece of clothing was on the cabinet floor. All the hangers hung on the rod, empty and still.

Laurel's pulse skyrocketed, and a chill shot through her entire body. Then her anger rose. *Katrina.*

She whirled to the door, ready to march out and confront the girl ... but she stopped herself, just short of reaching for the knob.

And what, look like a screaming harpy? You're the adult, here. Let her play if she wants to. You're here to observe. Keep it professional and lock the door next time. Or let her do what she wants and write it down. It's all part of the experiment in the end, isn't it?

She crossed back to the closet, knelt, and fished through the heap of clothes to find her purse. She extracted her cell phone and tried dialing 411. No signal, of course; she hadn't really expected there to be. She hadn't switched her service from Los Angeles and could barely get a signal most places even in town.

255

But she hadn't been spending much time on the phone—there hadn't been anyone to call.

She sat back on her heels, thinking.

So should I just get in the car, go to Dix? I might have more luck getting information just showing up anyway, and Raleigh is only an hour's drive or so from Five Oaks.

She and Brendan had agreed that no one was to leave the house except in case of emergency, but it was suddenly very urgent that she know more about Paul Folger. *I just want to know. Was he imprisoned here? How bad was he?*

She stood, opened the glass door to the balcony, and stepped out, with the faint hope that she could get reception outside. Mindful of the treacherously low balcony, she leaned back against the side of the house and tried the phone again—but nothing.

She punched off and looked out. The day was crystal clear after the hard rain; she could see straight to the white gazebo, with its crown of roses and frame of firs. A bird swooped through the garden, too small to be a hawk, but with the same graceful glide. The quiet was seductive.

Then she saw a figure moving in the tangled undergrowth of the boxwood labyrinth . . . no, two figures. Katrina and Tyler were walking together, meandering really, with no apparent purpose.

Laurel stood looking down on them. She glanced back through the door into her room at the mess of clothes on her closet floor, and another thought struck her. *Are they both conspiring to juice up the investigation—Katrina to please Brendan, Tyler for his own amusement?* It was more than possible.

She was both shocked and uneasy that Brendan was being so credulous, and she wondered if the whole experiment was already compromised beyond repair. On the other hand, they had carefully set up the project to be a study of the participants more than the phenomena. There was still an interesting study to be made here, if she could keep her own head.

Part of her whispered that she'd already lost her head, or she'd be gone from here, already.

And there's no mistaking who you've lost your head to, is there?

She pushed that thought away and looked out over the gardens again.

Tyler and Katrina had disappeared in the paths beyond the labyrinth. Now they reappeared suddenly beside the reflecting pool, two tiny figures, far away.

Tyler glanced back toward the house—*surreptitiously*, Laurel thought, and then led Katrina toward the overgrown garden house.

Looks like Tyler's about to execute Plan A. Miss White Sugar is toast.

But it's Brendan who Katrina wants—that's entirely obvious.

She stepped back inside her room and looked at the scattering of clothes, dumped out on the floor.

Someone did it. Both of them?

Time to find out.

Chapter Forty

Outside Laurel moved down the brick steps and onto the gray gravel path toward the garden house. The path meandered along the reflecting pond and she was startled to see large orange and white shapes in the murk: Koi, overgrown and bloated and barely able to navigate the snarls of weeds and straggling lilies, yet somehow still surviving.

Even as neglected as the pool was, Laurel could feel the power of that carefully designed meditative walk: the long pool on one side, the soaring wall of weeping cherry on the other. Ahead, the garden house was a hobbit den of river rock; the roof had caved in in places and the yellow jasmine had done its aggressive damage, working tendrils in through cracked windows and wrapping itself around the beams of the covered patio until the wood splintered and sagged, but the structure was still reasonably in one piece. Laurel approached it cautiously, debating ...

If they're only out here having sex, I definitely don't want to see it.

And it was a perfect spot for a tryst—given the social history of the house it had no doubt been used hundreds, even thousands of times for that very purpose.

She was about to turn back, when she heard Tyler's voice. There was something stilted about it, not his normal speaking voice, but almost a stage voice. She frowned and moved quietly up along the side of the house toward a broken window.

She inched closer, and could now distinguish Tyler reading aloud from something.

"'Every poltergeist haunting is a contract between the percipients, the investigators, and the house ...'"

Laurel felt a jolt of shock.

What?

She leaned closer to listen in at the broken window, fascinated.

"'In its first stages the poltergeist plays with ordinary reality. It breaks down the laws of physics, and in its very randomness creates a sense of helplessness and dependence among its human observers. As there is no predicting what the poltergeist will do, it is completely in charge of any given situation. Further, there is an order to the occurrences that is seductive, they have a logic all their own. A logic that is incomprehensible to the human percipients, yet undeniably a logic, and thus all the more fascinating—'"

Tyler broke off for a moment to break into an eerie "Mwah hah hah."

Katrina's voice overlapped his, an irritated drawl. "Shut *up*." There was the sound of a slap, though not very hard.

Tyler said something that Laurel couldn't catch and then there was a pause. ... Laurel suddenly smelled a strong, familiar green odor drifting from the cottage.

Oh, great—on top of everything they're getting stoned. And then she almost laughed. *That might have an interesting effect on the experiment. I wonder if Dr. Leish had this problem.*

Inside the room, Tyler spoke again. "Wait—this is where it really starts getting good—

"'The poltergeist has all the power, because the human percipients give it that power. It seeks to lull the percipients into a state of amusement and fascination and gradually seduces them into complicity.'"

Laurel moved closer to the door. There was something familiar about the ideas, the rhythm of the prose.

"'The percipients come to crave manifestations, and when they are not forthcoming, manufacture them, either by fraud

259

or by RSPK. The poltergeist ultimately takes complete control of reality. And like drug addicts, the human percipients cut their ties to the world and in effect become addicted to the whims of the poltergeist.'"

Laurel walked in. Tyler and Katrina reclined on the same dusty divan, one propped up against the armrest on one end, the other propped up on the opposite side, their legs entwined in the middle. Tyler held a sheaf of printed-out pages in his hand.

Katrina dropped her hand holding the joint behind the couch to hide it, but Tyler didn't bother to move.

Laurel strode forward and snatched the sheets out of his hand, scanning what looked like a professional article. The title of the article was "The Poltergeist Effect," which was intriguing all on its own. Then Laurel froze at the name of the author.

Alaistair Leish.

"Where did you get this?" she demanded, looking up at Tyler.

He shrugged. "The Net, where else?" His eyes gleamed at her, catlike. "Just thought we should know something about what we're getting into. Right, Dr. MacDonald?"

Laurel didn't answer him for a moment; she was too riveted on the pages in front of her, on Leish's name. The pages were from Leish's long out-of-print book, *The Lure of the Poltergeist.* In all her research she had never come across this particular excerpt and analysis.

She looked up from the pages. "You found *this* on the Net."

Tyler was watching her. "I thought you'd want us to do some research."

"You know the rules, Tyler," she said evenly. "We said specifically, no Internet." *He has an iPhone, of course,* she thought, furious. *I'm sure they both do.* And then immediately realized—*But he couldn't print it, unless he brought a printer, too . . .*

"I haven't been on the Net since we got here," he was protesting. "I looked that stuff up the first night you told us about the project. I swear, Sugar . . . I mean Dr. MacDonald,"

260

he said in that buttery voice that probably had gotten him exactly what he wanted for all of his life. "You wouldn't expect anyone to go out hunting or backpacking without knowing the lay of the land, would you?"

And all those innocent questions the other night about the difference between a ghost and a poltergeist. Total sham, she thought, but said none of that.

"What else do you know about Dr. Leish?" she asked instead.

"Who's—" Tyler started, and then seemed to realize what she was asking and glanced at the pages she was holding. "Oh, the—I don't know anything about the guy, except that you mentioned him. It just sounded like he got it right."

Laurel stared at him. "You just Googled 'poltergeist' and *this* is what happened to come up." She held up the pages.

Tyler looked back at her. "Well, yeah. I mean . . . no, it wasn't the first link. I read through a bunch of articles, but that one just kinda said it all."

Laurel stood for a moment, looking at him, then turned and walked out with the pages.

Back in the house she found Brendan in the small downstairs library, in front of his laptop at a marble-topped table. She put the confiscated pages down on the table in front of him.

"What's that?"

"Read it."

Brendan looked at her oddly, then leaned back in the chair and read. After the first few sentences he said aloud, "What the . . .?" and started to read faster; she could see his eyes skimming quickly through the paragraphs.

Laurel waited while he read it; she'd already been through the document several times on the veranda outside.

Brendan finally looked up. "Where did you get this?

"Tyler had it. He said he got it off the Net. I found him and Katrina with it. Getting stoned," she added.

An almost comically dismayed expression crossed Brendan's face, then he laughed. "Well, we didn't say they couldn't. Maybe

261

it will be good for the experiment."

That's a whole other experiment, Laurel thought, *but that's not the point.* "I never came across that article, did you?"

"No."

"It's not from Leish's book. Tyler said he Googled 'poltergeist' and that's what came up." Brendan looked at her curiously. She lifted her hands. "He just *happens* to come up with a theory of Leish's that neither of us has ever seen, and that's the one he *happens* to bring here?"

The corners of Brendan's mouth quirked. "Well, if you think about it, we did choose these two for their psi ability, didn't we?"

She stared at him. "Are you being serious?"

"I don't know," Brendan said. He sounded tired, and she noticed again that he had dark circles under his eyes. "Might be good for the atmosphere." She stared at him in disbelief. "We want them psyching themselves out, don't we? We've only got three weeks, and we're not here for our health. It can't hurt to have them amped up." There was an edge in his voice, too, and she wondered about that.

Laurel took the article back from him and read aloud: " 'The poltergeist ultimately takes complete control of reality. And like drug addicts, the human percipients cut their ties to the world and become addicted to the whims of the poltergeist.' "

She looked up from the article, at Brendan. He looked at her, puzzled. "What's bothering you about it?"

If she were completely honest about why it was bothering her, it was that she had a queasy feeling about Leish suddenly showing up like that, randomly.

Above them there was a scream, then muffled pounding in the floor. They both froze and looked up, and for a suspended moment Laurel knew exactly what Brendan was thinking—that something was finally happening ... something. And she saw his excitement—the almost rabid look in his eyes—before they both ran for the stairs.

Chapter Forty-one

Upstairs, Katrina paced in the little lounge with the slanted ceiling. She was beside herself, on the verge of hysteria. Brendan had bolted into the room just ahead of Laurel, and now he took Katrina by the forearms, stopping her wild circling. She was hyperventilating and trembling, her eyes dilated.

"Calm down, Katrina. Just tell us what happened." Brendan glanced at Laurel.

"My room. In my room," the girl gasped.

Brendan crossed the lounge in three swift steps and strode down the hall toward Katrina's room, Katrina trailing fearfully behind. Laurel followed with a building sense of anger.

They all crowded into Katrina's room, looking around them. The mirror above the hearth was cracked, as was all the glass in the framed prints.

Katrina was talking very fast, and her eyes were dilated with excitement (and pot, Laurel realized). "I've been outside since this morning. I just came back to my room and ..." She gestured grandly.

Laurel stared at the mirror and for a moment she was back in her dream ... *the sound of the mirror shattering behind her ...*

She shook it off, pushed it away.

Laughter rang out behind her and she snapped back to the present. She turned to see Tyler hovering behind her in the hall. He looked past her to Katrina and started clapping, slowly. "Good one, baby doll. How many points does she get for that, Professor Cody? 'Cause I definitely think she's winning."

Laurel had to turn away to cover a smile, but Katrina caught it and shot her a look of pure fury.

"You don't believe me and I hate you. I didn't do it. I didn't." She burst into tears.

What a little liar, Laurel thought, with a viciousness that startled her.

Just as Katrina was obviously angling for, Brendan stepped to the bed to soothe her, crouching in front of her, holding her shoulders. Laurel was appalled at the wave of jealousy that washed through her.

"Katrina, it's fine, you're doing just fine." Brendan squeezed the girl's shoulders lightly. "All we have to do is check the monitors—" he stood and stepped to the camera, but stopped, looking at it.

Katrina sniffled from the bed. "I ... I turned it off when I changed my clothes earlier ... I forgot to turn it back on. I'm sorry," she said winningly.

Laurel shook her head in complete disbelief.

Brendan took out his EMF reader and stepped to the wall to hold the device close to a shattered picture frame. The device was silent. To tell the truth Laurel had never understood what electromagnetic levels had to do with anything and was skeptical that it meant anything real.

"The levels are normal," he said in a neutral voice, and moved to the other frames one by one to check. "Three ... three point three ..." He shook his head. "Nothing."

And again Laurel heard the disappointment in his voice.

He turned to the girl and said heartily, "Katrina, I want you to journal this for me, okay? Fill out your mood sheet, and an incident description page. Tape record your thoughts and feelings, if you want. When you're through, bring it to me and we'll talk about it."

She brushed at the wetness in her eyes and nodded.

"Good girl." He turned to Tyler. "Mr. Bradford, I'd like you

264

to take a camcorder and film"—Brendan looked around at the smashed glass—"the damage."

"Sure," Tyler shrugged lazily. "It's your party."

It's someone's party, Laurel thought. She looked toward Katrina, who stared back at her stonily.

Laurel turned and walked out of the room.

She walked down the stairs, through the dining room, and into the great room, and stopped in front of the monitors. She looked up at the wall, at her reflection in one of the cloudy mirrors.

Then she looked at the monitors.

So Katrina just turned off the camera, so she could smash the glass and win points with Professor Cody. Can I prove that?

She stepped closer and found the Reverse button. She backed up the recording and hit Play . . .

And saw Katrina standing in a baby doll nightgown, standing in front of the closet, reaching in to choose a sweater and pants . . . turning toward the bed . . . then stepping forward and shutting off the camera.

Exactly what she'd thought she'd find.

It's a good cover story: shutting off the camera so she could dress in privacy.

Laurel reached forward and shut off the recorder.

This whole experiment is completely out of control already. Is there any salvaging it, really? Is there any reason to stay, and let it be hijacked by a spoiled rotten Southern princess?

And the answer came to her in a flash. *Uncle Morgan. No matter what else is happening, I have a chance to find out what happened.*

A voice spoke behind her. "Okay. Let's hear it."

She turned to face Brendan. He was silhouetted in the light coming through the tall windows. "I know you're having trouble believing—" he began.

"I'm not sure that there's any point in continuing this study," Laurel said in a low, brittle voice. "Not if all she's going to do is make things up."

"We don't know that," Brendan said, his voice equally low.

"Oh, really? 'Ah turned it off when Ah changed mah clothes earlier and Ah forgot to turn it back on?'" she mimicked Katrina savagely, Carolina accent and all, and was gratified to see Brendan flinch. "It's completely obvious that she did it herself." Laurel could see from the uncomfortable reluctance in Brendan's face that he agreed with her, but she kept going, anyway. "Tyler gave her a whole blueprint with that article. They were out there reading it not twenty minutes before this happened."

"Okay," Brendan said, soothingly this time, which infuriated Laurel all the more.

"No, it's not okay. They got high, they read Leish's article, and they staged a manifestation." Her voice was rising again. "And what you don't see is that you're encouraging it. We're not anywhere near the level of scientific objectivity we need to be to make this study viable." She saw him recoil again, and felt a mean triumph. She couldn't resist twisting the knife. "Unless it's now just a study about Katrina acting out. Which you're rewarding her for doing, you know. So of course she's making things up to please you."

Brendan's face reddened. "To please me? What does that have to do with anything—"

Laurel found her voice rising for no reason she could name. "Oh, *please*. Don't pretend that you haven't seen—"

"What is this, some feminine intuition—"

"Practically on her knees every time you walk in ... and you're feeding into it. 'Journal this *for me*, Katrina—'"

"And I'm supposed to pretend this has anything to do with reality—"

They were almost screaming at each other, toe to toe, and Laurel suddenly had the sense that she was not entirely herself, that someone else was screaming through her.

She caught a glimpse of them both reflected in the mirrors and it did not seem to be Brendan but a tall, lean blond man.

Laurel gasped and started back, away from him ... and then

266

the feeling was gone, and so was the anger. She looked at him shakily. "What are we doing?"

Brendan sagged. "I don't know." Laurel was walking, first in circles, then suddenly out of the great room—she had to be out of the room. She walked into the glazed brick entry hall. Brendan followed her.

"I'm sorry. I don't know what that was," he said.

She sat on the bench, across from the odd family portrait, and looked at him. All the blazing anger she had been feeling just a moment before was gone, completely evaporated, as if the rage had not been her own. Brendan looked faintly puzzled, as if he was experiencing the same confusion. Laurel took a breath and groped back to the point she had been trying to make, with less heat.

"She did this. Maybe *they* did this. They planned it." She sounded incoherent to herself and his hand was on her neck, gently kneading it.

"Mickey. It's okay. Really—"

She nearly melted at the touch of his hand on her neck, and all the sensations of the night before came back in a rush—the weight of his body on hers, the unbearable pleasure . . .

Didn't happen. Not real.

She pulled away from him. "No, you don't see. She's sabotaging the experiment. Look, she's been in my room. This morning she dumped all my clothes on the floor."

He was instantly alert. "Wait, what?"

"She came into my room and dumped all my clothes onto the closet floor. First it was my robe, then the blankets, then every single piece of clothing in my closet—"

He was standing, jazzed. "Why didn't you tell me?"

She stared at him in disbelief. "Oh, please. Because I know who did it. I *know*. There's nothing supernatural about it—"

"You just decided that yourself?" He was agitated now, barely holding back anger. "Mickey, for Christ's sake, you're supposed to report *everything*. How are we supposed to conduct an experiment if you're withholding information—"

267

"How are we supposed to conduct an experiment if you're allowing student participants to fabricate data—"

There was movement in the corner of her eye and Laurel turned her head to look.

Katrina was standing on the landing of the stairs, in front of the bay window, looking down on them with sheer hatred on her face. When Laurel caught her gaze, she spun around and marched back upstairs.

Laurel shook her head, shook off the out-of-control feeling. "This is never going to work if we don't stay objective," she said aloud, and she didn't know if she was speaking to Brendan or herself.

"Absolutely," he said, and he sounded shaken. "From now on we go by the book No assumptions. Let's just go back to straight, quantifiable testing." He took a breath, and faced her with something like calm.

"But you have to report what happens to you, too. No holding back. Everything that happens, every action and reaction, are part of this study."

Chapter Forty-two

They did card runs that night. Brendan insisted on it. "We need to monitor the levels of psi daily, for consistency."

Katrina's scores were higher and higher. She seemed on fire. Every card run she performed was better than the last, and she preened under Brendan's praise. Tyler did worse and worse; Laurel could see his frustration building even as he sat there. Finally he flung his cards across the room, without completing the run. The cards fluttered to the floor, enigmatic symbols.

"This is bullshit," he raged. "We're just passing time, waiting for something to happen that Miss White Sugar didn't make up."

Katrina rose, with spots of red flaming in her cheeks. "Just because nothing's happening for *you*—"

Brendan was instantly walking between them, intervening. "Katrina, why don't you take a break? Just step into the dining room and fill out your notebook about the tests you just completed." She was unhappy, petulant, but he smiled at her and Laurel could see her melt. "I'll come in and we'll talk about them just as soon as you're done."

Laurel had to admit, he had the touch. Katrina lit up and moved through the door into the dining room without protest.

Brendan turned to Laurel. "Dr. MacDonald, I'd like you to test with Tyler."

Laurel looked at him, startled. "What—"

"I want to mix this up; try a telepathy test. You sort through a deck of cards, and Tyler will write down his guesses of the cards you are looking at."

There was a hole in the pit of Laurel's stomach; she felt wrong about it in three dozen different ways, but nothing she could articulate.

Tyler looked at her from the testing table, a challenging look, and she walked over and sat down across from him. The lamplight was low, a soft haze around them.

He sat forward in his chair, and she realized he would be staring at her for the entire run. She reached for the first boxed deck and removed the cards. Her hands were trembling slightly. She forced herself to look down and think of nothing but the cards as she gripped the deck in her left hand and turned over the first card: a star.

After looking at the card she placed it face down, maintaining the original order, as Tyler wrote down his guesses on a pad.

Five runs of twenty-five cards each.

She turned over a card, and stared down at the black symbol, making the card the only thing in her mind. That part felt fine, for a while; it was a relief to lose herself in the imperative of the symbol: circle, square, star, cross, two wavy lines like water. With each run that she did, the symbols became larger, metaphorical, elemental. The circle, the square, the star, the cross, the waves: eternity, construction, celestial, religion, water.

And then something else began to creep in—she could feel Tyler's mind. Maybe it was just the sense of his eyes holding steadily on her face, but she felt that he was seeing what she was seeing, that they were looking at each card together, hanging in some space between them that was also inside them. It became more and more real, this space ... as if they were in a white room with each card suspended for a moment in the air between them, like a painting hung in a gallery.

It seemed to go by in a second—and last forever. The feeling was hypnotic, intoxicating—and dismayingly sensual. She was aware of his body just a few feet from hers . . . she could feel the warmth of him, the life force.

When she put down the last card she kept her eyes fixed on the table, unable to look at him.

Brendan cleared his throat—a gruff, uncomfortable sound—and stepped beside her to pick up the deck of cards, then Tyler's scorepad.

He walked over to the table he was using as a desk, and set the cards and the pad down, then returned with a second set of cards and another pad. He put the pad on the table in front of Laurel and handed Tyler the deck.

"This time Tyler will send and Dr. MacDonald will receive." His voice was flat, he almost sounded angry, and Laurel felt a stab of unease. *What's wrong?*

She looked up, then, and caught Tyler's eyes, still on her face, and this time he looked away from her.

The second run was even more intense. She didn't look at Tyler, but stared at the black screen dividing the table in half. Or maybe she had her eyes closed—she couldn't tell, because she was back in the white room again, the room in which she and Tyler sat and looked at a symbol suspended in the air between them, as tangible as a piece of art in a museum.

Her hand held the pencil and made the appropriate marks; she was barely aware she did it, and again, time had ceased to exist; it could have been five minutes or it could have been an hour.

Then the white room suddenly vanished as she heard a chair scraping, and Tyler said, "That's it."

His voice was strained. Laurel opened her eyes—or focused—and for a moment Tyler looked at her with no guile or amusement or mockery, simply looked at her without smiling.

Brendan stepped abruptly up to them, breaking the moment. He collected the cards and the notepad.

"Thank you, Tyler, that's all for tonight."

Tyler stood, and Laurel thought he looked disoriented. He

271

mumbled, "G'night," and walked a bit unsteadily toward the archway and out.

Laurel turned in her chair to look toward Brendan, who was already seated back at his work table with the cards and guess sheets in front of him.

She started to stand—and Brendan stood and said sharply, "Stay there and fill out this mood sheet." She sat back, startled at the edge in his voice. He crossed to her table and gave her a blank mood sheet, with its adjectives for assessing mood. She glanced over the sheet and half-heartedly circled a few words: *drained, lethargic, anxious, tense.* She wasn't going to write what she really felt, which was—weird. Like bursting into tears, like the vulnerability she felt after sex. She felt—open.

She glanced over the words on the page again and her eyes fell on the word *erotic.*

She pushed the page away, and was aware of Brendan turning around behind her at the desk. She stood, and felt wobbly. "How did I do?" she asked, trying to keep the question light.

"Right at statistical chance," he said briefly, not looking at her. "Both rounds."

Laurel stared at him, startled. "I—really? That's all?" She thought of the symbols that had been so clear, hanging in the space between her and Tyler; she'd been so sure that they were communicating on some level.

"Why?" Brendan asked, and his voice was wary.

She forced a shrug. "Oh, well. It doesn't matter." He was looking at her and she couldn't read his face in the dim light. She took the few steps over to his table and lay the mood sheet down. He'd already returned the cards to their boxes and the score sheets were no longer on the table.

"It wore me out, anyway," she said lamely. "I'll—see you in the morning."

"Good night," he said, without smiling, and she had again the feeling that something was wrong.

"Good night ... ," she said tentatively, but he turned away from her, to the desk, and she walked slowly across the room. Her reflection followed her in the mirrors like a ghost.

272

*

Upstairs in her room she took the desk chair and pushed the top of it up under the doorknob. When she stepped back from the door she felt sure that she was being watched. She turned to the balcony door and crossed to it, checked to see that it was locked. She undressed hurriedly, so self-conscious she pulled her sleep shirt over her head before slipping off her clothes underneath it. She felt open, vulnerable, that there were no boundaries anymore.

And are there? If I can walk into a room and share Tyler's mind . . .

But you didn't, she reminded herself. *You only scored at statistical chance. Whatever you thought was happening was all in your mind.*

She lay in bed for the longest time, exhausted but unable to sleep; with her eyes closed she saw the Zener symbols suspended in front of her, in a room that was not a place, in a space beyond time.

Chapter Forty-three

Laurel woke at dawn; they'd all gone to bed so early. The image of a circle card still burned a hole in her head.

She lay still and was relieved to realize she'd had no other dreams or visitations. The bedclothes were still on the bed and the chair was firmly propped under the doorknob.

Dressed now, she walked downstairs via the main stairs. Outside the arched window the garden was drifted with fog. She made her coffee in the main kitchen, avoiding the servants' kitchen so she would not wake Tyler; the last thing she wanted was to have to face him alone after their connection of the night before. She didn't want to talk about it. But at the same time she did; she wanted to know if he had had the same vision of the cards.

But what does it matter, if we only performed to chance? There was no uncanny connection going on there. It was all in your head, like everything else.

As the coffee percolated she drifted into the dining room, and felt again a faint but noticeable reluctance to enter it. The light was odd, very bright despite the fog outside the French doors with their glass arches, and weirdly contrasting with the dark paneling. There was an iron cookstove in the hearth, and a many-drawered sideboard that perfectly matched the dark wood of the walls, with a gorgeous gold-and-mahogany clock under a thin glass dome. Laurel paused in front of the looming grandfather clock, forever stopped at 2:59—and suddenly looked back at the smaller clock under the dome. It, too, was stopped at 2:59.

All right, now—what are the chances of that? What kind of an event stops nonelectrical clocks?

She felt a brush of unease, like fingers trailing her neck, and quickly walked out of the room.

In the great room she moved past Brendan's banks of monitors, looking over the static views of empty rooms. There was no one in any of the common areas. The new camera was up in Katrina's room—she could see the girl's sleeping shape, curled on her side under the blankets in the bed in the dim room. The only moving thing Laurel could see on screen was herself, in the great room. She felt a great detachment, looking at herself. *Is this how the house watches us, then?* she thought, and then shook her head to dispel the thought. But maybe she kept feeling that she was being watched because she *was*—by the cameras, by whoever might be looking at the cameras. *Maybe it really is as simple as that.*

And then she realized she was being recorded at that very moment, and later Brendan would be watching her looking at herself. She stepped away from the monitors, flushed with embarrassment.

The sky had lightened outside but not by much; it was overcast and gloomy. Suddenly she walked for the front door. At least outside she could think without feeling on display.

The air had turned chilly, and there was again the wispy ground fog, snaking between the trees, floating in patches in the air as Laurel walked between the trees, so she was not entirely sure of what she was seeing when a black-suited figure with a walking stick and a hat materialized from the indistinct grayness.

The figure from the garden.

Laurel stopped and stared, expecting it to vanish, but he—definitely a he—walked toward her, moving purposefully up the road from the gateposts. He got bigger and more real, red-faced and portly and sweating slightly, in his early sixties, she guessed, though his hair beneath the hat was shiny jet black. Always wary of any lone man when she was alone in an unfamiliar place, she glanced up toward the house, and could see no one stirring. Yet curiosity kept her rooted to the spot.

When he was a few yards from her the man in black removed his hat in a courtly gesture, revealing a full head of the black hair with only a few threads of gray, and a pronounced cowlick. "Morning, ma'am. I'm Pastor Wallace, from Five Oaks Baptist. We're just down the road a piece."

"Oh!" she said, startled. "Hello. I'm Laurel MacDonald." She hesitated, then extended her hand to shake his, and felt he held hers a shade too long. But then again, so many men did. He smiled, a yellow-toothed smile.

"I heard we had guests at Folger again, and I thought I'd come by to welcome y'all."

"That's very kind of you," she said, pleasantly, but she was on alert. *Very early for a social call, isn't it?* "You were here before, though, weren't you? The day before yesterday."

His eyes narrowed slightly. "Yes, I often make this my morning walk. Keep an eye on the place ... make sure tramps don't get in."

Tramps? Is that so?

"I had no idea the other day that the house was occupied. I hope I didn't scare you," he added, and his eyes gleamed in a way that belied his words.

Laurel's mind was racing: Did she want to ask him into the house? But here was a chance to find out more about the Folgers—how could she pass that up?

The need to know won out over caution. "Will you come in for coffee?"

He smiled. "I believe I will."

She had again a moment of unease, which she attributed to city paranoia, then turned to lead him to the house.

After all, there are four of us and one of him. It will be fine.

She brought the pastor through the front entry of the old main house, and he stopped before the staircase, and looked

276

up at the stairs as though he saw someone there. She shut the door behind them and when she turned he was still looking at the stairs.

Finally, he broke his stare and looked to her. "It's been a long time." Laurel thought she heard something ambiguous in his tone.

She was already realizing she'd made a huge mistake by inviting him in. With the cameras and monitors set in up the great room and their young research subjects likely to come down—likely half-dressed—any moment, it was going to be next to impossible to keep him from asking the wrong questions.

"We're not really set up for entertaining," she hedged. "Why don't we sit in the library, and I'll bring coffee."

"As you like." He walked ahead of her, as if he knew the house, into the middle entry hall, through the paneled door into the dark book-lined study.

"I'll be right back," she called after him airily, stepping casually out through the door again, then racing across both entries, the great room, and the dining room, to the kitchen. She grabbed the whole pot of coffee and two cups from the counter, and hurried back. She was breathless by the time she reached the library, feeling as if she'd just done the hundred-meter dash.

She stopped for a second to catch her breath before she walked back into the study.

It was empty.

She froze ... then strode across the room and through the door of the garden room.

The pastor was there in the tiled, airy room, standing, gazing out through the arches of the outdoor patio.

Laurel realized with dismay that she had brought neither milk nor sugar. She was not going to leave him alone again.

The pastor turned and his eyes shone at her as if he knew what she was thinking. "Black will be fine, my dear."

She set the coffeepot down on one of the counters under a window and poured two cups, then crossed the floor and handed him a mug. "We just haven't had much time to settle in, and—"

"And settling in is not really what you're here for," he said jovially.

She jolted slightly and he smiled. Her mind scrambled back for something he'd said when they walked in. "So, you've been here before."

"Oh my, yes. Yes, we are acquainted, this house and I." He walked the room, sipping his coffee, trailing his hand over the windowsills and counters, which gave Laurel an unpleasant shiver, but she smiled brightly.

"I would love to hear about it. We haven't been able to find out that much about the Folgers, after a certain date."

"And what you have learned has been odd. Even— unsettling." His eyes gleamed again, he was practically purring.

She swallowed her distaste, and thought of the article she'd found in the upstairs den. She sat in one of the rattan chairs and sipped her coffee. "Is it true that Paul Folger was confined to Dorothea Dix Hospital after he was discharged from the Army? And that he came back to live here after one of the main buildings at Dix burned down?"

The pastor sat, spread his knees and leaned forward. "You are curious, no? You even have suspicions, perhaps?" In the dimness of the room, his eyes took her in with prurient interest. "Suspicions . . . of perversity?"

She felt her stomach turn in revulsion. And even though it was exactly what she had wondered, she said, "No. Nothing like that." She had a sudden body memory of an unknown weight on top of her in the dark, of breaking waves of pleasure. She drew in a breath and the pastor looked at her as if he knew, as if he could see.

"But the question must be asked. A young woman, alone with her disturbed brother. Refusing to put him back into the hospital, where he belonged. Never leaving the house herself. . . ." His voice trailed off insinuatingly.

She kept her voice level. "Is that what happened?"

278

He looked at her. "What do you *feel*?" He smiled at her, with yellowed teeth and flat eyes. "That is why you're here, aren't you? Because you can *feel* it? Because you *know* things?"

What she felt were goose bumps rising, and a sickening feeling of vertigo.

"They can't leave it alone, can they—this house," he said softly.

"Who can't?" Laurel said in spite of herself.

"The University, of course. The so-called *scientists*." He stared out through the windows at the main house and seemed to be far away for a moment. Then he turned to her. "And what do you think you're going to find? Are you sure you want to know? The hospital claimed more than one, you know."

"The hospital?" she repeated, confused. "You mean Dix? What do you mean?"

"Perversity," he said. "Perversity is what I mean. It's here." He looked around the house, breathed in deep. "It is still here."

As creeped out as she was, he knew far too much for her not to probe. "You know a lot about the University study," she said carefully. "How is that, Pastor Wallace? Were you living here in Five Oaks at the time?"

He smiled at her. "Oh, I have my ways."

She calculated quickly. He was probably in his mid-sixties; he would have been the age of a student at the time of the study.

"Did you know Dr. Leish? Rafe Winchester? Victoria Enright?"

He turned on her so suddenly she took a startled step back. "They didn't get out. No one did."

She felt a chill, hearing the same words she got from Uncle Morgan. The pastor's eyes were dully gleaming again and she realized that something about him was not right. And still she pressed on.

"They didn't get out? You mean, they died?"

"You are playing with something you don't understand. Open the door to the devil and the devil will walk through."

279

Spittle had formed in the corner of the pastor's mouth and his eyes were unfocused. There was something familiar in the cadence of the rant, but all Laurel could think about was getting away from him.

"I think you should go now," she said, and heard the tremor in her own voice.

"You think you can study it? You think it will yield its secrets? *It will not be known*," Wallace thundered. Laurel was frozen, unable to move.

"It's been waiting," he said softly. "It waits, like a spider. And eventually, the flies come, the busy little flies, the busy bees. They fly in. They fly in and are devoured. No one leaves."

Laurel walked straight to the French doors onto the covered porch and opened one. "Get out. Now."

He planted himself truculently. "You get out. Before it's too late."

"Go," she said. Her whole body was shaking.

He smiled, and said very softly, "No one leaves."

The pastor sidled past her with a knowing smile and stepped through the door. She shut it and shot the bolt, and stood by the windows, watching as he meandered around the side of the house, turning once to smile unpleasantly back toward her. Then she ran to the front hall to watch through the windows by the door, making sure he really walked down the drive toward the gateposts. She was shaking with adrenaline.

When the black figure had disappeared through the gateposts, she stepped back from the door, and rushed for the stairs. She rounded the corner at the landing in front of the arched window and nearly screamed as she ran into Brendan.

Chapter Forty-four

He took her arms, steadying her, and the story spilled out of her as they moved together down the stairs. "There was a man. Pastor Wallace, he said his name was," she said in a rush. "From the Baptist church down the road." *Except that they hadn't actually driven by a church, had they?*

"He knew about the Folger Experiment," she continued, her voice shrill with tension. "And he knew that we were here from Duke, somehow. I think . . . I think he's been watching the house—" She stepped into the archway of the great room, and stopped still, mid-sentence. Brendan bumped into her from behind.

"What—"

Then he stopped, too, staring.

There was a pool of water in the center of the floor, in the same place that they had first seen the footprints in the dust, a shallow pool about a foot and a half in diameter. There was something odd about it, and it took Laurel a moment to identify it: the pool was almost perfectly round.

She felt a flare of fury, and started across the floor toward it.

"Wait!" Brendan caught her arm. "Mickey, wait. Let me measure and get photographs—"

Laurel shook herself free of his hold. "Why? *He* did it, obviously."

Brendan turned and looked at her. "Wait, Mickey, did you see him do it?"

281

"No, I—"

He interrupted her. "Where was he?"

"I put him in the library, and then I went for coffee," she started, defensively.

"So he was three rooms away?"

She opened her mouth to respond, then was silent. It was starting to sound odd.

"And you went through this way to the kitchen"—Brendan pointed, then turned—"and you came back through this room on the way to the library? Was there a pool here when you brought the coffee back through?" Laurel saw where this was going. Brendan lifted his hands. "If he'd followed you and poured water out, you would have seen it when you walked back through the room."

"He knows the house," she protested. She stepped to the tall back windows and looked toward the garden room, on its perpendicular angle to the main house. "When I went back, he was in the garden room. He could have gone out through the outside door and walked in through that one." She pointed to the French door of the great room.

Brendan walked to the door and tried the knob. It was locked.

"Then he has a key," she insisted. "He's been watching the house. I saw him in the garden the second day we were here."

Brendan looked toward the pool of water. "But why? Why would he do *that*? Specifically that?"

"Why would he come here at all?" she said, her voice raw. "He has some weird thing about the house, and he obviously doesn't like us being here—"

"All right, then, all right," Brendan said, and his placating tone just infuriated her more. "Why don't you start from the beginning and tell me what he said."

Laurel looked out the French doors to the veranda, the gardens beyond. "He knew all about the experiment, and about Paul and Caroline Folger, too. He thinks the house is evil." *Well, so?* She was already answering herself in her own head. *He's a small-town minister, it's not exactly a stretch.*

Brendan was already smiling. "Honey, that's what ministers say. These fire and brimstone guys down here ... I have news. You're evil, too, and I'm definitely evil. We're all going straight to hell."

"He knew about the experiment. He talked about the University being here, to study the house, and he knew that that's why we're here."

Brendan stopped smiling. "Well, that's interesting," he admitted. "I wonder what else he knows?"

No one ever got out, is what he knows, she thought, with a chill. And then she frowned, realizing. *But that's not right, because Rafe's sister said that Rafe was living on the streets in Atlanta after—* and then she stopped, and there was a thought there, just out of reach. ...

Brendan was speaking again, oblivious to her sudden turmoil. "But that doesn't mean he put that water there. That's what we have monitors for." He crossed to the bank of monitors and reached to rewind the tape—and his face darkened. "It's off," he muttered. He looked at the time code. "Stopped at 7:30 A.M."—he checked his own watch—"forty-five minutes ago." He stared at it, turned to her abruptly. "Did you turn off the cameras?"

She felt her face flush. "Of course not," she said in total disbelief. "I can't believe you'd even ask."

He turned back to the monitor without responding and backed up the recording. The screen image showed the room with no puddle of water.

Laurel was feeling a growing sense of unreality. "It was the minister ... pastor. He turned off the monitor, he poured water on the floor. He was right here when this happened, Brendan, of course that's what happened."

She could feel his impatience rising. "Why are you doing this?"

"What am I doing?"

"Why are you fighting this so hard?"

"We're supposed to be objective—"

"You're not being objective. You're looking for reasons to poke holes in everything that happens."

That stopped her for a moment, and of course the truth was, she was afraid. Things were moving too fast and she didn't know who she could trust, and she didn't like the feeling of skidding out of control.

She forced herself to be calm, forced quiet into her voice. "The pastor came in. At the same time that he was in the house, the monitors were turned off and that water poured on the floor. There's no mystery about it."

Brendan took her shoulders and forcibly turned her toward the pool of water. "Look at that water, Mickey. Look at it. Have you ever seen water poured in that perfect a circle? That's a characteristic of pools of water in the literature."

Now she was starting to feel crazy herself. Something was real that she'd thought was just in her imagination and it was wobbling her sense of reality. She pulled free of his grasp.

"All right, then he poured out the water in a perfect circle. He knows about the study, Brendan. He would know how it's supposed to look. You're seeing what you want to see."

Brendan looked at her with a stony expression, then turned his back on her without another word, returning to the monitors.

She stared at his back, then turned and walked out of the room, carefully steering clear of the pool of water.

Upstairs she stalked the length of the hallway, past Katrina's closed door, through the lounge and linens room, to Tyler's little room at the end of the house. She knocked sharply and he answered, "It's open," in an awake enough voice. She opened the door and saw him lounged back on the bed, with a book splayed on his bare chest. She jolted a little at the raw sensuality of the picture. He smiled lazily, seeing her, as if she'd come to service him.

"I need your iPhone," she said.

He assumed a look of injured innocence. "But Dr. MacDonald, you said phones were off-limits—"

"Just hand it over. Are you getting reception?"

284

He opened the drawer of the nightstand beside the bed, and tossed her the phone. She caught it with a steel resolve that surprised her.

"On and off," Tyler answered. "Outside is best. Anything else I can help with?"

"I'll bring it back," she said, ignoring his inviting look.

"Well, just let me know what I can do," he said, with a smile that was not a smile.

And for a moment they were together there in that little room of endless white that was no place on earth ...

She turned on her heel and walked out, closing the door behind her.

Back in her own room she locked the door and sat on the bed, dialed 411 to get the number for the Five Oaks Baptist Church. Tyler's phone did get reception and the cheerful church secretary confirmed Pastor Wallace had been with the church for ten years now.

Laurel sat with the phone pressed to her cheek, her mind racing.

Just ten years? *So how does he know about the house? Or more specifically, how does he know about the Folger Experiment? That was over forty years ago, and he's only been here ten. Leish's study, the Folger Experiment, everything that happened at that house was meticulously covered up. So how does he know?*

And why would he fake a poltergeist manifestation?

"Where is Pastor Wallace from, originally, do you know?" she said into the phone.

"He came to us from upstate New York," the secretary responded.

That doesn't fit, either, Laurel thought. *He has a Southern accent as thick as molasses. So maybe he was here before, and knew about the study?*

"Oh, so he's not from around here originally?"

"Not that I ever heard of, ma'am."

"Thank you for your help." Laurel clicked off the phone.

He's mid-sixties. He could have been a student at the time.

285

A lurking suspicion started to grow. *A Duke student?* she wondered. *He could have been ...*

And then the thought that had been just out of reach a moment ago dropped into place.

The pastor's religious ranting. *"Lewdness and perversity."* *"Open the door to the devil, and the devil will walk through."*

She'd heard it before.

She looked up at the raven lithograph above the desk. "Why is a raven like a writing desk?" she said aloud.

She stood, opened the door of her room, and walked down the hall to the library.

She crossed to the shelf where she had seen the Duke yearbook from 1965, and grabbed the navy blue volume. She dropped onto one of the window seats, opened the book, and flipped to the section that was so familiar to her by now—the section with the photos of the Rhine lab.

She stared down at the testing photos, at the black-haired young man she had identified as Rafe Winchester. Those unnervingly intense eyes, and the cowlick was unmistakable.

The same cowlick as Pastor Wallace's. The pastor was Rafe Winchester.

Could it really be? Had Rafe Winchester been in this town all along?

Doing what?

She looked out the window, out toward the gateposts. The yard was empty; no sign of the black-clad figure.

I keep an eye on the house, he'd said.

Was that actually, literally true? Had he set himself up as a guardian?

Of what? Against what?

She stood and put the book down on the window seat and circled the room, trying to work through what she knew.

Rafe had been here—a part of the original Folger Experiment. He had known Leish, and Victoria Enright, and possibly her Uncle Morgan. (And what had Uncle Morgan

286

said? *"They never came back."* And Rafe: *"They didn't get out. No one did."*)

But Rafe Winchester/Pastor Wallace did make it out of the house.

Or did he, really? Certainly he may not have made it out intact. Not with his whole mind. There were years on the streets, drugs, degradation ... and then apparently a turnabout at some point—a return to religion.

But not to sanity. He may have made himself a place in the community, but there was nothing right about him.

He had seen what had gone on in the house, had experienced it; he might know details of Leish's death, and details of Uncle Morgan's ... *breakdown? Shattering?*

Laurel was certain that the timing of the pastor's visit and the "manifestations" in the great room were not coincidental.

She felt a powerful need to find out more about him, and a sense that it couldn't wait. The pastor knew a lot about the house, and he wasn't right in the head. If he was lurking around, and even possibly had a key to the house, she wanted to know as much about him as she could find. She forced herself to think through the specifics of what he'd said.

Perversity. A young woman alone with her unstable brother. Laurel flinched at the thought, but it provided a motive for a murder/suicide, if there had been one, and the pastor had confirmed the story of Caroline Folger taking in and caring for a schizophrenic Paul.

And then that strange statement: *"The hospital claimed more than one."*

The hospital.

She sat at a round table, pulled Tyler's iPhone out of her pocket and called information again, this time asked for and was connected to Dorothea Dix Hospital.

"I'm Dr. MacDonald, from Duke Medical," she said, then took a breath and took the plunge. "I'm calling about a patient." She mentally crossed her fingers and said the name.

And maybe it was the Duke reference that did it, or maybe she was just lucky, because the receptionist actually answered

287

her, with a bit of information that floored Laurel ... at the same time that she had been completely, utterly sure that she would hear it.

Victoria Enright was committed to Dix mental hospital in April of 1965 and had resided there ever since.

There was no one in the upstairs hall, and Katrina's bedroom door was closed, as Laurel took an outwardly leisurely walk back toward her room. Inside her thoughts were racing. *Front stairs or back? How do I get out without drawing attention?*

Brendan was likely still in the great room, obsessing over the pool in the living room, which made the back stairs a safer bet. Then Laurel's stomach dropped as she realized: *If he's at the monitors, no matter which stairs I take he'll be able to see me walking down the hall. He'll know I'm leaving.*

She stopped at her bedroom door and stepped into the room, found her purse on the writing desk, and reached into it for her wallet and keys. Then she put the purse under the bed, slipped her wallet and keys and Tyler's phone into her pant pockets, and pulled a sweater on over her head to conceal the bulges in her pockets.

She opened her door and shut it behind her, and walked down the hall toward the back, again affecting an idle stroll. She moved through the den, pausing to browse at the titles of books on the shelf, and selected one without actually registering the title. It was all to show Brendan that she was not going anywhere. And the feeling of being watched was overwhelming; she felt as if she were a rat in a maze in a lab.

She strolled out of the den with her book and walked down the short set of stairs to the last part of the hall. The door of Tyler's room next to the kitchen was shut, as she had left it. She moved casually into the kitchen and took a minute there to rummage in the random snack food spread out on the table. She selected a green apple and bit into it, looking contemplative. Then she turned and walked down the stairs, again, with apple and book, pausing to look out the window at the landing, gazing out over the back garden ...

Then she walked down the last stairs to the back door, bracing herself for Brendan to call her name—but not a word.

Fuck the house quarantine, she thought grimly. *We're getting some answers today.* She eased the back door open, stepped out of the house, and hurried down the gravel drive toward her car.

Chapter Forty-five

Dorothea Dix was a large complex of buildings scattered over several hundred acres of gently rolling hills near downtown Raleigh. Laurel drove past a lush vineyard and a small cemetery as she wound the Volvo up the hill. The Romanesque buildings of the central compound looked more like a private university than a mental institution—until she got a glimpse of the spiral razor-ribbon wire layered on top of the abnormally tall fences.

Laurel had lucked out with her first phone call, but the formidable nurse at the reception desk—her name badge read "Delphine"—saw through her instantly.

"You're not Miz Enright's doctor and you're no relative. What business you think you got with her?"

Laurel opted for the truth. "She was involved in a study at the university in 1965 that I believe might have something to do with her condition." She held her breath, hoping against hope.

Delphine looked at her in disbelief. "What kind of *study* you figure would bring on catatonic schizophrenia?"

So it's schizophrenia. Like Paul Folger. Laurel didn't like the parallel one bit.

"I don't know," she said aloud. "That's what I was hoping to find out from her."

The nurse shook her head. "You're not going to be getting

anything out of her," she informed Laurel. "She hasn't talked in all the time I've been here."

"Can I see her?" Laurel asked, without much hope. "Not talk to her," she said quickly, as the massive nurse frowned. "I just want to see her." She could not have said why, except that Victoria was a living link to the past, even if that link was broken.

The nurse looked hard at Laurel, then to Laurel's vast surprise, she turned silently and nodded her head toward the stairwell.

Laurel followed the nurse's regally swaying bulk up two flights of institutionally green stairs. They came out on a ward with the familiar stench of urine and the faintly goatish smell of hebephrenic schizophrenia; Laurel had done a semester of field work in UCLA's psych ward and the memory of that smell was like an old and disturbing dream.

The doors of the patient rooms were locked and solid, with foot-square observation windows, the inset glass laced with wire.

Delphine stopped in front of a room and indicated the window.

Laurel looked in on a small, sad room. A stooped, elderly woman sat in the one straight-backed chair. She looked far older than mid-sixties ... her cheeks sunken and hollow, her hospital gown hanging on bony shoulders. But her hair was still thick, with traces left of the luxurious chestnut it must once have been. She did not move, but for a moment her eyes seemed to lock on Laurel's through the threaded glass of the window, and though her face remained still, her pupils dilated, with recognition or horror.

Laurel stepped quickly back from the window and found Delphine watching her. "I'm asking myself," the nurse said dryly. "I've been here fourteen years and in all that time no one's ever come to see Victoria. Her mama died twenty years ago. Then suddenly she gets two visitors in a month. How about that?"

Laurel stared at the nurse. "Who was the other?"

291

The nurse lifted her shoulders. "I wasn't here. Only heard about it. But it had to be a relative, I'm thinking. They let him in to see her."

Laurel herself had not been able to find any of Victoria's relatives; neither her Google searches, nor the Duke alumni records, nor the actual alumni she'd talked to had any leads for her. Laurel's mind raced through possibilities, something solid in the rush of confusing new information.

"Has Victoria been catatonic since 1965?" Laurel asked. Contrary to general belief, catatonia did not necessarily mean that a patient remained mute and frozen for all time—there could be phases of manic energy, or fairly normal movement.

The nurse shrugged. "Far as I know. She's a strong one, to last this long."

Horrible, Laurel thought. *What hell . . . to be trapped in your own mind, in your own body like that.*

The nurse fixed her gaze on Laurel and with her next question Laurel understood why the nurse had talked to her.

"What was this study that did that to Victoria?"

Laurel found herself suddenly unable to speak. "I don't know," she said finally, haunted. "I'm trying to find out."

Down the hall from them, a door opened and several orderlies herded out a group of about a dozen patients. Some were clearly medicated to the gills, drooling and shuffling. One wizened old man muttered and twisted a strand of unkempt hair. A tall black man with an overbite lurched forward, with his eyes rolled up in his head. Beside him a grossly fat woman cackled with laughter.

They stumbled toward Laurel and Delphine, a parade of mad souls.

Lost . . . lost and mindless . . .

Laurel felt her stomach drop. The walls felt as if they were closing in around her and she was flooded with a sudden terror that if she didn't get out now, she would never get out.

She inched backward toward the stairs. "I . . . I have to go," she barely managed to say aloud to Delphine. "I appreciate your help." She pushed through the stairwell door, escaping, the sound of the patients gibbering and catcalling echoing behind her.

The drive back to Five Oaks, and the Folger House, was just under an hour, and Laurel still felt the lingering, claustrophobic horror of the hospital as the houses and farms disappeared around her and she drove into the isolation of the pine barrens. The image of Victoria, locked forever behind that door, haunted her.

Committed to Dix in April 1965. *Like Paul Folger.* Catatonic. *What had she seen, that would keep her imprisoned in her own mind for forty-two years? What had she done?*

Leish: dead. Victoria: institutionalized. Rafe Winchester ... Pastor Wallace ... certainly unbalanced at the least. And Uncle Morgan: shattered in some way she could not explain.

She felt sick with a fear she was just beginning to identify.

Is there something in that house?

Did they see something, do something, experience something? Something that whatever it is causes—

Madness?

She saw again the parade of lunatic patients, and shivered.

We have to get out. I have to get them out.

She stepped on the gas.

Chapter Forty-six

The wispy fog of the morning had thickened to soup. When Laurel drove back through the stone gateposts, there was a fog beyond them that rendered the entire landscape insubstantial.

She motored slowly on the road, past the rail fence and the crape myrtles, all shrouded in mist. The gray pebbled path wound in and out through trees; there was no sign of the house in the fog.

And then suddenly it was there, in front of her, the porch so close that Laurel slammed on the brakes and the car came to a jolting stop beside Tyler's Maserati.

The house was silent as she let herself in. Walking into the entry felt like being swallowed.

Why? What's changed?

It was so quiet.

She walked across the first entry, and into the second, with the hearth and the family painting ...

Not a sound.

She found Brendan and both students in the great room. They had placed chairs at some distance around the pool of water, which seemed exactly as it had been when Laurel had left, and the three were seated in a circle, each holding a clipboard poised in their lap, just watching the pool. Someone had taped three straight parallel lines of duct tape on the floor beside the pool and marked each tape with inches, like a ruler.

There were notations handwritten in marker at various points along the scales. Brendan and both of the students held clipboards, and they did not move when Laurel stepped through the archway.

"What are you doing?" Laurel said, her voice hollow in the room, and was unnerved when for a prolonged beat, not one of them looked up. "Professor Cody?" she asked, more loudly, her heart beating faster.

Brendan finally pulled his gaze from the pool and looked at her blankly, without speaking.

"What are you doing?" she asked again.

"It keeps coming back," he said, and his voice was alarmingly vague. "We've wiped it up three times now, and each time it wells up again." He waved a hand toward a plastic tub with several sopping towels piled up in it. "It comes up from the floorboards. It takes forty minutes for the entire pool to appear, and then it stops growing. It doesn't get any bigger than seventeen inches in diameter—it just stops at exactly seventeen inches."

Laurel noted with unease that Tyler and Katrina had not looked up during Brendan's entire speech—they remained fixed on the pool. She had the sudden feeling that they were playing with her—that it was all an elaborate joke.

"So ... you've been doing this all day," she said, her voice brittle.

"Yes," Brendan said, puzzled. "Of course. This is what we're here for, Dr. MacDonald. It's a demonstrable anomaly, a classic manifestation. We have it recorded, too." He waved toward the monitors without looking away from the pool. "And the EMF readings are three times normal levels: they've been fluctuating between eight and nine-five for three hours."

Laurel looked toward the archway of the great room, and then toward the dining room. "The house is built on inclines," she said, keeping her voice even. "We'll need to check with a structural engineer or a geologist. It's very possible there's a perfectly explicable structural cause."

Brendan's eyes darkened with anger. "Of course," he said stiffly. "I'll make some calls tomorrow."

"I need to talk to you," she said, and glanced at the students. "Tyler. Katrina," she spoke more sharply than she intended. Again, the two did not look up. "Tyler. Katrina. You've been at that long enough." Suddenly it was very important to get them to look away from the pool.

Laurel stepped closer to them and looked down at Tyler's clipboard. There were random words scribbled on it—nothing like a sentence, just words: *shimmer growing round watching moving breathing*.

"I think we should break for dinner," she said, too loudly. "Tyler."

"Things are finally starting to happen, Dr. MacDonald," he said, without looking at her. "We can't break now."

Laurel stared at him in disbelief. *Is he actually being serious?*

Laurel stepped closer to Katrina, who just clutched her clipboard to her chest protectively and continued to stare into the pool.

Laurel turned to Brendan. "We need to talk *now*."

Irritation bordering on anger flickered across his face, but Brendan rose and followed her out of the room, through the entry hall, into the small library.

She closed the door behind him. Brendan hovered beside the door, not taking a seat, as if ready to bolt any second. "I think we need to leave," Laurel said, and immediately knew it was not the way to start.

He half-laughed. "Mickey, we're not leaving. The house is just starting to activate."

"It's a pool of water," she said.

"It's a pool of water that has formed itself in the exact spot, at the same rate of speed, in the exact dimensions—three times in a row, now." His voice was patient, logical. For a moment Laurel felt like screaming, just to break his impenetrable wall of calm. Instead she tried a different tack.

"Don't you want to know where I was, today?"

"Where were you?" he asked dutifully, without a hint that he'd even noticed she was gone.

"Dorothea Dix."

He looked at her blankly, and finally it registered. "The asylum? In Raleigh? Why?"

"I found Victoria Enright. She was institutionalized in April 1965, with a diagnosis of catatonic schizophrenia." In her mind Laurel saw Victoria again, slumped in her chair, hollow-cheeked, eyes dilated with horror . . .

"You left the house?" Brendan said, with a flare of ire. "We agreed not to do that."

"Brendan, are you not listening to me? Victoria Enright participated in the Folger Experiment in 1965, and she has been in a mental institution ever since."

Brendan sat on the edge of the peacock-covered love seat.

"Mickey, first of all, you don't know that this Victoria Enright had anything to do with the Folger House. She was in a photo in a yearbook. What does that prove? You're making huge logical leaps."

"It's not just Victoria," Laurel said. "It's all of them. We know Leish died. Rafe Winchester—"

"You aren't really going to tell me that Rafe Winchester is at Dix, too."

"Pastor Wallace is Rafe Winchester."

He stared at her incredulously. "How do you know?"

She hesitated. "The yearbook photo."

"The yearbook photo," he said again, as if that ended the discussion. "That's all the proof you have of all of this? A forty-two-year-old photo?"

"He's the right age. He knows about the experiment." She knew it sounded flimsy.

Brendan stared at her through the dim of the library, and his voice was suddenly gentle. "All right, stop. You are now officially freaking yourself out over nothing. This is not proof—it's wild speculation, Mickey."

"We can't take a chance. We're responsible for the well-being of two students. We're shutting this down."

His face closed and he stood. "You can leave if you want to. But I'm not."

He started for the door and she turned on him. "We can't keep these kids here when we don't know what might happen."

He halted by the door, in front of the ship in its glass case. He was looking at her with interest, now. "So you really think we're in danger? From what?"

She stopped short, confused. Was she really thinking there was a ... not a ghost, but some kind of danger, evil—in the house? Something that could actually cause madness, even death?

"I ... didn't say that."

"What, then?"

Yes, what?

"People died here. Paul and Caroline Folger. Leish ..."

"But that was over forty years ago," he said patiently.

"Leish died while doing the exact same thing we are doing." She was aware that her voice was rising, and that it made her sound unbalanced.

"We don't know it was while he was engaged in the experiment. You're making it sound like he died at the house, and you don't know that." He laughed, but there was no mockery in the sound. "Laurel, you've read all the same literature I have. People don't get hurt by poltergeists. They certainly don't get killed by them. Something may have happened, maybe even something terrible, but that part of it was human, not supernatural. What could that possibly have to do with us? I just don't see where you think the danger is, here."

"Victoria ..." She swallowed, felt her voice breaking. "She's been catatonic for over forty years ..."

His voice dropped, soft and comforting. "I'm sure it was unpleasant to see her. But mental illness is biochemical, Laurel. You don't develop schizophrenia from trauma. You know that. Whatever is wrong with her has nothing to do with this house, or with us. She can't do us any harm."

"The pastor can. Whoever he is, he's not stable," Laurel said, grabbing on to something tangible. "It's not safe for any of us,

298

having someone like that wandering around."

"A sixty-year-old man? How much of a threat can he be?" he said lightly.

But Brendan had not met the man, had not felt the madness emanating from him.

"You didn't meet him."

"No, I didn't. In fact I haven't even seen him," he said pointedly.

She felt suddenly short of breath. "Are you saying I made him up?"

"Of course not," Brendan said reassuringly, but it sounded hollow to her. She looked in the direction of the great room, where the students were.

"You can't afford to be dismissive when we have two students working for us," she repeated. "We're responsible for their safety."

"First of all, I haven't seen anything remotely like danger in this situation, and second, Laurel, they're adults. Being here is entirely their choice."

She wanted to laugh at the idea that their two subjects were adults. Twenty-one was barely the age of reason.

"But they don't know."

"Know what?"

They don't know what I know and don't know.

She lifted her chin. "They don't know any of this. It's time to tell them."

He stood looking at her for a moment, then turned up the palms of his hands. "All right. Let's tell them."

They found Tyler and Katrina standing over the monitors, their chairs beside the pool of water abandoned.

Brendan was instantly alert. "What? Did something happen?"

Tyler looked up with a scowl, and Katrina tendered Laurel one of her patented loathing looks. "No—it's stopped happening," Tyler said. "The pool stopped growing. It's been at ten inches for half an hour—"

"Since *she* came back," Katrina said pointedly, with a sideways glance at Laurel.

"The EMF readings have dropped back to normal, too," Tyler said, without looking toward Laurel himself.

"Good. We all need to talk," Laurel said firmly.

Chapter Forty-seven

The three of them refused to budge from the room, in case the pool "became active" again, so they were seated stiffly in the embroidered straight-backed chairs with the pool of water at their feet.

"We both feel you should know," Laurel looked from Katrina to Tyler. "There's more that's gone on in this house than we knew going into this investigation. There was a murder/suicide here—a sister and a brother, Caroline and Paul Folger. Paul Folger was discharged from the army because of paranoid delusions—he suffered from schizophrenia. The family kept him here instead of institutionalizing him. . . ." She glanced at Brendan, who was pointedly not looking at her. "They kept him in this house for fifteen years, until the sister killed him and herself on the same day."

She looked from Tyler to Katrina. They were watching her, Katrina with a blank and unreadable look, Tyler with a faint smile. He raised his eyebrows, as if inviting her to go on.

"The Duke group who came here in 1965 did so after a report of poltergeist activity. It was an experiment—the one that we're duplicating. It ended . . . badly. The researcher in charge of the investigation died, and as far as we've been able to determine, at least two of the student participants, maybe all three of them, suffered severe mental trauma." She paused to let that sink in, and looked again from Tyler to Katrina.

"I'm sorry for my part in bringing you here, because I feel strongly that we don't know enough about what we're dealing with and we need to terminate the experiment and leave this house." She looked around at all of them. She could feel Brendan bristling beside her, and Katrina's contempt, rolling off her in waves. Tyler was studying her, a thoughtful, curious gaze.

"This guy ... this researcher—" he began.

"Leish," Laurel supplied.

Tyler raised an eyebrow. "Leish. You mean the guy who wrote that article?" Laurel nodded. "How did he die?"

"We don't know that. But he died in the same month as the experiment." Laurel could hear the agitation in her own voice.

"And then what happened?"

"Well, the lab was shut down, and the files were sealed. They were only recently opened, in fact."

Tyler leaned forward, elbows on his knees, and looked intently at Laurel. "I don't think I get it. Those things happened—when?"

Brendan spoke before Laurel could. "Over forty years ago. Both of them."

Tyler barely glanced at him, his attention was completely on Laurel. "So you're thinking—we're in some kind of danger from that? Forty years later?"

Laurel found her certainty wavering, just as when Brendan had asked the same question. It did sound far-fetched when anyone said it aloud.

She looked at the reflection of the group in the cloudy mirrors on the walls.

"Is this because of that trauma imprint you were talking about?" Now Tyler did look at Brendan.

"It's one of the theories," Brendan answered. "That an imprint of trauma—an echo—can remain in a house."

"And it could *hurt* us?" Katrina was taking her cues from Brendan; her voice fairly dripped condescension.

"I have never read or seen any proof of that. Ever. We wouldn't be here if I thought that," Brendan assured her.

"So what do you think got imprinted, Dr. MacDonald?" Tyler asked. "Are you saying that the murder/suicide got imprinted on the house and somehow caused someone else's death? Or caused someone else to go nuts?"

I don't like the coincidence, Laurel thought.

"It is a creepy coincidence, I guess," Tyler said, and hearing her own thought voiced, she started, staring at him. "But it was forty years ago. Could an imprint last that long, Dr. Cody?" he said, turning to Brendan with that fake, interested-student look.

"It's a paranormal theory," Brendan said. "There's no proof about any of these things."

Laurel again felt caught in an undertow, mocked, and helpless to do anything about it.

"Well, seems to me that in the interest of science we should be staying right here and doing our job," Tyler said, with exaggerated seriousness. Without budging an inch, Katrina gave the impression of having moved even closer to Brendan. "Especially with what we've seen this afternoon," Tyler added disingenuously, giving Brendan an obsequious look, completely false. "We can't possibly abandon the mission now."

The three of them looked up at Laurel from their chairs, united. Laurel stood quietly, then dropped her head. "All right." She turned and walked from the room.

Just as she reached the archway, Tyler said behind her: "Where did they keep the brother, by the way?"

She stopped and looked at him. "I don't know, Tyler." She moved out of the room, inwardly flinching as she had to pass through the arched doorway.

As she climbed the stairs, Tyler's question echoed in her head. *"Where did they keep the brother?"*

"I don't know, Tyler."

In the entry beside the staircase, she stopped and looked out on the garden.

But don't you?

Laurel walked down the upstairs hall, now nearly dark in the deepening twilight. But instead of going into her room, she continued on toward the middle room with the narrow door. Brendan's room.

Paul Folger's room.

She reached out for the knob—then there was a flicker of white in the corner of her eye. She spun around—

And gasped at the sight of a pale figure standing in the dark of the hall. Katrina stepped forward. The blond girl looked Laurel over disdainfully.

"Why don't you just leave, Dr. MacDonald? If it's bothering you so much? Why don't you just go? Why stay? Just go."

Laurel was breathless from the venom in the girl's words.

Why don't I? I will.

So she packed. She stalked past Katrina, back to her bedroom, where she slammed the door behind her like a teenager and stood in the middle of the floor. The sun was sinking behind the trees outside, darkening the room, and she switched on the light.

Without giving herself time to talk herself out of it, she strode to the clothes cabinet. The door was shut and as she reached for the knob, she froze, suddenly overcome with trepidation, an almost paralyzing fear that she'd open the door and find ... something—her clothes on the floor again, some other sign of derangement.

And what if they are? she told herself impatiently. *What difference does it make, now? You'll be out in fifteen minutes. Just pack up and go.*

But she literally had to force her hand from her side. She twisted the knob and pulled open the door.

Her clothes were lined up on hangers, perfectly normal.

She pulled her suitcase off the floor, opened it on the bed, and grabbed an armful of clothes.

Downstairs she stopped in the archway of the great room with her suitcase and looked in on them without stepping through the doorway. They were lined up at the monitors, now looking at footage of themselves seated on chairs watching the pool.

Laurel cleared her throat. "I'm going now. If anyone wants to come with me, I'll wait."

The three of them simply looked at her, with no discernible expression.

She turned with her suitcase and went to the door.

Outside, twilight was darkening the sky between the tall spikes of pine trees. The cold, spicy smell of sap was in the air. Brendan followed her out into the drive. "Laurel, you can't drive in the dark. How will you even find your way out of here?"

She ignored him and got into the Volvo, beside Tyler's Maserati.

The car wouldn't start.

She sat in the driver's seat, with Brendan standing outside. She turned the key over and over again, but there was nothing but clicking. Brendan peered through the window from outside, tapped softly on the glass.

She put her head on the steering wheel. *They've sabotaged the car,* she thought wearily. *They're not going to let me leave.*

Brendan opened the car door. "Come on," he said. "Get out."

Defeated, she pulled the key out of the ignition, slid out of the car, and stood. To her surprise, Brendan took the key from her, got into the car. He turned the key in the ignition and it started immediately. He got out and held the door for her, but as she moved past him he caught her hand and held it. "Please don't." They stood in the dark, not moving, not looking at each other. She could feel his breathing, could feel his heat in every cell of her body. "At least . . . stay tonight."

And she knew that no matter what, she was staying: she was caught, and it was not the house that had caught her.

When Laurel finally stepped away from him and turned toward the house, Katrina stood framed in a window of the great room, watching them.

She didn't talk to anyone on her way up the stairs, just went to her room and stayed there. But when she heard them going up the stairs she slipped back down herself and checked all the doors.

Locking someone out—when in all likelihood whatever they had to fear was already in.

305

Chapter Forty-eight

Voices.

Laurel jolted out of sleep and lay with her heart pounding, her eyes wide.

There. *Voices.* Talking, ranting, raging.

She felt a frisson of blind panic, wild, random thoughts. *I should have left, I should have gotten out. Too late, too late ...*

Stop it, she commanded. *Pull yourself together.*

She strained to hear in the darkness. The voices had stopped.

She threw off her blankets and made herself stand, and fumbled for the light switch. The light went on ... which instantly made her feel better.

She unlocked her door and looked out into the hall. It was dark, and silent, and still. Beyond the arched doorway was pitch black. She left her bedroom light on, but they had not put bulbs up and down the hall; it would have taken several dozen for the upstairs hall alone.

There was another short burst of voices, very faint, seemingly from somewhere in the Spanish part of the house. She felt a rush of fear unlike anything she'd experienced since the random nighttime terrors of childhood.

How badly do you want to know?

She almost turned back into her room, and then had the horrible thought that Katrina had found Brendan, and they were laughing together somewhere in the house.

She steeled herself and stepped forward. The light spilling from her bedroom lit her way for the first few yards, but then the hall jogged and she was plunged into darkness again.

In the dark, the unevenness of the floor was magnified. As she edged forward, she could feel the floor rising and falling underneath her bare feet; it *rolled*. The floorboards were smooth as glass, though, like satin under her feet.

She jogged right again and carefully descended a set of steps, feeling ahead with one foot at a time. *This must be that little sitting room with the cabinets,* she thought . . . then something soft and cool brushed her bare calf and she almost shrieked. She put her hand out and felt leather; the smooth green leather divan.

Another jog to the right, and the archway at the end of the hall came into view. There was a thin spill of light coming from somewhere in the perpendicular wing.

She stepped through the arch and looked instinctively right, toward the library. The heavy dark door was closed, but there was a sliver of light underneath it . . . and Laurel heard a muffled burst of laughter.

She breathed in and walked silently to the door. She put her hand on the latch, and depressed it, pushing open the door.

Brendan was in the room, and a quick glance around it revealed him to be alone, sprawled in one of the big leather chairs, with a bottle at his feet and a full glass in his hand. His head was lolled against the back of the chair and he was looking up at the portraits. It was them he was talking to, singing to, a growly rowdy tune which Laurel recognized as an Irish traditional song popularized by several punk rock bands:

As I was a-walkin round Kilgary Mountain
I met Colonel Pepper and his money he was countin'
I rattled me pistols and I drew forth me saber,
Sayin' "Stand and deliver, for I am the bold deceiver!"
Musha rig um du rum da, Whack fol the daddy O
Whack fol the daddy O, there's whisky in the jar—

He jumped up suddenly, spinning toward the door. His face changed as he saw Laurel, and he swayed, just barely catching his balance. Then he beamed at her.

"Ah, lovely. Company. That is, 'Ah, lovely company.'" He corrected himself, bowing gallantly, with a little flourish. "Let me get you a drink." He staggered toward the built-in bar.

Laurel swallowed. This was drunk in a way she'd rarely had to deal with. *At least that hadn't been one of Matt's problems,* she thought, irrelevantly.

"We said we weren't going to drink while we were here," she said lightly.

"Ah." He pointed a finger at her. "But you see, I think we were wrong. This house was made for drinking. Much"—he slurred, so it came out *Mush*—"drinking was done here. The house likes it, that's my conclusion."

"I don't need one, really," Laurel said, trying not to let the alarm sound in her voice. "It's awfully late."

"Never too late," he said gaily, and poured a frightening amount of what looked like whiskey into a short glass.

"Let me get that," she said quickly, and crossed to him to take the glass before it could spill.

"Drink up, then," he said, and took a deep swig straight from the bottle. He looked at her expectantly. Laurel sipped from the glass and felt the amber burn.

"How about bed?" she suggested, and he smiled at her.

"I've been hoping you'd ask."

She blushed from her chest up, and he would not stop looking at her.

"Why don't you let me have that?" She reached for the bottle and he yanked it away from her.

"Oh no." He hugged the bottle to his chest and curled his arm around it protectively. "Oh no no no. Many before you have tried," he snickered.

"All right, then," she said carefully. "Let's talk." She sat on the wood bench of a window seat, watching him.

"Talk?" And suddenly his mood shifted, to something so dark she had no idea how she'd missed the transition. "What's

308

there to talk about? It's over. You're done, therefore we're done. We spent the day measuring a pool of water. A fucking pool of water. That's one for the books, all right." He drank again, and she winced. "S'not working, not working," he muttered agitatedly, and began a distracted prowl around the library.

He stopped, swaying, underneath the portrait of James Folger, and stared up at it. His eyes were hazy, as if he were seeing someone else. *Father?* Laurel wondered to herself. *Is that what this is about? It almost always is, with men.*

He laughed, harshly. "What's another failure, though, hmm? What else can we expect?" He slipped into a thick, savage brogue. "There's no belying birth, now, is there?"

He turned from the portrait abruptly. "Total failure. That's what you think, too."

"I don't think it's a failure," she said, and realized she didn't know what she thought. "I—just don't think we can afford to risk ..." Again, she was unable to say what she thought they were risking.

He suddenly turned and hurled his full glass at a blank spot on the wall, shattering it in a wide splash of amber liquid.

"Can't afford? Can't afford? Do you know how much is riding on this?"

Laurel stood in the middle of the floor, in shock. The glass had barely missed her; she smelled whiskey all around her. "No," she said softly. "What's riding on this?"

His face twisted, and for a moment he looked almost cruel. "You really don't see, do you?"

For a horrible moment she felt tears sting her eyes. The photographs and portraits looked down from the library walls. "I guess I don't," she managed, and started blindly for the door.

Brendan put out an arm to stop her as she pushed past him ... and then his arm was around her waist and he was pulling her against him. "Don't leave me ... ," he whispered, and then his hands were in her hair and his mouth was on hers and she was opening under him. His mouth moved down her

309

neck and she nearly passed out, sagging against him. He pressed his groin into hers and she could feel him throbbing against her. ... He was murmuring into her ear as he kissed along her jawline, "Oh God ..." and then his mouth was on hers again, and she was on fire. The couches were too small for two adult people but somehow they were on one, and somehow there was room, and his weight was on top of her, her hands were under his sweater, and her nipples were straining against his palms, and they were melting into each other.

"We can't, we can't," she said against his mouth but she was swooning. His tongue filled her again and his hand was between her legs and she was wet against his fingers, so wet ... and she didn't care.

Then suddenly, the room was plunged into darkness ... and a thunder of crashes shook the house, staccato hail, like the downstairs windows all being assaulted at once. Brendan and Laurel bolted up from the couch, staring into the dark, stupefied, paralyzed. The crashing went on, accelerating, deafening, and ending with a crash that was dissonantly musical, like a piano being dropped from a great height.

Then silence ... just the sound of their fast, harsh breathing.

Brendan was already reaching for his sweater, which had somehow come off, and Laurel pulled her sleep shirt back down over her breasts and her leggings back up around her hips, and they were running in the hall for the main stairs.

Brendan made it down first and was already disappearing through the archway into the great room as Laurel cleared the landing of the stairs.

She ran down after him ... and halted in the archway when she felt a sharp crackle of energy, like static. She gasped aloud, not sure what she'd felt. She blinked to focus.

In front of her the great room was a vast stretch of empty dark space—there was not even moonlight through the windows. The piano was a black shape in the corner of the room, where it had always been—and perfectly intact. The

310

room was darker than it should have been but she could not see why.

Brendan stood in the middle of the room, looking around him—at the piano, at the ceiling, at the walls.

"Was it in here?"

Laurel found her voice. "I ... don't know ... I thought so ..."

Brendan bolted across the room and disappeared into the dining room.

Laurel rushed across the floor after him, and gasped in terror at the sight of a white shape running beside her—then realized she was seeing her own reflection in the mirrors on the long front wall.

She stopped again in the door of the dining room.

Brendan paced the room beside the table, staring around in the dark at the clock, the mantel, the wood stove, the windows, the ceiling. "Nothing here, either."

A shadow loomed up in the opposite doorway and Laurel bit back a scream. It was Tyler, sleepily mussed but eyes wide. "What the fuck?"

"Did you see anything?" Brendan shouted at him.

There was a sound behind Laurel and she whirled again, to see Katrina in a baby doll nightgown, looking groggy, only half-awake, standing in the middle of the great room. "What happened?" she said, her voice fuzzy.

They all stood, staring at each other. The silence was deafening.

Then Laurel gasped aloud, her hand to her mouth, as the frozen grandfather clock in the corner began to tick.

Simultaneously a beeping started in the dark, faint, muffled. Brendan shoved a hand in his pocket and pulled out an object that Laurel realized was his EMF reader. He held it up in the center of the room. It continued to beep steadily, louder. "EMF is nine," Brendan said feverishly, reading the red numbers on the digital screen. He moved around to different spots in the room, the grandfather clock. "Nine ... ten ..." The beeping continued, shrilly.

311

"It's high," Tyler said warily. Laurel turned from the grandfather clock and came to a halt before the mantel, in front of the antique clock in the glass dome. Her heart plummeted as she saw it had started ticking as well, much more faintly. *Both clocks ...*

Brendan darted back into the great room and as the others followed he paced the room with his EMF reader, monitoring the levels. "Eight, nine ... eleven ..."

Tyler grabbed another EMF reader from the table beside the monitors and switched it on. It immediately started beeping shrilly in counterpoint with Brendan's. Tyler walked the room on the opposite side. "Nine ... ten ... the whole room is hot."

Brendan crossed to the equipment caddy and they all crowded in front of the bank of monitors. The beeping continued from the EMF readers, and Brendan said harshly to Tyler, "Shut it off," as he clicked off his own. Tyler followed suit. Brendan backed up the recordings for the cameras in both rooms and the group stood tensely, watching the double screens as the video recorders replayed.

Each showed a fuzzy picture of a dark room, the great room and the dining room, with faint video glow. After interminable minutes there was the sudden frenzied crashing through the speakers. The sound levels jumped crazily; but the video picture of the rooms didn't change at all. Brendan leaned closer, staring at the screen. "I don't see anything."

"Nothing," Tyler agreed tensely, his eyes glued to the screen.

Onscreen there was a sudden muffled pounding and Brendan ran into the great room, barefooted, hair mussed, his sweater hanging on him. After a moment Laurel ran in after him.

Watching herself on the screen, Laurel was absurdly relieved that she looked reasonably dressed.

One after the other, Brendan then Laurel ran across the great room on one screen and appeared on the next screen in the dining room.

Tyler ran in from the opposite side of the room and they all

312

stood shouting at each other, Brendan looking up at the video screen. Katrina appeared onscreen in the great room.

Brendan leaned forward abruptly and backed up the recording. They watched the same sequence again, in slow motion. Aside from the crashing sounds, there was no other sign of anything going on.

Brendan hit Replay and they waited in silence for the recording to back up.

But no matter how many times they watched there was nothing to be seen.

Chapter Forty-nine

She lay in her narrow bed, trying not to let on that she was awake. A man ... she knew it was a man ... stood in her room, a man with a clipboard, standing over her, watching. There was a heaviness beside her, holding the blankets down—

Laurel forced open her eyes. The room was filled with gray light, and empty. No sign of the man with the clipboard. But there was something cold and hard in bed with her, pinning the blankets so she couldn't move. She gasped and shoved out, and there were multiple loud *THUMP*s on the floor. She froze, fighting against panic.

Some of the heavy pressure was gone, but not all. She reached out gingerly—and her hand found a rough hard lump. She closed her fist around it.

A rock?

She sat up and in the dim light from the window she could make out several lumps of rocks in the bed beside her. She looked over the bed and saw several more on the floor, the ones she'd shoved off the bed. She was alone in the room. But there had been someone. There had.

What? Who?

She threw the blankets off her and stood.

She tried the door—it was locked from inside, but she hadn't propped the chair under the doorknob when she'd come back upstairs, after they'd all stayed up for hours waiting vainly for more crashes.

314

She turned to the balcony door.

She opened it and stepped out on the balcony into the chilly morning air, under a sky blanketed by dark layers of clouds. She looked to her left and right. Both of the other doors leading out to the balcony were closed. In front of her, fog snaked through the garden, through the pines . . .

Laurel edged cautiously to the low railing to look down—and gasped.

The brick patio below her was littered with rocks. Hundreds of them.

Back in the upstairs hallway, Laurel pounded on Brendan's door. When there was no response, she hesitated, then took the knob and twisted it, shoving open the door.

Brendan sat up groggily in the narrow bed. His face was gray and his eyes were dull; he was clearly hungover. Even so, Laurel's body flushed with heat. She could smell him, too: the warm scent of skin and the faint aftershave he'd been wearing the night before. Her heart beat faster and she clenched her hands against the vertiginous feeling of desire.

"Something happening . . . ," he slurred, not yet awake.

She forced herself to focus. "You need to see. Now."

As he grabbed for his pants, she turned away and lifted the digital camera from the small writing table under the window.

They stepped out the French doors of the dining room and Brendan stopped on the bricks, staring stupefied at the rocks. There were even more than Laurel had thought from looking down at them, hundreds and hundreds, from pebbles to baseball-sized stones to rocks as big as her head.

They both walked slowly around on the brick veranda, Brendan clicking off photo after photo. His whole body was tense with excitement. "It's exactly as in the 1965 police report—the sound first and then the stones later."

"Yes, exactly," Laurel said in a thin voice. But Brendan seemed oblivious to her—all he could think of was the rocks. He had already pulled out the EMF reader and was waving it around.

315

"Two-two ... three point three ... ," he mumbled, and she had the sudden and disturbing thought that he looked like a mental patient, measuring his own unquantifiable reality. "I'm not getting any raised levels. It must have happened hours ago." There was disappointment in his voice; then his face brightened. "But the sound displacement is classic. I should have had a monitor out here, damn it. Maybe something will have recorded through the windows. ..."

She had said nothing for some time, and finally he turned to look at her. "What's wrong?"

"It's a little too perfect, isn't it?" she said slowly. "*Exactly* like the police report?"

His face closed, but she could read his thoughts perfectly. She was resisting again, she was fighting the evidence, and he hated her for it.

"I'm going in to check the monitors," he said flatly.

There was a man with a clipboard in my room, she thought. *I know it.*

But she said nothing as she followed him into the house.

The playback of the rest of the night showed no movement, and registered no sound, either in the great room or the dining room or upstairs—although the clocks in the dining room continued implacably to tick. Brendan stared into the monitor screen with a intensity that unnerved Laurel, but there was only dark beyond the windows of the dining room; no sign of movement, no bodies sneaking around placing rocks.

In her head Laurel was thinking of a dozen ways it could have happened. After all, Brendan had taken the DVDs out of the computers after the crashing incident and replaced them with new ones. The DVDs could have been switched and replaced with a recording of a previous, quiet night, or could simply have been stopped, while someone crept around outside setting out rocks. Laurel kept thinking of Katrina watching her and Brendan from the window, thinking of how the crashing sounds of the night before had oh-so-

316

conveniently put a stop to her encounter with Brendan.

She was worried that Brendan was far too invested in the occurrences, when another explanation should have been obvious: they were in a house with two unprincipled, self-centered adolescents who more than had their own agendas. And there was Pastor Wallace/Rafe Winchester—who wanted God only knew what from them and the house. He'd been in the garden before, and he would have known about the rocks from the police report of the 1965 rock incident.

But Laurel bit back her objections and watched.

Tyler and Katrina surfaced within the hour and were suitably bowled over by the rocks. Their surprise seemed genuine, but Laurel was aware that they were expert manipulators: the more sincere they were, the more she doubted them.

"You mean we heard the rocks first and *then* they fell?" Katrina asked breathlessly, all blue-eyed innocence. She was practically batting her eyelashes at Brendan, who visibly brightened at her interest.

"Sound displacement is a commonly reported characteristic of poltergeist manifestations," he explained, and excitement was a crackling current in his voice. "For some reason no one's ever been able to explain, the sound often seems to be out of sync with the actual breakage or falling."

"That's so awesome," Katrina said, practically swooning.

Tyler was uncharacteristically silent, walking slowly around the rocks. "Of course, we didn't ever go outside on the veranda last night," he pointed out. "The rocks could've been there all along and we wouldn't have known."

Laurel was surprised at his return to skepticism. She found herself both suspicious and strangely relieved that someone besides her was not swallowing this latest occurrence whole.

She could see Brendan bristling, even as he struggled for a neutral tone. "I've watched the recordings ten times by now. There's no movement through the windows."

Tyler half-smiled. "It was dark."

Tyler was clearly intrigued, but at least he was fighting

317

against instant belief. Laurel could see him struggling to maintain objectivity. Brendan and Katrina, on the other hand, were off in their own fog of fascination.

Laurel left the three of them to their obsessive viewing of the night's recordings (it would take hours ... hours). They didn't even notice her leaving.

She walked first into the dining room ... and felt a frisson of unease when she was face to face with the newly ticking grandfather clock. To her side the antique clock in the dome ticked along in tandem.

Explain that; something whispered inside her.

Well, it's a great parlor trick, isn't it? she argued back. *A clock that has wound down ... set the other clock to the same stopped time ... for all I know it could all be set up so it would just take the slightest tremor to start the clocks again, and in the moment, it looks like magic.*

She continued out of the dining room, through the kitchen to the stairs. As she climbed she was strategizing. Yesterday's paranoia—maybe it had even been fear—had faded and she was feeling a different kind of paranoia. She felt *played*. She had the unmistakable feeling of being set up. And not by any paranormal entity.

Last night she had been almost desperate to get out of the house. She had almost had herself convinced that there was something supernatural in the house ... some amorphous evil. And yes, she could go—her suitcase was packed, she could be in the car in five minutes. But now she was angry. Now she had the cold and implacable desire to know what was going on.

She reached the small upstairs servants' kitchen, started the coffeepot, and sat at the table, forcing herself to slow down, to go over everything.

There was a human element to this—a human trickery. She *knew* it. But what had changed, since yesterday, since her frantic, nebulous panic to get out?

The knocking and crashing of the night before ... again, so suspiciously like the reports she had read.

And Tyler was a sound technician. How hard would it be to fake?

318

And there was a man in my room last night.

That was it most of all. The presence in her room—the man with the clipboard. As bizarre as it seemed, she could not believe that was a dream. The house was being monitored. So, who? Brendan? Tyler? Pastor Wallace, haunting the house in his own way?

And who was visiting Victoria Enright, forty-two years after the fact?

No, there was definitely someone human out there, with a very human interest in the house.

And Laurel was angry. She was furious. She was being manipulated again, cheated, just like with Matt. She could feel the heat of rage burning through her, energizing her. And this time she had no desire to run. She wanted to *know*.

She held her coffee cup in her hands, and was resolved. From now on, she was watching *them*.

Chapter Fifty

When Laurel stepped back into the great room she found Brendan and both students were in their chairs in the center of the room again. The pool of water was back, exactly in the same spot, and the three were back seated in a circle around it, each holding a clipboard poised in their lap, just watching the pool.

"It started again fifteen minutes ago," Brendan said to Laurel, without taking his eyes from the pool. "EMF levels are back up between nine and ten."

Tyler spoke, also without looking away from the pool. "We're wondering if it's going to go through the same cycle again: the pool, the pounding, the rocks."

"But it's speeding up," Brendan added. "The pool is growing at one-third again the rate it was yesterday. If it continues at this rate it should be complete in half an hour instead of forty minutes."

Laurel looked around at them. They all were entirely mesmerized by the pool. *That can't be a setup, can it? They really believe this—whatever this is—is happening.*

But before she could speak, she felt the tingling behind her ears, and a sudden jolt of adrenaline ran through her. The hair on her arms was standing up . . . and she had no idea why. She looked around the room in confusion. Fog drifted against the windowpanes . . .

At first Laurel wasn't sure if she even heard it, it was so on the periphery of her consciousness. She saw Brendan frown slightly, no more reaction than that, as if he had a headache. *What is that?*

Then Katrina stood, dropping her clipboard to the floor with a clatter that made Laurel jump. "Don't you *hear* that?" the girl demanded. And as if saying it made it so, the knocking was suddenly unmistakable, loud slow thumps, coming from the middle of the house, Laurel thought, the crooked corridor above the dining room and great room.

The thumps continued, building in volume, shaking the ceiling. Brendan was frozen in his chair, listening intently. Then he and Tyler both shot to their feet and were out the door, running through the dining room. Katrina was not far behind, but far enough to be delicate about her haste. Laurel could hear their footsteps pounding in the kitchen, up the progressive stairs and rooms and jogs.

Laurel stood in the center of the great room, her mind shouting *Go* at her ... and she didn't know if that meant after them or out the door or what.

Then inevitably she followed, running.

Upstairs they were all stopped in the hall outside the room, Brendan's room.

Of course, of course ... that room ...

The three were very still, hovering in the hall, listening so intently they seemed about to shatter.

The knocking had stopped.

Laurel watched from farther down the hall as they waited, suspended ...

Someone said, "It's stopped." Laurel's heart was pounding so loudly she had no idea who had spoken.

Brendan grabbed the doorknob and pushed open the door. Laurel cringed back against the wall. The other three crowded around the door to look in. The room was seemingly untouched: the bed unmade, papers strewn on the writing table—but a very human disorder.

"It was in there," Katrina said, looking through the door at the room.

321

The knocking started again. This time it was downstairs, muffled ... curiously the sound seemed the exact same distance away. Slow, steady thumps.

Listening to it, all of Laurel's suspicions about a human source fled her. She could feel in her marrow—this was *other*. It was mind-shattering, soul-shattering. Her whole body was in revolt against the essential wrongness of it, the irrationality, the impossibility. She could feel the same reaction in the other three; they all stood still and poised in disbelief, in outrage, in awe.

Brendan was the first to break the paralysis. He and Tyler strode down the hall, in the direction of the main stairs, Katrina right behind. By the time they reached the doorway to the next hall, they were running.

Laurel stood and looked through the doorway of Brendan's room at the white walls, the narrow, monastic bed. The knocks continued steadily downstairs. She felt the hair on the back of her neck rise, and she turned and ran for the hall.

As she reached the bottom of the main stairs, she realized that the knocking had stopped. Voices came from the dining room, a few sharp sentences, then silence. Laurel darted across the entry hall toward the great room.

She passed through the archway and again felt a shock of static electricity that made her gasp aloud. *What is that?* She halted on the threshold ... but the tingling was gone. She forced herself forward, walked across the wide expanse of the great room.

The other three stood around the long central table of the dining room, heads lifted toward the ceiling, not moving ... just listening in the stillness.

Katrina started, "I don't—"

Brendan lifted a warning hand and she fell silent.

The thumping started again—this time in the library, upstairs and on the other side of the house. Again, Laurel noticed that it sounded exactly the same distance away, not any closer or farther than any of the other knocks had been.

No one ran this time. Tyler's face tightened, and Brendan looked resolute. They all walked back slowly, even deliberately,

322

out the doorway of the dining room, across the floor of the great room toward the stairs. Brendan held the EMF reader up as they walked.

Laurel braced herself as she stepped back through the arch, but there was no sting of static this time. She saw Katrina glance at her speculatively and wondered if Katrina had felt the shock, too—but Laurel was too keyed up to speak. The EMF reader began beeping steadily as they all headed up the main stairs.

Brendan, in the lead, paused on the landing and they all stopped behind him, listening. The knocks continued, the slow, heavy raps. "Is this recording?" Brendan asked Tyler.

Tyler glanced back toward the first floor. "I don't know. I mean, the cameras are on, but I don't know if we're picking up audio."

"Go back down and check—" Brendan started.

"*No,*" said Laurel violently. "No one goes off on their own." She didn't know why but it was imperative that they stay together.

After a moment Brendan nodded curtly and they all continued moving upstairs toward the slow, steady knocking, Tyler taking two stairs at a time. "Slow down," Brendan snapped at him.

Tyler instantly flared up. "What are we doing, sneaking up on it?"

Brendan grabbed Tyler's arm, halting all of them. "Just slow down. I want to see when it stops—"

At that moment, it did.

All four of them were still, heads raised, holding their breath . . .

"It heard us," Katrina whispered, and no one laughed. They followed Brendan up the remaining stairs and across the hall to the library.

The heavy wood door was closed. *And that's weird,* Laurel thought. *Who would have closed it?*

Brendan reached for the knob—then rattled it. He pushed on the door. "Locked," he muttered.

"Is there a key?" Tyler asked.

"Maybe. There were some extras on the ring."

On impulse, Laurel reached to the knob and turned it herself. The door swung open. Brendan looked at her and she shook her head, mystified. Then they all moved into the room.

It took a moment to grasp—then Katrina gasped. The framed photographic portraits along the whole back wall were askew, as if someone had brushed by the entire length of the wall, or an earthquake had jarred the house and deranged them.

The electromagnetic frequency reader in Brendan's hand started beeping louder and faster. "It's reading twelve," he said, excitement crackling in his voice. "That's extremely high." Tyler had the camcorder up to his shoulder and was shooting footage of the pictures on the wall.

"Is it still here?" Katrina whispered. Laurel knew exactly what she meant. It felt exactly as if they were chasing a presence from room to room, as if a child were playing hide-and-seek with them.

"Let's see." Tyler lunged for the heavy round table with the lazy Susan built in, and knocked his knuckles sharply on the wood surface. The sound was very loud in the room.

There was a pregnant silence . . . then the knocking started again, on the far side of the house.

"Goddamn it," Tyler swore. He turned to the library door and took off running.

"No!" Laurel called behind him, but he was out the door, footsteps pounding in the hall.

Brendan and Katrina followed, and again Laurel found herself a beat behind, trailing, as they ran into the upper hall of the main house.

Running down the hall she was very aware of the pitches and tilts of the floor. It rolled, a feeling like a wave, like seasickness. One moment she was running down it and suddenly she was tripping, flying, and sprawled on the floor—right in front of Brendan's room.

The door was closed again, though she knew it had been

324

open when they left it. She stared up at it, and felt chills start from the base of her spine, a feeling of pure, black terror. She scrambled away from the door, and up to her feet, and bolted after the others.

They all arrived in the servants' kitchen, breathless, to find Tyler standing in the middle of the floor. The knocking had stopped.

Tyler kicked the table.

A skillet jumped off the hook where it hung on the wall and crashed to the floor behind him. Katrina gasped; they all spun, staring ... and waiting ...

The knocking began again in the dining room, below.

Tyler tore out of the kitchen like a madman and pounded down the back stairs. The others hurried behind ... down the stairs, through the house office. They had just bolted into the downstairs kitchen when the knocking stopped, followed immediately by a cry of rage from Tyler in the next room.

Laurel and Brendan dashed for the doorway. Tyler was in the dining room, shouting at the walls, at the ceiling. "Show yourself! Come on! Come out!"

There was silence ... and then knocking began from all the places they had heard it before, except the one they were standing in.

"You made it mad," Katrina said to Tyler breathlessly. The knocking grew louder, waves of it, pounding around them.

"It's trying to get in," Katrina said, and the blankness in her sweet, light voice was chilling.

"It *is* in. Isn't that the point?" Tyler said roughly.

Brendan spoke, and his voice was very distant. "No—it's trying to get *over*. Over, or through."

He had his clipboard out and was writing down the numbers from the EMF meter, which had gone off again, beeping frantically. Now he strode to the doorway to the great room. "I'm checking the audio ..."

He stopped just inside the door.

Laurel came up behind him to look, and felt her stomach drop, a vertiginous jolt.

The paintings hung on the walls in the great room were not crooked, but upside down.

"Whoa," Tyler said behind them.

Laurel felt a sudden pressure in the air. She gasped for breath. Katrina cried out beside her, a strangled sound. "Oh my God!" The girl raised a trembling hand. And then Laurel and Brendan saw what she was pointing to. The screens of the monitors were shattered. Glass glittered on the table and floor around the table.

Brendan ran to the monitors.

"Did it record?" Tyler demanded.

At the monitors, Brendan's back stiffened. He checked the power cords, jiggled switches. "*Damn* it. The equipment's off. Completely off."

Tyler strode to the monitors and checked.

"Look." Katrina pointed again. The lamps on the mantel of the fireplace were shattered—the glass bowls lying in heaps of glass on the marble.

Laurel felt a wave of disorientation. *But they weren't broken when we walked in. I know they weren't. And I didn't hear any crashing, either. . . .*

Brendan started forward, holding up the EMF—but something had changed. The device was silent. Brendan stared down at it, flicked at the switch. "It's gone dead."

Tyler hefted the camcorder, checked it, and paled. "Camera's dead, too."

"But—that's not electrical," Laurel heard herself saying.

"It fried the equipment?" Tyler muttered, and Laurel thought in that moment that he looked more confused and vulnerable than she had ever seen him.

Brendan strode toward the archway. The rest followed. "Watch out!" he cautioned. There was more broken glass on the floor, and on the butler's table under the lamp. Laurel could see bits of broken glass under the sconces on the stairs, and gleaming shattered pieces in the hallway. *When did this happen?* she thought wildly. *Why didn't we hear it?*

And then all around them they heard the sounds—like

lightbulbs popping and bottles shattering and glass cracking—all at once, a prolonged destruction ... and completely aural. There was no movement, no sign of anything stirring or breaking, just a reverberation of sound. Katrina pressed her hands to her ears and squeezed her eyes shut, trying to block it out.

And then silence.

Chapter Fifty-one

They chased it for hours, on and off all day, until they were exhausted and shaking. It seemed like an hour ... it seemed like three days. But wherever they were in the house, the knocking was somewhere else. They never saw anything move; whatever it was they were chasing was always a step ahead of them, as if deliberately taunting them.

They were being played with, completely. Several times they tried waiting in a room, *not* following the knocking. And the knocking would start in one room, then move to another, then back to the room it had just left. Slow, leisurely, taunting, until at one point Katrina screamed at the ceiling, "What do you want?"

There was a silence ... then the knocking started in another room.

It was like being under siege. But by what?

There was a force of personality there, undeniably.

It's the randomness that feels so insane, Laurel thought. *It does seem to be communicating, trying to communicate, but what? Or at least—it seems to have intention.*

There was no further assault of sound after the glass breaking; in fact, the knocking slowed down considerably after that auditory blowout.

When finally it stopped, Katrina had curled up and fallen asleep on the couch in the great room, like a fatigued child.

Brendan found the digital camera was working, and they had no idea if it had been working all along, as they had not thought to use it. He went around the house clicking off photos of the damage, which was really nothing more than some upside-down paintings, broken lightbulbs and lamp fixtures, a few shattered bowls. Whatever *It* was, *it* seemed not to like glass; or perhaps it only wanted to leave them in the dark

And no one thought of leaving.

While there had been pockets of terror throughout the day, there had been nothing at all like an assault, or physical threat. They were all spacey from the adrenaline rushes and crashes but they were also raw with impatience for something else to happen.

They all drifted in the house: Brendan prowled relentlessly with the digital camera and the EMF reader, checking and rechecking levels. Tyler disappeared into his bedroom, and when Laurel went to get a broom from the narrow closet by the servants' kitchen, she could hear soft snoring from his room. There was glass everywhere and she wanted to get it up before dark, or at least pushed into corners.

She started in the servants' kitchen and the back part of the hall, and when she stepped through the lounge into the central part of the hall, the door to Brendan's room was still closed. She hurried by it, putting as much distance between herself and the room as she could before she resumed her sweeping.

It took more than an hour to make her way all the way around the house. Twilight was descending and she could see the white nymph at the tip of the circle of lawn through the windows as she walked across the front hall, toward the great room in the fading light. Katrina sat on the couch, curled up in blankets; she was awake, staring out through the windows. She did not look up when Laurel stepped in. Tyler stood in front of one of the upside-down paintings, looking absurdly like a quizzical patron in a modern art gallery.

Brendan was at the desk, writing by candlelight, which

startled Laurel, until she realized that they had no electric light anymore. Every bulb had been shattered.

Was that intentional? she wondered. *Will we do something about that?* But she was too tired to think clearly about it.

She stood in the middle of the room, feeling like a ghost, but also feeling no desire to speak, to make her presence known. Finally, Brendan glanced up and noticed her. "No manifestations for two hours," he said.

"No," she answered. "What do we do?" she asked, like a child herself.

"We wait," Brendan said, and returned to writing.

Chapter Fifty-two

Everything was moving. The wind played hide-and-seek through the trees outside, a constant rushing swirl of motion; bushes scraped their branches across the windows, screeching and scratching, nails on the glass. The draft breathed through the chimneys, and curtains stirred in front of the windows.

She woke and did not know where she was, or who. She was very still in the dark, listening to the moving and scraping.

And something else ... the piano. A single note, over and over, then dropping a third, then back to the original note.

She sat up and looked around her.

She was in the indistinct white room that she'd been in with Tyler during their testing. The Zener card table was there, and instead of Tyler, another young man sat in one of the chairs: broad shoulders, round and ruddy face, Carolina blue eyes ... only she only sensed their blueness, because he and the whole room were in black and white; it had the faded, grainy quality of a newsreel. She stared at the young man.

I know him.

He reached to the table in front of him and picked up a card, a Zener card, and held it up so she could see: a card with a thick, black circle on it. He looked intently across the white room at her, holding the card ...

She stared back at him.

So familiar, those eyes.

And she stared at the card, trying to glean the message . . .

A circle.

Chapter Fifty-three

She bolted up from sleep ... to silence and grayness.

Who am I? Where is this? What year is this? What century is this?

Terror pulsed through her, instinctive, immediate.

She was not in the white room, but rather, on a sofa downstairs in the great room. The room was dim and there was no color in it; it had the faded, grainy black and white of a newsreel. There were lumps of sleeping shapes around her, and her skin started to crawl. *Who are they? Who am I? Which reality is this?*

She forced herself to breathe, forced herself to focus on the objects around her. The computer monitors, with their smashed screens. The sophisticated control board. The black-and-white newsreel quality faded and she saw the room in dim color, in the present.

Brendan, Tyler, and Katrina slept on sofas and mattresses. Now Laurel remembered.

We brought the furniture in last night so we wouldn't be sleeping alone.

She looked around at the arrangement of furniture and bodies. No sign of the young man from her dream.

God, it was real. So much more real than anything else was feeling right now. She had to ride out another wave of disorientation, of displacement.

Outside the tall windows it was dark, not the dark of night

but the deep gray of rain, which was what had leached the color out of the present. As she focused, *Laurel* focused, waking, she could hear the pounding and splashing of rain on the bricks outside, and the rumble of thunder in the sky.

She sat up and the blanket that was covering her slipped down, and something white fluttered to the floor. She looked down, and down.

It was a card, a white Zener card—with a thick black circle on it. An electric realization shot through her.

The card. He gave me the card.

The others woke, slowly. She watched them—saw their jittery jolts as they came into full consciousness and registered first where they were, and then began to remember what had transpired. Each of them looked up to the ceiling, then to the walls, where the paintings still hung upside down as in a surrealist exhibit.

They all looked around, and no one said a word.

They sat around the dining-room table, with the dark paneling and the tall glass windows around them. They were in a bubble. Laurel knew that there was a garden outside, that there was air and sky and trees and a road, but the thought of going outside didn't even occur to her, and it had nothing to do with the heavy and dismal pour of rain.

Brendan had set up a wide white board on the mantel of the fireplace, turning the room into a parody of a classroom. Laurel was reeling from the absurdity at the same time that she was finding comfort in the familiarity, the attempt at order.

She was so shaky, her whole body trembling ... her whole sense of reality shattered, really. Nothing she thought was real was real.

But there was no thought of leaving anymore—none whatsoever. She felt as if she were part of the house, as if she had always been part of the house. It was in her blood. No one else seemed to have any intention of moving, either.

"So today," Brendan said. "We need a game plan."

334

"A game plan," Tyler snorted, though without anywhere near his usual panache. "It's not our show, though, right? We wait and see what it decides to do."

"On one level," Brendan agreed, and his voice was even, but Laurel had the fleeting thought that he could have killed Tyler in that instant, and an accompanying thought that that was not good. "But we can also analyze what happened yesterday, and I think we should. Let's first review the major theories of poltergeists."

He picked up a red marker and went to the white board. Katrina sat, straight-backed, with her hands primly folded in her lap, the perfect teacher's pet. "Anyone?" Brendan said, lifting his eyebrows.

"A noisy ghost," Katrina said promptly.

"Excellent," Brendan beamed, as if this were kindergarten, and wrote the phrase at the top of the board.

1. A noisy ghost.

"What else?" he demanded.

Slumped in his chair, Tyler shrugged listlessly. "A particular aspect of a traditional haunting."

"Which aspect?" Brendan asked, and waited, marker poised upon the board.

"A particularly kinetic aspect," Tyler shot back, and Brendan turned to look at him.

"Good answer, Mr. Mountford." Brendan wrote it down as number 2:

2. Kinetic aspect of traditional haunting

—and turned back to the room. "What else?"

"An imprint of a violent emotion on a place," Katrina volunteered. Her eyes were shining, her lips full and wet.

"Yes, good." Brendan wrote it down.

"We also have the agent theory," Tyler said, his voice dripping with innuendo. "The repressed emotions of an

335

adolescent . . ."—his eyes slid toward Katrina—"girl, gone wild and manifesting externally." Katrina kicked out at him from underneath the table. But Laurel noticed their sparring was forced, it lacked any kind of energy or conviction.

Brendan was already busy writing on the white board.

3. Agent

"And fraud," Laurel said suddenly. "Let's not forget fraud." She looked at Brendan, and saw his face tighten. "A proven factor in many cases," she added, holding his gaze. She didn't even know why was saying it—it wasn't what she believed. After yesterday she didn't even know what she believed anymore, but it was what she was compelled to say, and it was out.

Brendan turned stiffly to the board and wrote,

4. Fraud.

"Anything else?" he asked, and there was a touch of fury in his voice.

To Laurel's surprise, Tyler spoke again. "'A dynamic between the percipients and the house,'" he said, and Laurel realized he was quoting from the Leish article. "The Poltergeist Effect."

"Yes," said Brendan slowly, and wrote on the board. "Anything else?"

"Something else," Katrina said quietly, and Laurel felt a chill. "Something else entirely."

"Like what?" Brendan said, but without as much force as before.

"Entities," Katrina said after a moment. "Something . . . extradimensional. Just something *else*."

There was a silence that felt cold. Brendan turned to the board and wrote it.

"None of the above," Tyler said, and Laurel knew he meant it as a joke, but the ice was not broken. Brendan continued to write, making his own notes on the list. Then he put the marker down and rubbed his hands together, delighted. "Excellent list. Let's break it down now."

He stepped back to survey the list on the left-hand side of the board:

1. **A noisy ghost**
2. **Kinetic aspects of a traditional haunting**
3. **An imprint of violent emotion on a house or place**
4. **The psychological projections of a human agent (possibly adolescent, possibly female)**
5. **Fraud**
6. **An agreement between the house and the observers: The Poltergeist Effect**
7. **Some other discarnate entity**
8. **Unknown**

"Let's take number one. A noisy ghost. An angry or mischievous spirit," Brendan embellished, and added the words to the board. "Certainly we had a taste of that yesterday, no?" His voice was hearty. "In fact, let's talk about that for a moment. Would you characterize the manifestations yesterday as a: 'angry'; or b: 'mischievous'? Or, c: 'other'?"

Or d: 'insane'? Laurel thought, wildly. *I vote 'd.'*

Brendan turned from the white board, and looked expectantly at them. "Let's just throw out some adjectives. Descriptive words."

"Teasing," Katrina said promptly. "Sly."

"Excellent!" Brendan leaped to the board and wrote down the words.

Teasing / Sly

"Indeed," he nodded, looking toward the upside-down paintings. "Keep going," he ordered.

Beside Laurel, Tyler spoke, to her surprise. "Seductive. Manipulative."

Brendan turned and looked at him. "Interesting. Why do you say so?"

Tyler shrugged. "It got us all going, didn't it? We were chasing it around for hours." He looked sidewise at Katrina. "Might as well add 'feminine.' I've spent less time chasing a girl."

Katrina gasped and hit him, automatically. "Prick."

Tyler smiled lazily. "I'm just sayin'."

"It's not feminine, though," Laurel heard someone say, and then realized that it had been herself who had spoken aloud.

"No," Katrina said, and looked at Laurel for perhaps the first time ever without a trace of rancor. "It's not feminine."

"No," Brendan echoed. They all sat for a moment, contemplating.

"Childlike," Katrina said, thoughtfully. "Playful."

Laurel felt they were going down a dangerous road, suddenly, but could not have said why. The grandfather clock clicked softly in the corner. The sound felt ominous.

Tyler was nodding, also thoughtfully. She looked around at all of them, their almost dreamy focus. Outside, the rain was a soft, hypnotic patter.

Lulled. We're all being lulled.

"Intelligent," Katrina said suddenly. "You know? It's *trying* to communicate."

"But what is *It*?" Tyler asked.

"I don't know," Katrina said slowly. "But It *is*."

"This is good," Brendan said, pacing the floor in front of the fireplace. "This is good. Yes. There's an intelligence. A . . ." He turned to Laurel and pointed. "A *personality*. It's all of the same . . . mind." He paused, rethinking. "Mind isn't the word. But one intelligence."

Katrina and Tyler were nodding.

"We're agreed, then?" Brendan said intensely. "It's one. Just one."

Laurel felt at this point that she had to put a stop to it. There was something wrong—*what had the pastor said?*—something *perverse* about talking about this . . . *thing* . . . as if it were human, as if it were friendly, as if it were knowable.

"It's also room-specific," Tyler said suddenly. "It had us

338

going on a circuit, yesterday. The library upstairs, the little room in the center hall, this room"— he glanced around the dining room—"and the one next door." He nodded toward the great room.

"Yes, it is," Brendan agreed, nodding thoughtfully. "I wonder why?"

And what if the point is, there is *no why?* Laurel thought.

"So are we done with this analyzing yet?" Tyler said.

Brendan turned to him, with a cold look. "And what would you suggest instead?"

Tyler shifted on his chair. "Well, are we just going to wait for it to make some kind of move? We could try to make something happen."

Brendan's voice was neutral, but Laurel could tell he was intrigued. "What exactly did you have in mind?"

Tyler looked up in the direction of the upstairs library. "Instead of sticking around together, we could stake out the rooms. Things are only happening in a few of them. Why not divide them up, hang out, and see what happens?"

"I don't like it," Laurel said immediately. Everyone looked at her.

"Nothing dangerous happened yesterday," Brendan said, placating. "No one was hurt. I think it's a good idea. We wouldn't be far from each other . . ."

"Or we could try talking to it," Katrina said.

Brendan turned to look at her, intrigued. "How would you propose to do that?"

"The same way it talks to us. The rapping."

Laurel felt a current go through the room. She looked at Brendan and Tyler, and could see the light in their faces, burning hot. The two clocks ticked behind them: the grandfather clock in the corner, and the gold clock in its glass dome.

"I think Miss Sugar is onto something," Tyler said slowly.

Laurel suddenly realized what the feeling of danger was. *We want fireworks again. Even I do. We got a taste of it yesterday and we want more.* She thought of the article Tyler had been reading by

Dr. Leish: *"In effect the percipients become addicted to the manifestations."*

But of course, it had already been decided.

Rain fell in a dark curtain outside as Brendan and Tyler carried the long dining-room table into the great room, and they set up four chairs around it, while Laurel watched with a growing feeling of unreality.

Brendan looked to Katrina.

"Katrina, this was your idea. Do you want to try?"

Laurel saw Katrina straighten her back and lift her head. "Yes, I will." She walked across the dully gleaming floor and seated herself at the center of one long side of the oak table . . . and looked to the others expectantly until they took their seats.

So she's a medium, now? Laurel thought. That was exactly the role Katrina seemed to be assuming as she placed her hands flat on the table, closed her eyes and took a breath, and sat still for an extended moment. The weight of the great room settled around them, the heaviness of place out of time. Rain fell steadily, a soporific rumble. Then Katrina opened her eyes and looked off into the gray distance.

"We want to talk to . . . whatever is in this house," she said in a firm, clear voice. "We know you're there."

There was a long, deliberate stillness, which not even Tyler tried to spoil.

Katrina suddenly leaned forward and rapped her knuckles sharply on the center of the wood table, as if she were knocking on a door.

"Are you there?" she demanded.

Again, stillness. But Laurel felt something else in the air now. That quality of listening, of waiting . . .

Katrina's eyes shone in the dim room. "I know you're there," she breathed. "I can feel you." She leaned forward and knocked again, and Laurel saw Tyler flinch in his chair. Brendan was staring at Katrina, mesmerized.

"Talk to us," Katrina commanded. "Answer us." She

340

knocked again, so hard that Laurel cringed. *She's going to tear her knuckles apart . . .*

Katrina seemed oblivious. "Are you here?" she demanded. "Answer me!" Her china-blue eyes shone with the intensity of madness.

And from the ceiling, or deeper than the ceiling, from the center of the house, came an immense, hollow *THUMP*. The sound reverberated through the house, through the room, through Laurel's body.

All four of them jumped in their chairs. "Whoa," Tyler muttered, through a dry mouth. Katrina's eyes blazed with triumph. Brendan looked stupefied.

"Thank you," Katrina breathed. "Welcome."

Through her fear, Laurel felt a rush of absurdity. *Welcome? We're the outsiders here.*

"How do we do this?" Tyler muttered feverishly. "One knock for yes, two for no?"

Brendan leaned toward Katrina from his chair at the head of the table. "Were you here when the original experiment was done here?" he prompted her.

"Were you here when the original experiment was done here?" Katrina repeated aloud.

There was another reverberating *KNOCK*. Laurel could feel it through the floorboards, hear it echoing in the walls.

"Whoa," Tyler mumbled again, and he looked a bit sick.

"One knock is 'yes'?" Katrina clarified.

Another hollow *KNOCK*. Laurel felt her pulse racing, her heart pounding in her throat, the same dizzying thrill as being on a roller coaster.

"Are you a ghost?" Katrina demanded, her eyes alight.

"It's not—" Brendan started, but another single *KNOCK* boomed through the house, silencing him.

"Yes," Katrina said.

Brendan's face darkened with confusion.

"Are you Paul Folger?" Laurel said suddenly, looking at Katrina. Katrina stared back at her without expression, and for a moment Laurel thought the girl would simply refuse her.

Then Katrina turned her eyes to the ceiling again and asked in her clear, firm voice:

"Are you Paul Folger?"

Another booming *KNOCK*.

"Yes," Katrina breathed, her face glowing. At their sides of the table, Tyler and Brendan were electrified, practically vibrating with excitement.

Laurel said sharply, "Wait." Her thoughts were racing, questions forming. Now she spoke aloud, projecting as Katrina had. "Are you Caroline Folger?" she demanded of the air.

A single, reverberating *KNOCK*. "Yes," Laurel said, and looked around the table. Katrina's face was stormy, Brendan's confused. Laurel felt an electric thrill. *I know what you're up to.* She leaned forward on the table.

"Are you Alaistair Leish?" Laurel asked loudly.

Another *KNOCK* shook the house.

"You're all of those people," Laurel said, her eyebrows raised skeptically.

Now two thundering *KNOCK*s.

"That's 'No'," Tyler said.

"Are you Paul Folger?" Laurel asked again.

Two *KNOCK*s. "'No,'" Tyler repeated. He looked toward Laurel with admiration.

"Are you Alaistair Leish?" Laurel demanded.

Two *KNOCK*s again.

"Are you Caroline Folger?"

Two *KNOCK*s.

Laurel sat back, and they all looked around at each other, stymied at the contradiction.

"Are you dead?" Laurel tried.

Two *KNOCK*s . . . then another.

So all it's doing is playing, Laurel thought. *Or maybe it doesn't understand English.* But she didn't say it aloud.

Tyler suddenly said loudly, "Show us something. Show us what you can do."

They waited in breathless silence. Nothing.

Katrina shot an oblique look at Tyler and leaned forward,

her cornflower eyes wide and appealing. She said to the center of the table, in an enticing voice, "Please show us."

The girl's words hung in the silence, and the four of them sat poised at the table, upside-down paintings and shattered mirrors around them. And then Laurel felt something change.

"What's that—" Tyler began. Brendan held up a warning hand.

"Shh ..." said Katrina. Her face was glowing. Everyone sat still, not even breathing ...

The air changed, turning both heavy and cold around them ... and then the temperature plunged, as if the room had suddenly frozen. Katrina gasped and hugged herself. Laurel shuddered violently. All their breaths were showing in the air in misty white puffs.

"Jesus Christ ..." Tyler said, through chattering teeth.

And then rocks began to fall from the ceiling. Not a violent shower, but as light as rain. Large rocks, small rocks, fist-sized, pebbles. They materialized from just below the ceiling and fell softly to the floor, as slowly as drifting leaves. There was no noise, no sound at all as the stones hit the floor, not so much as a muffled thud. But Laurel could see that on the floor, some of the rocks were steaming, wisps of white mist.

"Oh my fucking God ..." Tyler said, from miles and miles away.

Katrina clapped her hands like a child. Her face was glowing, and she laughed, that tinkling, musical laugh. Brendan and Tyler were simply frozen, staring around in awe.

Laurel reached out as if in a dream and held out her hand. A rock fell on her open palm and for a moment it was light as a feather—and then all she felt was heat. She pulled back her hand and the rock fell with an audible thud on the floor.

"Hot ..." she said. Her voice sounded faraway to her.

Tyler stood slowly. Katrina was already on her feet, and she opened her arms as if to catch the falling rocks, embrace them. "Yes ... yes ..." Her face was ecstatic. "More!" she cried out. "More!" She spun in the room like a child.

"No," Laurel said, and a black wave of dread crashed over

343

her. "No!" She grabbed Katrina and shook her, shouting in her face. "Stop it now."

Katrina stiffened in Laurel's grasp. Her eyes were dilated to black saucers ... but as Laurel dug her fingers into the girl's forearms, she saw Katrina slowly returning to awareness. It was warmer around them—the intense cold was fading. Laurel was suddenly aware that it was pouring rain outside, storming, with thunder and lightning cracking through the sky in brilliant bursts of illumination.

"No!" Brendan's voice suddenly burst through the room.

Laurel turned to look. The rock showers had stopped. The stones lay around the room, steaming, but still.

Brendan turned on Laurel and the rage in his eyes was terrifying as he advanced on her, through the rocks littered on the floor. His whole body was shaking. "What are you doing? Why did you do that?" He was nearly screaming at her. "What the hell are you thinking? We were there, we had it—" Even Tyler cowered back from Brendan's fury, his eyes suddenly haunted, as if he were seeing someone quite else.

Laurel was so stunned at Brendan's anger she couldn't speak, but she was certain, certain, that it had to be stopped, that to go further would be to lose themselves in something from which they might never return ...

Lightning split the sky again, a burst of white light.

"Get out of here," Brendan shouted at Laurel. "Get out!" And behind him, Katrina looked at Laurel, her eyes glassy with triumph.

Laurel backed up from Brendan, then turned and ran from the room.

344

Chapter Fifty-four

Even then she didn't leave, though; she had no thought of the front door, of her car, of escape. Instead she ran up the stairs like a chastened child ordered to her room, past the window overlooking the drenched garden, and up ... She didn't stop until she'd reached the upstairs hall, where she halted in the middle of the floor, panting, half-crying, barely able to breathe.

Her knees buckled and she realized she was shaking from head to foot with adrenaline. She was barely able to lurch to the green leather divan against the wall in the hall, where she collapsed, leaning her head against the back of the seat, swallowing against a sudden wave of nausea.

My God ... my God ... did that just happen? What *just happened?*

With her eyes closed she pictured the softly falling rocks ... and felt chills through her body at the sheer unreality of the memory. It was like a painting, like a dream ... only it wasn't.

She felt exhilaration ... and terror. Her mind battled between the two. *We have to get out,* one part of her shouted, while another part of her wanted to cry out, just as Katrina had: *More, more, more!*

But Brendan ... His rage ... the desperation of his rage ...
What was that about? What is going on?

And suddenly her uncle's voice was very clear in her head.
Pay attention.

Laurel bolted up to sitting, as if she had been slapped.

Pay attention.

She drew in a deep breath. The nausea had passed, but she was still shaking. She wiped her sweating palms on her skirt . . . and felt something stiff inside her front pocket.

She reached in and drew out the Zener card with the thick black circle on it.

He gave me the card . . .

But what was it trying to say?

Something stirred in her memory, and her eyes widened. *A circle . . .* She looked down the hall to the closed door of Brendan's room.

She stood from the divan and held still for a moment, checking her balance, then walked slowly toward Brendan's door. She reached for the doorknob with trepidation, as if it would burn her. She breathed in shallowly, tried to slow her racing heart.

It's a room. It's just a room.

Then she grasped the knob and twisted it, swung open the door.

She stepped in quickly so as not to lose her nerve, and pulled the door shut behind her. She stood with her back against the door. The walls were white; the room was cold, and dim from the curtain of rain outside. The sense of claustrophobia was instantaneous and sickening, but she steeled herself and walked across the narrow expanse of floor to the window, leaned over the writing table, and pushed back the gauzy curtain . . .

. . . to reveal the thick circle scratched in the glass, filled in with black ink: a circle just exactly like the circle of the Zener card—the exact same size and thickness.

But what does it mean?

She pulled her eyes away from the circle in the glass and looked down at the writing desk. It was a mess, the familiar clutter of academia . . . so many notebooks, so many pages of notes Brendan had made already. Diagrams, including several sketched floor plans of the room she was in. There was a file of floor plans of the whole house, dozens of copies, each labeled with a date and time, and mathematical notations in each room. *The EMF readings?* she wondered. *Or some other obscure formula of his own?*

There were journal pages, too, and paging through them made her heart start to beat faster. While they started out normally, with dates and time entries and margins and spaces between entries, by the middle of the first book the sentences were continuous, from the very top of the page to the very bottom, from one far end of the page to the next, a dark tidal wave of writing, with no margins, no line spacings, no pauses, and in later pages, no punctuation or capitalization either:

The smell again today bad eggs rotten yellow odiferous no order odor yellow stink sulfer sulfurous sulfa

Laurel's mind was reeling. It was familiar, this writing, she knew what it was ...

And then she could smell the stink, faint ... horrible ... the smell of goat. She turned in the room, holding her breath against the smell, fighting the rising tide of panic.

I know it didn't smell like this before. I know that smell.

The smell of the schizophrenic ward at Dorothea Dix. The smell of schizophrenia. It was like a living thing in the room.

And then she thought she finally understood, and the thought was terrifying. Bile rose in her throat and she turned to bolt for the door, to get out, when Uncle Morgan's voice spoke sharply again in her head.

Pay attention.

Laurel stopped.

It was so real, that voice.

Pay attention to what?

She forced down her claustrophobic feeling and turned where she stood, looking around the room.

Her eyes fell on the closet door, and her ears began to tingle.

She stepped forward and opened the door.

347

It took a moment for her eyes to adjust to the darkness, then she was startled to look in on a much deeper closet than she ever would have expected. Brendan's few clothes were pushed to one side of the clothes rail, leaving a blank space that revealed a length of at least ten feet back to the back wall beyond the rail.

It's almost like a—

Passageway.

Laurel stepped forward and ducked under the clothes rail, and walked back toward the back closet wall. She squinted in the dark and then reached her hand forward, put it flat against the wall, and pushed.

The wall swung open, and Laurel looked up ... at a narrow, steep stairway.

Chapter Fifty-five

Laurel stepped through the back of the closet, and climbed the dark and narrow stairs, one cautious footstep after another, carefully, noiselessly.

As she reached the open doorway at the top, she held her breath, and eased forward, an inch at a time . . .

The stairway opened into a large attic with slanting rafters and small, high, dirty windows.

Laurel swept her gaze quickly over the room, but there was no one human in the attic space. It was empty except for a bed, a chest of drawers, a camp toilet, a square mini-refrigerator, a table and chair set up as a desk with a metal filing cabinet beside it—and against the far wall, a bank of monitors and computer equipment that was the twin of the one downstairs, but with double the equipment, double the screens. Laurel moved forward to it in a daze, and drew in a sharp breath seeing her own room with the narrow bed and the raven above the desk on one of the screens. Each of the other bedrooms was being recorded as well.

We're all being watched. Who? Who?

She could see the great room on another of the screens, with rocks now scattered all over the floor and on the long table in the center. Brendan and Tyler and Katrina were back to sitting beside the slowly growing pool of water, watching the puddle form again.

Laurel could tell from the angle of the cameras that they were set high, almost on the ceiling. *The cameras must be in the molding,* she thought, even as she reeled with the shock of the discovery. *In those medallions on the crown molding.*

Still moving in a trance, she stepped to the desk. A file folder was open on top, and she looked down at a collection of brochures, some of them plain flyers, others glossy four-color versions, some formal applications. Words jumped out at her:

Prize. Grant.

She picked one up, and then another, and read with increasing disbelief.

Abraham Kovoor's Challenges, Prize: 100,000 Sri Lankan Rupees
Alfredo Barrago's Bet, Prize: British £50,000
Center for Inquiry West, Prize: U.S. $10,000
Association for Skeptical Enquiry, (United Kingdom) Prize: £13,000.
Stuart Landsborough's Puzzling World, Prize: NZ $50,000.

All were international prizes for conclusive evidence of the paranormal.

Laurel looked up from the brochures, reeling. She suddenly leaned over the table and picked out one bold-lettered flyer:

The James Randi Educational Foundation Prize: One Million U.S. Dollars.

Laurel jolted in disbelief.

There was a handwritten notation on the sheet: *"May be combined with the Sima Nan Prize from China—for a total of two million two hundred thousand U.S. dollars."*

350

Laurel put a hand to the desk to steady herself. She was staggered. *Two million two hundred thousand. Enough money to make someone risk . . . anything.*

She felt ill.

He's using you. He's been using you all along. He's in this for money. He might even have faked it all.

There was an overpowering sense of familiarity about it.

Betrayal. Lies. Used. Again.

She could barely stand, now; she was adrift, loose from her moorings. Nothing real or solid or rational.

Don't think about it. Don't think about it.

But underneath the disbelief, anger was rising, blood flooding into her face.

There was a disorienting scraping as a file drawer suddenly slid out in the file cabinet.

Laurel whirled and stared at it. The cabinet was motionless, the drawer open as far as it could go without falling.

What? What?

She started to back up, filled with an overpowering urge to run. She turned—and gasped. Behind her in the dark corner of the room was the man with the clipboard, standing, observing, a shadow in the dim light of the attic. He studied Laurel with clinical detachment.

"Who are you?" Laurel whispered, stunned. And then her eyes focused in the dimness and she recognized the dark man. The lecturer from the Paranormal Research Center. "Dr. Anton."

The man smiled, white teeth in a swarthy face. "That's right, Dr. MacDonald."

Her mind scrambled to make sense of it. "How . . . how long have you been here?"

He gestured casually with the clipboard. His voice was relaxed, unstressed. "Since the beginning, of course."

"It's your experiment," she said, with dawning realization.

"That's right." He half-smiled. "And I might add— successful beyond anything I dared hope."

Laurel stared at him, grasped at a thought. "Have you faked everything, then?"

351

His eyes widened in mock surprise. "Oh no. I may have primed the pump in the beginning ... but the house ... the house is coming alive. You've all exceeded my wildest expectations."

She was fighting for composure, fighting not to scream. He had been inside her room, and inside Katrina's—he had watched them as they slept, had recorded their every move. It was monstrous, and he was unbalanced, quite possibly dangerous, and she was trapped in a secret attic with him and no one knew where she was, and he was between her and the door. She swallowed her panic, groped for an air of detachment.

"I suppose you had to keep us in the dark to keep from tainting the experiment," she said, colleague to colleague.

"Naturally."

Something occurred to her and her eyes flicked to the wall. "The monitors up here weren't damaged. You have it all recorded? The glass smashing, the rock showers ..."

"Oh yes. Everything," he agreed, and for a moment, a feverish light burned in his eyes.

A familiar voice suddenly spoke from the stairwell. "What the hell?"

Laurel's knees went weak with relief. *Brendan. Thank God, thank God ...*

But as he came forward from the narrow attic doorway he was looking at her with reproach and regret ... and she knew.

He stopped some distance from her and shook his head sadly. "Mickey. I wish you hadn't done this."

She was cold all over, but she looked from Brendan to Anton. "So this was your experiment all along, both of you. You're doing it for prize money."

"We'll cut you in, Mickey," Brendan said, and his smile was sickly. "It's just that we needed you to be here with no expectations—"

"It's hardly just the money," Anton interrupted, and there was a fervor underneath his words that froze her marrow. "This is an active, powerful poltergeist manifestation. It's

352

bigger than anything ever documented, and we have it all recorded."

"It's real. You know it, Mickey. You know it," Brendan said softly.

It was true, but it was wrong. The rough attic walls seemed to be closing in on her.

"We're making history," Anton pontificated. "There's something monumental, here—"

"Don't talk to me," she said to Anton, and turned to Brendan. "It's not too late. We need to take Tyler and Katrina out of here. We need to get out—get out now."

She tried to keep her voice calm, professional. "I think I understand what's going on. There *is* an imprint in this house, just as in the theories. It's an imprint of Paul Folger's mental state. An imprint of schizophrenia. The symptoms are all here. Hallucinations. Obsession. Delusions. The feeling of being watched. The smells." She looked into Brendan's eyes. "I know you've experienced them. It's in that room, the room you've been sleeping in. That's the center of the house. It was Paul Folger's room. All those years, the hallucinations, the paranoia, the emotions, his madness—it soaked into that room, and into the walls."

She was listening to her own voice, and somehow the thoughts that had seemed so coherent to her in the room downstairs were not having the effect she intended.

"The house is delusional," she said. "We see its delusions."

"A fascinating theory," Anton said. "I'm impressed. We'll have to take that under consideration."

"We don't have to prove *why*, though, Mickey," Brendan explained patiently. "We only have to show that it *is*."

She wasn't following, and then she was. "For the money, you mean."

"We could live like this, Mickey," he gestured vaguely, indicating the house. "In a house like this, a life like this ..."

"You don't understand," she heard herself saying. "Don't you see? Rafe Winchester, Victoria Enright, my uncle ... whatever is in this house, it imprinted them, too. There's madness

353

here, and it's contagious. We have to get out."

Brendan looked away from her, and her heart dropped.

Anton shook his head. "We simply can't let you do that, Dr. MacDonald. We are in the midst of a breakthrough study and we can't let you interfere."

She turned again to Brendan numbly.

"Just one more night, Mickey." His voice was a raw plea. "The children are doing so well; the house responds to their intentions. You saw what Katrina did this afternoon. We just need one more night to film it, to make sure we have everything documented."

This is crazy. I have to get out. I have to get them out.

She made a desperate attempt. "I can understand that. I'm of no use to you, though. You don't need me anymore . . ."

She looked to Brendan, pleading . . . desperately seeking the person she'd thought she'd known. And for a moment, he met her eyes.

"We do need you, Mickey," he said. "We might need you most of all."

She stared at him in a new confusion.

Brendan walked to the file cabinet and pulled a file from the already open drawer, approached, and handed it over to her with a bizarre formality.

This is absurd, she thought, as she opened the file. *I'm a hostage and they're standing around discussing it as if we were in a lab—*

Then she froze. What she was looking down at were test charts: the familiar charts for Tyler and Katrina, the initial results of the Zener card tests.

But there was a third chart, and the scores were higher than Tyler's or Katrina's. She stared in disbelief at the numbers before the name of the test subject finally registered. She was looking at her own chart.

She paged through the charts again, thinking there must be a mistake. Even as she did it, she was remembering the tests she ran with Tyler, and Brendan's strange, distant responses when she asked about the scores. *Nothing there,* he'd said. *Perfectly average. Right at statistical chance.*

354

But the scores told another story. Her own psi levels were 85 percent above chance, higher than Tyler's, off the charts.

Her head was ringing—and Uncle Morgan's voice whispered in her ear: *Runs in the family.*

She looked up, and Brendan was smiling at her sadly, and with a touch of awe. "What are you going to do?" she managed.

"But you know that, Dr. MacDonald," Dr. Anton said with exaggerated patience. "The group was very close this afternoon, before you interfered. We're going to finish what the group started. Make contact. The same as the first group did."

"How do you know that?" she said automatically, curious in spite of herself.

Dr. Anton smiled at her. "Victoria Enright," he said.

For a moment Laurel flashed on the dingy green halls of the asylum. "You visited her," Laurel realized. "You were the one."

"She's actually quite accessible with the proper techniques."

Laurel remembered that Anton had been a hypnotherapist. "You hypnotized her."

"Yes, a very pliant subject. She told me all about their séance. It is truly a loss that none of their recordings survived."

She tried to keep her voice steady. "Not all of their group survived, either. And not one of them is still sane."

"Ah, yes, this extravagant theory of yours," Anton sounded amused. "Do you really believe that whatever happens tonight will drive everyone in this house mad?"

"You've seen how Victoria is," she said, and she heard her voice shaking. "Did you meet Rafe Winchester?"

He smiled faintly. "Oh yes."

She felt a chill of unease at the insinuation on his face. "What did you do to him?"

"He's somewhere he can't interfere," Anton said lightly. "Amazing that the old fellow has been the self-appointed guardian of the house for all these years. Who would have thought we could have found the house so easily, if we'd just followed that particular trail?"

"So you know about Rafe, and you know about Victoria—" She was not going to mention Uncle Morgan, but Anton added—

"And your uncle, of course, yes." He met her eyes and she knew that this man would stop at nothing, let no one stand in the way of his goal.

She swallowed. "So—then how do you explain what happened to the original group?" She was keeping him talking, but she was also genuinely curious.

"Simpler minds in a simpler time, unprepared for the expansion of consciousness they experienced."

His clinical detachment frightened her. *He really only sees people as lab rats, to be used for his purposes.* Aloud she asked, "What makes you think this group is any more prepared for what they might see?

He looked at her, puzzled. "But as a scientist, how can you not go forward and learn for yourself?"

Laurel nodded thoughtfully … and lunged for the staircase, running as hard and fast as she could for the door.

Chapter Fifty-six

Brendan bolted after her, grabbed her around the waist. She flailed out at him, punching and kicking, but Anton seized her arm from behind, twisting her around, and both of them tackled her, holding her struggling and screaming between them, only Anton's hand was clamped hard on her mouth and all she could hear was her own muffled grunting.

Brendan held her down on the floor as Anton duct-taped her mouth shut and tied her hands with some silky rope. The agony of having Brendan's hands on her like that forced tears to her eyes and she clenched her eyes shut, clenched her jaw, her legs, her body. ... She was sick with fear, that they would leave her upstairs, trussed and helpless, possibly to die. But instead of tying her to the chair, or a pillar, the two of them hauled her up from the floor and marched her down the narrow stairway. Brendan eased open the back closet panel at the bottom and they brought her through the dark closet, out the door into Paul Folger's tiny, white room.

They muscled her toward the bed and she stiffened, fighting them.

"That's right," Anton told her. "I think you might be more of service to us here."

Anton threw back the coverlet of the bed and for one terrible second her mind went to the worst ...

No no God please no don't hurt me don't—

Then something at the edge of the bed brushed against her

calf. She gasped and twisted in Anton's grasp.

The horror she felt on looking down was instant and complete. Welded to the metal frame of the bed were three thick iron rings.

For restraints.

There were three identical protuberances on the right side of the bed, beside the wall—which was actually forcing the bed out several inches away from the wall, instead of it lining up flush.

Somehow it was those iron rings that made it real: Paul Folger's long years of confinement. The room seemed to close in on her, with a rush of all that it had seen, all that it had absorbed, the sodden, stinking madness—the horror . . .

She bit back a scream. She wanted to scream, to scream her lungs out, but she wouldn't give them the satisfaction of her muffled, impotent howls.

Anton pushed her down on the bed and held her down. "Do it," he snapped at Brendan.

"We don't . . . have to hurt her," Brendan mumbled.

"Don't be a fool," Anton said sharply, but his voice never rose. "Tie her." And Brendan did, loosening the rope from her hands and, as Anton held her, looping it through the iron rings, fastening her arms by her sides, one on each side of the bed.

When Brendan stepped back, Anton straightened and looked down on Laurel with nothing like lust, or pleasure at her captivity—only the detachment a scientist would show a lab animal. "I trust your experience here will be illuminating. For you—and all of us." He glanced around the room with an enigmatic smile. "I think we are in for an interesting night indeed. Perhaps even—life-altering."

Brendan gave Laurel what seemed for a moment like a stricken look—ambiguous with misery—then the men moved away from the bed, and out.

She heard the lock turn in the door.

She was dizzy and gagging, fighting to breathe through her nose. Her eyes darted frantically around the room.

The room was stark and cold, the magnetic malevolence was heavy in the air.

Scream kick bounce shake make noise get them here make them help. Her mind was shouting at her, fast, panicked thoughts.

No.

Why?

Because Tyler and Katrina can't help you, she found herself answering herself coldly. *You'll only put them in more danger. Shut up for now and figure out what you're going to do.*

She breathed through her nose, breathed through the heart-pounding panic, until her pulse slowed. Her eyes went again to the side of the bed, to the rings. *So Brendan knew that, too, had known from the beginning that it was true, about Paul Folger, that they . . . they kept him here, that he was what they said he was. . . .*

Get hold of yourself. Now is not the time to freak out.

Brendan had lied to her, betrayed her. *It's worse than with Matt. That was just an engagement he broke off. This is jeopardy. This is criminal.*

And then the anger came, and that was good.

Chapter Fifty-seven

What if you slept? And what if, in your sleep, you dreamed? And what if, in your dream, you went to heaven and there plucked a strange and beautiful flower? And what if, when you awoke, you had the flower in your hand? Ah, what then?
—Samuel Taylor Coleridge

The anger rose and fell in waves, and she rode it like the gentle rocking of a boat on the ocean. It was both calming and powerful. She breathed and burned as she lay tied to the bed of a madman, and tried to force her thoughts into some kind of order.

Think. Think. Think.

You have to get out of here, get Tyler and Katrina out before they start that séance. That cannot happen. It must not happen.

How can I get out?

She yanked and pulled at the ropes. She could move her hands, her fingers, but her arms were bound tightly.

She twisted on the bed, looking around the room. Her eyes fell on the circle cut into the window.

Uncle Morgan.

The card was in her pocket—the one she pulled from the dream. The realization of it stopped her racing thoughts.

I saw him and he gave me the card.

Somehow, wherever that was, it was a real place. Real enough. Can I get to it now?

She lay still on the bed and thought of the white room. She closed her eyes, breathed in ... and saw it in her mind's eye: the room she had been in when she walked among the file boxes and found the Folger test charts, the room she had been in when she tested with Tyler, the room she had been in in her dream, with Uncle Morgan as a young man. She saw its dreamlike whiteness, felt its indistinct contours, felt the coolness of the air, saw it becoming substantial around her ...

Her heart beat steadily and slowly and she became aware of the pulse in her wrists. Then she realized she could move not just her hands, but her arms. The ropes were no longer binding her. She opened her eyes, lifted her hands, and sat up from the bed.

She was in the white room ... it glowed faintly around her. All of the furniture and details of Brendan's room had disappeared, but there was a door at the other side of the glowing white.

Laurel stood from the bed and walked across the whiteness to the door. She felt light, insubstantial; she moved with a dreamlike detachment.

She reached out and opened the door—

And found herself looking in on the great room.

She was standing in the archway. The room before her was recognizably the house but its contours were indistinct— nothing seemed clear. *Is this a dream?*

The dining-room table was set up in the middle of the room with four people around it.

They've started the séance already, Laurel thought in a panic. But something was wrong. There was the bank of equipment across the room, only it looked different, primitive, and the screens were intact, not smashed. And there were several arrangements of sofas and chairs and tables in the room, and carpets as well, three separate conversation areas in an elegant arrangement. The gilt-framed mirrors were there, too, intact on the walls.

Laurel understood with a jolt that she was looking at an entirely different group seated around the dining-room table.

Two young men and a young woman of college age were

seated at the table. An older man stood with a clipboard, blond hair and high cheekbones. *I know him,* Laurel thought, electrified, but she could not think from where.

As Laurel hovered in the archway, fascinated, she saw the young woman speak, but Laurel could not hear, only see it, like watching a television with the sound turned down.

Across from the dark-haired young woman was a black-haired young man who also seemed familiar—the slant of his eyebrows and the prominent cowlick. At the far end of the table was another young man who was strangely familiar as well—with crystal-bright eyes in a round boyish face. They were all dressed in clothing that was instantly identifiable as from a previous era because of its formality. The young woman's short dress and Jackie Kennedy bouffant decided it. The sixties.

There was something odd and distancing about the entire room and the people in it ... and Laurel realized there was no color. Everything was black and white.

I'm on film, then, Laurel thought, and promptly forgot there was anything strange about that.

She tried to look around the rest of the room, to get more details about the group, the time, the situation. She felt that she was looking through a fog: though some details were sharp and clear, the perimeters of the room were hazy. But as she stared harder, trying to focus, she suddenly recognized some familiar pieces of equipment: the dice machine with its oblong Lucite tube, and the black felt-covered particle board with its Zener card displays.

It's the Duke group, she thought in a rush of understanding. *Leish's group. Dr. Leish ... Victoria Enright ... Rafe Winchester ... and the crystal-eyed boy is Uncle Morgan. What are they doing here? What am I doing here?*

The young woman was speaking again, but Laurel couldn't hear her. She watched as all three men watched the young woman covertly; there was a sexual charge that Laurel could feel from where she was standing. Then suddenly a *RAP* sounded, reverberating through the room. All four at the table

362

reacted with excitement, looking up, talking quickly. Laurel heard the *RAP* but not the voices. The tension was electric in the room.

And suddenly she felt a chill, like a cold draft.

Laurel.

She stiffened. Someone had spoken her name very clearly.

She looked around the room. No one in the room was looking at her. The round-faced boy was looking down at the table, at a pack of cards he held in his hand.

Laurel.

She heard it again. And then she realized: the voice was in her own head.

She glanced around the room surreptitiously. Who was it? Who was speaking to her?

She stared toward the table. Victoria was speaking, soundlessly. The round-faced boy with the electric eyes was concentrating on the cards. The Zener cards. There was one card in front of him—the bold black **O**.

Laurel, the voice said again in her head, and now she knew. Young Uncle Morgan.

He said her name again, quite clearly, but she saw that he had not moved his mouth. Somehow, he was speaking inside her head.

Play the cards with me. Come sit and listen.

She glanced at the others warily.

They can't see you.

Laurel's eyes lingered on Leish, with fear.

He can't hear us. It's his great anger—he has no ability at all.

Laurel stepped out of the archway, walked across the misty room to the table, and sat down across from him. None of the others acknowledged her. The cards were spread out between them.

She looked back into the boy's eyes—so familiar ... and even through the strange black and white she knew they were blue, Carolina blue.

She had no idea how to express the things that she wanted to say—she had no idea how to begin.

363

Just ask, he said, and his thought was as warm and comforting as a caress. *Concentrate on the card and say what you want to say to me.*

She concentrated all her being into the words, and thought at him: *Is this the past?*

She felt immediately exhausted from the effort, but was rewarded with the tug of a sad ghost of a smile at his lips. And then a haunted look that wrenched her heart.

Somewhere between. Half-life, he said enigmatically. Then his face darkened and he glanced at the others around him.

But where is this? How can you see me? she thought at him, frightened.

A jumble of thoughts came from him then: *Vortex whirlpool threshold gateway timeless limbo.* She could feel his frustration at the inadequacy of the words.

Dimension. He finally ended. *Dimensions. There are so many more than one.*

She could hear everything he said clearly in her head. But no one around them heard. Leish never turned toward either her or Morgan.

The round-faced boy was looking at her intensely.

What happened? she thought at him. He glanced surreptitiously at the tall, blond man.

Dr. Leish wanted big results, violent results. He wanted to see the poltergeist effect at full force. He thought—hoped—that our psi ability would bring the force out into the open.

Laurel felt a chill, realizing how very closely they had followed Leish's example. She looked at the table, at the séance—so eerily similar to what her own group had just been doing

And he—made contact? she asked silently, her own voice hollow inside her head.

Not him, the young man—Morgan—said. *It was a dynamic, between the house, and us—*

Another *RAP* reverberated through the whole of the house ... through the foundation, through Laurel's body. Everyone at the table looked up, electrified. Laurel clenched herself, thought at the young man at the table.

364

What is it?

He glanced for a second toward her. What she got from him was not words but a black wave of fear ... it made her cold all over. Her teeth began to chatter and her breath came shallow and fast, she could actually see it in the air, but she pressed on.

Morgan ... Uncle Morgan ... I need to know. Is it madness? An imprint of madness on the house?

For the first time she saw the young man across from her flinch. Again he did not speak, but the voice in her head was raw and urgent.

It is dangerous to think you understand. It is many things. It is pure irrationality. There is no answer. It is a mistake to think that you know. It will not be known.

The young man at the table closed his eyes briefly. Then he opened them and Laurel heard in her head:

We opened a door.

She looked toward the striking blond man with the clipboard. *Is that how Dr. Leish died? Because of something you saw? What?*

Morgan shook his head, a quick, surreptitious shake. *You must get out before it is summoned again. Stop it before they open the door. You must get out.*

How? she said, frightened beyond anything she had ever felt before. *How?*

At the table beside her Dr. Leish and Rafe Winchester started arguing, without sound—the blond older man with the clipboard and the black-haired younger man across from Victoria. They both stood, soundlessly screaming at each other across the table,

And then the knocking started, and that Laurel could hear, and feel, too; feel it reverberating through her ... and everyone in the grouping froze, looking upward ...

One by one the mirrors began to shatter on the walls, exploding outward into the room.

And the electric-eyed boy lunged across the table and seized her hand—

365

Chapter Fifty-eight

Laurel jolted and her eyes flew open as she gasped, tried to gasp ... and couldn't. Her chest was on fire ... she couldn't breathe, couldn't get a breath ... but then she felt the duct tape binding her mouth and remembered, and she drew a shuddering breath of air through her nose. She lay in the small bed with her heart pounding like the waves of knocking from her—

—Dream?

She was on the bed, in that small, cold, white room, and it was dark—not black, though, not full dark, more gray dark, and she realized it was raining, black, roiling clouds outside the window.

She was still bound to the bed, the rope through the rings. There was a smell of burning around her, although she could see no flame.

She breathed shallowly against the smell, fighting the rising tide of panic ...

She heard a *RAP* that reverberated through the entire house—through the foundation of the house, through the floor, through the bed, through her body ...

Oh God, they've started ...

She felt panic, terror—she writhed and fought against the ropes.

Helpless. Helpless.

She felt a rush of blistering anger and did not know if it was her own or Paul Folger's.

And then she realized there was something in her hand.

Laurel curled her fingers around it and felt a sharp pain. She lifted her head from the bed and looked down the length of her body toward her hand.

She was clutching a long, sharp shard of mirror.

What? What?

She thought of the mirrors in her dream, shattering outward, of young Morgan lunging across the table and grabbing her hand . . .

A wave of confusion hit.

He gave it to me?

Don't think. Just use it. Hurry.

She clutched the spike of mirror, curled her fingers toward the rope that bound her arms, and found she could just reach the rope with the edge of the mirror. It was a camp rope and sliced easily with the razor-sharp shard. In a few slices she had cut through and pulled her arm free. She sat up and ripped the duct tape off her mouth, not caring about the pain, and then used the mirror to slice through the rope on her other arm. Adrenaline gave her a push . . . she tore off the remaining rope and jumped off the bed.

She flung herself at the door—locked, of course. She looked wildly around the room and grabbed the coat stand, hefted it in both hands, aimed the heavy base at the door underneath the doorknob, and ran at it with all her weight.

The door cracked open just as another *RAP* shook the house.

Laurel whirled back to the bed and seized the mirror shard, slid it gingerly into her skirt pocket as a weapon. Then she stumbled out into the hall, amazed at her freedom. *No time to think of that. Two ways, two choices. Main stairs or back?*

Main stairs led to the front door. They were all downstairs, she was sure.

Have to get them out.

She pulled the mirror shard from her pocket, wincing as the

367

sharp glass cut her again. She held it carefully and ran as silently as she could down the hall, halting to ease around the corner into the entry at the top of the stairwell, to listen. She heard no voices ... no rapping ...

Where is Anton? Would he be in there with them? Can't can't can't get caught again ...

She moved onto the stairs and crept downward toward the landing. Rain pelted the gardens outside the huge arched windows beside her, and the sky was black.

Still no sound from downstairs.

She poked her head around the corner of the landing. She could see downstairs to the front entry hall. A dark man hovered beside the archway of the great room, watching whatever was inside.

Laurel's pulse skyrocketed and she pulled her head back and stood pressed against the wall, trembling, clutching the mirror shard in her fingers.

Dr. Anton.

He was standing just outside the great room with that damned clipboard.

So they all must be inside.

He was right next to the front door, too close for her to get by him, even if he didn't see her until she was right on top of him. *And I can't leave Tyler and Katrina in this house.*

Do I go back? All the way up and around, down the servants' stairs? Do I have time?

She eased her head back out and looked down at Anton, assessing the bulk of his body. She studied the mirror shard in her hand. *Can I sneak up on him, go for the jugular? If I run at him, with downward momentum, can I possibly shove him against the wall, knock him out?* She glanced around her for some other weapon, but all she saw within reach were a few small paintings hung on the walls. *Useless.*

But there was a recessed alcove in the wall next to the lower landing where she could stand and be hidden from Anton's line of sight.

Laurel stuck her head out again. Anton still hovered below.

368

She took a breath, then moved swiftly and silently around the wall, and slipped down the remaining stairs to the lower landing.

She ducked into the shallow alcove, pressed her back into the recessed wall, felt her heart pounding through her ribs against the plaster. From her new, closer hiding place she could make out the murmur of voices from the great room. She held very still, forcing her breath to slow, straining to hear.

"I still think we should wait for Dr. MacDonald." Tyler's voice sounded agitated.

"She's not coming back, Tyler," Brendan's voice answered patiently. "It was her choice to leave. Please don't interrupt. Katrina?"

"We're here. We're waiting. Are you there?" Katrina called out, her voice clear and energized.

A *RAP* shook the house. Laurel felt the wall she was leaning against shake to the foundation.

There was an excited murmur of voices, words indistinguishable, then Brendan's voice called out from the great room: "Is there an imprint in this house?"

The air was suddenly suffused with a rotten smell, the stink of goat. A sound like harsh breathing began, coming from everywhere and nowhere . . . in and out.

Laurel saw Anton stiffen below her, electric with excitement. He started for the archway.

Then Laurel's eyes widened as a small dark splotch began to grow on the wall in front of her. She watched it, riveted . . . and it burst into flame. She pressed her hand to her mouth to stifle a gasp. The spot burned for a moment, then flickered out, leaving an oval scorch mark on the wall.

All around her she could hear whispering—many voices, from the walls, from the ceiling . . . from nowhere and everywhere, whispering and mocking, with no words . . .

Brendan's voice suddenly called out from the room below, "I want whatever is in this house to show itself. I want to see."

No! Laurel thought, her pulse spiking. *No!*

The house began to shake. Laurel had grown up with

earthquakes and the feeling was the same—like an immense, invisible animal lashing in the foundation, convulsing the entire house. Something ripped through the entire building, like a wind that was not a wind. The mirror shard fell from Laurel's grasp as she flung out her arms and pressed her hands against the sides of the recessed space in which she stood, bracing herself against the sickening roll of the house. It was coming from the great room, the convulsion, and she heard Katrina screaming, Tyler and Brendan shrieking . . .

There was a great rushing roar that was like a vacuum, a thundering absence of sound, a vortex of wind that was not wind.

Laurel heard herself screaming now, screaming her voice raw—but the sound was swallowed in the vacuum.

It went on forever, a rush of nothingness. She shut her eyes against the pressure, the violation of it. She felt her breath being sucked from her, her mind sliding toward madness, her whole being screaming, screaming—the house was screaming . . .

And then it stopped.

Chapter Fifty-nine

Laurel gasped for breath, for consciousness.

Am I alive?

Her mouth was dry, her ears ringing, her body shaking with adrenaline ...

The house was preternaturally still.

Laurel felt her arms shaking now; her hands were still braced so hard against the walls that her whole body ached. She opened her eyes ... lowered her hands from the walls, and took a jerking step from her alcove.

Every framed painting on the wall in the entry was sideways or otherwise torqued. The entry hall was empty below her. There was no sound, no sound ...

Fear flooded through her and she stumbled down the remaining stairs, across the entry hall to the archway of the great room.

She burst into the room and stared around her ...

... at total chaos, everything overturned, paintings ripped and mangled on the walls, as if a tornado had hit. The piano was upended and mashed up against a wall, on its side. Anton was nowhere to be seen. Only the long table was still in its place, with Katrina, Brendan, and Tyler slumped in their chairs around it, all three of them slack-jawed and staring. Laurel took a staggering step, felt a chill of horror, recognizing the vacuous looks of the catatonic schizophrenic.

The room was completely silent—and live. The feeling of being watched was paralyzing.

Laurel bolted forward—and almost fell over Dr. Anton, slumped on the floor against the wall with legs sprawled out in front of him, head lolling on his neck ... vacant-eyed and drooling.

She found her voice and screamed, "Brendan! Tyler! Katrina!"

The three slumped shapes at the table were still. Not a blink, not a twitch of a muscle in response. Lightning cracked in the sky outside the house, illuminating the room in blue white light. The trees lashed in a frenzy of wind.

Laurel ran to the table, leaned over, and slapped Brendan hard across the face, and then again. "Do you see me? Answer me!" she shouted. No response. She took his shoulders and shook him.

"Brendan, I need you to hear me." He slumped to the side of the chair, his head lolling against the chair back, his eyes were all black, staring blindly at the ceiling.

Laurel turned to Katrina and shook her, shook her hard, until her teeth clacked in her head with a sickening crunch. The girl was as limp as a doll, frighteningly light.

Laurel heard a rustle of movement and froze. She turned ... looked toward the side of the room. A clipboard that had fallen from the table started to tremble, then abruptly slid a few inches across the floor. Laurel started back.

All around the room objects began to shift and move around her, slightly, slyly. A pencil started to roll across the room in teasing slow motion. On the mantelpiece, a china cupid that had somehow remained intact suddenly exploded.

Laurel spun toward it ... and saw that the pool of water had begun to seep from the floor again, growing. She felt an unbearable sense of something gathering.

Get out. Get out now.

She whirled back to the table and lunged across it to grab Tyler's wrists.

His eyes rolled with a blankness that dropped her heart to her stomach.

372

Laurel held his wrists, digging her fingers into his flesh, and looked into those eerie eyes. "Tyler, you need to come back to me now. Can you hear me?"

The rasping voice that came back to her inside her head was nothing human. *Of course I can hear you. I am in you. You belong to me.*

"I'm not talking to you," she said vehemently. Her eyes fell on the scattered Zener cards on the tabletop, and suddenly, instinctively, she switched to the inner voice she had used with the blue-eyed boy in her dream.

Tyler. I need you to hear me now. I need you to come out. Wherever you are, follow my voice.

She shut her eyes tight against the shifting movements of the room, shut her mind against the sly creeping sounds ... and imagined the white room—the room they had shared during their test run. She forced herself to breathe, to let go ... and saw herself in the room. When she opened her eyes, she was alone in the white room with Tyler. He sat at the table, slumped slackly in his seat. Laurel pulled out the chair in front of her and sat before him, across the table. He was still, limp, unfocused.

Tyler. I'm here. I'm here.

She stared into his eyes and saw nothing.

Tyler, listen to me. Hear me. Follow my voice. Come toward my voice. Come out.

She thought she saw something in his face, saw a flicker, or maybe it was an illusion, but she jolted with hope. She leaned toward him urgently.

Tyler, look at me. Look at me. See me.

She reached out and grabbed his hands, squeezing hard. *Tyler. Come out of there. Now.*

All at once the young man in front of her gasped, a long, shuddering breath as if he'd just surfaced from deep water. He panted raggedly.

The white room faded around them as Laurel shot to her feet, moved around the table, and knelt beside Tyler, reaching up to stroke his face. "Breathe. Breathe. Tyler, are you there? Can you answer me?"

373

He answered thickly, but it was his own voice. "God." He looked around them wildly. A painting shifted on the wall. The piano suddenly fell forward onto its legs without a sound and slid several feet across the floor, then stopped, hovering . . .

A low, deep groan shuddered through the foundation of the house . . . the floor beneath Laurel's knees slithered like a serpent.

Now what she saw in Tyler's eyes was pure terror.

"Oh God," he managed. His teeth were chattering so hard he could barely get the words out. "Where is it? Where'd it go?"

"Talk to me. Talk to me," she commanded, digging her fingernails into his forearms.

"Jesus." His voice was weak, and thick, but his eyes were lucid. He looked across the table at Katrina, then at Brendan; slumped lifeless and staring at the table with those black, vacant eyes. "What are we going to do?"

Laurel stood. "We're going to get out of here," she said grimly, and hoped that he believed her. "Can you move? Can you stand?"

He leaned his arm over the back of the chair and shoved himself up to standing. He promptly doubled over and retched, dry heaves.

She caught him and held him as he heaved. "I know . . . I know." Her eyes were scanning the room even as she comforted him. On the back wall, a window cracked, a long, slow split. "But Tyler, we have to go. We have to go now, before . . ." She did not know how to express the unformed horror she felt. She looked to Brendan and Katrina. "We have to get them, and we have to get out."

"There are no doors," he said, looking honestly bewildered.

"Yes, there are. Come on, Tyler. Take Katrina. Pick her up if you can. Drag her if you have to. Grab her and run," she commanded.

Tyler seized Katrina's arms and pulled the girl's limp body from her chair. Laurel had to not look at the idiot look on Brendan's face as she reached for his arm. He felt like a snake in her grasp, but she held his slick skin firmly, slipped her arms under his armpits, and yanked him up from the chair.

She glanced back at Anton, sprawled against the wall, slack jaw dropped open, then turned back to Tyler.

"Go!"

They both heaved forward and half-ran, stumbling, half-dragging Katrina and Brendan through the archway, into the entry hall.

Laurel dropped Brendan's limp and heavy body to the floor and lunged for the front door, twisting the doorknob. It was locked and solid, would not budge even a fraction of an inch as she pulled and shoved at it. Around them, she could hear the house breathing, that rasping, live breath. Tyler barked behind her: "Out of the way!"

She turned to see Tyler had dropped Katrina, who lay crumpled on the floor. He grabbed an end table and lifted it. Laurel pulled Brendan's dead weight aside and Tyler hoisted the end table and ran at the long vertical window set beside the door with an inarticulate cry. The table smashed through the glass.

He hit again and again, breaking the remaining glass out. Behind them from the great room came a cackling of voices, whispering, and ranting, a frenzied cacophony.

"Get out!" Laurel said through chattering teeth. "I'll hand her through."

With Tyler outside and Laurel inside, they carried/passed Katrina through the broken-out window. Laurel's mind was screaming at her.

What if they don't recover?

And then,

What if we don't get out?

The house began a long, slow rumble again, and the rapping began to shake the walls, rolling through the house in waves.

Tyler lunged back in through the window, and together they muscled Brendan toward the window frame, straining with his weight.

The voices in the great room jabbered, louder and louder, and a man's voice began to shriek, raw, horrible screams. Laurel cried out and shoved Brendan through the window. As Tyler pulled him through, Laurel squeezed through the window herself, feeling the remaining jagged glass rip her skin, feeling blood seep from her face and arms and legs.

Outside the rain was pouring down, splashing on the porch and path. Wind lashed the trees above them, whipping water against them. The wet was the most welcome thing Laurel had ever felt; she turned her face up to be drenched. Lightning branched through the sky.

Unbelievably, their cars were still lined up in the slate-pebbled drive, and Laurel felt for a moment as if she were in a painting, in a dream.

Then she dropped to the porch beside Katrina, pulled the girl's soaked and prone body into her arms. "Do you have car keys?" she shouted at Tyler over the thunder. Tyler shoved his hand into a jean pocket and a look of salvation lit his face as he pulled out the keys.

"Let's fucking go." He zapped the doors unlocked.

Katrina was shivering, convulsing in Laurel's arms. The girl's eyes suddenly flew open.

"Run," Katrina whispered. "Run run run run run . . ."

A wave of terror crashed over Laurel and she hauled Katrina up to standing, ran with her for the car. The sky opened and hail began to pelt down in marble-sized chunks, bouncing whitely off the car.

Laurel pushed Katrina into the backseat of the Maserati and ran back to help Tyler, who was stooping to pick Brendan up by his armpits. Together they dragged him across the gravel to hoist him into the car, both of them straining to lift him, straining not to listen as the house loomed and shrieked and raged behind them. And as lightning cracked across the sky, Tyler gunned the engine of the Maserati and drove like the wind.

Chapter Sixty

The hospital was small and pretty—if a hospital could be called pretty—with light, airy open spaces, and arches, and views of rolling hills and fields out the windows.

Laurel knew the views well. She had been there for nearly a week.

The intake doctor in the emergency room, Madsen, had been suspicious but competent. He started Brendan and Katrina and Tyler on IV fluids, and stood with Laurel to take their reports. Katrina was still conscious; Brendan was not.

Laurel and Tyler recounted as little as possible: a break-in at the house they were renting while the two of them had been out, returning to find the house ravaged and Katrina and Brendan in the condition they were in, no idea what happened to them, leaving the house with them, frightened out of their wits. Dr. Madsen listened and watched and wrote, without speaking.

Then Brendan, Katrina and Tyler were taken on gurneys into the hospital, and Laurel sat down to wait.

Brendan came out of his catatonia on the fourth day. Laurel was not sure how, but when Dr. Madsen was taking Brendan's intake report, Laurel had said on impulse, "There's a history of schizophrenia in the family." Her heart beat faster at the chance she was taking, and the doctor looked at her sharply, but after a moment said, "Interesting," and made a note on Brendan's chart.

They let her see him on the sixth day. She had not left the hospital for any of that time.

He was pale and thin, tubes snaking from his arms, but his eyes were clear as he looked at her from the hospital bed, and the range of emotions on his face was painful to see. His voice rasped as he said, immediately:

"Tyler . . . Katrina . . ."

"Conscious. Recovering," Laurel said, standing in the doorway. And she added silently, *Thank God, thank God.* "Faster than you, actually. They're young. I visit them and they . . . they're starting to talk. I'll be there when they do."

Brendan looked as if ten years had dropped from him. Then slowly his face tightened. "And Anton?"

Laurel's eyes clouded; she felt a range of emotions she could not name. "The police went to the house." Laurel had emphasized the possible danger to the cops, the destruction she and Tyler had seen. But she had not gone with them—not that they would have allowed it—but she was certain in the core of her that they were safer without her. She was afraid to activate the house.

Folger House had been empty. The great room was in chaos, but a chaos still attributable to the random destruction of a criminal, though Laurel had wondered more than a few times what the police had made of that inexplicable scattering of rocks. There was no one else in the house—living, dead, or otherwise.

Brendan stared at her, stupefied. "But where . . ."

She lifted her hands. She had no idea. *Did he revive and get out somehow? Did the house—or whatever was in it—take him?* She remembered the horrible screaming at the end . . .

"The police said there was no trace," she answered.

"And there's no record at all, is there? The cameras . . ." Brendan asked, and added quickly, "Don't take that the wrong way. I just meant . . ." He stopped, swallowed hard. "There's a lot I don't remember, and what I do . . ."

She knew what he was going to say. She'd heard it from Tyler and Katrina, and when Brendan spoke he sounded as young as they were, lost and groping.

"Did it really happen? I ... don't know what's real anymore."

"I have no idea," she said simply.

He nodded, looking faintly ill.

"There was nothing left," she said. "The hidden cameras in the great room and system in the attic—they burned. Electrical fire, the police said." *Only the electricity had been off for a day.* "Completely destroyed."

Brendan closed his eyes ... then opened them and looked at her.

"Why did you even bother to take me out? Why not just leave me? It was what I deserved."

She looked away from him and said slowly, "I know what it is to be out of your mind. I've spent some time there myself." She looked out the window, and found with faint surprise that the thought of Matt didn't cut her heart open anymore.

"I was lost for a long time. I came out of it." She looked at him briefly. "I believe people can change."

He bowed his head. "I swear. I ..." He looked up, and there was real pain in his face. "It was never supposed to be about hurting you."

She nodded, abstractly. "The thing is, I *knew*. I knew about—someone else, and I knew about you." She stopped. "I need to trust when I know."

"Mickey," Brendan said softly, and despite everything, she felt it in her heart. "What will you do now?"

"I have no idea," she said again. "I doubt either of us will have a job by the end of the week, but ..." She thought of Uncle Morgan. "Somehow that doesn't seem so important anymore. There are other things I need to do."

He looked at her probingly. And then she smiled, with a tremor, and quoted softly. "'How can we not devote our lives to pursuing that question—of whether a thing like this could happen, and how?'"

And she looked away from him, out the window at the sun, the sky, and the rolling hills.

Afterword

The Unseen was inspired by the work of parapsychologist Dr. Joseph Banks Rhine at Duke University from 1927 to 1965. The history of Rhine's ESP experiments has always fascinated me; I can still get a thrill just from seeing the Zener card symbols on a page. As the daughter of scientists and educators, I am drawn to the idea that such an elusive thing as ESP could be scientifically proven. And as a thriller writer I know a good story when I see one.

Though *The Unseen* contains some factual circumstances, I have of course embellished the real-life history in all kinds of ways, and will take a brief moment here to delineate the facts from the wild ravings of my imagination.

Dr. J. B. Rhine (1895–1980) began his scientific career studying botany, earning advanced degrees at the University of Chicago, but after a brief stint of teaching he switched fields to study psychology at Harvard under Professor William McDougall, a colleague of celebrated philosopher and psychologist William James. In 1927 McDougall was named the head of the new Duke University psychology department in Durham, North Carolina, and Rhine and his wife and colleague, Dr. Louisa Rhine, moved to Duke with him.

In the psychology department at Duke, Dr. Rhine began his soon-to-be world-famous ESP experiments using Zener cards, and psychokinesis experiments using automated dice-

380

throwing machines. Rhine's intention was to use rigorous scientific methodology to test and prove the existence of ESP, and Rhine and McDougall coined the term *parapsychology* to describe the study of paranormal psychological phenomena such as telepathy, clairvoyance, and psychokinesis.

Rhine's work led to the establishment of a dedicated parapsychology laboratory at Duke, headed by Rhine, in 1935. Over his thirty-eight years at Duke, Rhine tested thousands of students for ESP ability, using the Zener card method depicted in *The Unseen*, and employing the new science of statistics and probability to analyze the results. Dr. Rhine identified test subjects who were able to predict the cards with an accuracy far higher than statistical chance, which led him to conclude that ESP really does occur.

In 1934 Rhine published his findings in his monograph, *Extra Sensory Perception*, which was published in several editions in many countries, and which made Rhine internationally famous. He is now credited with almost single-handedly developing a methodology for parapsychology as a form of experimental psychology.

In the late 1940s Dr. Louisa Rhine began to collect reports from all over the world of spontaneous psi experiences, further contributing to our understanding of clairvoyance, telepathy, precognition, and crisis apparitions.

In 1957, William Roll, a parapsychology researcher who studied at Berkeley and Oxford, joined the staff of the Duke parapsychology lab, and he and Dr. Rhine's longtime assistant and researcher, J. Gaither Pratt, conducted field studies of reported poltergeist occurrences, including the famous Seaford, or "Popper" case in 1958. Roll developed the theory of "Recurrent Spontaneous Psychokinesis," RSPK, to explain poltergeist phenomena; that is, that the random movements, noises and breakages characteristic of a poltergeist manifestation are not the work of ghosts or spirits, but are caused by a human agent, usually a prepubescent child or a teenager, who consciously or unconsciously was projecting mental energy outward to cause the movement of the objects.

As in *The Unseen*, the Duke parapsychology lab did close down completely in 1965, when Dr. Rhine reached the age of mandatory retirement, and seven hundred boxes of original files from the lab really were stored in the basement of Duke's Perkins Library on the Duke campus, and have only recently been made available for public viewing. It was the idea and the existence of those boxes that crystallized the story I wanted to tell.

However, from there my story diverges completely from reality, in more ways than one. There is no such person as Dr. Alaistair Leish, or the nefarious Dr. Richard Anton, nor are they based on anyone in real life. There is no such place as Dr. Anton's Parapsychology Research Center.

The parapsychology lab files that exist at Perkins Library have been neatly catalogued by librarians; you will not find petrified cans of peanuts or Sen-Sen breath mints in the boxes.

North Carolinians may be able to guess the house that was my model for the Folger House; on the other hand, there are many such houses tucked away in forests in the South, houses which may or may not be haunted, but which most definitely feel as if they should be.

Finally, there was never a Folger Experiment, and certainly not ever one sanctioned by Duke University, the parapsychology lab, or any of its administration, faculty or staff, or that caused the closing of the parapsychology lab.

I based the poltergeist manifestations depicted in the book on the kinds of manifestations that have been reported over centuries, in countries all over the world. There has never—to my knowledge!—been such a concentrated attack as the one I portray in the book (despite the interesting embellishments of incidents that you can find in some supposedly factual reports), but I have tried throughout to be true to the spirit of the—well, spirit.

Reports of actual poltergeist investigations are maddening to read because there is never any real explanation. There is no restless, departed ghost who brings crucial information to a loved one or demands retribution. There may be fraud, there may not be. Inexplicable things happen and remain frustratingly inexplicable ... and thus all the more seductive.

It is the very mystery of the phenomenon that enthralls.

For those interested in reading further in the field of parapsychology and on the work of the Rhine Lab, I highly recommend Dr. Sally Rhine Feather's *The Gift*, an illuminating study of real-life ESP occurrences, which also details both her parents' work in the field; and William Roll's *The Poltergeist,* for detailed accounts of his poltergeist investigations while at the Duke parapsychology lab and after. Deborah Blum's *Ghost Hunters* provides a fascinating historical perspective of the work of the American Society for Psychical Research and the British Society for Psychical Research to find scientific proof of ghosts and psychic phenomena, and Colin Wilson compiles some of the most entertaining poltergeist stories in his book *Poltergeist!* (among others). Tony Cornell's book *Investigating the Paranormal* is a useful study of fieldwork.

For further information on current studies, and for an extensive bibliography of parapsychological topics, I recommend The Rhine Research Center's Web site: http://www.Rhine.org/.

Acknowledgments

I am indebted until the end of time to:

Dr. J.B. Rhine, Dr. Louisa Rhine, and William Roll, for their groundbreaking and inspiring work in the field of parapsychology.

My editor, Marc Resnick, and Sarah Lumnah, for always making all things better.

Sally Richardson, Matthew Shear, Harriett Seltzer, Ellis Trevor, Talia Ross, Mike Berry, Matt Baldacci and the entire St. Martin's team. I especially owe Jennifer Enderlin for pointing me toward this one!

Scott Miller—not just a great agent but a great guy.

Frank Wuliger and Sarah Self, for doing the Hollywood thing in a non-Hollywood way.

My partner, Michael Bradshaw, the least likely person to keep me sane, and yet . . .

The awesome Sheila English and Michael Miller at Circle of Seven Productions for the trailers, and double thanks to Sheila, for her constant support and advice.

Adam Auerbach for his mindblowing cover art.

Beth Tindall, webmistress extraordinaire.

My family, Alexander, Barbara, Elaine, and Michael, for constant support and inspiration.

Kimball Greenough, for his encyclopedic knowledge and understanding of parapsychology and the paranormal.

Michael Bradshaw, for airport shuttle services.

Margaret Maron, Diane Chamberlain, Katy Munger, Brenda Witchger, Mary Kay Andrews, and Nancy Olson, for their friendship, writing support, political comradeship, and hilarious spooky times in the "Folger House."

Nancy and Jim Olson and the entire staff of Quail Ridge Books for being a home away from home.

The Weymouth Center Writers Retreat.

Michael Bradshaw, keeper of the cats.

Martin and Sue Hatcher, for their stories.

Susan Bradshaw, for everything.

The Rhine Research Center and Dr. Sally Rhine Feather.

Stan, Phil, Neisha, and the Bodhi Tree Bookstore for such a comprehensive education on all things paranormal.

Heather Graham, Dennis Pozz, and all the Pozzessores for being the best gypsy traveling players second family I could ever ask for.

Sarah Langan and Sarah Pinborough—my dark sisters and personal muses.

The Coven, for the magic.

The wild extended family of Murderati.com for being there, 24/7.

Doris Ann Norris, Mary Boone, Elaine Paquette, Kathy East, Robert Lambert, Clare Bass, Linda Adams, and Karen Kiley. Librarians rock!

The authors, officers and staffs of Sisters in Crime, International Thriller Writers, Horror Writers Association, Mystery Writers of America, Romance Writers of America and the Heart of Carolina Romance Writers for those incredible communities and for taking care of all of my cross-genre, multiple-personality needs.

Michael Palmer, Heather Graham, F. Paul Wilson, and Ken Bruen: idols, inspirations, and friends.

Ira Levin, forever a shining light in this dark field.

Watch out for other novels from one of the most exciting
voices in supernatural fiction –

Alexandra Sokoloff

The Harrowing
(978-0-7499-4158-1)

The Price
(978-0-7499-4163-5)

THE HARROWING

Baird College's Mendenhall echoes with the footsteps of students heading home for Thanksgiving and Robin Stone, who won't be going home, swears she can feel the creepy, hundred-year-old residence hall breathe a sigh of relief. As a massive storm approaches, four other lonely students reveal themselves to Robin: Patrick, a handsome jock; Lisa, a manipulative tease; Cain, a brooding musician; and Martin, a scholarly eccentric. Each has forsaken a long weekend at home for their own secret reasons.

The five unlikely companions establish a tentative rapport, but they soon become aware of another presence disturbing the building's ominous silence. Are they the victims of an elaborate prank, or is the energy evidence of something genuine – something intent on using them for its own terrifying ends?

Together, they'll face three long days and dark nights before the world returns to find out what's become of five students nobody wants and no one will miss ...

978-0-7499-4158-1

THE PRICE

Boston District Attorney Will Sullivan dreams of becoming the next governor of Massachusetts. With his beautiful wife, Joanna, and adorable daughter, Sydney, Will seems destined for greatness ... until Sydney becomes seriously ill. Now both parents resolve to do *anything* to save their daughter's life.

But in the twilight world of the Briarwood Medical Center, nothing is as it seems. Patients on the brink of death are not only surviving but thriving, while others wither away – and the recoveries all revolve around the ministerings of a mysterious counsellor, who takes an unsettling interest in Joanna. When Sydney's health miraculously improves, Will suspects that Joanna made a terrible bargain to save their child. Now Will must face a powerful, unknown evil before he loses ... everything.

978-0-7499-4163-5